The Promise of Tomorrow

A Man's Struggle Between The Life He Loves and The Love of His Life

A.D. Haywood

About the Author

[Client will be providing details]

Page Blank Intentionally

Part One

Chapter One - The Note

Charlotte Medical Hospital – May 20, 2000 – Five days after Injury

Visiting hours had expired well over an hour ago. This is what prompted the pale-skinned 5'6", 300-plus-pound balding man to waddle his way out of the hospital room at such a late hour. The same room in which he had spent the majority of the past eight days filled with fear and anger.

Sleep deprivation was the culprit of the heavy skin drooping below his red-shot eyes. A noticeable look of concern is evident by the painful wince on his scrunched-up face. The deep thought trance he was in allowed his mind to be absent as his body found its way to the nearby elevator. The man is leaving behind a brother who is wearing the standard issued white hospital attire with tubes and wires going in and out every hole that the gown left exposed. Despite the bandage on his head and a cast on one arm, this will be the patient's first night without a family member by his bedside in days.

The periodic stops in the elevator's nine-floor de-escalation to the hospital lobby only allowed the heavy man more time to speculate about the circumstances of the accident and what it had to do with a family vacation when the two men were just teens.

The weak but conscious patient was sitting upright in a bed placed in the center of a room at Charlotte Medical Hospital. Numerous different machines beeping and blinking gave confidence that the patient's body was functioning properly. The terrible accident that almost took his life has caused a parade of family, friends, and co-workers to drop by. The brown-haired man is engulfed by flowers and balloons, expressing deep concern from well-wishers and loved ones. They have served their purpose and given the man a reason to smile more than once.

At this moment, though, they were just the backdrop to his viewshed.

The only action that he was taking was a non-stop glare at the envelope bearing his name. As directed, his brother had propped it up against a flower-filled vase that was sitting on a table that was closely located to the bed. The envelope is within reach, but he can't bring himself to grab it. He is afraid of what is inside.

Before long, the injured man has company in the form of an older African American woman. She has been his main caretaker for six of the past eight nights. She strolls in with a happy face that does not match the tone that was left by the previous visitor.

"God bless! It sure is nice to be able to talk to you. God is amazing. You know, there was a time I wasn't sure if we would ever get the opportunity to speak to each other," she states in almost a jolly voice.

The patient ignores her.

"You need anything," she offers.

The man is wide awake and alert. The scolding from his brother left him in a state of bewilderment.

He responds by saying, "I'm fine."

But it's apparent that he isn't too interested in what she is saying. He is still in deep thought. Maybe even shock. He is not mad at his brother's reaction because he knows that his brother is right. Or... is he right about what he thinks is going on? Caught in a daze, he can't take his eyes off the envelope.

"OK, you'll be fine. But I'm fixing to leave you and won't be back for a while. I am going to take a couple of days off. If you need something, Nurse Megan will be the one helping you. She might be younger, prettier, and quicker, but she doesn't have the 35 years of TLC that I have. So, honey if you are in any pain, please let me help you," the concerned nurse offers assistance one last time.

Appearing agitated, the middle-aged man responds firmly, "I'm fine."

The slightly hefty nurse takes it in stride and offers, "You know what? I am going to give you a pass on that attitude. I know you have had a rough week. Besides, your family is too beautiful and nice for you to really be a mean person. I am going to chalk this up to the meds. So, I accept your apology."

The man is taken aback for a moment and retraces his actions.

"I'm sorry. I didn't mean to be rude. I just got a lot on my mind."

"Ah, don't think anything about it. Like I said, I have already forgiven you. I probably gave you too much of that crazy juice. I don't always measure, you know," the jovial lady jokes.

He gives her a smile and explains, "I just got a lot to think about. You just don't know."

"You never know. I have been around this hospital long enough that the walls talk to me. And guest too," the lady with Alice attached to her nametag responds as if she knows all about his problems. She turns and picks up the paperwork that is attached to a clipboard on the back of the room door and starts to fill out the top portion by writing in the initials ALW.

The injured man seems to be intrigued by what she knows or thinks she knows about him. Who has been talking to her, and what have they been saying? Is she judging me? Anger creeps into his body. A body that is already filled with a melting pot of emotions. The suspense is eating away at him, and he decides that he is going to discover what she really knows. "So, what do you know about me? What have the walls told you?"

His curiosity makes Alice smile. But she realizes that she may have said too much and shuts down the conversation. "Nothing. Nothing at all." She never raised her head from the clipboard.

Her smile was filled with insinuation as if she did know more and refused to share. This only intrigues the man. Or is this agitation he is feeling?

"Do you have something to say?" he asks.

She shakes her head, no, but before she can continue, he adds.

"Because I think you do."

Alice laughs and says, "I have nothing to say."

The man is ready to concede and is beginning to dissolve back into a restful position. Turns his eye back towards the envelope.

Words that he thought he said to himself came out loud enough to reach the nurse's ears.

"I didn't think you knew anything."

The patient tried to sit back up as he realized that his thought had escaped his mouth. He turned his head towards her.

"I'm sorry. Didn't mean that. Maybe you did put too much of that crazy juice in me."

Trying to play off his obvious stupid mishaps.

Alice's demeanor and appearance scream that she is someone who is not afraid to share what is on her mind. She reminds him of his own grandma. He looked at her sheepishly, just as he had done many times before to his grandma, using his charm to get out of a scolding.

"Mister that is number two. I will let you slide once again. The good lord says to turn the other cheek."

Alice raises her head and looks in heaven's direction.

"You are testing me. Dear Lord, I thank you for sending me this test. Now get your book out and mark that your child of God, Alice Lucielle Wilson, has passed this test."

She looks back at her patient.

"You see. I think I have been getting behind in my scores with God. My time is drawing near. I understand. God sent me someone like you as extra credit. Thank you for allowing me to get those bonus points."

The man chuckles, but the slight movement enflames some pain in his arm and chest area.

Alice makes her way over and comforts the man.

"So, you are a good God-Fearing woman. Are you?" he asks.

Alice smiles and responds.

"I try. Some days better at it than others. But lord knows I try."

"Does your God look down on you lying?"

The man blind-sides Alice as if she were a witness at a murder trial, and he is the chief prosecutor destined to get the truth.

Sensing she is being attacked or being backed into a corner, the incredulous woman responds.

"Of course. But I don't lie."

"Right…" he responds in a dragged, over-exaggerated tone.

One that left no doubt that he didn't believe her.

"What in the tarnation would make you say that?"

She looks at the medication that is on a nearby sink to highlight her next statement.

"My God, I really did give you some crazy juice."

Then, once again, she raises her eyes to the lord, "Lord, go ahead and erase my name from that book. Imma about to lose those extra credit points I just received."

The man gets a giggle out of her response. Once again, causing him to wince in pain.

"If you don't lie, then tell me the truth."

He responds in a way that is more playful and challenging than an attack of anger.

"Mister, I have no idea what you are talking about" the puzzled nurse responds as she moves some pillows around to comfort the man that is antagonizing her.

The man continues in a calm, measured voice.

"Earlier, you said the walls tell you things. People too. Your mouth said you had nothing to say, but your eyes and body said something different. I tend to believe the eyes over the mouth. So, are you going to lie to me again? Or you gonna say what you wanna say."

She looks down at him, and he returns the glare back up.

Her eyes spoke to him one more time. It said that this woman obviously knew something. And she is about to share.

Alice takes an exaggerated deep breath while pondering how to answer her patient's question. Her eyes looked over at the letter and returned back to meet his glance. She must respond now. The words liar never came from his lips, but that is exactly what she heard. Alice is a lot of things, but a liar she is not. She has every mind to let him know that nobody calls her a liar. Because a liar, she is not.

Her demeanor changes from jovial to serious as quickly as possible.

Now, she is going to let him have it.

"You know what?"

She takes a deep breath in preparation to allow all the venom that a godly woman can release without earning a direct flight to hell. But that moment of inhalation brought wisdom with it. Thus, she decides the better of it and stops herself.

He reaches up and grabs her hand. For some reason, she does not withdraw.

"Tell me. I want to know what you have heard. The truth. I need the truth."

Once again, Alice takes a deep breath. But this time, it's more of a surrendering breath, as if she needs to get this off her chest.

"I know you got yourself in a heap of trouble. I know the past couple of days, a lot of good people have been worried sick to death about you. Now, I ain't one to judge, but something doesn't smell right. I think that your brother, the one who has been here every day. The one who just left. He knows that, too. Just being honest. I know you have a lot of good people worried about you, but I'm not sure if you are worth it. They keep saying you are a "Good Man".

Freeing her right hand, she puts up the imaginary air quotes around the good man portion of the message just to highlight the idea that maybe she doesn't believe this to be true.

"I am a god-fearing woman and believe in giving people the benefit of the doubt. But I am not sold. I am not sure if you are a "Good Man" (once again with the air quotes) in a tough situation or just a man trying to take advantage of a situation."

The man is shocked and offended by her honesty. Forgetting that he was in pain just a second ago, he decided he would protect his character as he rose with his back even straighter.

"Whoa! Hold on here. I don't know what you think you know, but I really am a good man."

"Never said you weren't," the nurse snaps back. "I just said I don't know. Nothing's wrong with your hearing. You didn't hear me call you any names. I think there is a chance that you could be a good person, but I don't know. What I do know is that wolves are often hidden in sheep's clothing."

The agitated man fires back, "I'm no wolf. What would make you say that? If you knew me, then you would know better!"

Alice takes her hands and straightens her nurse gown out as if it was full of wrinkles. Then lends back over to the man in his mid-20s and grabs his hands.

"Son, I am not the one who gets to decide that. Nor am I the one who needs to know if you're a good person or not. That's for the big man above. I think there is goodness in everybody. I saw that little girl crying over your body. Thinking her daddy was never returning. That broke my heart to the point that I was crying. Not for you, but for her. But to be honest, I also saw who gave your chubby brother that envelop you been staring at. I don't know, nor do I need to know what it's about. But this much I gather, that envelope was too secretive for it to be something good. Hmm... I don't need to know all the facts to know enough."

The dumbfounded man was a total loss for words as tears started slowly rolling down his face. He knows that she is right. No matter the message in that envelope, somebody is getting hurt. When his body heals, his heart will remain broken because he is about to hurt someone that he loves so much. The question is, who is the one that will be getting hurt? And can he live with the answer?

Alice knows she hit her mark but is not sure she is proud of her actions. She is sworn to help as a nurse and a child of God. Instead, she is walking out of the room with the man in worse condition than when she walked in. She starts to walk towards the door, and guilt is settling in.

To redeem herself, she offers, "I am going to keep you in my prayers. Nurse Megan will be in soon."

She heads out of the room.

"Ma'am, hold up."

Alice turns back towards the broken man.

"Just letting you know; I am a good man. I'm just a good man put in an impossible situation."

Alice walks back to his bedside to reengage in the conversation with a puzzled look on her face. But there is joy in her heart. She can't help but think that God is giving her another chance to be a better person.

The man continues, "I don't know what to do. What do you do when you have to choose between the love of your life and the life you love?"

Even more intrigued than before, Alice tells him, "Son, I going to need more than that if you want a straight answer."

"Do you have time?" he asked.

Alice thinks about the answer for a second. Closes her eyes. She says a short, quiet prayer that includes a request for the right words to say and a promise to get her extra credit points back. She turns to her patient with a little bit of excitement.

"Tell you what sugar. Let me make my rounds. Clock out, and then I'll be right back."

Chapter Two - The Return

Shortly after leaving the room, she returns dressed in a sweater thrown over her hospital uniform. But she was not alone. She is accompanied by a sharply dressed African American bald man.

"Sir," looking at her patient. "This is Marcus," Alice introduces.

Marcus is professional in his demeanor and comfortable with completing the introduction. He walks over and extends his hand. He shares that he is the hospital chaplain.

The injured man introduces himself as "Bo." "Bo Hawes," he repeats, adding his last name on the second go around.

Using the hand that is free from the cast, Bo grips Marcus's hand as opposed to the traditional handshake. Marcus and Alice take a chair right beside the bed as if they were family or friends.

"Marcus is a pretty good listener. Hope you don't mind that I invited him to sit in."

Bo is a little puzzled about how this man just ended up in the room. He didn't ask for a chaplain. The expression on his face betrayed Bo, and Marcus could see the discomfort.

"If you would prefer that I not be in the room, I do not have to be here. Alice said you have a predicament, and I find myself speaking with people in predicaments quite often."

With perfect timing, all three look in the direction of the envelope.

The envelope bearing the name "Bo Hawes" is in the same spot it was 30 minutes ago. The envelope that no doubt Alice had told the chaplain about prior to them entering the room. The same one that reminded him that he needs all the help he can get.

"I appreciate you making time for me. I am certain you are a busy man. Not sure if this is chaplain quality work," Bo responds.

Alice can't help but get some satisfaction that she did the right thing.

Just then, Marcus responds, "Son, all things that are the matter of a man's heart and soul is exactly why God put me on earth. This is of no bother."

Bo was taken aback by how his anxiety seemed to drop a level every time the man spoke.

He relented and took a deep breath, "So where do we start?"

Alice replied, "From the beginning. I am in no hurry."

She pulled out a can of Pepsi and took a sip as she prepared for the man's tale of the impossible situation.

Marcus said, "The best way to solve the problem is to know as much as possible about the issue. Therefore, I agree with sister Alice. From the start."

Giving them the "You asked for it look" to serve as a warning to them that this may take a while, Bo again swallows a gulp of air. He is fully aware that he is about to tell strangers things that he has never shared with anyone else. For the next couple of hours, he never breaks stride in his story.

From time to time, Nurse Megan would come in and give him medicine or check his vitals, but he never slowed down. He was telling the story, trying not to leave out a detail. He was telling the story of his life as if he wanted someone else to write the ending.

Part Two

Chapter Three - Family Trip

Summer of 1989

We hated sitting behind my dad in the car! Every time we got in the car as a family, my brother and I would fight over who had to sit behind my dad. He was a two-pack-a-day Marlboro man, and he couldn't endure a thirty-minute drive without smoking, little lone a three-hour drive. During the drive from our house to the mountains of North Carolina, Joe Hawes would inhale about five to seven cigarettes. This means whoever sat behind Dad was doing the same.

Dad would crack a window to flick ashes and allow smoke to exit the three-year-old candy apple red 1986 Mustang window. But in reality, the crack in the window just created enough wind to blow the smoke and ashes into the face of whoever sat behind him.

Today was my turn. Phillip and I have been fighting the same fight ever since he was born 13 years ago. This time, I decided that we needed to work out a plan. I had to endure the smoke for the drive up to Chimney Rock, and he would battle the conditions for the journey back to Indian Trail, NC. This treaty agreement meant we wouldn't start our vacation with a fight, plus it displayed me in a more mature nature. This was important since I was about to turn 16 and get my license in around seven months.

Camping is my family's thing. And the mountains of NC is our spot. Plus, camping fits my parents' very limited budget. We normally go camping a couple of times a year in either Myrtle Beach or the mountains. I liked the beach better, but my parents (mostly Mom) preferred the mountains. Plus, the beach displayed a whole bunch of half-naked jezebels walking around, according to my mom, which is why I believe we end up in the mountains most of the time.

I will admit that every year, I would rather be at the beach when we begin the trip, but I end up being very happy with whatever they (Mom) decided. Having two brothers and a set of really involved parents made every trip unique. Even though we always visited the mountains of North Carolina, we would often find ourselves in different parts of the mountains and involved in many different adventures. We would go to Maggie Valley and visit "Ghost Town" or Grandfather Mountain and walk across the "Swinging Bridge" or walk into one of the local Caverns and walk through the mountain. A couple of days of every trip ended with the Hawes Family Tradition of telling ghost stories by the campfire under a moonlit sky. This is something that Mom was very good at. I believe she would research the whole year just to tell us ghost stories during camping trips, but she swears that she just makes them up on the fly. Either way, she can really paint a picture and scare the crap out of anyone within earshot. Normally, anyone that Phillip or I made friends with while camping would be invited to join us on our nights of fright. The bigger the audience, the better Mom would perform.

The long drive to the mountains often felt like a lifetime. Dad always focused on driving and smoking. Mom would give her best effort to keep three boys crammed in the back seat of a sports car active and not fighting. As a member of the Oak Grove Church Choir, Mom never ran out of gospel songs to sing. She implored us to sing along. This trip was no different. "Wane Got the Power" and "Old

Rugged Cross" were just two of many songs that we would sing during this and every trip.

Anita Hawes's dark eyes almost always sit atop a smiling face. The 5ft 6-inch red head was raised the daughter of farmer C.J. Craig and had five older brothers. She always said that God gave her three boys because he knew she could handle it after living on a farm with five brothers. Fighting with her brothers and the morning chores that farm life required explained the thick-built frame. Normally, the term "country strong" is a description that is reserved for men, but the term has been tossed in her direction a time or two. Being the daughter of well-known hell raiser C.J. Craig and being a part of the Craig Clan empowered her with the self-confidence to never be one lost for words nor afraid to share her opinion. That is just the Craig way. She is quick to inform you that her faith in God has given her the power to put some distance from that reputation. Occasionally, the Devil will gain power and bring the old life to the forefront. But the church community has accepted her as a good, kindhearted, God-fearing woman. This could be the same way you would describe her mother, who shared the same first name and very similar body features.

Like every vacation we ever took, my parents didn't make any reservations. And like every other vacation, we were on a wild goose chase trying to find a campsite. This being the week of the fourth, finding a place to camp was becoming very irritating, especially since Dad was sucking down a cancer stick for every campsite that rejected our efforts to stay.

The senior Hawes was not much for planning, which didn't partner with his struggle with patients very well. He was a proud countryman who had worked hard his whole life. Nothing is given; everything is earned.

Joe Hawes was born in 1943 to a hard-working lower-class family.

He quit school in the 6th grade so he could help support the family. He got a job picking cotton all around the county for local farmer Horace Plyler, making $1.20 a day. The oldest of seven siblings (3 brothers and four sisters), he felt obligated to assist the family financially when they were in need. The family struggles were due to Grandpa Hawes getting hurt while working in a mill. Dad had to assume the role of sole financial provider for a couple of months. The plan was for Dad to be out of school until Grandpa got healthy. Then, he would go back to complete his education. But somewhere along the way, Dad forgot to return. Judging by the stories, my grandmother would tell me about my father's school days, I believe this became a convenient way for Joe Hawes to leave the North Carolina Education System. Grandma once told me not sending her oldest son back to get his education was a heavy burden for her to carry. Then she recalled that he was so happy that he did not have to return to that "Worthless Crap." She smiled when she recalled that the teachers at Waxhaw Elementary School weren't too disappointed that he didn't return.

At the age of 16, he left the cotton fields and started working in a plant across the NC border in Fort Mill, SC, called Springs Mills. They made sheets, shirts, and underwear for the local company that sold their product all over the world. That has been the source of income for my family ever since. The hard manual labor awarded his 6 ft body with good definition. Well, enough for Dad to catch an eye or two from the fairer sex, as long as Mom wasn't around. Of course,

Dad often discounted the good shape he was in and transferred the credit to his greatest asset. His dark black hair and prized handlebar mustache.

Finally, we found a campsite right below Chimney Rock at a place called Lake Lure Campground that looked promising. We sat in the car with Mom while Dad went inside the cabin looking office to secure us a spot to spend the next week.

I could tell that that Stevie was becoming giddy with excitement. He started pointing out all the things that we could do during our time at this site. He pointed out a pool, game room, and a creek. All were placed between the office and the campsites, which was a bit unique. Campsites surrounded most campsite offices. This office was within the eyesight of campers, but they weren't nearby. It really didn't matter. When camping, the more isolated, the better.

Phillip interrupted, "Hello," and pointed at two girls who were walking by.

I responded, "Nice catch. You and I will be looking them up very soon." Knowing full well that this was almost certainly not the case. But it helped me with my macho persona. There is also the fact that Phillip lacks confidence, and I am well aware that they were way out of our league.

Which at the moment made me think, is that a lack of confidence in myself as well?

Confidence or not, my attention was fully gained by the two beautiful teenage girls walking in front of us in their bathing suits.

They were walking gingerly across the rocks to get to the pool, which was on the other side of the office and game room.

Then Stevie chimed in, "WOW! Look at those Boobies."

Phillip and I were thinking the same thing; we just knew better than to let it leave our brains and exit our lips.

We started dying of laughter as Mom started to scold our five-year-old brother, "Boy, you don't talk like that!" Then Mom started in on Phillip and me, "Boys, look at the things you are teaching your brother. You have to be a better example than that."

Mom went on and on with the same speech that Phillip and I heard every time Stevie did ANYTHING wrong. Lord knows, he learned it from us no matter what it was. If it's bad, we taught him.

The ironic thing was Stevie didn't learn this from us. He got that word from Dad. "Boobies" was our father's word. He used that word a lot, but never in front of Mom. Dad would point out hot women (or at least what he thought was hot) all the time when Mother wasn't around. My Dad must have pointed out a thousand pair of "Boobies" to me. Weird thing; I always felt uncomfortable about that. I wasn't sure if he was pointing them out for me or him. But since my uncles and other men I was around had done the same thing, I gathered that this was some form of Father/Son bonding or just plain "being a man" tradition. After all, Dad was very loyal, and I know he loved Mom. I never witnessed him cheating or even flirting. It always stopped at "the point," the comment, and recognition.

Mom turns back to Stevie; where did you learn that word? I knew Stevie was about to spill it. If Stevie told Mom that Dad said that, this vacation would be OVER!! Mom would make Dad's life a living hell the entire trip. Dad provides for the family, but Mom is the queen of the castle and everyone in it. Including Dad! Living with five brothers and being her daddy's only little girl, Mom had gotten her way pretty much her whole life. This was not going to change just because she picked up a husband along the way.

Mom was a very Godly woman. Dad, not so much. He was very Godly around Mom but not so much around others. I heard Dad say curse words many times. I asked him once did he believed in God. He said sure. I wasn't convinced. He said I believe in believing in something. I believe in your mom. She is a good woman, and if believing in God makes her happy, then that's what we will do. Still wasn't convinced, but in some weird way, I understood. It's the law that the Hawes have always lived by: KEEP MAMA HAPPY.

I bit the bullet and accepted the blame.

I quickly covered Stevie's mouth and interjected, "Sorry, Mom, we won't use that word again. We will be careful what we say around him."

This led to another stern lecture until Dad returned to the car. Right before he entered the car, Mom said that she was not going to start our vacation off on a bad note, so she was not going to tell our Dad. Just don't let her hear it again.

Chapter Four - Found

As soon as he entered the car, she changed her tone, "Anything available, honey?"

With a huge smile of relief on his face and another puff on the cigarette, he gave us the great news that they had a spot available at the back of the campground. He explained that it was not the ideal spot, but it was all they had available.

Then, with a little excitement in his voice, "There is a pond on the other side of the campsite, and they rent fishing poles. This really might work out."

"This is meant to be. This is where God wants us to be. I knew he would watch out for us," Mom suggested.

Mom kept talking about how God had blessed us as we were leaving the office to find our campsite. Meanwhile, Phillip, Stevie, and I looked back to see if we could see the brunette and red-headed beauties that had just passed. But they were gone.

Relieved that the ride up was over, Phillip, Stevie, and I unfolded from the back of the Stang. Dad was right. The campsite was not normal. To get to the site, we had to cross over a creek via a wooden bridge. It was a single site tucked back into the woods with a huge rock on it. I climbed on the rock and noticed that you had a clear view of the sky.

"Mom, this is an awesome spot to tell ghost stories."

"I know! I can't wait," Mother returned in her "scary" voice as she was walking away from the campsite.

"Where are you going?" Dad asked.

She responded that she was going to the restroom. Then you heard a yell, "I'll be right back."

The restroom was a good distance away but still in eyesight if you looked hard enough. The tin-roofed, wood-planked-sided building backed into the woods a little. One side was for the men, and the other was for the women. It was one of five community restrooms on the campground, with four toilets and showers on each side per restroom.

"Right, I mean, as soon as we empty the car and set up the tent," Dad gripped.

Again, words he would never say in front of Mom. Then he ordered us to assist him in getting everything out of the car so we could set up the dark green 6-man tent.

A little while later, you can see Mom's 5'4", 165-pound frame walking up a path toward the campsite.

As she is about to step on the wooden bridge to cross the creek, Dad asks, "Where in the world have you been?"

Mom answers as if she didn't even recognize the agitated tone in Dad's voice, "Honey, look what I found."

She holds up a shiny gold necklace with a charm that is half a heart with the letters "Be" on top and the letters "Fri" right below. Obviously half a "Best Friends" charm that's very popular with teenage girls.

"I found it on the floor of the restroom as I was walking out. AND (with a little tone of her own directed back towards Dad) it took me so long because I was trying to be a good God-fearing citizen, and I took it to the office to see if anyone was looking for it. I was sure that some little girl would be missing this."

Everyone gathers around the newfound item, except for Dad, who continued to work to get the site set up stopping long enough to put one cigarette out and ignite another.

"If you took it to the office, then why do you still have it?" I questioned.

"They told me that nobody has come to them about a necklace. Told me to keep it. If someone came looking for it, they would send them down to our site. This way, they won't be responsible. Actually, he told me that I didn't even have to return it, but I told him I just wouldn't feel right. I made him promise to send anybody that was missing their necklace to me. I just wouldn't feel right. Lord knows."

"Shoot, as soon as he told me that I didn't have to return it, it would be mine," Phillip offered and then very quickly realized that the statement he just made was not the right answer, even if it was the honest answer.

You could see the fire in Mama's eyes as she turned towards Phillip and spewed some verbal heat in the direction of the husky 13-year-old.

"Boy, you know that ain't right. We don't steal."

"It's not stealing if they say we can have it, right?" Phillip questioned.

She changes her tune and turns back to the teaching Mom, "Phillip, it's not theirs to give away. What if it was your Dwight Gooden rookie card that was lost, and I had it? Wouldn't you want me to give it back?"

Phillip quickly reacts, "Two things! One, I wouldn't be dumb enough to leave my Dwight Gooden rookie card on the floor of a bathroom," everyone but Mom laughed. "Two, yes, I would want you to give it back."

The senior Hawes had been working throughout this whole conversation and was beginning to look frustrated by the lack of help from his family. With the cigarette dangling from the side of his mouth, he announced in a stern-feed-up type of tone, "Phillip, we are giving it back. That's the bottom line. Now, everyone, let's pitch in and get the site straight before it gets dark."

Everyone got to work, and everything was set up rather quickly.

It made it possible for Phillip and me to offer to take Stevie to the swimming pool. Stevie had been hooting and hollering to go swimming ever since we drove into the campground and saw the pool. Taking him would give Mom and Dad some time to rest. Plus, this allowed Phillip and I to find the two hot girls we saw earlier.

Chapter Five - Story Time

As the darkness started to appear, we made our way back to our secluded site. Phillip and I were disappointed in our lack of success in finding the girls, but we still had some time to bond. We walked all around the site, the nature trail, and the fishing pond, and even went to the office and got some information on all the activities that the site offered. Campsites were very good at holding family-orientated events like swimming races, dances,and pool tournaments just for the kids of the camp. This was really something that we looked forward to every trip.

Phillip and Stevie really looked up to me, and I took great pride in being a role model for them. This was installed into me by my parents and my Sunday school teacher, James Simpson.

I have a girlfriend and promised Phillip this would be the year that we would get him one. We made a pact that this would be the goal of this trip.I told him that this was his practice field. He could put the moves on the girls in the mountains of NC because nobody here knows him. He didn't have to worry about rejection because we will never see these people again after this week.

After we ate some of Dad's World-Famous BBQ wings cooked on the open fire, we started to settle in for the night. We started to explain to our parents how awesome this location was, which included the suggestion that we may not have to leave the campground the entire week. Mom was beginning to turn off the radio right when my favorite song was coming on, "I'm Going to Love You Forever and Forever" by local hero Randy Travis.

Randy was born in Marshville, which is less than thirty minutes from our house, and supposedly, my uncle Richard used to hang out with him when he was a teenager.

This song is my girlfriend's favorite song. Kimberly Simpson is a beautiful brown-headed 15-year-old and has been my girlfriend for about three months. She is my Sunday school teacher James Simpson's daughter. She still wears braces and looks like Jaclyn Smith from "Charlie's Angels." Kimberly is very conservative. We haven't really kissed a lot, but that was OK with me. I could really see Kimberly and me in the future. It's very important for me to have a beautiful woman as my wife.

But more important, I want a good woman to be the mother of my children. I knew at 15 this was too early to start thinking about family. But when my dad awkwardly gave me the "sex talk," he told me never to be with someone unless I could see myself with them for the rest of my life. When he said to be, he highlighted the word "BE." To ensure I got the true meaning of the word "BE", which was never said but understood as sex.

"Don't fall in love and know that it would be impossible to stay that way," he said.

I took that to heart.

Mom waited until the song went off, and then we started huddling around the fire for the night of frightening ghost stories. The fire was close to a big rock. Stevie and I sit on the edge of the rock while the rest of the family sit in yard chairs surrounding the fire. This was the perfect spot to tell ghost stories. There wasn't another site on this side of the creek, and the rock was big enough that it created an opening in the trees that made a direct path to the moon.

Stevie wanted to start roasting the marshmallows, and Mom reminded him that we just ate. She told him we will do the marshmallows later in the night. After he persisted, Dad had to put his foot down and remind him that what Mom says goes. Period! As soon as Dad put his foot down, Stevie's whining stopped per standard practice.

The ghost stories Mom often told seem even more real because she would use our current surroundings in the story. This story was about the bridge that connected our site to the rest of the campground and the creek that ran beneath it. We were told about a young woman who was walking across the bridge many years ago when someone came from behind and snatched her baby from her arms. Then disappeared into the woods. Mom said that the woman dashed into the forest searching for her baby and its abductor.

Never to find either. Ever since that date over thirty years ago, if you listen carefully on a night when there is a full moon, you can hear her walking through the woods, and sometimes you will even hear her yelling out for her baby.

"Helen," Mom explained in a slow, scary voice.

"H..e..l..e..n," Dragging out every syllable.

At that moment, Mom pointed her hand towards the heavens and Stevie, Phillip, and I looked into the sky at the full moon. She requested us to be quiet to see if we could hear the young lady walking through the woods yelling out her baby's name.

Dad always played along and said, "Listen, I hear something."

At first, I thought he was doing his part, but then I really did hear something. My mind started running. I first thought my mind was playing tricks on me, but when Stevie jumped in my lap, I knew he heard it, too. Then we heard voices in the distance that were coming closer. It sounded like they were saying "Hellen." And it was truly the voice of a young lady.

"What in the tarnation?" Dad jumped up from his chair.

Phillip pointed to the bridge, and we could see two figures walking towards us. Suddenly, we realized that we had let our minds get the better of us; there really were two young ladies walking toward us. They were real people, not aberrations.

It was "Hello" we heard coming from one of the figures.

Quickly, Phillip and I sat up straight as we realized that these were the two girls we spent the majority of the evening looking for.

Stevie whispered in my ear, "That's the big booby girl."

I threatened him not to say a word, and I covered his mouth. Stevie has no filter. He will say whatever comes to his mind.

Mom, being the host of the family, said, "Well, hello, you just scared the devil out of the boys."

I gave my mom the "Are you serious look" as I informed them that I wasn't scared.

Then Mom told them the situation and how ironic it was that they were walking up at that particular moment.

Finally, Mom got around to introducing everyone. The two girls introduced themselves as Binki and Margaret. Binki was drop-dead gorgeous! Easily the most beautiful human being I had ever seen. She had brown hair, a golden tan, stood about 5'8", and, as my brother had pointed out several times, had big boobs. She was wearing a white tee shirt that was thin enough that you could see the Bra under her shirt. She had cut-off jean shorts and a pair of flip-flops that showed her lime green painted toenails. In between the shorts and the flip-flop were a set of impressive, tanned legs. If there was one imperfection on her body, I couldn't find it. And I was certainly looking. I concluded that they just left the shower because Binki's hair was still wet, which made her look even hotter.

Margaret was attractive, but it was more of a simple beauty. She had light brown/reddish hair and a perfect smile that hung below lightly visible freckles that sprinkled across her nose. Her skin was pale, and you could see that she didn't tan but instead burned. Her body was above average for a girl her age, but her features were not as distinctive as Binki's. She was about an inch taller and had her hair up with the ponytail hanging to the side. She was wearing big earrings and a black Madonna tour shirt. The jean cut-off shorts, flip flops, and lime green toe nails were an obvious attempt to match her friend's style.

"We are just telling some ghost stories. Why don't you sit down and join us?" Mom asked without ever even asking why they came to our site in the first place.

There had to be a purpose. This was not just a site you stumbled across.

Binki responded by saying, "No, thank you, Ms. Hawes. We just came by because I lost my necklace earlier today, and the man at the office said you may have found it."

Before Mom even answered, "We found it," Phillip interjected.

Mom said, "Hold on, what does it look like."

As Binki described the piece of jewelry, Margaret was displaying the other half of the shiny gold necklace with a charm that was an obvious match that Mother had found earlier in the day. This half had the letters "st" on top and the letters "ends" right below inside of a heart charm.

A perfect match.

Mom explained that she had to be careful. She wasn't just giving this to anyone. The two girls seemed really happy to have found it.

"I bet you were worried to death," the concerned Mrs. Hawes said.

"I was. Where in the world did you find it?" Binki responded.

Mom went on to explain the whole event of the day, not leaving out one detail. She even threw Phillip under the bus about him wanting to keep it.

Then, just to make sure she got him good, she said, "Two pretty girls come up, and then he is ready to return it."

You could see Phillip was pissed at Mom, but he said, "No, we talked about it, and you said returning it was the right thing."

I think Mom's version is a lot closer to the truth, but that was a good attempt at a save by Phillip.

Make no mistake, nobody was buying Phillip's version.

"Ok, I hid it. I will go get it. Hang out right here." And with that, Mom walks into the tent.

There was an odd moment of silence, but I felt compelled to break the lack of noise by asking, "Where are you from?"

"We are both from Gastonia", Binki responds. "How about y'all?"

We explained that we were from the Indian Trail.

Dad did the math for us, "Gastonia and Indian Trail are only about 45 minutes from each other.

"Really?" Binki sounded surprised.

"How do you know each other?" I asked as I was really starting to enjoy the conversation.

Margaret, getting involved in the conversation, tells us that they are best friends, and her family comes to this site every year and often brings Binki. But this is the first time that Binki's family came with them. They both start talking and talking. It became apparent that they were true southern young women who liked to talk.

As Mom came out with the necklace and handed it to Binki, the two of them told us their entire history together. We learned how they met five years ago and live in the same town, but they go to different schools. They have both been here for about a week. Margaret said she was leaving the day after tomorrow, and Binki said she would be here for another week, which I thought was odd and lucky. Who gets to go on vacation for two weeks?

Stevie, out of nowhere, said, "My brother can move his boobies without moving his arms, can you?"

Directed towards Binki.

At that very moment, I wanted to die.

A loud scream came from Dad, "Stevie! What is wrong with you?"

"What? Bo does it all the time," Stevie explained, not knowing what the big issue was, but he started to cry because he could feel that he was about to be in BIG trouble.

Anita Hawes was ready for the good Lord to take her home and she was certainly going to take Stevie with her. The red on her face matched the color of her hair.

"Girls, I'm really sorry," an embarrassed Anita Hawes said. "Stevie, you should be ashamed of yourself. I'm so sorry."

Stevie ran towards Mom and cried even more.

You could see that Dad thought it was a little funny as he smiled while sucking on a cigarette. He turned his back to the group for the pretend purpose of not wanting to exhaust the smoke in our direction but really to hide the smile. He never minded the direction of the cancerous gas before.

I knew what Stevie was asking, but I really wasn't sure how to explain it. I often can flex my chest muscles and it impressed my brothers so much. No matter, the situation was very awkward.

"It's OK. I have a little brother too, and that is so something he would say." Binki offered.

As Margaret nodded her head in agreement.

She added, "He says even worse. Trust us. Mitch is the devil."

I tried to explain that I could move my chest muscles without moving my arms and that Stevie thought that it was impressive. Not sure if they were really getting it. Then, they challenged me to show them. I really wanted to, but instead, I declined.

Changing the subject, Mom invited the young ladies to sit and join us in our family tradition. They said they had something planned with some other people but would love to join us another night.

I thought, "Anytime!" and before I realized it, that thought came out of my lips just like I said it in my head. It was filled with obvious excitement and everything. The girls smiled and thanked Mom for returning the necklace. Said their goodbyes, and they walked back towards the bridge.

We then decided that we were ready to bring out the marshmallows and start roasting, much to Stevie's approval. Before we got started, we saw Binki and Margaret walking back towards us.

I said, "You aren't scaring us this time."

The girls laughed.

"We didn't mean to last time; we are really sorry," Binki said, looking sheepishly sexy.

"We just came back to see if you wanted to join us. We are meeting some friends on the other side of the campground and thought you might want to join us?"

I was shocked.

"Really?" I thought for a minute and then looked over at my dad.

He had overheard the conversation and said "Sure" without me even having to ask.

Then, my overly protective Mom stepped in.

"What time is your little get-together over?"

"No certain time. It's just a bunch of our friends that sit and talk and listen to music," Margaret reveals.

"We promise we will watch out for your boy; we aren't killers. We will personally walk him back home," Binki offered with a bit of playful sarcasm.

Dad stepped in, recognizing that Mom was being too protective and was going to embarrass me if this conversation went on much further.

"Bo, go on. Have fun, and don't worry about your mom. Just be safe."

I could see Phillip off to the side, looking like he was sad that he didn't get offered to come, so I thought I would ask, "Hey, Phillip, you want to come? If that's alright with you," looking back at the girls.

Phillip was excited when he heard the girls give their permission for him to join us.

He got up and walked up beside me. I heard him whisper "thanks" as he was putting on his shoes.

This was the first time that Phillip had been out with me and teenage girls. It was like a mini double date. I knew he was excited, but I was a little nervous for him. Phillip was a little husky, shy, and naïve about what teenagers do. Truth be known, Phillip was ten years old in worldly experience, trapped in a body that had been around for 13 years. Either way, I planned to show him the ropes.

Stevie thought he would give another stab at talking and said, "Can I go?"

Before I could answer, Mom stepped in and said no. She told him it was because she had already gotten the marshmallows out and needed someone to eat them with. Roasting marshmallows won out as he thought about it.

After we went across the bridge, I questioned, "So where are we going?"

"First, we are going back to my site to change, get some goodies, and then we are going to a spot up the mountain to meet some of our friends," Binki responded.

"Oh, okay," I answered, but I was truly intrigued and a little weary.

"Goodies, what kind of goodies," Phillip asked.

"Cigarettes, cards, and some cups," Binki said.

You could tell that Binki has changed a little since we left our parents. I had the feeling that the angelic girl who stood before my mom turned a little devilish as soon as we crossed over the bridge. You could also see that this made Phillip extremelyuncomfortable. But I found myself even more attracted to her.

Chapter Six - Party

Our campsite and family faded in the distance as the two girls continued to talk about a couple of different people as if Phillip and I were not even there. Their conversations continued to include a lot of curse words. A couple of times, I would join in their talk, but the ladies certainly dominated the conversation. Phillip never said a word. The more we walked, the further behind he would lag.

"Is Scott going to be there tonight," Margaret asked Binki.

"Hell yeah, this is going to be fun."

Phillip's eyes grew every time Binki said a curse word. Phillip has never been around teenage girls, especially not teenage girls like these two. Free-speaking teenagers who looked like angels but spoke like sailors. The only teenagers he was ever around were the ones at church, and they didn't curse.

"Do you smoke?" Binki casually asked.

Phillip's eyes grew to the size of golf balls at the question.

Trying to play it off as if it was just a routine question, "No, neither of us do," I responded.

Binki then questioned, "Have you ever drunk beer?"

He could not hold back anymore.

"No!" Phillip chimed in louder than needed. His face was covered with "the get me the heck out of here look".

"Is it going to bother you if we do?" challenged Margaret.

I stepped in quickly and said, "No, you have the right to do whatever you want to do. What kind of beer?"

"The drink of the night is whatever Scott brings," Binki said.

Finally, we arrived at a campsite that was isolated by a row of small, purposely planted trees that separated their site from their neighbor. The beige pop-up camper was placed in the rear of the plotted-out area. The foundation of the camper was in the middle, with canvas sides that popped out on each side where the sleeping area was. The girls walked in while Phillip and I stayed outside.

Phillip leaned over to me and said, "Bo, I know these girls are hot. I know that I'm not the one they are interested in. I'm scared. I'm going back to the site."

I understood how he was feeling out of place. Every conversation we had was without him being involved or even questioned. Plus, he was not used to this. Truthfully, neither was I, but I was way too intrigued not to follow through. I really wanted to go with the girls and knew that if he didn't go, I would have to take him back to the site. Mom would kill me if I let him walk back by himself. I made a half-hearted effort to make him stay because of my promise to try to find him a girlfriend. But knew that I would be better off if he didn't go. He would just ruin the night because he didn't want to be there, and I would have to watch over him the entire night. The guilt of the promise suddenly changed to fear. The fear of what the girls have already said. Beer, cursing, and smoking. If Phillip goes back and I leave, he will tell. I might as well just tell the girls neither of us can go.

"I understand. Hold on, I will tell them that we aren't going."

Phillip already had it worked out.

"You can still go; I will find my way back. You can tell them I was feeling sick, and I will tell Mom and Dad I was just too tired. Bo, I won't tell Mom or Dad about beer or smoking. I promise. You can trust me!!"

It hit me like a rock. The whole time, he was lagging behind awkwardly and not being involved in the conversation with the girls; he was strategizing. Trying to figure a way out. If I left him behind, I would feel so guilty. But I really wanted to go with the girls. Either way, he can't walk back by himself. Plus, he heard them talk about beer and smoking. He said I could trust him, but I wasn't too sure. But... my mind started to run a scan of historical events. Trying to recollect the last time he ratted me out.

Nothing came to mind. But I normally didn't do things worthy of getting ratted out. Finally, I made up my mind. I can't take the risk. I can't go.

"That's okay; I will tell them I can't go tonight."

I knew once I did this, I would never see them again.

"No, then I'll stay," Phillip gave in.

There was a moment of celebratory emotions. Maybe he just needed the chance. Maybe he would have fun. But that moment was short-lived as I looked in his direction. He was scared. First, I thought that his fear was due to the girls. Then it hit me that maybe he was scared because he didn't want to let me down. Or maybe it really was about the beer and cursing. I concluded that it was probably all of that combined. It just overwhelmed him. More than ever, I knew he couldn't go. He was only doing this for me. It would be miserable for him. He would make the whole night awkward. Time to do the deed. I tapped on the outside of the pop-up camper as if I were knocking on the door of my neighbors and said, "Hello?"

I then heard Binki's voice say, "Come on in."

I told Phillip to stay outside as I walked into the camper. Phillip sat on the wooden picnic table as I opened the camper door. As soon as I walked in, there was Binki with a different set of jean shorts around her ankles, standing in her panties.

I said, "Oh, sorry. I thought you said come in."

Binki laughed and continued to pull on her shorts.

"I did say come in. I just had to change shorts. I hated the other ones."

Then she changed the direction of the conversation, "You look like you have never seen a girl in her underwear?"

Trying not to look like a wimp, I responded, "Of course I have. I was just trying not to be rude."

Really, though, that was the first girl I had ever seen live in their underwear. And I really liked what I saw. I knew there was no way I wasn't going with them tonight. My brother just had to understand.

"We are coming. Impatient, are we?" Margaret said.

"Well, I just came in to tell you that my brother doesn't feel too well, and I need to take him back to the camp. I really want to go but understand if you can't wait," I explained.

"Are you scared? Did the beer scare you away? Or is it seeing a girl in her underwear?" Bikini asked in a bullying tone.

"Of course, I'm not scared," I said, making a highly offended face.

"I really want to go, but I would feel bad if I made him go and he didn't feel good. Just tell me where the location is. I'll find it," I fired back.

Feeling like my manhood was challenged.

"You will never find the place. We will walk with you to take you brother back," Margaret said.

"I can't. You go with him; I have to wait for Scott. He will be here soon. He can't be here when Mom comes. She will have a shit fit. We will meet you at Devil's Head," Binki said.

Margaret and I walked Phillip back to the camp. You could tell that Margaret went into Binki's pop-up tent and worked hard to increase her looks. She put on some additional makeup and some perfume that was strong but smelled pretty nice. I complimented her on her perfume. She seemed impressed and grateful that I noticed.

As we drew closer to the campsite, I was afraid that if I went across the bridge, Mom might try to talk me into staying. Or get into this huge dialogue about something. Or Stevie would start begging to go with me. We conspired on a plan that had us taking Phillip to the bridge and dropping himoff. I reminded him with my best big brother voice that came across as more of a plea than one of force.

"Don't let me down. Remember what we discussed."

"I know, I know! You can trust me, I promise," Phillip said with a hint of frustration mixed in with a bit of relief.

Phillip played his part as being sick and slowly made his way back in the direction of comfort and familiarity, holding his belly the entire time.

I saw Mom and Dad sitting around the fire with Stevie on Mom's lap. They were still roasting marshmallows, and it looked like Dad had gotten the chocolate and graham crackers out to turn them into smores. I waved as I turned and walked away before they could call me over.

Chapter Seven - Devil's Head

We walked in the opposite direction until the road was swallowed by a mountain of trees. We reached a shallow stream that displayed a defined path on the opposite side. Large rocks were laid as makeshift steps to cross over the water.

"Hmm... who knew, man can walk on water," I said in jest.

Margaret's laugh was more the obligatory form, but it did its job and appeased me for my lame attempt at a joke.

"He wasn't sick. He just didn't want to go. Right?"

I surrendered the truth and told her that he wasn't that comfortable. I explained that I really wanted to help him become more outgoing, but for some reason, he is very insecure.

I didn't divulge that I was insecure about this situation, too. I have never smoked or drunk any form of alcohol. I don't hang around people who do. People at school call me the "Pope" because I stick to the values that my parents have instilled in me. I don't go to parties where people smoke or drink. I don't even get invited to parties where people do. I felt guilty walking up this mountain with Margaret, who may have participated in these activities. I felt like I was betraying the trust that my mom and dad had given me, not to mention the fact that I had a girlfriend back in Indian Trail.

But with all that said, I couldn't stop myself from going with Margaret to find Binki. I felt adrenaline flowing through my body. It was very similar to the excitement I felt as a linebacker for Sunny Ridge High's junior varsity squad during a game, but at the same time, it was different. I knew what I was about to do might get me in trouble, but I felt like this could turn out to be one of the greatest nights of my life. I'm never in trouble. One time might not hurt. The thing I liked the most was that I could recreate myself. Back in Indian Trail, I was the church boy dating the Sunday schoolteacher's daughter. With whom I have not seen any skin above her knees, but here I have already seen the most beautiful person alive in her panties. Even if it was for only 2 seconds. Those two seconds had me hunting for more time. I can be whoever I want for the next week and then ride back down the mountain and go back to being choir boy with my conservative girlfriend.

We continued to find out more and more about each other as we walked. I learned that Margaret likes to ride horses and is an A/B student in school. She wants to be a vet after school. I also found out that Margaret's parents really don't like Binki because they think she's a bad influence, which is probably true according to Margaret. She offered that the only times she ever seems to get in any real trouble is when she is with Binki.

"What's her story," I asked.

Then she hit me with the news I didn't want to hear.

"She dates a 20-year-old dude named Scott!"

I could not believe how stupid I was. The entire night, they spoke about Scott, and I never put it together. I was devastated. I think Margaret saw my disappointment.

"What, do you like her?"

I lied, "No way. I'm more the conservative type."

Which was true, mainly because that's the only option I ever got. Then I let the cat out of the bag, and my frustration overflowed.

"Conservative Blond or Conservative Brunette? Pick and choose! The preacher's daughter, the deacon's daughter, or the Sunday school teacher's daughter. A wild and crazy bunch!"

Margaret started to laugh extremely hard.

"You are really funny!"and then asked the question I didn't want to answer, "Do you have a girlfriend?"

I told her I just broke up with my girlfriend. Of course, this would really hurt Kimberly if she heard me say that. But I knew there was no way she would ever know about this discussion.

The path led us to an opening where the trees disappeared to the left of us, and in its place was a cliff that served as a floor to a window of awe-inspiring beauty. The view was enchanting. Almost like God was showing off. I slowed to admire the sight when Margaret stopped once she observed my gaze. "Pretty view," she says, acknowledging my admiration.

I shook my head in agreement, but before I could say anything, she continued, "Be careful. They say this view is a killer."

I was intrigued, so I bit at the mystery, "What do you mean?"

Still speaking in code, she says, "Just because she is pretty, doesn't mean she ain't dangerous."

Mischievously, I examine, "Are we talking about the view or you?"

The surprise and delight could not be hidden. She does a large inhale and fans her face as if she is about to faint.

In her best southern voice, "Well, be still my heart. That is so sweet." Then turns serious in a jovial way, "And true."

We both laugh as she leans into me. Nesting her shoulder under my arm. I move my arm as it makes its destination on top of her shoulder.

Margaret awkwardly pulls back and points at a large boulder that is about the size of a car. The huge piece of stone rested about seven feet from where we were standing.

"That rock is known as the "Sweet Spot" by the locals. Obviously, because of the incredible view, and that is where people come up here to be sweet with each other if you know what I mean."

She once again lightly bounces into me with her eyebrows raising a couple times. Which apparently meant make-out.

My smile widens as I say, "Oh yeah."

Mainly because I assume that is what every man is supposed to say when talking about sex.

"That's pretty", she offers.

"But make no mistake, she is dangerous. Behind that big old rock and right in front of the pretty view is the cliff. That is not an ordinary cliff. This cliff does not have a sudden edge. That cliff turns smooth. Like a slide. Thus, that spot is called the Suicide Slide. Either because it would be suicide to go too far or because of the Lover's Legend."

Margaret points at a big blue sign right beside the rock with large white letters that reads, "Nobody Beyond This Point".

Without taking a breath, she carries on, "Legend has it that a young couple died trying to get a view over the cliff while holding hands. Holding hands as they fell to their death."

She closed her eyes and dipped her head to rest on her shoulder in an exaggerated display of heartbroken love that was no more, just for special effects. It was working. I felt empathy for them.

Margaret taps the breaks on the story for dramatic effect but does not stall too long. Moments later, the foot is once again planted firmly to the floorboard as she continues.

"Some say the couple was fighting. He got mad and pushed her off."

She does a fake falling scream, "AAAHHHH – Thump."

In true storyteller fashion, she scrunches her forehead and points a finger to the sky.

"And the momentum from his push made him slide to his death." Once again, "AAAHHHH – Thump." Which is one version.

In a soft storytelling voice, "Others say she fell over backward when he was trying to take a picture. Just like Romeo and Juliet, he could not live without her. So, he decided to join her in the afterlife."

She looks to the sky as if she can see them in heaven together.

The stories and her way of painting the picture impressed me. Thosesound like the stories my mom would be telling my brothers right now. I almost expect my father to jump out from behind the big ole rock to scare us.

"Which story do you believe?"

With a flirtatious smile sneaking across her face while her hands met at her heart. She rolls her eyes towards the sky in a dreamy fashion, "I am a romantic. The Romeo story is obviously the right one. Mainly because I dream that someday, my Romeo could not live without me."

Just like before, she went from dreamy to stern in a playful, deep, matter-of-fact voice.

"Plus, when they found the man, his camera had a picture of the girl standing right beside the Sweet Spot."

She motions her head to the rock just in case I forgot the rock's name.

"That is an awesome story. You should put that in a book. I bet you would sell a million copies," I proclaim.

She said in a gleeful manner, "I might just do that. But I'm not sending you any of the money, honey."

Laughter fills the night air once again.

The view was breathtaking, but I decided that I was not going on a suicide slide tonight. I started back in the direction that we were heading before the scenic distraction.

Margaret quickly catches up and picks up right where we left off.

"You are full of shit. You have a girlfriend. I'm not stupid."

"What about you? You got a boyfriend?" I said, trying to change the subject without answering the question.

The "Nobody serious" that came from her mouth was a mixture of hopeless self-pity and an invitation to take the role. Knowing she was being honest, I decided to flatter her anyway.

"Bull Crap, you are too pretty not to have a boyfriend."

Using a page out of my book, she changed the subject as smoothly as I did.

With a grin on her face, she asked, "Did you just say bull crap? You are too cute. Bull crap?"

Going back to old reliable, I again took us in another direction. "Wait, if her boyfriend is 20, then how old is Binki?" I asked.

"15," was the answer.

When I asked what her parents thought about the 20-year-old lover, another layer of Binki was unraveled. Margaret made me swear not to tell Binki and then proceeded to inform me how her parents were in this big fight. She told me that Binki's Dad was part of some gang. He was always partying and drunk. Binki's dad is an angry drunk who is abusive verbally and physically. One night the abuse was so bad that Binki's mom almost died. So, Mrs. Wallace gathered everyone up and left. They are camping here to hide out from Binki's dad. Her Mom is afraid of her dad. She has been working at a restaurant up the street, putting in extra hours until she can save enough to rent an apartment.

"Her mom is hardly ever at the site," she concluded.

We walked for about ten minutes, going deeper into the woods and higher on the mountain with every step we took. Out of nowhere, Margaret then turns her body towards me, getting right in front of my next step.

"Do you really think I'm too pretty?"

She didn't wait for a response. She leaned in as if she were going to give me a kiss. I was shocked and wasn't sure what to do.

I tilted my head back and said, "Sure, you're beautiful".

Really thinking she was pretty, but beautiful might be a stretch. Beautiful is Binki, Margaret is OK. Binki has a great tan, and Margaret has a burn instead of a tan. Binki has a body like the women I see in the posters hanging on my bedroom walls, like Elle Macpherson, Christie Brinkley, and Kathy Ireland. Margaret has the body of, well, a 15-year-old girl. I feel like I know Margaret. She is every girl I have ever known. Conservative and okay. Binki is mysterious and anything other than okay.

"Sure, beautiful? What does that mean?"

"It means I think you are really pretty. Wait a minute, how do I call a person I barely know beautiful and then she acts offended?"

Margaret allows a sense of peace to slide over her face and then offers, "Sorry. It's just that everybody we meet likes Binki. Then that is all I ever hear. Binki this! Binki that! I guess I should have taken that compliment better."

"That's cool," came from my mouth, but in my head, I was thinking, Holy cow! She just read my mind.

She grabbed my hand, and we returned to our journey to the top of the hill. My mind was racing. I looked over at Margaret and saw a big smile on her face. She was glowing. She laid her head on my shoulder as if we were now a couple. I thought, why not?

Chapter Eight - Scott

The path became more defined the higher we climbed due to heavy traffic in the past. It was apparent that this was a place that had been visited many times by many people. Finally, I saw an opening up ahead. As we drew closer, heavy metal music was roaring louder and louder with each step. Upon our arrival, we passed a small group of people and went to the edge of a cliff that stood atop our campground. It was impossible to make out the identity of people, but you could see movement and the overall layout of the place, including the road in front of the campground and the lake that covered one side of the site. When I looked up, the spot's namesake appeared. A rock structure that resembled a "Devil's Head".

An arm came from behind. One from each direction meeting at my stomach.

"Amazing, right?"

Margaret pushed her chest against my back.

"Unbelievable," I responded.

I turned around and grabbed her hand as we walked towards the group. My mind was racing from the unknown of what the night had to offer. I was digging how happy and really forward Margaret was being with me. How do I take a walk in the woods with a stranger and come out with a "girlfriend," or so she thinks? Just because I told her she was beautiful. Really? Maybe those Gastonia city folks do move faster than we do in the country.

I noticed five people sitting around a campfire. All of them were drinking from red Dixie cups while the scent of cigarette smoke filled the night air. A blonde kid that looked younger than the rest had his arms around a girl that looked order than everyone immediately caught my eye. Behind the group sat a jacked-up yellow off-road bike that proudly displayed the words "Yamaha" on the side.

Margaret and I walked towards the group. Upon contact, Margaret grabbed Binki's cigarette, took a draw, and released the air from her lungs as if it were the greatest feeling in the world. Then she introduced me to everyone. Binki swiped the cigarette back from Margaret and took a draw of her own. I could not get over how stunning she was with her white mesh shirt that was covering her black bra seductively hiding in plain sight. I was afraid I was going to get caught staring. Especially since "Scott" is sitting right beside her. Plus, I had my new "Girlfriend" sittingbeside me.

Scott was wearing a black bandanna covering his dirty blond hair, a pair of jeans, and an Ozzie shirt.

He responded, "S'up, dude."

I answered with a head nod and a "S'up" of my own.

I was surprised. I expected some muscle freak, but he was more of a skinny rocker guy. As every guy does, I sized him up very quickly. I was thinking that I weighed more than he did, had a bigger body frame, and certainly more muscle mass. Net evaluation: I could kick his butt.

I came to discover that beside them was Mitch, Binki's brother. You could see the resemblance because he had her tan and facial features, but his hair was as blonde as it could possibly be. My first thought was Rick Flair, my wrestling idol. The color was the same, but Mitch had his hair a lot shorter and parted down the middle. He came across as cocky and didn't acknowledge me. He dressed like a model for some preppy magazine. He had a pair of khaki shorts, a red collared shirt, and was bare footed. I wondered where his shoes were. He was trying to kiss the girl to his left during the entire introduction.

Holding Mitch's hand was someone introduced as Mitch's girlfriend, Becky. She tried to acknowledge me but found herself fighting off Mitch's playful kissing attempts. She was a pretty girl that was obviously older than him. I quickly came to the conclusion that she was probably older than everyone here except for Scott. She had long dark hair and was wearing shorts that were so high that everyone had a good view of her thighs. She wore a half shirt that covered her breast and her breast only. The thing that stuck out was how much makeup she had on. She was covered. Her eyes looked like they were painted blue, with long fake eyelashes, and her face looked like it would crack if you touched it. My mom would describe her as trashy!

Then, there was another teenage boy who looked out of place. He sat around the fire with everyone else but was by himself. Nobody was directly on either side. He looked disinterested in the whole group. He was dressed in dark-colored jeans and a tank top. It was apparent that Margaret had met him before but didn't remember his name. She asked him his name, and he informed us that he goes by Jared. He told us he was Becky's brother. He was not an appealing guy and a little scary. His curly hair looked dirty, and his round, freckled face had a 2-inch gash across the cheek that looked like it needed stitches at one time but was never addressed by a doctor and had scarred. He looked a little older than me.

I saw Margaret whisper something in Binki's ear, which I assumed was about me. They both were smiling so I assumed this was a good thing.

Binki handed me a Dixie cup and said, "Drink up."

This was going to be my first sip of any type of alcohol. I really wasn't sure what to expect.

I asked, "What's this?"

"My good friend Bud," Scott said with his chest stuck out.

I had no clue what that meant, but I gathered that it was beer. I looked around and saw a cooler sitting behind Binki and Scott. The cooler was surrounded by a couple of empty beer cans, which quickly made me wonder how are there already empty beer cans.

Binki offered, "You going to babysit it or drink it?"

Her poke at me got a laugh from everyone around the fire except for Jared. Who, now I gathered, got up here early or somehow started before we did because he was already drunk and getting closer to passing out with every second that went by? I noticed that he had his own small glass bottle of something darker in color that was about empty in his hands. The glass, his hands, and his head were just waiting for gravity to pull them all to the ground.

Too late to turn back now. I put the small Dixie cup up to my lips and emptied the cup. I had always heard about beer and how good it was, but I didn't feel that way after drinking that cup. It really didn't taste good. I also expected to be drunk after that sip, but I was feeling fine.

They offered me a cigarette, but I knew that was something I couldn't do.

We talked for a while, often learning about each other. I found out that Scott was just up here for the night, and it took him 3 hours to get here. He was supposed to be at his job at a motorcycle place by 9 am in the morning, and he had to be there on time because they didn't know he borrowed the motorcycle he rode up on. He said he would get fired if they found out but informed us that he really didn't give a shit.

The whole time I was thinking, I didn't see it. I have no idea what someone as beautiful as Binki is doing with a loser like him. Binki's Mom felt the same way because she had "pure hatred" for Scott, mainly due to many nights like this where he got her drunk or kept her out too late. The general consensus is if they are spotted together, Binki's mom is going to call the police on him.

When Mitch became the subject, the picture was painted as him being a real lady's man despite being just 14 years old. He often spoke about his many girlfriends back at home, with Becky sitting right beside him, holding his hands. Binki offered the words "Male whore" to describe him. He talked about Becky as if she wasn't there. Mitch thought a lot of himself and nothing about the girls he was talking about. He said Becky understands that after this week, they will probably never see each other again. So, they decided just to have fun.

Which I thought was interesting because those were pretty similar to the words I said to Phillip at the beginning of our vacation. All men might really be dogs. I couldn't help but think that at least he was being honest with Becky. That's more than I was with Margaret.

It was determined that Becky was 16 but looked a lot older. All that make up did its part in making her look older than she really was. And her brother Jared was actually the older of the two. He was 19 years old and lived in a mobile home down the road from the campsite. The trailer is owned by their parents but allows him to stay there. Becky was a rising sophomore at some school in Tennessee and was spending a couple of weeks with Jared. Mitch and Becky had only known each other for four days.

During our time talking, Margaret kept rubbing my hands, my back and my legs, which I must admit did feel nice.

"OK, let's stop all the Walton's Family Moment Talk and let the games begin," Scott said loud and looking like he might have already drunk more than he should have.

"What do you want to play? Spin the bottle, truth or dare?"

After what seemed like 15 minutes of discussion, we decided to play a game similar to craps. But we used rocks instead of dice. They called it "Mountain Quarters". Scott drew a line near our campfire and then placed a big rock about 10 feet from us. Everyone gets their turn to step up to the line and throw quarters at the rock. The one that got the closest to the rock without touching it was the winner. The winner gets to choose to either drink or make someone else drink.

Everyone was playing except for Jared, who was just lying flat on the ground. He was done for the night. I also noticed that the brown stuff in the glass bottle was gone, with the bottle lying right beside his head.

I was pretty good at this game and believe my football background helped. The alcohol was beginning to have some effect, but I was still alert. Margaret, on the other hand, was not doing as well. Her inability to speak without slurring was evidence that she was past the buzzed phase and was rapidly ascending to the drunken zone. The higher the alcohol intake, the more aggressive she got. She was pushing her body all over me. She kept giving me sloppy, octane-flavored kisses. I was shocked! I did not know this girl a couple of hours earlier, and now she can't get her hands off me.

We played for a while, and the more we drank, the dumber people were getting. Scott, Binki, and Becky had their share, too, and you can see that it had done some damage to them as well. I recognized that the drunker Scott got, the meaner and more aggressive he became.

Chapter Nine - Bitch Fight

Scott would talk about his past girlfriends and tell us stories with a sense of pride of his many drinking adventures. Including the time in which he was arrested for drunk driving and public indecency when he got caught pissing on the side of a Seven/Eleven. He talked loudly and cursed with almost every sentence. Several times, he would refer to Binki as "bitch".

He would say, "My bitch" got it going on or "Bitch, grab me a beer".

I could not comprehend why she would allow him to call her that, but she didn't seem to be bothered by it.

After quite a bit of time, we stopped playing the game, and it turned more into story time again, which allowed Scott to tell us more stories using incoherent, slurring words. The stories got more and more outrageous and made less and less sense. Still, everyone was laughing or engaged, mainly due to the buzz. If not, just stone drunk!!

This included me. I think I was on the buzz side. Then again, I could be drunk. Never been either, but knew that all night, I was trying to be conservative with the amount of beer I drank because I had to go back to camp that night. Knowing the potential danger that awaited, I still was intrigued to know where the night would lead because Margaret was all over me. The more I drank, the more the idea of being with Margaret seemed to be justified. It was shaping up to be the greatest night of my life.

Scott told yet another story, no doubt, with the intent to prove how macho he really is. Every word is filled with the goal of reminding everyone that he is tough and a real badass. This particular story talked about how many times he has broken the law without getting in trouble.

Mitch, trying to be funny, jabbed at Scott by saying, "Rocker Romeo, you better not let mom know you are with Binki. She will go crazy, and you will go to jail".

It was said in jest. Scott was offended and didn't find his humor funny even though everyone else was laughing. The combination of an offended Scott, people laughing at him, and a lot of alcohol apparently made him even stupider.

I didn't think that was possible, but he tried to prove me wrong by stating, "I don't care; I will tell that bitch. I will do it tonight. Binki is my Bitch. And I will tell your Bitch mama."

"Shut up," the equally alcohol-impaired Mitch interrupts as he seems to get offended. "Don't call my mom a bitch!"

I looked over to Binki, and for the first time, I was disappointed. I was disappointed that she didn't defend her own mom. Her mom being called a bitch didn't even bring a flinch. Just didn't register. It is almost as if Binki had come to the conclusion that it is OK for women to be called Bitch.

Especially in that family.

Things went from zero to 100 miles per hour really quickly!!

Scott decides it is time for him to prove his manhood. The twenty-year-old Scott goes towards the fourteen-year-old Mitch in an aggressive manner.

"Punk, you don't tell me to shut up. I'll knock the blonde out of your hair."

Mitch stands up, but it's not straight. The alcohol has given his stance a lean that alternates from one side to the other.

Scott staggers towards Mitch and gives him a hard shove, resulting in Mitch landing flat on his back. Scott stalks Mitch as if he were a lion that is about to finish off a deer. With his chest puffed out, he puts one foot in front of the other in an uneven line. It was evident that Scott was moving closer to Mitch as if he were going to jump on top of him and start pounding him. To finish him off.

Binki's fear had hit a catastrophic level as she sensed that this was about to get out of hand. Her eyes filled with fear, and in a moment of bravery, she grabbed Scott's arm while simultaneously yelling for him to stop. Scott takes a drunken, unsteady, over-exaggerated turn. His head was the first to make the turn, with the rest of his body slowly following. It took him a moment to gather his wits and recognize who had just put their hands on him. Then, with a smile on his face, he allows his venom to be directed towards his girlfriend.

"Oh, Oh, HELL NO, you didn't."

He launches his body directly towards Binki with redirected hate and pushes Binki to the ground.

"Shut the hell up bitch. Do you know who you are talking to?"

He steps over her body to demonstrate his dominant position.

I couldn't believe what I was seeing. It was quickly going from the greatest night of my life to a nightmare!! Who is this Scott dude? Is this some crazy killer that nobody knows about? My heart was pounding as if it was outside of my body. I could feel the pulse in my neck pounding. Scott took his right foot and put it across Binki's neck, restricting her from breathing. I thought I saw him crack a smile in her direction as she had both of her hands on his boots in an effort to release the pressure from his boot on her neck. She started making whizzing sounds as she was struggling to breathe.

Adrenaline kicked in as I jumped up and gave him a hard push. A hard push wasn't needed. Nevertheless, that is what I administered. The shove did its job and allowed Scott to lose balance and fall to the ground. Which in turn allowed Binki to regain her ability to breathe.

My actions coincided with a loud "back off. What the hell is wrong with you? You better not touch her again."

As if I was some great protector. I couldn't help but think, am I drunk? What am I doing?

"You stupid shit. If I want to, I will. That's my bitch!! You can't do nothing about it," Scott slurs his words as he directs his attention towards me this time.

Blood is flowing through my body so fast that I think my heart is going to explode. Scott slowly gains his way to his feet, and now the tornado of evil known as Scott has found his third intended target within the last sixty seconds. He gathers himself and turns his body in my direction.

That's when I had the self-confidence that I was bigger than him despite the age difference. I also noticed that he didn't make a move toward me, though he was talking to me. That was the first time tonight. He rushed towards Binki and Mitch. I think he recognized that I was bigger than the 14-year-old Mitch and his girlfriend, whom he had just shoved to the ground. When I was sizing him up earlier, I bet he did the same. No matter the lack of forward movement with his body, his mouth didn't stop. After a couple of verbal exchanges that included him using every hill billy/redneck insult he could think of, his drunk courage mounted to the level that allowed him to start walking toward me. I got in the fighting stance as if I was Mike Tyson in the middle of the squared ring.

Right before he reached me, Scott fell with his head landing at my feet. Originally, I thought he fell into a drunken stupor. Then, I noticed traces of blood leaking through his long blond hair. I took my eyes off the fallen body long enough to look up and see Mitch standing there motionless as if he were playing a part in a horror movie. He was in a trance, or his body had been possessed. Or he was having an out-of-body experience as he just stood there. Frozen. My clouded mind was trying to make sense of the situation when I caught a glimpse of the cause of the blood. Mitch had a large rock in his right hand. The same hand and rock he used to hit Scott in the back of the head.

My focus shifted back to the body that was lying at the base of my feet. Scott is dead! Or that was the first thought that entered my mind. The thought became even greater by the fact that he was moving no more than the tree limb that was sitting nearby. I felt the same possessed motionless trance that Mitch was in when reality started to settle in. The trance came in and took over my body. The surreal moment began to come into my vision. I just witnessed a murder. Wait, was I part of a murder?

As "Holy Shit" came across my mind, "What the Hell" entered my ears as Scott displayed the first sign of life.

I never thought I would be happy to hear his voice, but I was so relieved. I left the trance state I was in and bent down to help. At first, groggy Scott accepted my help while he gathered himself. I assisted as he slowly made his way towards sitting up. I took the black bandanna that had fallen nearby and tried to plug the gash caused by the rock. He had no idea what happened to him. A rebalancing of his eyes towards me allowed him to remember that it was probably my fault. He swiped his hand across his head, ensuring that it went under the bandanna as if he were wiping off sweat.

When his hand reached the front of his face, he saw it was covered in blood. Scott caught me looking at Mitch in a manner that said it wasn't me. My eyes betrayed Mitch by informing Scott that it was him. Scott turned his head and recognized who the culprit was due to the rock still sitting in Mitch's hand. At that moment, I saw hate, revenge, and pure evil right before me.

There was FIRE coming out of every pore of Scott's body as he stood up to get retribution for the damage that was done to his skull. Mitch suddenly awakens from the comatose and dropped the rock. He started stumbling down the mountain with Becky chasing after him.

Scott started in the direction that Mitch had taken, but his steps were wobbly. He was struggling to put one foot in front of the other.

The knock to the head with a rock, the large consumption of alcohol, or a combination of both had really enhanced his rage but impaired his ability to do anything about it.

Binki's tear-filled face jumped in front of him, yelling for Scott to stop. Scott allowed the alcohol to assist him in insulting Mitch as loud as he could and decided that he was going to get his revenge. His body told him that he was in no condition to get the retribution that his mouth was promising. Or, at least, not tonight. Scott crumbled to the ground.

Binki grabbed the bandana from me and picked up where I left off.

She used it as a towel to wipe the blood from his head. It quickly started to soil up the bandana. Though it was black, you could see the imprints of where the color was leaving, and the soaked blood was taking its place.

Upon command, she does as she is instructed by her fallen lover and hands him another beer to help calm him down. It is obvious that beer had done enough damage; thus, giving him another didn't seem too wise. Yet Binki was just trying to de-escalate the issue and appease him.

For the next several minutes, Scott constantly tries to give another shot at finding Mitch. Failing every time. Eventually, Scott seems to give in and folds himself down on the ground near a passed-out Jared. Who was circled by empty beer cans, an empty whiskey bottle, a host of cigarette butts, and oblivious to any of the action that had just taken place. Though his legs were not taking him anywhere, Scott's mouth never stopped sharing what he was going to do once he got his hands on Mitch. Scott starts to chug another beer and then turns his attention to Binki, telling her how sorry he was for pushing her. That she knows that he would never hurt her because he loves her too much. She just soaks it in as if he were complimenting her.

I walked towards the edge of the cliff, looking over the campsite with my mind racing. Thinking how she could accept this. He just threatened her brother, insulted her mother, and physically assaulted her. Yet she is over there cuddling and mending his wounds by kissing him on the cheek and hugging his neck.

Looking towards the stars and trying to clear my mind, I realized that he was about to fight me. He might have had a gun or knife. He still might!! HE COULD HAVE KILLED ME!! Heck, he still might want to.

He may still come back for revenge once he sobers up. Wonder if he even remembers tonight when he sobers up?

I decided no matter how beautiful these girls are; this is not for me. I started walking toward the path back to the site when Margaret walked over and put her arms around me. I could smell the alcohol oozing from her mouth as she leaned around and kissed me. We stood there in silence, embracing each other. I realized that Margaret was scared and found comfort in my arms. Made me feel manly to be standing there like her security blanket.

The silence is broken rather quickly, with a couple of curse words exploding from the lips that I have quickly grown to hate. Here we go again, I thought. When I found the commotion, it came with a sense of regret that I didn't leave when I had the chance.

Scott is trying to get on his bike, and Binki is trying to stop him. I am conflicted. What is the right thing to do? The alcohol consumption obviously put him in no condition to drive. Add the alcohol consumption to the bloody head, and it's obvious that he should not be driving anything tonight. On the other side, he is an asshole and deserves what he gets.

My morals start getting the best of me. The POPE in me returns.

Nobody deserves to die. Plus, he is so messed up he could hurt someone else. I start walking towards them to help Binki convince Scott not to drive.

Scott notices that I am walking towards him. I'm not sure if he is scared that I might be trying to fight him or if he has just had enough excitement for the night.

But before I get there, Scott pushes Binki to the ground and yells, "You will regret this!!"

He gets on his bike and flips us a bird as he weaves down the mountain.

Binki was lying on the ground crying uncontrollably as the Yamaha's taillights disappeared down the trail with the same staggered side-to-side motion that the driver displayed when he was trying to walk just a couple of minutes earlier.

Chapter Ten - The Aftermath

Almost as quickly as the taillights disappeared, Mitch and Becky reappeared. I gathered that once they noticed that they weren't being followed, they snuck back up the mountain and hid in the shadows.

Mitch walks over to Binki and gives her a hug. This moment brought the realization that Mitch and not her father has always been the protector of the family, despite his young age. He wiped her tears away and gave some comforting words as Margaret and I made our way toward them.

As we get close, I hear Binki say the words, "Kill her."

"Whoa, hold up!! Someone needs to explain this to me. Kill? Kill who? Kill what?" I stated in a concerned voice.

"Nothing you need to worry about," Mitch replies as if I were a child not needing to know what the parents are talking about.

"Nothing to worry about! Dude, I just got in this dude's face. He just attacked you! Attacked your sister! And called your mom a bitch! Oh yeah, not to mention, I just heard SOMEONE (looking at Binki) say the words KILL. There is a lot to worry about!"

"You have nothing to worry about!" Binki sternly informed me. "Scott was just drunk. Tomorrow, he won't remember anything. Even if he did, he doesn't know you or where you are staying. You are good."

In a matter-of-fact tone as if I'm the lucky one.

Binki tries to defend him.

"Plus, he really is a nice guy. That was just the alcohol."

Binki could see that I was not convinced and gave a great effort to make me feel different. But the words were meaningless to me because I didn't hear the goodness in him. What I gathered was he was a nice guy when he wasn't drinking, but he was drinking quite often. Thus, he is not normally a good guy. This was confirmed when she spilled the beans that tonight was not the first time something of this nature had happened.

The only difference from the other events was the rock and blood. Which only brought about more concern on my part for everyone's safety. The rock and blood are a huge difference.

There was a moment of silence which allowed me to sneak a peek in Binki's direction. The look covering her face told of fear and concern.

Contradicting the brave words spoken just moments before. The fearless façade starts to crack when Binki admits that she is concerned about how Scott may react tomorrow when he discovers his lacerated head serving as a reminder of the night's events. But she shares that she is not afraid of Scott physically trying to hurt anyone who was at Devil's Head tonight. Her body is shaking due to Scott's threat that he was going to tell her dad where her mom is staying and tell him that she is shacked up with some guy.

"Just to get him good and pissed off," she quoted.

Binki said that she begged him not to contact her dad. Yet Scott kept holding her mom's location over her head, and eventually, she couldn't hold her anger in and called him a "dick".

Which only infuriated him even more. This is when he got so angry that he pushed her down and drove off.

Margaret went over and put her arms around Binki to comfort her.

Telling her that Scott is not stupid enough to tell their dad about the location. Reminding everyone that he did attack you and Mitch. Plus, Scott would have to share that Mitch was the one who cut his head. We all know that he is too cool to let anyone know a 14-year-old beat him down. This seemed to draw a smile from everyone. The group bought what Margaret was selling. She was making sense. The thought of him having to tell this story to others is not possible. Everyone conceded that he will not remember tonight when the sun rises tomorrow. Scott will explain the dent in his head in some manly fashion, like a bike accident, while trying to do some never-before-done trick in order to keep all his cool points with his groupies.

It was settled that Binki would call him sometime soon and make things right. After all, that is what true love is about, according to her.

Sticking with your man through the good times and bad, no matter the faults.

The tension that was hanging in the night air started to dissipate as Margaret started ribbing Mitch about the "hit and run" he did with the rock. Binki chimed in that Mitch was her hero and then gave me kudos for stepping up in her moment of despair. It was as if the whole thing wasn't real. Like we were talking about a TV show. The group recapped each person's acts of heroism or the lack of in the case of Margaret. The excitement of the evening slowly gave way to other topics. Topics that were more typical for teenagers.

After a little deliberation, everything seemed to be back to normal and Mitch was ready to get on with his life, "What now?" as if he were looking for the next adventure.

Margaret gave her two cents, "Let's go back to the campsite."

Binki suggested. "We can go to the pier."

"That's what you can do. Becky and I are going to her place," Mitch responded.

You could tell Mitch was already over the events and had Becky back on the brain.

"What about Jared?" I asked.

"He'll eventually realize that he is up here alone. He'll wake up soon and drag his ass down the mountain." Slurs his sister.

"Won't be the first time he will wake up alone. Which might be why he is alone."

Everyone laughs. Including me but not sure I got the joke.

You could tell by the blemish in everyone's speech and the moist haze in their eyes that not everyone had fully recovered from the consumption of alcohol. I wondered if this was the case for me, too. Was my speech impaired? Are my eyes red? Oh well, nothing I can do about it now.

I took a spot between Margaret and Binki as we started walking down the hill. The ladies turned playful as they started playing bumper cars, with me being the constant battering ram, which I did not mind even though I acted as if it was a bother. Then they got this wise idea that I had to take turns carrying them. I didn't think I wanted to do this until Margaret came up with the idea that they would pay me for the ride. It would cost them a kiss per ride. I quickly agreed!

I would alternate between them every so often. Sometimes carrying them like a baby or giving them piggyback rides. One time, I just picked Binki up and threw her over my shoulders as if she was a sack of potatoes, with the result of every ride being me receiving a kiss. I got the wise idea to make each ride shorter and shorter, allowing me to receive more and more action. I am sure they caught on to this, but neither complained. Instead, they just insisted that it was their turn.

Every kiss had that distinct beer smell. Though I did not like the taste of beer, I did not mind this flavor. Margaret would kiss me on the lips, with every kiss getting more intense and lasting longer. Binki started by kissing me on the cheek, but with every kiss, she got more creative. One time, she said she was trying to give me a hickey on my check. It was incredible. I didn't want this to end. Having Binki's and Margaret's bodies rubbing against mine drove me to carry them down the whole mountain.

The last ride at the bottom of the hill had me carry Binki.

When it was time for her to pay up, instead of kissing me on the cheek, she whispered in my ears, "Thank you for standing up for me," and kissed me on the lips.

The only thing that crossed my mind was "Holy Shit!" The kiss added fog to an already clouded mind. Really wasn't sure what that meant. Was she just kissing on the lips to reward me, or did that mean something more? Why did she whisper it? Margaret was ahead of us, and I couldn't see if she noticed. Or if she even cared. I thought Binki had a little too much to drink and didn't think she did it on purpose. But I realized that I really enjoyed it, even if it was only for a short moment. And not on purpose.

We headed towards the lake to sit on the pier as we had planned once we reached the campground. It was the same pier that Phillip and I were swimming at earlier in the day which reminded me that I needed to check in. I told them that I should go by and let my parents know I was OK.

They offered to come with me. I knew no matter how drunk I was, those two coming with me were not a good idea. There was no way I was going to take them to the site. I couldn't risk my parents knowing that I had been drinking, and I was afraid that Binki or Margaret might give it away by acting weird or something they might say. I, on the other hand, felt sure I could pull this off. Nice as possible. I declined their offer. But I did get a couple of pieces of gum off Margaret in an effort to mask the beer breath the best I could.

The confidence I had just a moment or two before rapidly grew into fear with every step I took in the direction of the campsite. That fear manifested itself into downright terror as my thoughts started to get the best of me. Mainly because I was concerned that Phillip told on me. What if he didn't keep our secret? What if they smell the beer? I decided that keeping my distance was the best way to hide the beer smell. I will just talk to them from a distance. Genius, I thought. Wait? What if they so I can't go? What do I do then? Ever being the planner, I concluded that I would act like I was mad and storm to the tent. Just so I won't have to get close to them.

Hmmm.... Mom might see through that plan. Maybe I'll just fall asleep on the rock. It's decided; if they say I can't go, I will do which of the two options allows me to stay the greatest distance.

Right then, I saw Dad walking towards me in a hurry. Oh no, he looked mad. Am I drunk? I asked myself. I've never been drunk, so I don't know how that feels. If you are asking yourself if you are drunk, you might be drunk. Ahh, Hell!! Do drunk people know when they are drunk? Then Scott came to my mind. He didn't know he was drunk. Shit, I might be drunk. Oh crap, I said shit. And Hell!! I really might be drunk!! Dad was getting closer. I took a couple of steps back to keep my distance per my previous plan and stood as straight as possible so he wouldn't smell the beer breath or suspect me of anything.

"Hey Dad, looking for me?"

"Nope," he said in a short, quick tone as he walked right by me. "I got to go to the restroom. The beans from supper do not agree with me."

"Too much info," I responded in a disgusted tone.

I yelled as he kept walking towards the restroom, never breaking stride.

"I'm going down to the lake; I was just checking in."

Dad said, "Okay," and flipped his hands as if to say he was too busy to worry about me. He walked right by me as if his butt were on fire. Which apparently it was.

That was easy. All that worrying for nothing. Shifting my thoughts back to Binki and Margaret, I made my way towards the lake. The fact that I was more intoxicated than I thought came to light as I struggled to get my sense of direction. Which way was the lake?

Chapter Eleven - The Lake

I approached the swimming area and noticed that there was a chain blocking the entrance. Normally, I break no rules. To hell with rules tonight, I thought! Plus, the risk of getting into trouble was worth the reward of spending more time with the two girls who really seemed to like me. I climbed over the chain and jogged towards the pier. The jog turned into a smooth, cool walk as I got closer to the destination, just in case the girls noticed. I didn't want them to think I was too excited. Which I just might be as the pounding of my heart was confirming!!

I stepped to the edge of the pier only to notice that nobody was there. I waited for a little while, just mentally recapping the night that I had already experienced. Soon, it became obvious that nobody was here or coming. I couldn't believe it. Did I say or do something wrong? Did they just trick me? I began to get angry as I started walking back to the site.

Then I was startled as I heard a voice, "Gotcha!"

I turned and noticed Binki jump out from behind a tree that she was hiding behind.

"For a big country boy, you sure do scare easy," she said as she noticed the relief on my face.

Lying, I informed her that she didn't scare me. She didn't believe me for a minute.

"Where is Margaret?" I asked as we walked back towards the pier.

Binki told me that Margaret's parents bumped into them at the drink machine and smelled beer on her breath. So, obviously, she will not be joining us tonight. I wasn't sure if I was happy or sad about this news. I really like Binki and liked the idea of just the two of us. But I didn't want Margaret to get into trouble. I was starting to like the idea of an aggressive girlfriend. Margaret was growing on me.

Binki told me the details so matter of fact. No emotion. I got the feeling this was not the first time they had been caught doing something wrong, maybe even drinking.

We got to the end of the pier, and I sat with my feet hanging over the edge while she lay flat out on the pier.

As if the incident with Margaret's parents never happened, she quickly shifted directions.

Binki asked, "So, do you like her? Apparently, she really likes you."

"How well could you possibly like someone that you just met?" I responded and then asked, "Are you still drunk?"

"Maybe, but Margaret's mom scared me alert, to be honest. That bitch was yelling at me and Margaret, telling us how disappointed she was in us. How she knew better than to trust us. She mentioned that she was going to call the police."

My heart fell out of my chest.

"What?"

I saw myself in the back of a Police car being driven to the campsite. What were my parents going to say?

Binki saw the fear in my eyes.

"Oh, don't cry. Chill out. She won't call the police. If she called the police, she would have to tell them that her daughter was drinking, too. And that's not going to be happening."

That made sense to me. There was a moment of silence, and then she asked again, "Well, do you like her?"

"She's okay."

"Okay? Is she prettier than your girlfriend?" Binki asked as if someone told her that I had a girlfriend.

"What? Who told you I had a girlfriend? I mean, I don't have a girlfriend," I found myself fumbling over my words.

"Hey, don't have a heart attack on me. I don't care if you have a girlfriend or not. Who am I to judge? By the way, I won't tell Margaret or your girlfriend. So, who's prettier?"

You could tell that Binki was enjoying the interrogation. I am not sure if the enjoyment was coming from my squirming or the self-gratification of being right. She spoke as if she knew Kimberly's name. I was retracing my conversations the entire night and knew I had never said her name or spoken of her. I was VERY careful not to say anything. But then there was the alcohol factor. I have heard people speak of "Alcohol Talking". Did my alcohol make my mouth say something that my brain doesn't remember?

"I think Margaret is really nice."

Binki sat up as if she was highly agitated.

"Okay, now I see who I am dealing with. I thought you were some Mr. Clean, Nice, Honest Guy, but now I realize that you are just like all the other guys. Full of shit."

I couldn't tell if she was being serious or playful.

"Me?" I point to my chest. "I am the most honest person you have ever met."

As soon as those words came out of my mouth, I realized that I was lying. This was not going how I thought the night was going to go. I'm not sure what I expected, but this wasn't it.

To salvage a conversation that was going south very rapidly, I offered, "Okay, here is how our relationship is going to go from this day on. I promise you NO LIES, NO SECRETS, and JUST HONESTY, no matter how much it hurts, as long as you promise the same."

"Easy for me; I have nothing to hide," she agreed as she laid back on the pier, this time curling up as if she were ready to go to sleep.

I confessed that I had a girlfriend, but I really wasn't sure if it was more than just a namesake. We never went "out" together and pretty much only saw each other on Sundays or talked on the phone. After her constantly hounding me, I relented and told her that Kimberly was prettier. I tried to balance it out by sharing that I believe Margaret was more fun to be around.

We traded questions and answers, finding out more and more about each other. I was surprised to find out that she gets good grades and wants to be a fashion designer. I discovered that her father wanted a boy with his firstborn child and wanted to name it after him. He didn't get a boy, but still gave her his name. Billy Wallace. She said she got the name Binki from the ghost in the Pac-Man game. She only smokes when she drinks and when she is nervous. She said she learned to smoke from her dad. Being the father of the year candidate he was, he taught her that smoking after you drink keeps you from getting so drunk. She had drunk a lot of alcohol in her lifetime and told me that her father allowed her to take her first sip when she was 9 years old.

I informed her that tonight was my first-time drinking alcohol and told her about my pretty boring, conservative life on a farm in Indian Trail that consisted mainly of farm work, football, and church. She was shocked to find out that I was still a virgin, but I was not brave enough to ask her. Mainly because I really think I know the answer and felt that it would be uncomfortable. She got a kick out of my nickname, the "Pope".

Binki reminded me I had to tell the truth as she asked, "So who is prettier, Kimberly or me."

Trying to keep my promise to tell the truth, I responded as politically correctly as possible.

"I think you are prettier, but I think Kimberly is more girlfriend material."

"What does that mean?" she responded in an offended tone.

I reminded her about our promise of "NO LIES, NO SECRETS, and JUST HONESTY". But she still seemed offended.

Then I explained probably more than I should have but told her the truth as I saw it.

"When I first saw you, I thought you might be the most beautiful person I have ever seen," I started out. You could see that she liked the compliment, and she let her guard down a little. "Then, as I got to spend time with you, I began to believe you to be mysterious and dangerous. Which I dig!! That's cool for a girlfriend for a while, but not really for a girlfriend for life."

"What? Screw you," she said.

I responded with the goal of letting her know that she deserves better.

I'm not sure if it was the alcohol or just pent-up emotion that I have been wanting to share. Nevertheless, the reaction lacked the tactfulness that I was seeking.

"That's exactly what I mean. Said like a girlfriend for a while!! A girlfriend for life doesn't say, "Screw you," and doesn't allow me or anyone else to call her bitch. You are beautiful and should be treated with respect. Nobody should disrespect you like that. NOBODY!!" I responded. "Especially not some cheap Def Leopard wannabe who obviously doesn't respect you or your family. You are SO much better than that! I just don't comprehend what in the world you could see in him."

The tears made their way down her cheeks, displaying the pain that she was in. Or displaying that I just hurt her feelings.

"Who are you to judge me? You don't know what I have been through. Mitch, my mom, and I are lucky to be alive. You live in the perfect little world. You have a mom and Dad that love you and love each other. You don't know how it feels to live in fear that your dad is going to beat your mom to death. Or lie in bed at night praying that your dad doesn't come home drunk and take his anger out on you or your brother? Or having to…"

At that moment, she stopped. She realized that she had said more than she wanted. I realized, I heard more than I was prepared to hear.

I stuttered the words, "I apologize. I shouldn't have."

I stopped because I wasn't sure where to go.

She sat up straight. Pulled out a cigarette and lit it as she moved closer to the end of the pier so her feet could hang off.

"Ah, fuck it. The cat is out of the bag now. But I SWEAR I will kill you if you share this with anyone. My Mom, Mitch, and Margaret are the only ones that know."

I thought it was interesting that she didn't say Scott, but I had no interest in bringing that topic back to light. Smoke escaped out of her nose and mouth at the same time.

It was followed by the words, "My dad. I hate that man. He is pure evil."

She confirmed Margaret's version of events and told me the entire story about how her dad is a "piece of shit drunk" who is verbally and physically abusive to his family. She said her mom used to be an alcoholic. A really bad one.

She told of her dad wanting to join a local gang. At the initiation party, a friend of her father's raped her mom. Once her mom realized what happened, she told her father, thinking he would confront the friend. Maybe kick his ass. But that is not what happened. He said she wasn't raped at all. Instead, he gave his wife to his friend as part of the initiation. Said that her mom was irate. Her Dad's response of "Sorry, I thought you were too drunk to care" brought to life the type of man he really was.

That was the last straw. He had beaten her, insulted her, shamed her. But to her, that was the act that was over the line. So, she got help. Along the way, she found God. She stopped drinking and started going to church. Her mom thought that finding God meant the beatings would stop. This seemed to enrage her father even more. The beatings got worse. She explained that he would often start abusing her or Mitch, but then her mom would step in and get the worst part of the beating.

She said her dad would come home and beat them because he lost a bet or because he got kicked out of a bar. It would be things they had no control over, but they would get the blame and whatever punishment he felt should come with it.

"You have no idea how hard it is to live in fear. To have a monster greet you as you wake, eat beside you, or kiss you good night. To lay in bed and hear your mom in the next room begging for her life. Sometimes, I would go to sleep and wonder if my mom was alive. Often, I would hear my dad mock her religion. Saying, I am your God. Or get your God to help you now."

She took another puff of the cigarette.

Took a moment to collect her thoughts. Then continued to share that a couple of times, he beat her in front of his friends, and they would just laugh as if it was a game.

She snuffed out the cigarette on the pier and looked out into the nothingness of the night. She saw visions in the darkness that had vividly been playing in her head for quite a while. These were images that were burnt into her memory.

Just the thought of this took my breath away!! I could see that this was hard on her, and I could not even come close to putting myself in her shoes. Weirdly, though, it seemed like she was getting some form of relief by sharing. Once she started, she just kept talking. I'm not sure if it was to me or just the comfort of getting these visions out of her head.

"The scariest night was when Dad thought Mom locked him out of the house on purpose. He went out with some of his friends. Probably one of his whores he described as friends. Either way, that isn't relevant. It was late, so Mom locked the door. No different than all the other nights, especially since our neighborhood is popular for its share of crime. Dad has his own set of keys and normally comes in sometime in the middle of the night. However, he has had his share of nights where he didn't think coming home was important. We were all asleep. At about 3 am, we heard a loud banging on the door. It scared us to death. I mean, we were awakened from our sleep. We didn't know it at the time but either Dad couldn't find his keys because he was too drunk, or he had forgotten his keys. Mitch and I ran and met Mom in the dining room, full of fear. How were we supposed to know it was him? He had keys! Why would he be the one beating on the door!! The slamming on the door quickly escalated to him breaking the door open and walking straight to Mom. Yelling, why did she lock him out of the house? Before Mom could answer, he punched her straight in the face. No remorse. As if he was hitting a worthless punching bag at a gym. Mitch jumped on Dad, and Dad slung him across the room. Mitch was just lying there, scared to death. Dad walks back towards Mom, and I get between them, thinking I am his daughter. His pride and joy. He didn't care. Uncontrollable rage was already in place, and someone was getting their ass kicked tonight for supposedly locking him out of a house. He grabbed me by the arm and pushed his beer-stained, breathed face so close to mine that our noses collided. The collision was so hard that my nose started bleeding. Get the hell out of the way! You trashy bitch. I'll beat two asses as quick as one."

Just listening to this made me sit in total horror. Could not imagine living it. I have seen things like this in movies but didn't know people really had to live like this. Trying to take her side and show her I was empathic, I offered some sarcasm.

"Really brave of him to offer to beat up two women."

Almost like I didn't understand the seriousness of the situation, Binki looked at me and said, "Not two women. His daughter, whom he called a trashy bitch, and his wife. That is who he was threatening. His own flesh in blood. Maybe the only two people on earth who really loved him. That night ended that for me."

"So, did he stop? What did he do?"

I was beyond the point of being worried about being perceived as nosey.

"Like a dumbass, I thought he would listen. I told him that he needed to stop. He slapped me so hard that I think I blacked out. I laid on the dining room floor and saw his anger shift from me to Mom without a thought, as if I was barely a speed bump on his way to the target. I heard the fight shifting from the living room and noticed him dragging Mom by her hair into the bedroom. Ungodly noises. The beating may have been just minutes, but it felt like a lifetime. All of a sudden, it was totally quiet. No sounds of a fist hitting flesh. No sounds of crying. Nothing. The scariest moment of my life. I was afraid that my dad had just killed my mom. Soon after, I heard footsteps followed by the image of my dad walking out the front doorway. I assume Dad had done what he thought was enough damage and left the house. This gave me the confidence to go check on mom. Entering the room is a vision I will never forget. Mom's lying on the bed with her clothes ripped. Blood spewed from her lip. Her left eye is swollen, something horrible. I didn't know that bruises could be so vivid, so fast. I just sit there holding her. Eventually, I leaned over and asked if she wanted me to call the Police. Mom uttered the word no. Mitch brought a blanket and a couple of pillows and joined me on the floor. The three of us stayed there the rest of the night. Mitch and I hugging Mom with God and the rest of the world freely able to walk into our home due to the door being caved in."

Amazed by the incident, "Man, I feel so bad that you had to go through that. That is horrible. Just wondering, why didn't you call the

Police? Why didn't your mom want you to call the Police? Is that why you are here?" I asked.

She seemed to be getting agitated that I did not understand the gravity of the situation.

"YOU DON'T UNDERSTAND!! My dad is fucking crazy, man. We fear him. We are deathly scared of him. That's why we are here. Dad had said many times that if we ever called the police on him, it would be the last thing we ever did. He didn't mince words. No misunderstanding what he meant. I heard him tell Mom that he would kill Mitch and me in front of her, then kill her. Who says that about or to their wife and kids?"

Agreeing with her, "You are right. I can honestly say that I have never had that type of fear in my entire life."

Obviously, wanting to finish what she started.

"Dad returned the next day as if nothing had happened. Walked in just like it was just another day and fixed the door. No apologies, nothing. We never spoke of that night again. It was just another night in the Wallace house. We have had many nights that resemble this. But none as bad! But similar episodes on a smaller scale. Dad, he didn't even know the difference. He couldn't give two shits."

I was lost for words. I wasn't sure how to react. Before I could respond, she just kept telling her story.

"We didn't leave right after that night. But I know that was the moment that Mom knew that Dad was not changing. That night confirmed that if she doesn't do something, he is going to kill us.

Weird thing, Dad was actually pretty good for the next couple of weeks. Then came the night. This is the reason that we are staying here. It was another incident, but this time, we called the police. It all started when Dad came home in the middle of the night drunk again. I was sound asleep, and he came into my room and woke me up. He was crying. I asked him what was wrong. The moment I looked up, saw the red eyes and smelled his intoxicated breath that I had seen and smelled too many times, I knew this was not going to be a good night. I was SCARED to death of the answer. He said, I lost my bitch. I was terrified. I had heard Dad refer to Mom as bitch so many times; I thought he was talking about her. I asked Dad if he had hurt Mom. I thought he had hurt Mom, and guilt was making him confess to me. I should have known that man does not have a heart. He is incapable of feeling anything, a little lone guilt. As if he was talking to one of the guys at the bar, he angrily said no, not that bitch. My side bitch. I yelled for Mom, and she came running. After I explained what had happened, she confronted him, which we both should have known better. Never argue with a drunk person, especially my dad. Per his standard, he started deflecting. Calling me a liar and whore. Then, blaming Mom for not being interested in him anymore. Giving him no choice but to look for love from another person. Then accusing her of cheating on him with the preacher."

She goes on to explain that the massive verbal confrontation got physical and led to her dad beating her mom using his fist, a belt, broom handle, and then he pulled out a gun. He said he was going to kill Binki, the preacher, and then Binki's mom. But before he got too far in his plan, he passed out on the couch in the living room with the gun right beside him.

But not before Binki's mom had received the beating of her life. Bruises and cuts everywhere. Both of her eyes were swollen shut, blood running from her nose, and apparently broken ribs that hindered her from being able to breathe without making weird sounds. She admitted that for one fleeting moment, she thought about picking the gun up and blowing that sack of shit out of their lives. But she couldn't. Their mom was just lying on the floor. Bleeding and struggling to breathe. Binki was afraid she was going to die. This time, they didn't ask. Mitch did as he was instructed by his big sister and called the ambulance. And the ambulance brought the police.

Binki explained that was the hardest decision she ever had to make. The first thought that came to her head was her dad's threat. But fear from that threat only got superseded by the love for her mother. Binki thought her mother was dying. She admitted that she thought her mom was going to be mad, but they had to call the police. She also shares that when the Police arrested her dad, he didn't hide his intentions. Even in handcuffs, surrounded by police officers, he looked straight at Binki and Mitch and reminded them that they needed to remember his promise. He mocked a clock as he went by, "Tic-Toc. Tic-Toc". He was saying that the clock is ticking on the amount of life they have left.

As soon as her mom got released from the hospital, they got their stuff together and went to stay with someone at the church. Margaret's parents just so happen to go to the same church. Concerned the church would be the first place he would look, Margaret's parents suggested that they stay in this campground for a while. The church is paying for the site and helping them find a house nearby. She said they have been living at this site for over a month.

Knowing the answer, I asked as if I was clueless, "Can't your mom get a restraining order or something like that?"

"Sure, my naive country bumpkin, she can definitely do that," she sarcastically responded. "Of course she did. That paper won't stop my dad's fist or a bullet. My dad doesn't care about no piece of paper or no law."

Offended that she took that tone. I was about to say some smart response, but then I looked over and saw tears going down her face. At that moment, I realized that she had really had a hard life, which explained a lot. You could tell that my family life and her family life were two different worlds. She was right. I have no clue what her world is like.

She went on to explain how her mom has talked about leaving her dad numerous times before but never could go through with it. Her tears seemed to be coming to a halt. My emotions, on the other hand, were at full blast. I felt like I should have helped her. I felt guilty that my life was better and easier. Why am I feeling guilty for something that I didn't even do?

She told me that the worst part is that she is afraid that her brother is going to turn into her dad.

Knowing that I have already opened the gate, I might as well walk on in and let her hear my entire feelings.

"I can understand your fear for your brother, but I think you need to look out for you, too. You told me you have a dad who is a drunk, and yet your boyfriend is a drunk. You said your dad disrespects your mom, and yet Binki, your boyfriend, does not respect you. It sounds like you are destined to live with a drunk who does not respect you. That would scare me. This does not have to be your life. Have you ever thought about how you ended up here? At a campground. Paid for by a church. Maybe this is God's way of giving you another chance. You can break the cycle. Where does it go? Think about it. In 20 years, are you and your child going to go in hiding from Scott? I know this sounds overly dramatic, but the thought is not too farfetched. Right?"

"That is a horrible thing to say."

Regaining my thought process, "Maybe, but true. Here is some more truth. You are beautiful and obviously very smart. I would imagine that the main reason that your mom doesn't like Scott is because she sees you making the same mistake that she made. She sees your dad in Scott. I have never met your mom, but I would imagine you have a man like your dad as a boyfriend or Mitch growing up to be a reincarnated vision of your dad would be the unhappy ending to a horrible nightmare. Have you ever thought of that?"

"Screw you again," she spews in my direction between sobs.

At that moment, I got the feeling that I was put into this situation by God. I was put here, on this pier, to experience the events of the evening just to give her that message. Felt like it was my mouth, but some greater power was feeding me the vocabulary.

"I believe that God may be giving your mom a second chance. I noticed that your brother really does look up to you. He feels the need to be the man that protects you. As he bravely did tonight. He also succeeded in protecting your mother's honor. There is good in him. But I also saw the fear of a scared little boy as he was running away. What happens if that rock killed Scott? I can't get that thought out of my mind. I think he reacted and then had the same thought. What have I done? Did I just kill someone?"

Then I thought, I might be getting overly dramatic now. Maybe my honesty was too honest. I apologized for being too honest, and there was a long moment of awkward silence in between the sniffles. During the silence, I couldn't help but think Mr. Simpson would have been proud of me. I think this may have been my first real-life testimony to God. All I need now is to call her to the altar and ask her to give her life to God. But oddly enough, I did all this after cussing and drinking. Wait, does the good word I put in for God outweigh the drinking and cussing? Was it really God talking through me? Could God be working through a drunk? I bet there is something similar in the bible. Doesn't it say God works in mysterious ways? Could I be one of God's modern-day disciples? Disciple is overkill. Disciples don't drink and curse. Hmm… If I died now, am I going to heaven for the good words or hell because of my sins?

Looking over at her and seeing her sad made me feel guilty for the second time since we had been sitting on this pier.

"You hate me? It's okay. You are right. I have no right to judge," I offered as an apology.

"No, I am the one that should be apologizing. You just told the truth. I shouldn't blame you for having great parents and for me not having real loving parents. I know Scott drinks too much. My life sucks!!" Binki rambles on as if she were sitting in a pool of self-pity.

Chapter Twelve - Pier Pressure

I wanted to put my arms around her and give her a hug. But I didn't. I was afraid that would have been unwanted. After all, she does have a boyfriend. So, we sit in silence for a moment. Each of us was searching for the next thing to say. I was at a loss for words. Do I say you are right? Your life does suck. Decided that probably wasn't the correct route to take. It was abundantly clear that she had indeed had a rough life. That she was tired of hurting. He wasn't sure if talking about it was opening wounds that were already infected or therapeutic and allowed her to relieve some stress. But decided a change of topic was what was needed.

"Boy, this spot is awesome. The moon looks like it is posing for a picture sitting on top of the lake. If God created a more beautiful spot, I have never seen it."

She smiled, obviously recognizing my lame effort to change the subject, but responded as if my last words were not heard.

"OK, that's the last time we will talk about that," as she wiped her face.

There were a couple more seconds of silence before she attempted to take the discussion in a different direction. That direction was pointed to me.

"What is the perfect life for Bo Hawes? Do you want to get married?"

I thought for a moment.

"All I want in life is to have a good job that allows me to have a house worth $100,000. I would love for my job to be in football as a player or coach, but I know that is a long shot. Maybe I can coach? I really don't know a career yet. But I will have a beautiful wife who is confident yet respectful. Someone who can be good friends with my mom because I believe if my mom likes them, then they must be a good person. I know this sounds strange because I'm only 15, but I really want to be a father. Just a simple life: A house worth $100,000, a beautiful wife, and two kids (one boy and one girl)."

She smiled as the mood changed. Binki could envision the picture I was drawing.

"That sounds nice," as if the goal that sounds simple to me would be a miracle for her.

Before I gave real thought, I turned the question on her. I asked her if Scott was the man for her.

She surprised me with her response when she said, "No. I think you are right. He is my boyfriend, not my boyfriend for life. I have never dated anyone that resembled a boyfriend for life. I want someone who is everything my dad is not. I want someone to treat me right. To love me no matter the mistakes I make. I want a good father to my kids and a provider. Money doesn't hurt. I promise that neither my children nor I will ever live with the fear that my mom, Mitch, and I currently live in. I know you may not believe this, but I am smart. I will have a good life, I swear."

I was not sure if Binki is trying to convince me or herself?

"I am sure you will," I said as I turned my head towards her and noticed that her eyes were closed.

She had a small smile stretching across her face. I couldn't help but wonder what is causing that smile. Maybe she could see herself in the vision that she just described to me. A vision that was not unlike mine. Just her vision seemed to be sitting at a further distance away. Yet, there was a renewed effort to make sure this happens.

The silence seemed therapeutic as we were just soaking in the atmosphere. While her eyes were closed, I was captivated by her beauty. I couldn't take my eyes off her. Then she opened her eyes and caught me.

Showing off a mischievous smile that many country songs have been written about, she said, "Ever been skinny dipping."

My heart fell through my chest.

The answer was an easy "NO".

It was the next question I was afraid of.

Then she said it. "Want to go?"

"I don't think I can do that," I said.

"Sure, you can. Just take off your clothes and jump in. What are you afraid of?" she challenged.

My heart was racing. My body said YES, YES, YES.

My consciousness, the way I was raised, and everything I believe in said NO, NO, NO!

"Nobody will know. Ever! Except for you and I," she taunted.

She is beautiful, and she is right; nobody else will ever know.

"What the heck?" as the thought of seeing her naked body won over the embarrassment of being naked myself.

I slowly took off my shirt and shorts and laid them on the pier.

Folding them just to make a show of it. I walked to the edge of the pier. Then, as quickly as possible, with my body in the opposite direction of her. I took off my underwear and JUMPED in.

I poked my head above water because I could not wait to see her do her part.

"Your turn," I yelled back.

Then I noticed she was laughing.

Uncontrollability laughing.

What is she laughing at? Do I look that funny naked? Then it hit me!! I have seen this in the movies. She is going to take my clothes and run.

To her credit, she doesn't run. Instead, she walks to the end of the pier and sits down with her feet hanging over. She takes her finger and motions me to come closer.

"I can't believe you did that," she said.

"Wasn't that the plan? I thought you were going to do the same," I questioned.

"What type of person do you think I am? I haven't even known you for a day."

I could tell she was using our previous conversation against me. I guess I look pretty stupid. She could see the disappointment, maybe embarrassment, on my face.

She starts gathering my clothes, "What would you do if I took these little goodies and hid them somewhere in the campground?"

Hoping she was playing, I stated, "You wouldn't."

She saw the fear starting to show on my face.

"Like I said earlier, you don't know me," she badgered.

The thought that she was right started to place genuine fear in my heart. Panic was setting in. How in the world was I getting back to my site? How would I explain this if I was caught? By the police, my parents, or worse- both.

She saw the seriousness in my face.

"I will make you a deal. I will give you the clothes if you come and get them."

"OK, deal," I quickly agreed since she was right at the edge of the pier.

I can just swim to the edge and grab them. Then she gets up and walks back, placing the clothes in the middle of the pier. Knowing that the only way I can get my clothes is by her seeing everything God gave me.

Feeling like I just got played, "Ahh... Heck", I said out loud. "That's not fair. At least turn your head."

"Nah… The first time, I didn't get a good enough look," she said, smiling with a playful look.

"I can be in this water all night," I announced with conviction.

"Me too, the only difference is in the morning, I will have my clothes on when the people come. You will be in the water naked and looking like a perv."

"Darn," came from my mouth as I came to the realization that she was right.

Not wanting to give in, we sat in the current situation of me holding on to the side of the pier while she sat in the middle with a big smile on her face and my clothes by her side.

Man, I didn't know what to do.

She crawls to the edge of the pier as if she were some type of jungle cat.

"You know I gotcha. You are just going to have to man up and show up. If you get my drift."

Pissed at myself for getting myself into this situation and beginning to get a little angry, I didn't let it show. Too much. I kept my cool and did what any man would do. I begged for my clothes as if she were holding a gun to my head. She never weavers. Eventually, the theme of this trip came back to me. WHO CARES!! I will not see her again after this week.

"Okay. You win. Here I come."

The closer I swam to the ladder, I noticed the distance was further from the clothes than the side of the pier. I thought I might look pitiful if I tried to get up on the pier in all my glory and failed. Therefore, I am just going to use the ladder and walk like a man proud to show off what he's got. And that's exactly what I did. Pride and Glory for all to see. I purposely march with a cadence and put on my underwear. Then she grabbed me from behind and pushed me back into the water.

"What the heck?" I said.

"What the heck? So cute."

Again, she is finding joy in my southern dialect.

"Oh, don't cry. For an innocent conservative country boy, you sure do get naked fast. And you don't mind showing it off. I know I am just a simple mind from Gastonia, but that doesn't sound too conservative to me."

Noting this is at least the third time that she has used my words against me. This time, I had to come back with something witty. It really wasn't too witty.

Frustration was building, and the male ego started to show.

"Number one, you are from Gastonia. You are just as country as I am. Number two, if you got it, flaunt it as I did. Lastly, I was totally hoodwinked in this deal."

"Are you getting mad? Stop crying."

She bawled her fists up and placed them over her eyes, mimicking a baby crying.

"I plan to join you, but I'm not getting naked. After all, I just met you."

Faster than I wanted, she took off her white mesh shirt and striped down to her matching black laced panties before jumping in.

She was still laughing as she swam next to me and repeated, "I really can't believe you just did that. I can't believe you just gave me a show. That is normally reserved for the third date."

"Okay, Okay. You got me."

"Are you mad? Is the baby mad?" she taunted me with her beautiful face, imitating a baby, which seems to be her theme at the moment.

I responded that I just feel like a fool. Then she said in a sarcastic tone, "Well, I guess I might not be the girlfriend for life, but I'm thinking you might not mind me being your girlfriend tonight."

There she goes again, using my words against me. Mental note: talk less - listen more!! But I have to admit. She was right. I thought I was a better man than that. As I was wallowing in my own stupidity, I noticed her getting closer. She got right beside me with her face almost touching mine. She had one hand holding the side of the pier and placed the other on my shoulder.

"Don't worry, I still think you are a great guy. I think you may be the boyfriend for life type, especially with that body."

Then she grabbed my face with both of her hands and kissed me straight on the lips. Then put her head under water and swam under the pier.

I smiled and thought that was the second kiss on the lips tonight. But I'm not sure what they meant. Were they playful, or was there some meaning behind them? I suck at this. Why doesn't she just tell me what she wants? Then I realized that she just kissed me, and I was still holding onto the pier. Maybe I should follow her underneath the pier.

We settled right in the middle of the pier, where a couple of wooden boards shielded me from the clothes that I was so desperate to get just five minutes earlier. I saw her looking up as if she were reading something while using the beams from the pier to assist her in holding her head above water. Upon inspection for myself, I noticed there was nothing to read. She shared her idea to carve our names in the wood, but that plan quickly unraveled as I informed her that we had nothing that could be carved into the wood. We agreed that this is on the menu for later this week. How do we go from kissing and finding out that she thinks I have a great body to carving things in wood? I want to go back to kissing.

"So, you think I have a GREAT body?" I said, trying to use her words to my benefit for once.

"Never said that. I said you are a great person with a body," she replied with a coy look on her face.

"Okay. So, you don't think I have a great body?"

With a smile on her face, she said, "I never said that either,"

She let go of the beam and placed one arm around each shoulder until they locked around the back of my neck. She pressed her body as close to mine as possible, and then she gave me a kiss that I knew

I would never forget. I was in absolute heaven. Never have I had that feeling before. For the first time tonight, I knew what this kiss meant.

Almost immediately, we heard someone walking onto the pier.

"Binki," said a lady's voice that I recognized from earlier.

It was Margaret. Binki takes her finger and covers my mouth.

"Shhh," Binki whispers in my ear while hanging onto my body with her arms wrapped around my neck and legs around my waist.

I was holding on to the back of the wooden beam for dear life, trying to be as still as possible.

"Hello, I thought you were going to be…" then Margaret stopped.

She was right above us and noticed the clothes.

"Are you swimming with…"

Then, the tone changes from inquisitive to angry.

"Are you serious? Really? I know y'all are below the pier. Probably naked!! I snuck out from my parents just to find out that my best friend is a whore!! I always knew it. I always defended you. Never again!! I told you I liked him. But you couldn't resist. Well, that's it. I will never speak to you again."

Just then, we heard an adult male voice yell, "Margaret Lynn Helms! You better get your butt back at the site right now. What is wrong with you?"

At that moment, you could hear Margaret stomping her way off the pier, reminding Binki rather loudly to never call her again and that the friendship was over.

"Binki whispered, "We need to leave. Margaret's dad yelled so loud I know someone is going to call the campground security."

That was certainly a mood killer.

As soon as we thought she was gone, I said, "I'm sorry. I really didn't mean to break up your friendship. I really feel like crap."

We were talking as we swam from under the pier and climbed up the ladder to put on our clothes.

"She won't be mad for long," Binki responded as if this was nothing new. "I will tell her I don't know what she is talking about, and she will...Holy Shit!! She took our clothes."

We didn't miss the ironic twist that both of our clothes had been taken.

"Karma is a bitch," she enlightened.

Just then, we hear Mitch calling, "Come on. Don't mean to break up this little Hallmark moment, but Mom wants you to come to the camper. You were supposed to be there before she got there. Remember?"

Then he noticed that we both were in our underwear.

"I know what y'all were doing."

Quickly, he turned his head toward Binki, "Tramp!! Mama is going to be mad!!"

Binki fired back with an authoritative voice, "Mom is never finding out, or I will tell Mom about Becky."

"Take a chill pill. I'm just playing."

106

Then he turned his head towards me, "You dog. I underestimated the hick."

I know I was just insulted by a kid I could beat to a pulp, but I didn't think that was my main concern at the moment. I am currently wearing just my boxers.

Then Mitch looked around, surprised and in a mocking type of tone, "Hmm... Where are your clothes?"

After suffering through the embarrassment of telling Mitch our story, he agreed to go back and get us some clothes. Binki and I ran to the closest bathhouse and waited for him to return. It would really be embarrassing if we had to tell this story to security. Who in return would probably share with my parents.

Thankfully, that was not the case. He brought me some crazy Hawaiian shorts that were so tight I think I stretched the elastic. Didn't bring a shirt. Once dressed, I walked outside to wait for Binki. Mitch was already waiting and thought he would fish for a compliment.

"You guys are lucky I came down."

I agreed to satisfy his ego as Binki came out in some pajama pants and a tank top that made her look even sexier.

We got started walking through the dark, with the only source of light being the moon and a couple of stray nightlights throughout the campground. Once we got within eyesight of the campsite, I think Mitch got the feeling he was intruding and ran ahead. We could see him jump into the camper.

"Really sorry about Margaret," I said, offering another shot towards an apology.

Binki leaned over and kissed me on the cheek.

"You did nothing wrong. Trust me."

Our slow walk ground to a halt.

"Hold up. Let's sit here for a moment," she directed.

She grabbed my hand and gently directed me to sit on the asphalt road that was within eyesight of her camper but not close enough that our conversation could be overheard.

"Did you mean that? Like, do you really believe that God is giving us another chance?"

"Of course I do," I said as if I was almost offended. "I mean, you have a church helping you. A church that is, no doubt, powered by God!!"

I'm not sure if you can see someone thinking, but I saw her thinking. I'm not sure what the thoughts were, but the act of thinking was there.

"Binki, you believe in God, don't you?" I asked.

You could have pushed me over with a feather when she said, "No."

I am not certain I have ever heard someone say "No." I know people who don't practice the same religion as I do or who don't live their lives accordingly. But I have never heard someone say "No".

"What? How is this? Didn't God save you and your family every time the devil got in your dad and assaulted your family? Didn't God help you get away from him? Tonight, I think God was watching over us with Scott."

"I am not trying to be argumentative, but I have a lot of questions about God. Just letting you know. If he is real, he must hate me."

"How can you say that?"

"Well, why me? I didn't choose this man to be my dad. Why couldn't I be the one who was born into a loving family? Did I do something to deserve this? I am only 15 years old, and my life has already had more trauma than most people have in a lifetime. Why me? If we are all God's children. That makes me one of his children. Yet he selected this asshole to be my dad. God allows my mom, my brother, and myself to sustain unimaginable abuse. That's child abuse, right? Allowing your children to be abused!"

I was way over my head answering that question. I didn't know the answer. I thought for a second in a way that allowed her to see that I was contemplating how to respond, but secretly, I was saying a quick prayer for God to take hold of my vocabulary once again.

"First of all, I am not certain that I can answer that question the right way. I just know that God does everything for a reason,"

This solicited an eye roll from her.

I was stalling to give God time to express mail me the right words.

From God or not, I ended up recycling what Mom would say.

"I can't understand the reason. But what we know is what happened in the past is horrible. What we do not know is what is in store for us in the future. The Bible is filled with stories of people who took a struggle and turned that struggle into a reward. Like Noah's ark, Moses parting the Red Sea, or David and Goliath. Those miracles started as hopeless situations and turned into victories that we are still talking about. Many, many years later. Maybe the church helping you is just the beginning of your miracle story. Every blessing from God doesn't have to be a story told for thousands of years. I can't explain why you were the one put into this crappy situation. But have you thought that maybe it's God's love that you are not in that situation tonight? This moment here could be the start of your miracle. I think," I say as I take a finger and playfully touch her nose. "You should start thinking about the promises of tomorrow instead of the pain of yesterday."

I looked over and saw her in deep thought. A stray tear was falling down her cheek. I couldn't help but think, and maybe even hope on hope, that this was a tear of hope. Not one of despair.

I added, "Even if you don't believe in God, believe in Karma. You have had enough bad things to happen to you. Boy, when the good comes, it's going to overflow."

"Binki," I heard Mitch doing a quiet yell as if he were scolding someone in a funeral home.

"I have to go," she said as she stood up, and we started to separate, with her going in the direction of the voice that yelled once again but a little louder and more agitated.

I couldn't help myself from watching her walk away.

Before I could make my first steps towards my site, she redirected herself back towards me, "Hey, something to think about tonight. Can you have a girlfriend for a week?"

She covered my lips with her index finger as if not to speak. She removed her finger placed her lips where her finger just rested, and kissed me.

She ran away and said, "Tell me tomorrow."

"Tomorrow," I yelled and turned around to start walking back towards the site.

Reflecting on the greatest and scariest night of my life. More action had just happened in one night than has happened in the past 15 years of my life.

My mind was wandering and finally landed on an earlier thought. If I die right at this moment, am I going to heaven? Is that really how that works? I am so confused. I have always thought that God has a scale that balances the good and the bad. Drink beer and cursing. 20lbs to the bad.

Witnessing God's word to the non-believer, easy 50lbs to the good. I told myself that I had to win today!! Wait a minute. I prayed that God would give me the words, and he obviously came through. Does that mean it's not 50 lbs of good because God had to help? No matter, I asked for help, and he came through. It is obviously not too mad. He still helped!! It may not be 50 lbs, but it has to be more than 25 lbs, right? I sighed at the thought.

I got back to the site, almost forgetting that I was wearing Mitch's shorts. And that it is well after midnight. I quickly thought of a cover story of how I lost my clothes. Something like I fell into the water and had to borrow Mitch's clothes. And Dad never gave me a time to be back? So, that should work.

I saw my dad sitting alone in a lawn chair by the fire as I was walking across the bridge. This was a relief because my dad couldn't remember and didn't care what I was wearing. As I got closer, I noticed he was asleep.

Even better.

I quietly grabbed a pair of shorts, a toothbrush, toothpaste, and mouthwash and went to the nearby spigot to brush the smell of beer off my breath. Then I changed into my own shorts right under the moonlight. I woke him up and told him he was going to hurt his neck. We put out the fire, and he climbed inside the tent for the night.

Meanwhile, I was thinking to myself how lucky I was that my parents were asleep. I couldn't believe Mom didn't send out a search party for me. And maybe most of all, Phillip obviously kept his word.

I tiptoed inside the tent in an effort not to wake up the family.

Especially mom. She might question the time no matter what Dad said. Everyone had grabbed their position in the tent for the night. Mom and Dad slept on an air mattress with Stevie in between them on the east side. I grabbed a spot in a camouflaged sleeping bag on the opposite side of my parents, with Phillip between us.

The noises of the darkness could be heard as Mother Nature was closing the curtain on the day. The echoing of the night, nor Phillip's snoring could hinder my mind from thinking about Binki and the night I just had. A million thoughts were flying through my head like the kiss under the pier, how beautiful she was, and how far I would have "gone" if we had not been interrupted. Am I in love? Could that happen in just one day? Is it possible that I loved her the first time I saw her? Then I thought about what Dad had once told me: never to fall in love, knowing it's impossible to stay that way. Am I setting myself up for a great heartbreak? But there is also the saying, better to love and lose than to never know the feeling of love. Wait, we can't be in love? I bet she doesn't really like me. If Scott came back tomorrow, would I have to play like I don't know anything? Hold up! Am I "the other guy"? If so, I might be able to live with that. Or is she going to tell Scott?

What would Scott do? Want to fight me or worse? What does a girlfriend for a week mean? Could this possibly last beyond this week? Man, I wish she lived in Indian Trail or somewhere close to our house. I am almost 16. I will be able to drive in 7 months.

My thoughts shifted towards how horrible Binki and Mitch's life must be. By comparison, how lucky I am to have the parents I have. I concluded that I didn't tell my parents thank you enough. I decided in the morning I would let them know.

My thoughts drifted to the question she asked me. I thought I answered it as best I could, but it doesn't make sense. How could God put such a beautiful creature on earth and then give her that man as a father?

How could any man hit a woman or beat their children? How could God allow that to happen? Aren't they his children, too? If he does everything for a reason, as my pastor says, then what's the purpose of this? Then I was wondering if I was going to hell for questioning God because my preacher said we are not allowed to question God. I quickly changed my tune within my thoughts and asked God to note that I was not questioning. I'm just asking. Said a prayer that included gratitude for allowing me to meet Binki, forgiveness for my sins of the day, and the strength to be a better person tomorrow. Thanked him for helping me with the right words and reminded him that I might need some more guidance tomorrow.

I thought about how much trouble Margaret must have gotten into. Then I became afraid. What if Margaret told her mom about me, and her mom didn't go to the Police but instead came and told my parents? Holy cow! I think I would rather she go to the police. But wait, that's stupid because then the police would come and tell my parents anyway.

Eventually, the sounds of the crickets and wind blowing on the nearby treetops put my mind at ease enough for me to fall asleep. As I went to sleep, my ears heard the music of the night provided by the stream rushing and the animals of darkness singing, but my closed eyelids were only seeing visions of Binki.

Chapter Thirteen - The Morning After Feel

Waking up in the middle of God's wonder never ceases to awe me.

Camping displays the evolution of the Earth in its simplest and yet most beautiful form. The start of each new day begins fresh and peacefully quiet. The day slowly comes to life as different sounds and smells from the camp's surroundings trickle in. By midday, all systems are full steam ahead as families race to different sorts of excitement and nature displays its full arsenal of species coming out to play or work. Then as the sun finds its way to hide behind the mountain tops, the impending darkness brings the action back towards the same peaceful quiet in which the day had begun.

Today was no different. The birth of this day was confirmed with the sounds of nature expressing its excitement for a new beginning. The birds chirping and the stream flowing beside our campsite confirmed that life was moving forward once again. The screeching of the giant zipper going straight down our tent had the same annoyance to me as fingers sliding down a chalkboard for others. This sound in the camping world took the place of the alarm clock back at the house. My mind was awakened from sleep, but my body stayed in place as it lay dormant on top of the sleeping bag that it was supposed to be inside of. I recognized the sound of children playing from afar way. By the clanging of pans and the sizzling sounds, I could tell that breakfast was being prepared nearby. With all that was happening, Dad was making the greatest argument for me to get some blood moving in my body. That wonderful bacon smell was enticing me to open my eyes and go devour Dad's handy work.

I rolled over and snuck a peak to discover that I was the last person left in the make-shift canvas castle. I decided I would just lay and be lazy for just one more minute. Quickly, I started to think about the previous night. Did I dream last night? Or did that really happen? I looked beside my sleeping bag and saw the Hawaiian shorts that Mitch gave me. That was all the confirmation I needed. My dream night was real.

Right in the middle of my dreamy thought, I heard a voice that sounded just like Binki's. What? Man, I must be in love. Everyone sounds like Binki. Soon after my mom spoke, I heard it again. I sit straight up. My blood was rushing now! Oh no! She is talking to my mom. Right then, the zipper floated upward. I was shaking. Afraid of who was on the other side of the tent door. Then, just like at our Christmas play at church, the curtain doors opened and …Dad stuck his unshaven face through the door.

"Bo, you might want to get out here. If you don't stop your mother, you will have no secrets in about thirty minutes."

"I heard that, Joe. I'm just making conversation," Mom informs him.

This is a nightmare. How does this happen? My hair is a mess. I have been drooling in my sleep. And my breath probably still got the smell of beer. What could they be talking about? I could hear them talking but couldn't make out what they were saying. I was certain I heard my name on several occasions.

I really like Binki and love my family, but I felt certain that these two worlds were not meant to co-exist. My mom and Binki are about as opposite as two people can get.

I ran my hands through my hair, trying to push down anything that was sticking up. Tried to wipe off the drool from around my mouth or any sleep that had built up in my eyes during the night. I grabbed some clothes and my plastic bag of shower tools. Took a deep breath in preparation for my grand exit from the tent.

I closed my eyes and said a quick prayer to God for mercy. Then I walked towards the light shining through the gap in the doorway. While my right barefoot was making contact with the earth, my eyes found their way to the person who dominated my every thought throughout the night. Binki was sitting at the picnic table talking to my family, sitting and smiling with my mom as if she were her best friend.

"Look what I found," Mom said with a little excitement.

Mom has three boys and I think she always wanted a girl. She says that having three boys is God's plan, but I feel certain that she would love to have a girl to dress up or cook with. In fact, she told us that the doctor said that she was having a girl when she was pregnant with Stevie. I always thought that my mom was hoping that Stevie would turn out to be a girl, but she took it in stride when it turned out she had another boy.

She is a good mom, and I honestly wish she had the chance to have a daughter. It just wasn't meant to be. I know that as the oldest child, whomever I marry will be in for a bit of a culture shock. Mom will treat them as if they were her daughter. Lord help us if she ever gets a granddaughter. The little girl will be the apple of my mom's eye for sure.

"Good morning, sleepy head," the voice of my new-found love said to me.

I replied with a grunt, trying to be cool. Acting like I was rubbing my eyes for only the first time today.

I stretched my arms out wide and asked, "What are y'all doin'?"

Meanwhile, I walked by my dad and whispered quietly, "Thanks for the heads up".

"I was just telling your family about last night. About how much fun we had," Binki said as she turned her coy smile in my direction.

Mom added, "Sounds like y'all had a lot of fun."

I couldn't help but glance at Phillip and notice that the whole truth never left Binki's lips. But once again, she had my head racing. What in the world could she have told my family? I felt certain that beer, kissing, and skinny dipping had to be left out, or my mom would have gone off on her. Then proceeded to beat me half to death before I ever heard the first chirp from a bird this morning.

I was getting familiar with Binki. I knew she didn't say anything to get me in trouble, but I was intrigued and felt a rush!! I wanted to know what she said but had to act as if it didn't even matter. She was enjoying the game of cat and mouse with my parents, which coincided with me being psychologically toyed with.

I smiled and played my part, "I am sure it is all lies."

I turned towards the bridge.

"I have to go take a shower. I will be back very shortly."

Knowing that I was risking leaving Binki with my parents even longer.

I was about to ask Phillip to walk with me so I could get the dirt on what was being said, but a better option came up.

Binki commanded, "Wait, I'll walk with you. I have to run by and ask my mom."

She said something to my mom that I didn't understand. But I heard my mom instruct her to let us know.

Mom yelled back, "Don't take too long. Breakfast will be ready in about 20 minutes."

I waved my hand in the air as confirmation that the message had been received. My eyes caught a glimpse of Binki walking toward me wearing black cotton shorts, a yellow t-shirt with the peace symbol on the front, and a matching bandanna covering her head. I couldn't help but smile because my dream night had been extended for at least one more day. We walked towards the shower area, and she grabbed my hand.

"So, you been thinking about me?"

"Who? You? Hmmm...Maybe? Just a little bit," I responded while noticing a hint of flirtation in her tone.

Her eyes told me that she spent the entire night thinking of me. My smile gave away my excitement. The sweet scent of her perfume closed the deal. I leaned over and kissed her on the cheek, even though I knew that my family was watching. I did not look back to see if they noticed. Honestly, really didn't care if they did.

Along our walk, Binki filled me in on what type of perfume she was wearing that gave off that hypnotic scent that commanded my recent actions. It was somewhere between flowers and strawberries. Rather quickly, our conversation transitioned to how she met my mom at the community restroom and that mom invited her down for breakfast. Binki said she told my family how our night went, but she gave them the "Church version," as she named it. She told everything we did but forgot to inform them of anything that would hinder my choir boy image. Binki informed me that she never lied. Just didn't give them all the details.

I was made aware that we were going on a family picnic that included fishing and swimming down by the lake. My mom took it upon herself to extend an invitation to Binki. But she had to ask her mom for permission.

Which is where she is supposed to be heading right now and yet, we are not going in that direction. Instead, we are walking towards the showers.

When I confronted her that we were not walking towards her site, she said her mom had already left for the day. No need to ask because her mom is meeting somebody that their church set her up with about a house. Her mom informed her this morning that they may be moving into a nearby house in a couple of days. She just told my mom that because she didn't want my family to know about her situation. Then she reminded me that I promised not to tell anyone about her family situation. Even my parents! I reassured her that she could trust me.

She walked me to the shower and told me she was going back to her camper to put on her swimming suit. She said she might just work on her tan if the fishing thing doesn't work out. We agreed that after I got done showering, I would go by her camper to pick her up on my way to the campsite.

After showering, I started the walk away from my site towards Binki's. Along the way, I noticed the empty campsite that was occupied by Margaret's family the previous night. By the road were two white bags of trash with clothes hanging out of them. Upon further inspection, I noticed that they were Binki and my clothes from the previous night. I wasn't sure if I wanted to get them out. After a little thought, I decided that I deserved this. I might mess up karma or something if I got those clothes out. Not counting the fact, how pitiful would I look trying to get clothes out of someone else's trash? Even if they were my clothes. The feeling of guilt for breaking up their friendship started hitting me again. I quickened my pace past the site, making my way towards Binki's beige make-shift home.

I approached her camper and noticed that there was nobody outside. After I knocked on the side of the camper, a soft-spoken voice invited me inside. I remember she said she was going to change into her swimming clothes when she got back to her camper. I stepped through this door as images of me walking in as she was changing the last time ran through my head. I was praying I got that lucky again.

But that was not the case. She was fixing her hair in front of a small black mirror that was resting between her legs, wearing the same clothes. She was trying hard to improve on what I already thought was perfection. I walked in and sat on the bed that doubles as a sitting area that she was already using.

After a couple of minutes of pushing her brush through her hair and making faces in the mirror, I had a thought. We are in this camper ALONE! I am going to kiss her. I scooted closer to her.

Then she said, "Let's go."

"I thought you were going to change," I questioned.

"I did. I have my swimming clothes under these," she responded as she pointed to her shorts and shirt.

She obviously put on more of the perfume that I just complimented her on. This helped confirm my decision to make my bold move. I pulled her in and gave her a kiss. I was really beginning to enjoy this kissing thing.

Then she pulled away.

"We need to go", she said.

"Where?" I spoke.

"To breakfast with your family, remember. We shouldn't make them wait," she replied.

"Oh yeah," my mouth said, but my body wanted to stay.

I was about ready to make a case for staying a little longer, but then the camper door opened.

"Not again?" I heard Binki's little brother say. "Well, at least this time, you will not need me to bring you clothes."

"We were not doing anything," Binki informed.

"Anything? Maybe "anything" has already been done," Mitch said, using his fingers to put air quotes around the word anything.

Binki cursed at him and told him to shut up. She picked up a black cloth bag that had a towel, a book, and suntan lotion in it and proceeded to push him out of the way as she exited the camper.

Mitch was taken aback by her hostility.

"Chill out, woman; I was just playing."

Binki acted as if she had never even heard him.

We started our walk back towards my family.

Before we got too far, Mitch ran up behind Binki and said, "Don't forget to call that other guy. You know, the asshole some people call Scott." He didn't even care that I (the other - other guy) was standing right there.

"I got this. Worry about yourself", she yelled back, and we went on our way.

I felt like a load of bricks just hit me when the realization of what Mitch had just said registered in my head. I am a fool. Is she playing me? Wait a minute, she never promised me anything? But she is holding my hand. I am totally confused. I have no idea what is going on here. Am I her boyfriend? Or am I the other guy? Am I jealous that she is calling Scott?

"Okay, hold up. Let's stop for a second. What is the deal with Scott? Is he coming back? What's the plan? What are we doing," I asked, expressing my concern.

Binki stopped. She pulled me towards a nearby picnic table that was absent of people but not their camping equipment. She inhaled loudly. "Okay. I'm just letting you know that this is really hard for me. Real hard. I wanted to tell you this later, but here it goes."

She swallowed another large gulp of air. She took her right hand and rubbed her forehead, maybe to wipe away the stress she misunderstood as sweat. The seriousness of her tone began to make me a little uncomfortable.

"I have been thinking about the events of last night. The absolute chaos!!! Then combine that with our talk by the pier and outside the campsite. Every word we spoke has been replayed in my head many times. The realization that the chaos of last night was there because I allowed it. I welcomed that chaos. Your impression of me is probably the same impression others have. You just have the balls to come out and say it, and they don't. I wonder how many guys have thought of me as a girlfriend for the night, not a girlfriend for life? A whore or a bimbo. Reflecting, I'm pathetic."

Feeling the good mojo of a couple of minutes ago going in the wrong direction, I corrected her.

"You are not pathetic. That's NOT what I said."

"I know. I know. Let me finish. You made me think about my future. What the hell is the plan? Is this my life course? Am I really going to allow my dad to be right? Am I going to be a trashy bitch? I never really thought about my future like that and never realized the similarities between Scott and my dad. Unfortunately, I think you are right. I can't be around people who are anything like my dad, and my dad can't be right about me!! Nor can I end up like my mom. I love her more than life itself, but I refuse to take the same path she took. Her path must be my lesson. She has lived a hard life. For most of her life, she has lived either drunk or in fear. Certainly, that wasn't her plan when she met Dad. But I could envision that the abuse between mom and dad started with events very similar to last night. Or with mom allowing dad to degrade her by calling her bitch and whore. I don't want that. Soon, I am calling Scott to tell him not to come back up here."

I could see that our conversation the previous night really hit her hard.

"So, you are breaking up with him?" I asked.

"Yes. I can't do this anymore. He treats me like shit!" she mutters as a tear makes an appearance in the corner of each eye.

I leaned over and softly wiped the moisture from her face.

Binki then stood up and said, "I am alright. I'm just not sure why I am crying. I decided last night that this is what I was going to do."

She put both her hands in front of her, not touching her face. She wiped down in an imaginary attempt to remove all emotions. Then, as if it was all resolved, she changed the subject and commanded that we get back.

Along the walk, she kept sharing the obvious, which was why she had to break it off with Scott. It felt like she was still talking herself into this decision or looking for me to give her even greater validation for making the choice. You could tell that this call was going to be very difficult, and she was dreading it already.

The fact that we discussed the Scott situation but never answered the "what are we doing" question did not elude me. Did she just say we are boyfriend/girlfriend? I never heard anything about us, only about them.

Am I supposed to deduce that with her getting rid of him, it is obvious that I am the one? I decided to wait and tackle that question later.

Chapter Fourteen - Family Time

My family was already eating, and mom gave us a hard time about taking so long. They had two plates already made for us. Bacon, eggs, and grits were sitting on a Dixie plate beside a napkin with a plastic fork. They left us an empty spot on one side of the table with a plastic cup filled with orange juice. Stevie decided he had to sit between Binki and me. So, we made the necessary arrangements.

The entire walk from Binki's site and all through breakfast, I couldn't help thinking about the decision that she made. There was joy in knowing this life-changing decision was based on my conversation. I took a minute to secretly thank God for giving me the right words and guidance. It was satisfying because I knew she could do better than him. Anxiety and worry charged into my brain. What if Scott got mad and came up here anyway to start trouble? That is all she needs. More problems. Or what if he blames me and comes after me? He is crazy! Can't worry about that now. After all, God seems to be on my side at the moment.

My mind shifts to what if she really, really likes me. Could our relationship go past this week? That's not possible. Right?

I realized that I had been with her for almost an hour, and she had barely cursed, nor had I seen her smoke. Then she stopped me from kissing her when last night I didn't think she was able to or wanted to stop. Plus, she got mad at Mitch for acting as if we were having sex. All this plus she has been nice to my family. She was nice the previous night, but today is different. She seemed like she really cared about what my mom said. Could she really be trying to change? This mysterious girl of today was equally intriguing as the one I met last night, but in a different way.

After breakfast, we cleaned up and headed to my dad's favorite part of vacation: fishing. We started the day by fishing off a pier whose backdrop was a heavily wooded area. However, it was within eyesight of the swimming area—the same swimming area that housed the pier where Binki and I had spent the previous night.

It was just a matter of time before Stevie would want to go swimming.

We always selected a spot that had both fishing and swimming areas. This allowed my mom to take Stevie swimming while my dad fished within earshot of one another. Making it seem like we are all in the same spot and keeping the spirit of family time alive. Truth be told, the two spots were not that close together because Dad did not like fishing too close to the swimming area due to all the commotion and noise the swimmers would make.

It was obvious that Binki had never been fishing before. This was mind-blowing for my family and myself. We just assumed that everyone went fishing several times a year.

My father kept with tradition and eventually moved further from the swimming area as he set up along a nearby bank that had several trees leaning over the water. This isolation allowed him to smoke his Marlboros without harassment from the rest of the family about the smell. He was catching fish like crazy from the moment he cast the first line under the shade of the trees. My mom and Stevie started out on the pier but saw the success my dad was having, and before long, they invaded his spot. I know this really bothered Dad because they made so much noise. Especially Stevie who couldn't help but to be loud. Dad would never complain. He just welcomed them with open arms.

The clan repositioning themselves from the pier was prefect because it allowed Binki and I to have more time to talk. Phillip every so often would toss in a topic like what type of fish we might catch or ask what was Binki's favorite TV shows. You could see that Binki's beauty totally intimated Phillip. As the day grew, Phillip was getting more and more comfortable.

Every so often, Stevie and my mom would make appearances; mom to be nosey and Stevie just because he was Stevie. Mom would say she just wanted to make sure we were OK. Stevie had different motives. Stevie would ask Binki something silly like if she ever owned a fish or what would she name her dragon if she ever had one.

I let Binki use my rod, but the bites were far and few. Even though we were not catching fish, we were having as much fun as you can have fishing without catching anything. At first, she would not put a worm on the hook. But after much harassment from my family, especially Stevie, she tried it once. Which was the first and last time she touched the worm. You would have thought it was the nastiest thing anyone could ever do. The only time she screamed louder than when she touched the worm was when she caught her first and only fish of the day. The screams were for two totally different reasons. The worm was out of disgust, and the barely four-inch brim provided the sounds of pure excitement.

It was my first-time going fishing with a girly girl. The only girls I ever went fishing with before were my mom and my cousins. All my cousins were raised on a farm, and my mom has three sons. I thought it was cute that anytime my brothers or I gave Binki a hard time about boyish things, my mother would come to her defense. Binki was as girly as a girl can be, and I could not have found that more appealing.

A couple of hours in, it became apparent that the sun was directing Binki's ideal of a perfect day from fishing to sunbathing. We agreed that she would lie out on the pier beside me while I kept fishing.

She grabbed a towel out of her bag and laid it across the wooden pier. By removing her shirt and shorts, she immediately shifted from something that she was not accustomed to, like fishing, into her natural habit of tanning. As she was transforming into her 2-piece yellow bikini, I could not take my eyes off her and didn't even care that she caught me peeking. This was a vision that resembled a scene from one of my mom's favorite soap operas, and I was in it. I felt like I was Greg, and I had my own Jenny for All My Children lying right beside me. She put on a pair of sunglasses as if she were about to get serious. Rubbed Coppertone suntan lotion all over the exposed skin and laid flat on the towel. Every so often, she would rise and splash water on her body, then retake her position back on the towel.

Flipping herself over from time to time to make sure each side got equal time exposure to the sun's rays.

The sun had to be happy because it knew that today it was making a masterpiece. For that, I was grateful. My focus on fishing easily shifted to trying to get as many looks as possible at the beauty that was lying right beside me. Then I noticed that I wasn't the only one who noticed!

Phillip and Stevie kept staring. So much that mom had to nudge Phillip. As mom poked Phillip with her right finger and bent to whisper in his ear something that certainly had to do with reminding him not to stare, I was wondering what mom was thinking?

All those times I heard her call the girls at the beach jezebels just because they were wearing something like the two-piece bikini that Binki was wearing. Today, she didn't seem to mind. She isn't calling Binki any of those names that we have heard for so many years. I always thought it was because she was jealous that her time wearing this attire had passed. Or maybe her father never let her wear things like this. Or maybe it was because of the whole "not the church" way idea? The truth is more likely to be because she never knew any of them. If she knew them as her daughter, her friend, or her son's girlfriend, maybe she wouldn't choose those descriptions.

In between interruptions, I was able to learn even more about Binki. I made sure I paid close attention to things like her birthday on March 26 and her favorite color, which is purple, because Mom always gets mad at Dad for her having to remind him of those types of things.

We spoke about our perfect places, and she informed me that if she could be anywhere, it would be on a deserted beach with hot chocolate, good music, and a good book. I was trying to be a smooth talker and told her that today, on this pier with her is about as perfect as it gets. I could tell she really liked that response because she leaned up long enough to tell me that it was sweet and kiss me on the cheek.

This led her to bring up the question she asked me the previous night about the "girlfriend for the week idea". We agreed that we are just going to have fun this week without titles, and there will be no future expectations. We decided not to worry about our future together. When that time comes, we will either adjust or go our separate ways with no strings attached. We will just live in the moment.

I knew that this was our agreement, but that's not going to be easy for me. I am falling for her so fast, and I can't stop the fall. With every action, I want another. With every word, I wanted more. The thought of not being around her or never seeing her again makes it hard for me to breathe. I really don't understand what is happening, but I am confident that I don't want it to end.

My perception went from a wild child who really didn't care about herself or anyone else in the world to discovering she really does have a depth and a caring side. The change was so great, so quick, I wasn't sure if it was who she really was. Could our night on the pier really make her reassess her own life, and this is her new vision of Binki? The saying, when in Rome, do as the Romans came to mind. Is it possible that she is a human version of a Chamaeleon? Whomever she is around, she can just adapt. I found that thought ironic, seeing as I, the choir boy for Indian Trail, was more like a misfit from anywhere but church last night. Drinking, cursing, fighting?

It made me wonder if maybe she's just playing me, telling me what I want to hear, or if she is playing some type of mind game.

After a while, fishing started to bore Stevie, and the pretty girl on the pier had gathered his full attention. Stevie, being Stevie, came over and asked if he could lay out beside her. He splashed some water on his body and then laid his 40-pound body beside her, using the wood pier as his towel. He thought he was in heaven.

The mind of a child often comes with the greatest of ideas. Stevie asked her if she wanted to play numbers, letters, or drawings. He explained to her that he would lay on his belly, and she would have to draw a number, letter, or picture on his back. Then Stevie would have to guess it. This was a game that my mom would play with him often to keep his attention while she was watching something on TV. Never had I wanted to play this game more than at this very moment.

We played several rounds, alternating turns. Allowing our backs to be canvasses for things like hearts, numbers, flowers, and cars. When it was my turn to draw on her back, I made sure I drew the most descriptive, horrible drawing of all time just to prolong my being able to run my fingers across her skin. The drawings were always big and came as close to the top of her bikini bottom as possible, often bringing a giggle from Stevie.

Never did it fail that when it was my time to be drawn upon, it ended with Binki doing something sneaky and playful.

Once she told Stevie she saw a shark, and Stevie looked away and she pinched my butt. The next time, she and Stevie tried to tickle me to death. Finally, the last time, they told me to close my eyes as they pushed me off the pier into the water. This ended the game and brought the attention back to just tanning.

Stevie's desire to be tan was not as strong as hers. Not too long in the process, he discovered that he was hungry. His constant nagging prompted Mom to go set up the picnic table in preparation for lunch. Stevie's need for food was justified since it was well after normal lunchtime. Binki impressed me when she volunteered to assist. I didn't really need to eat. I could have watched her sunbathe the entire day.

Soon after eating our sandwiches and chips, we decided we were going to go swimming. That was except for my father and Phillip, who wanted to stay and fish. Normally I stay with Dad, but this time I decided to go swimming. I knew that my dad would understand the reason.

I was proud of Phillip because he chose to stay with Dad. My father told him he didn't have to, but he made it seem like he wanted to stay. A little one-on-one time with Phillip and Dad would do a lot to enhance Dad's relationship with Phillip. Phillip isn't active, and being the middle child, it seems like he gets lost sometimes between the newness of the first child's every activity and the babying of the youngest child.

Chapter Fifteen - Cheese Whiz

The end of the perfect day was becoming inevitable. The trees started to cast long shadows as the sun was ever so gracefully falling out of the majestic frame. Binki was the first to throw in the towel when she said she had to go check in with her mom. She asked if I wanted to come. I glanced at Mom, who gave me the go-ahead nod. I walked over, gave Mom a kiss on the forehead, and whispered love you in her ear. Mom said she probably will not be here much longer, either. If she is not here, she may be back at the site. We agreed that I would probably hang out with Binki as long as I could and not wait up.

I dried off and put on my tank top as Binki grabbed her yellow sunflower shirt and pulled it over her bikini top. Then, she shimmied into her shorts before we made our way up the trail. During the walk, Binki told me how awesome my family was and reminded me of how lucky I was. Once we had created enough distance that my family was no longer in sight, Binki grabbed my hand and admitted that her mom was not at the campsite. She said she was done with the tanning since the sun was starting to set but didn't want to be rude.

The plan was for me to drop her off and tell my family that her mom wanted her to do something. She wasn't going to go back. I understood.

The sun was the excuse given, though I informed her that it would have been okay just to say that she was tired of swimming for the day.

We constantly question each other about simple things like the type of cars we want to own, movie stars that we admire, and music. When we got to the site, she invited me in so she could let me hear some of her type of music. After all, I'm not sure I have ever given Madonna a fair chance, according to Binki. Apparently, I just needed to be more open-minded. I obliged. Mainly because I discovered that I was impressed by her range of music fandom; no matter the style, she could talk about it. Rap, Country, rock, and even gospel.

She entered first, switching on a batter powered lantern very much like I do the light switch to my kitchen at home. I followed her in and pushed some clothes out of the way as I grabbed a seat on the side of the camper that was clearly hers because it had make-up, teen magazines with Madonna on the cover, a beatbox, and her clothes thrown all about. The other side was neater and better organized, with folded boy's clothes, a wallet, and a red gym bag. She caught that I could see the difference.

"Yes, Mitch is a lot neater than I. But I guess you can see that. He has always cared about his image more than me. Guess you came to that conclusion on your own as well," she said with a wry smile.

Trying to make her feel more comfortable, I lied and told her that I am the messy one in my house. When in reality, I must be the neatest one in my house. I am certainly the only one that cares about their image. Image is nothing that has ever concerned my parents or brothers.

I think she caught the attempt to appease and rolled her eyes, "Of course you are."

Not breaking stride in her conversation, she took off her tee shirt and threw it to the floor. I knew her mouth was moving, but my mind started to wonder about the possibilities that might be in my foreseeable future. I had the most beautiful woman in the world within reaching distance in a pair of shorts and a bikini top. Just her and I. Before my manly thoughts went too far down the road, Binki reached over me and grabbed a red flannel button-up long-sleeve shirt and put it on, buttoning the bottom four buttons. She then put both of her arms inside her shirt, very much like a turtle hiding in their shell, only for her hands to resurface a couple of minutes later with the bikini top that she had worn the earlier part of the day. She threw the bikini top on the floor and folded her sleeves up until they reached above her elbows.

"Hello, do you want one or not?" were the words that broke my trance.

I am not certain what I was agreeing to, but I said, "Of course."

There was a small blue cooler sitting on the direct opposite side of the entrance with a couple of bags of snacks stacked on top of it. This genius idea was no doubt that of a teenager because it was the quick stash for the bigger cooler sitting outside to allow people in the camper not to have to continuously enter and exit. Binki pointed the fan in my direction and reached into the cooler for a Pepsi for each of us. What I have now gathered is what I agreed to receive. Grabbed a box of crackers and a can of cheese whiz that she called Easy Cheese and took a spot right beside me.

We both slide back as far as we could using the side of the camper as support for our backs.

I would grab a cracker, and she would spray some cheese on it as I informed her that Randy Travis was my favorite singer and Forever and Ever Amen was my favorite song, but Three Wooden Crosses, I Told You So, and others had real meaning. Listen to the words because I think country music is God's way to speak right to the soul, I explained. Besides, there is nothing more romantic than dancing to a slow country song. She smiled but was ready to make her case for music domination. She reached over and turned on her radio, which had the cassette from Madonna already in place. "Like a Virgin" came through loud and proud. Followed by "Papa Don't Preach", "Crazy for You", "Like a Prayer", and every big hit Madonna had made. No doubt that Binki had bootlegged a cassette of all her favorite Madonna songs.

I had to admit that I did like it. So, I confessed this to her, "Why have you not liked it before?"

Getting another heaping of cheese sprayed on a cracker allowed me to ponder the question. Almost like a revelation from my pastor at church, it hit me. I shared that the reason I never liked this before was because I was never exposed to it. In the world I live in, Madonna is a sinner. She is a disciple of the devil. She sings about the devil, I thought. Just listening to her music was like purchasing a ticket to hell. But I don't know why. I have never listened to one song. I made this assumption because I was raised to think this way. This is what I was told of Madonna and that type of music.

Someone else controlled my mind. Pretty much told me how and what to think about music.

This brought about deep conversation about how many people don't like other people just because they are not exposed to them or their ways. Often, we judge people because they have different skin colors or believe in a different religion. Wonder how many people go to church because that is the only life they know. Or don't go to church because they never have been taught the ways of the Bible. How many boys grow up to be drunks or abusive fathers because they grew up in this environment and were taught this is how a man is supposed to run his family? Immediately, we spoke about rap music and how people immediately class them as thugs. Or how we generalize people who listen to country music as rednecks or people who listen to rock music as druggies. The thought was thrown about who set these stereotypes. Wondered how many people are being judged by the clothes they wear, the cars they drive, or the music they listen to. Then, the hypocrisy of this settled in as we did some self-reflecting. We wondered how many times we have made that same assumption about someone using those same facts. Weird how we judge people without really knowing them.

She admitted that the term redneck and that stereotype were the exact words used by her friends to describe me. Before she could finish her thought and I could act self-righteously offended, we heard something outside.

Binki immediately recognized the sound and yelled, "Cuddles," as she shot out the doorway.

Before I could get up, she returned with a full-size cat.

"What the heck?" I asked.

Proudly, Binki introduced me to a black and white cat named Cuddles. Cuddles is technically the property of the people who manage the campsite, and Binki playfully informed me that she is the great protector of their land. Therefore, Cuddles has full reign to explore and protect the campsite because she is a furious cat. And this is her jungle. I most certainly had my doubts. Cuddles was not here to explore or protect. Furious was not in this cat's nature. But eating was. I have lived on a farm long enough to know animals return where they are fed. Mom often joked, just like men.

She asked me if I wanted to hold Cuddles, and I refrained. I like animals but do not really like them all over me. She told me that she wanted to have a house full of cats. As she was telling me this, Cuddles set right beside her and would lick the excess cheese off the nozzle of the can after every spray.

This confirmed my suspicion of why Cuddles was a frequent visitor and cemented the fact that I was done with the Easy Cheese for the night.

As she had done just moments before, Binki sprayed some cheese on a cracker and placed it near my lips.

I said, "No thanks," as I turned my head away as if she was trying to feed me poison.

"That's rude. What's wrong with you," she said.

"I can't eat after no cat," I explained.

"Are you serious?" she says with a bewildered look on her face.

"Yeah, I am not eating after an animal."

Binki informs me that cat's mouths are cleaner than humans. She leans down and kisses Cuddles right on the lips as some form of verification. I challenge them by telling her she has no proof that Cuddles didn't just do his duty of protecting the land by eating some dead rat. She laughs. She notices the true uneasiness and starts to turn it into her own personal game of torture.

"Go ahead, just one little bite for me?" she says in a sexy voice.

"Never happening," I protest. I smile as if I think it's funny, but I know this is my line in the sand moment. I am not eating after some cat.

A sneaky, conniving smile comes across her face.

"I bet you that I can make you eat after a cat."

I stood firmly in my tone, with my head going side to side just in case she didn't understand the words that were leaving my lips.

"I am telling you, I can NOT and will NOT eat after a cat."

A mischievous smile appeared on her face.

"Yes, you would."

Knowing there was NO way I was going to eat after Cuddles, "Unless you have a gun, that cat-infested cheese ain't touching my lips."

The amusement of my disgust stretched across her face as she made her way back to the blue cooler.

"I need something different. Sometimes, Pepsi is too sweet. I need water or a spite."

She opens the cooler with one hand while Cuddles is still in the other.

"Damn, they are in the outside cooler," as she slams the cooler lid.

She throws the feline on my lap and instructs in a taunting way, "Hold Cuddles for a moment. Unless you are afraid that you will catch cat cooties."

"I am not afraid of cats. In fact, I like cats. I just refuse to eat after one."

Sounding holier than intended, I explain while she goes outside, carefully closing the door to make sure that the captive cat does not escape. I hear her rambling around outside for a second, and soon after I hear the cooler top slam, I notice a crack in the door as Binki uses the same caution to enter back the camper that she used to exit it.

The sound of the words, "Dammit. We don't have water or Spite," accompanies her body back inside.

I offered to go to my site and get water, but she said she would settle for the Pepsi.

Binki reclaims her position on the camper bed, sitting Indian-style directly in front of me, as Cuddles runs to the lap of her hero. Binki and Cuddles pick up where they left off by sharing the Easy Cheese and crackers.

Binki took the Easy Cheese, sprayed a little extra, and let Cuddles do his thing. This was being done in a taunting fashion as she looked to make sure I saw Cuddles licking the cheese off the nozzle. The sight of this cat licking the excess Easy Cheese almost made me gag.

"So where were we before my water break?" asking the question that I felt sure she knew the answer to. "Oh yeah, you said that the cheese from this can will never touch your lips."

I reminded her that this was the case while she was spraying the cheese on her pointer finger and letting Cuddles lick it. I could tell that she was about to try to wipe my lips with this same finger, so I turned my body to face her, sitting Indian style as well.

"Don't think about it," I said as I waved my finger from side to side.

With a devilish smile she mischievously whispered, "What?" and then stuck out her tongue and licked the cheese off her finger.

Cuddles once again, licked the spray cap. She placed another portion on her finger, and this cycle repeated itself as our conversation went back to music. We ventured to the topic of Michael Jackson as she stood up to make her way back to the cooler.

Suddenly, she said, "Gotcha," and threw her body on top of mine with such force I fell backward as her cheesy finger came in a direct path toward my lips.

The sudden movement caught me off guard momentarily, but she was laughing so hard it was easy to catch her finger before it hit my lips. I kept a tight grip on the hand with the cheesy finger as she positioned her body with her legs straddling my waist.

"I am not letting you up until you lick this cheese off my finger," she said with authority.

I reminded her that I was a lot stronger than her and could get up at any time I wanted. She laughed and agreed, but I still held her hand away from my face. Then reminder her, that this was an impressive effort, but I was not going to lose focus again by her tricks.

Trying a new tactic, she stops laughing and gets serious.

"Let go of my hand."

I could tell I was going to be played again as she struggled to free her hand.

"I will once you let me up, or that cheese leaves that finger."

Cuddles find his way towards the finger, but the commotion caused by Binki trying to free her hand gives him second thoughts as he surrenders towards the door.

She explains that she is not letting me up until that cheese hits my lips.

"I am stronger than you think," she declares.

Loving the fact that she was sitting so close to me, I played along.

"No doubt, you are strong. But you will need an Army to make that cheese hit my taste buds."

After another great effort to free her hand, she concedes, "Okay, okay."

Instead of her hand going towards me, she lifts her hand and licks the cheese off her finger with a sexy taunt.

"See, no cheese."

She turns her finger towards me as proof.

The smile of victory that I was wearing seemed to rekindle Binki's effort not to give up.

"You think you have won, don't you?" leaning towards me, confirming that this battle was not over.

My forehead wrinkles as my mouth renders its most cocky, playful told-you-so tone, "Of course. I mean. I was right."

"It looks that way. For the moment," she concedes.

I began to try to sit up in preparation for another attack effort, but I was too late as she pushed me back flat on my back. I quickly took my hands and covered my mouth.

As if this was her plan all along, she sprayed the cheese on my neck.

As seductive as possible, she licked it off.

That feeling was something I had never felt before.

She leaned up and wiped her mouth. My mind, my body was in a place it had never been. In movies, this was the go moment. But this was real life.

Binki didn't offer resistance this time as I sat up and gently pushed her to the side. I stood up because I was afraid of what I was about to do in my swimming trunks if she did that again.

I notice Binki sitting up with her legs folded under her, smiling as if she recognized the situation. I looked down and noticed that my trunks were bulging in a way that confirmed her suspicion.

"You okay?" was asked, but Binki knew that I was more than okay.

Heck, I might as well just pull it out. My shorts were doing me no favors by trying to hide any dignity that I may have had left.

I gave her a reply in an attempt to restore some type of pride, "Oh, yeah. Just making sure that cheese does not touch my lips."

Once again, that devilish smile came across her lips. Without saying a word, she slowly unbuttoned her shirt until each shirttail sat on each of her thighs, and there were no buttons left to unbutton. The flannel shirt was closed enough to cover her breasts but exposed enough for me to confirm what I already knew. There was nothing under that flannel. She took the can and started to spray right above her belly and continued to spray until the cheese made its way between each breast. Reached up and grabbed my hands.

"Last chance. Are you sure you won't eat the cheese?"

The perfect day just got perfecter as real life intersected with my dreams.

Chapter Sixteen - Mills and Fields

I immediately went to my site, got clothes, and took a shower. I'm not sure if sex smells, but I was going to wash away all evidence just in case. Fearing that Binki had the same thought, I used the community restroom/shower on the opposite side of the camp. Not sure why. I just knew I didn't want to run into her, thinking that would be too weird. Not sure what I would say.

The extra walk prolonged the battle I was having with my emotions. I was all over the place and could not get a grasp. It started with me retracing our every move. I could close my eyes and retrace every inch of her body.

This caused a sensation as I was getting excited just thinking about it.

It was hard to believe that this happened to me. Just a good ole country boy. I have called myself a good old country boy a thousand times, but am I really? Do bad people think they're good? That's not the problem; I am a good person who did a bad thing. Hold up, is that what a convict's mom says about their children right before they go to jail? My anxiety went to the next level. This isn't a bad thing. Sex is natural, right? Holy cow!

Not in the eyes of God. Sex out of wedlock is a sin. I could not walk anymore. Once I got close to my site, I sat down on the bridge just to gather my thoughts.

Moral values rushed their way into my thoughts like a Florida thunderstorm. Fast, violent, and without warning. Did I just take advantage of her? Guilt overcame me. I should have said no. I should have been stronger. My head lifts towards heaven, and I ask God why he didn't stop me. Wait, why didn't God stop me? He is the all-knowing, all-seeing. He could have sent Mitch or her mom back early if he wanted to. He could have done a lot of things not to allow us to be in there alone. Am I blaming God for my actions? The heck!! What is coming over me?

I have heard my pastor say several times that God has a plan for me. This can't be the plan unless… She got pregnant. Maybe God wants me to protect her. That is stupid. Why would she have to be pregnant at 15 for me to protect her? Or anyone to protect her. Pregnant!! Did that thought just enter my head? Holy Shit, she could be pregnant. I remember hearing my pastor speak about the choices you make and how one choice could change the course of someone's life. Of course, he often talks about being saved and accepting Jesus Christ as your saviour for your eternal life, but I think this is different. Wait, it is the same. Could I be a father at 15? Well technically. History is filled with 13-year-old brides and teenage moms. I must get control of my head. She said she was on the pill. I must trust that to be the case. Of course, no way to change what was done.

A smile crosses my face. I couldn't help but think that the devil put the smile there when the phrase 'How could something so bad feel so good?' came to mind. Does the devil have control of my thoughts? Yep, he's in my head. I am convinced that I need to fight him off.

Just then, a deep voice explodes through the air, saying my name. It is pretty loud but not close. Unquestionably directed straight at me.

Could this be God? Could this be the Devil? I wasn't sure I wanted to answer the call.

I have read that God talks to people and maybe it's my time. The second call was a little louder and a lot more recognizable. I see Dad making his way towards me asking in a concerning way if something was wrong. I noticed that he was coming in the direction of where the car was parked.

My body took a straight posture with great speed. Much like a suspect being hit with the flashlight of a peace officer in an attempted burglary. The surprise was confirmed with the high-pitched tone "Never better" that escaped from my body.

I got the feeling that my father didn't believe me. He encouraged me to walk with him while he interrogated me and lit a Marlboro.

"Why are you here, by yourself. Something wrong?" his eyebrows raised. Scrunching the skin on his forehead together.

I explained that I was just thinking, but he wanted more.

"This has something to do with that girl, right? Is she mad at you?"

The smile on my face told more than the three-letter "Nah" that I used to respond.

"Oh, so it's like that. You like her."

"Dad, she's almost perfect," was the response that intrigued my dad. He took a draw on his cigarette, and smoke flowed from both nostrils.

"Hmm… Almost isn't perfect." He brought out the old country saying I have heard a thousand times. "Almost is only good in horseshoes and grenades."

We both smiled because we both knew that was coming.

After a moment of silence, he continued, "Perfect is a high standard to hold someone to. I see all the reasons she is almost perfect." Dad kept the cigarette in his mouth and used his hands to put air clouds around the words "almost perfect". Just to emphasize the point even further, he used a different, almost sarcastic tone when he spoke the two words "almost perfect".

"What stops her from being perfect."

This type of talk is not an avenue my dad and I travelled to too often, but lord knows they're the greatest talks. These moments of openness and caring, I am certain, separate my dad from others. He grew up picking cotton and working in mills his whole life. He is not a philosopher or a physiotherapist. But somehow, I learned more during these talks than any book could ever educate.

"Nothing, she is perfect," was given.

Fearful that whatever I said would go from my lips to mom's ears.

Dad is not giving up that easily. "Nothing implies there is something. But I understand if you don't want to share."

Another moment of silence as he turns his head towards the sky, allowing the smoke from his last inhale to exit his lungs and disappear into the clouds.

"I know this; she sure is pretty," I agreed.

"Your mom is smitten." A moment of silence is broken when he adds, "Just between you and me. Your ma is going to be in love no matter who you or any of the boys bring home. As long as they are good to you."

I agreed again.

"Something to keep in mind. Whoever you date or eventually marry, they need to know they are marrying our family, too. That includes your mom. In fact, your mom isn't much different than mine. I think your grandma was more broken-hearted when I would break up with girls than I was," he laughed as he slowed down slowed down long enough to discard the old cigarette and replace it with another.

"Those things are bad for you," I say.

"That's the rumour."

We both smile because we both know that he has heard this too a thousand times.

The understanding that we were just walking in circles came to light when we walked past the path that took us back to our site. Either Dad was enjoying this talk, or we were walking until he made a point that he feels is important.

I come clean, "Dad, if you are wondering. I really am okay."

The next words that came from his mouth is when I understood that he wasn't waiting for me to say something. The cigarette, the walk, this is because he wants to say something.

"First of all, I will beat you if you tell your mom about this talk." This was my dad's way of getting into difficult conversations. "I know you are ok. I see you with that girl. That is not Kimberly."

"What does that mean?" I say with some offense in my voice.

"Stop, that is not what I am trying to say. I do not know this girl, but..." he hesitates. "Man-to-man, you and I know that is not a deacon or preacher's daughter. I am just saying."

Before I get angry, I decide that I should hear him out. After all, he said man-to-man. I guess hearing people out is what men do!!

He takes a deep breath and discards his second cigarette of the night with an exaggerated drop towards the ground, and smashes it out with the tip of his shoes.

"Listen, you are different. You are smart. Your mom and I didn't grow up with the same opportunities that you have. Just be careful."

"She is awesome."

"Son," he interrupts. "I think you are missing the point. I have no doubt she is awesome. That is not for me to decide. My concern is not her; my concern is you. I genuinely don't care who you date or how many you date. Just don't let today's mistake be the cross you have to carry for the rest of your life."

That caught me off guard. "Mistake of Today". How in the world did he know?

While I was working to solve this mystery, he continued, "All I am saying is that the financial problems of my parents didn't allow me to choose my career path. I was relegated to working in the fields and mills. That is not your situation. That circle of the Hawes Clan always working in mills and fields can stop with you. You are smart. You can be a preacher, a teacher, policeman, or whatever you want to be."

In an effort to find out if he truly knew what I did, I returned my own interrogation.

"Did I do something wrong?"

He took a deep breath as I braced myself for the response, "No, again. Please hear what I am saying. I believe that you are amazing. I am so excited to see the man you are going to become. I have no idea what road you take. I trust you'll figure it out. No matter the road, I know you'll be great. Like I said before. I am excited because I know that the path you choose will be your choice, unlike mine. I was restricted in my travels. I wasn't really able to chase my dreams. That's not you. We are not rich, but none of my boys will ever have to stop schooling to help their families. Not like I did. Not as long as I am breathing."

This hit me hard. I always knew my dad worked, and he worked a lot. Never have I stopped to think or consider that this is not his dream. The hardest-working man I know is not working for his dream. He is working to allow me and my brothers to pursue our dreams.

From my fifteen-year-old body came a sheepish six-year-old voice, "What was your dream?"

The far-off look in his dark eyes told of a man drifting back thirty years earlier when his dreams were possible.

"I would've liked to play for the Yankees. I wanted to be "The Mick," Mickey Mantle." He dove deeper into his memory when he laughed. "I had this white tee shirt that I drew on to make it look like a Yankee Uniform. I put the number seven on the back with "Mantle" above it. I wore this all the time. When I got home, I would hide it. I was afraid to wash it because it would take away my great artwork. Eventually, it stunk so bad my mom literally stole it and washed it. I'd just redo the artwork all over again. I bet this cycle went on for years. Or at least it felt as so."

Our laughter bleeds into a calm, satisfying silence.

"I am sorry you didn't get that chance."

He hissed with a wild, loud laugh at the notion, "Son, the odds on me playing for the Yankees weren't good. First of all, you have to be really good to play for the Yankees. But more importantly, I never knew it was even possible to do anything except what my dad did. Because that's what his dad did. Our family has always worked in mills and fields. ALWAYS. I didn't know any other way. Heck, that is just how it has always been. Kinda Family tradition. I was never told that we could do anything except work in mills and fields. That is just what people like us, Hawes, do. It is almost an unspoken family rule for the oldest child to forsake their education and help the family out financially. Always starting at a young age. Never able to finish any basic schooling. Lil lone doing any university studies. But if you get anything from tonight, understand this. That circle is broken with you. You have the greatest potential of any Hawes in our family history. Think about it. Never has Hawes gone to a university or anything of that nature. All my brothers and sisters, along with their families, still live in Union County. Working in mills and fields. That changes with you and your brothers. That is my new dream. For the record, I believe my dream is your destiny. Remember that, son. You are destined to break the cycle."

Dang, I thought to myself. He did it again. Once again, he had me thinking about how such a simple man could come up with such powerful words. I am destined to make his dream come true.

"I love you, Dad. I will not let you down," is all I could say as pride and responsibility swelled inside me.

"Not a doubt in my mind" came from my father's mouth.

That same mouth that had painted a vision that has always been there, but I have never taken time to notice. My dad truly believed in me. Dang, again!! My head bowed as emotions erupted inside me!

A moment of silence allowed me to gather myself. The elder Hawes interrupted the cricket signing in the nearby woods. "That's your destiny as long as no beautiful little vixen comes alone. Captures your heart. Changes your mind. Or any of that good stuff."

When I looked at him, I noticed an expression on his face that displayed his own pleasure in tying this all back to the original topic. That girl. Maybe he is not so simple.

Taking advantage of Dad's philosophical mode and the reintroduction of Binki to the conversation, I changed the subject. I went in heavy on the topic that has been weighing on my mind. "Dad, do you believe in God?"

The sudden change took him by surprise. He realigned himself, and he went straight for the generic line. "Of course."

"Common Dad. Do you really believe?" I decided to use his own words against him. "I mean, Man to Man. I won't tell Mom. I know her feelings. I am not so certain of your "REAL" stance." Adding a little extra on the word "REAL".

He takes a deep breath and slows the pace. "I gotta admit. I didn't see this coming. Why the sudden concerns? Why now? Something happen?"

My brain flares into action as concerns about the "why" this is a concern. This isn't a topic that you normally just bring out of the blue like I just did. I want to ask him how God could give Binki this miserable set of parents. Explain that she lives in a world that has her deathly afraid of her own father. Yet, he gave me a father who just went out of his way to stress how much he believes in me. How is that fair? Why can't God just strike Binki's horrendous dad dead or at least remove him from her life? Like, snap a finger. Boom- He is in the jungles somewhere, running for his life. Living in fear of snakes or something. How does someone so miserable get to father someone so amazing? I am about to share this with him, but I just can't. Suddenly, I had a different way of asking real questions, almost like God had put words in my mouth.

"Just thinking. How is it that God placed you in a situation where you weren't able to go to college and chase your dreams? Yet, God chose me to be able to do both. I mean, how does God choose who gets born in a life of ease and who lives in fear? Who is born broke or born rich?"

He puts his hands up in the air as if he were a school crossing guard, yelling for the kid not to cross the road in an exaggerated motion. This is done in an effort to add humor to a serious topic.

"Hold up, Hold up! That's a lot to answer. The good book says that we shouldn't question God."

With a serious look, I respond, "Dad. I am confused. I am not questioning. I am asking to learn. That alone doesn't make sense. Why can't I question if I don't know the answer?"

He takes a puff on his cigarette and blows smoke through his nose.

"Ok, Man to Man." He turns to me as if I am about to hear the most important words he has ever spoken. "I honestly don't know. Just don't. I see holes. I mean. Just like you pointed out. I am sorry. My parents have always taken me to church. I married a woman who always wanted to go to church. So, we always take you guys to church. But I see your questions."

I wait for more, but nothing is coming.

"Honestly, Dad! That is a horrible answer. I believe in God because everyone else does." I realized that I may have just disrespected my dad. I threw in the safe words of the day: "I mean, Man to Man—that is a horrible answer."

As if adding that last statement allowed me to say whatever I wanted, no matter how disrespectful.

I feel a sense of relief when I see a wry half-smile emerge, almost like he noticed that he was being called out for that generic answer.

"Bo, I believe now more than ever that you have the greatest potential of any Hawes ever. As I said, it's destiny," he said in a proud tone as if I had just answered a great riddle.

Maybe he respected that I called him out on words of wisdom that he has shared with us many times. He would often tell us that we were smart, independent boys and that nobody would ever convince him that we did something because someone else did it. He would tell us we have our own brains. Remind us not to be the sheep; instead, be the shepherded.

"You deserve a better answer. Here it is. Man to Man. No BS," he adds. "I don't wanna be wrong. What if there is a heaven and hell? What if I never exposed you to God or taught you to live right? I can't take that chance. So many years ago, I went to the altar with my concerns. God and I made a deal. I am going to go to church with your mom. I am going to raise you boys in a Godly way. I am going to live a good life. No promises of perfection. After all, I am just a good ole country boy from Union County. But I promised to live in a good, Godly manner and raise my family as such. When my time comes." He takes a moment to ponder. "If my boys and your mama don't end up in heaven. Send me to hell. I have no desire to live this life or the next life without you, your mama, or your brothers. Y'all, my whole world. That's the deal."

Dang! Dad said that to God was the thought bouncing around in my head. Then, he rendered the closing arguments in the case.

Summarizing the agreement to the other participant as he looks towards the sky with the goal of speaking directly to him.

"Yep. That's our deal. I am going to live the best way I can. In the end, if that doesn't warrant a spot in heaven. Then I will live with the consequences."

He turns his attention back to me.

"I mean... you know. Our lives are based on the Bible. That is our daily map. I always thought that God sent your mama to me to make sure I followed those guidelines. I guess you can say she is my beckon in the night. We are truly honest and caring people. I am a better man every day, mainly thanks to your mom."

We walked a little while to allow each of us to digest what was just said.

"By the way. If you ever tell your mama about my deal with God, I'll kick your ass. I mean, Man to Man," he says with a playful grin.

Dad smoked a couple more of the nicotine sticks as we passed the path to our site a couple more times that night. We stopped for a Diet Coke, which was his go-to drink. Which I always thought was kinda weird, and I thought now was the time to bring this up.

"So, I am not sure if I get to use the phrase man-to-man ever again. But ... do real men drink Diet Coke?"

He burst out laughing.

"First of all, don't get too big for your britches, son," he says with a smile on his face. "But I understand your concern. Me drinking this Diet Coke is not my fault."

"What? I just saw you buy it. It was most certainly your fault. You could have chosen a manly Coke or Dr. Pepper," I return the jovial volley.

"That, my son, is very true. But the reason I bought this Diet Coke is because, number one, your mama wants me to be healthy. Well, healthier? Number two, because I can't drink water," he states in a very concerning way.

Puzzled, I ask. "The heck? What do you mean you can't drink water? You use water in tea and in coffee. And... Well ... EVERYTHING!"

With the largest grin he can muster, I see that he set me up to ask this very question, "Well, God could have made water a little tastier, and don't you know that water rusts pipes? I don't need anything to rust my pipes. Remember reason number one: your mama wants me healthy."

We laugh, and I say, "It always goes back to Mama and God."

A look of resolution comes across his face as if we have just solved the impossible question.

"Son, it always has and always will. Can't go wrong with Mama and God."

That night, I realized that my dad was more than just a simple man from Union County.

Chapter Seventeen - Say Nothing

What had to be our last trip around the campsite, we ran into Binki at the drink station by the game room. Dad knew I wanted to go over. To his credit, he did not guilt me into staying with him, unlike Mom. Who would have either gone with me or guilted me into continuing to walk with her? Dad understood the bro code and followed the path back to our site without me. Binki caught a glimpse of me out of the corner of her eye and sat on the steps. She opened a can of Pepsi and took a gulp.

I kissed her on the cheek but didn't know what I was supposed to say. "Hello, Darling", like I am Conway Twitty. "What's up?" as if I was some cool cat in a Michael Jackson video. I settled on a simple, meek "Hello".

She extended the can in my direction, asking if I wanted a sip without saying a word. I took the can, and she laid her head on my shoulder.

I was looking for the right thing to say when she whispered in my ears, "Say nothing; enjoy the moment."

That is exactly what we did—said nothing and enjoyed the moment. Who knew that nothing was almost better than anything else?

Eventually, we walked towards her site and made plans for tomorrow that included neither of us waking the other before noon. I gave her a kiss and then headed back to my site.

I lay on the big rock in the middle of our campsite, my eyes focused on the moon. My every thought was once again on Binki, thinking about the night that was, wondering if this wasn't love; it must be how love was intended to go. But I also know that this is going to be over soon because we only have a few more nights before we head back to Indian Trail.

My mind started to wander and play games with "what might be" situations, trying to figure out how to make this work.

Could we have a long-distance relationship until we turn 18? I guess if it lasted until we were 18, then it was destiny. Wait a minute. What if I talked her mom into moving closer to our house? That's just stupid!!

Could my mom and dad take her in? They will love her. That sounds good to me, but I am not sure everyone else is going to approve. Especially my mom. Then I cracked a smile thinking about what the people at church would think. I could see the church ladies gossiping now. Then, I got sober, remembering the talk that Dad had just given to me. Shacking up at 16 cannot be destiny.

Quickly, my mind shifted to Kimberly. Holy cow that is the first thought of her all day. I can never go back to our relationship, seeing how Binki and I have something totally different. Or could I? Obviously, Binki and I can't make it past this week. Wait, am I cheating on Binki? Oh lord;

I'm not sure who I'm cheating on, but I know that having both of them in my thoughts does not seem right to either of them.

My thoughts of the here and now with Binki outweighed the great unknown that could happen when I return to Indian Trail. Thus, the smile on my face coincided with the image of her sitting on that step, waiting for me with a Pepsi in her hand. That should be a commercial one day.

Thoughts of her swirled around until, eventually, my mind went quiet long enough for my eyes to find rest.

Chapter Eighteen - Moms

I had planned to sleep until noon. Those plans went all to Hades when I realized that I forgot to inform my mom or get her approval. She woke me up before the crack of dawn with breakfast already cooked. She informed me that we were going tubing down the creek. My plans to sleep in didn't go over very well with her, especially when it started with the guilt trip. Her favorite tactic. She reminded me how lucky I was to have the family I have. How blessed we are. Blah, blah, blah. Of course, she is right, but I don't need a replay of this same speech that I have heard hundreds of times.

Her case was getting even stronger when she added that if I wanted to stay out late like an adult, I needed to be an adult and get up at a reasonable time. In other words, do the crime, do the time. I'm not really sure I understood that logic because don't adults wake up whenever they want to? But I wasn't dumb enough to bring that to her attention and prolong the fight. I wasn't winning, no matter what.

This morning, my relationship with my mom wasn't warm and fuzzy, which meant an unhappy mom, which in turn made an unhappy dad. I began to settle in and understand their point. I wasn't going to press my luck and ask for Binki to go, even though I wanted to.

We started to clean up from breakfast when I noticed Binki walking our way. I thought this was perfect timing. She can go with us. As if she was reading my mind, Mom walked over to me and reminded me this was a family trip. She doesn't get to attend this time. In other words, Mom is getting frustrated or jealous of the time I am spending away from her. I told her to just give me a minute. I will let her know we are going somewhere.

No big deal. But it was going to break my heart.

I met Binki before she got to the family, and I gave her a hug and a quick peck on the check.

"I thought you were going to wait until noon to wake up?" she asked.

"Yeah, about that. The next time we make plans, we may need to ask my mom first."

She laughs and says that it is so funny because she had the same problem. Her mom woke her up today and wanted her to go shopping this morning. I asked her if she had bought me anything and she told me they hadn't gone yet but were soon to be leaving. Before they went, she wanted to come by and ask me something. I was intrigued.

"My mom wants to know if you want to go out with us tonight?" she asked.

"Your mom is asking me out? I have never met her. That's kinda weird. If she is as pretty as you, I guess I could go," I said in a joking manner that resulted in a playful slap to the chest.

"No, silly. I want to go out with you tonight, but my mom has to go. The whole thing, somebody has to drive and pay. Unless you want to steal a car and rob a bank instead," she returned in jest.

"Robbing a bank and stealing a car sounds really appealing. If the car is a Ferrari and I get to drive, count me in. If not, I guess I will take the first option. Wait, we are going tubing, so…"

"Don't worry, it's tonight when we get back from shopping. We will wait if we have to. It's no big deal. It's my mom's only day off this week, and she wants us to do something together. I asked if you could come."

"Somebody has been talking about me? Awe, ain't that so sweet," I pick at her some more.

"Don't make this too hard. I do have options. I could ask Stevie to go in your place," Binki spouts back.

"I would love to go, but I must admit that I am a little nervous about meeting your mom."

Binki enjoyed my discomfort and seized the opportunity to stick it to me: "Big, strong country boy, scared?"

"There is a problem. I think my mom is getting a little jealous of our time together. Not sure she is going to approve," I responded.

"I got this!" Binki replies as she confidently walks towards the site and puts on a smile that conveys warmth and sincerity.

"I would not disclose that we may be robbing a bank. I'm pretty sure that would be a deal killer," I remind her, which results in another playful slap to the chest.

Approaching the site, Stevie approached Binki and requested a hug. She was more than happy to oblige and added a kiss to the cheek, which resulted in Stevie's favorite response to things he likes: "Oh Yeah!!"

Binki says hello to everyone and gives my mom a hug. Binki asks how she is doing, and Mom replies that we are headed out on a family trip, making sure the word "family" is heard. Binki replies, "I know Bo told me. That's very exciting. It should be a lot of fun. My mom and I are going shopping." You could see a bit of relief coming from my mom.

"In fact, I need to be heading back. I just wanted to say hello to everyone and thank you for such a great time yesterday. Your family is amazing. Something to really be proud of. I think you guys are perfect." She waves to everyone and starts to walk away.

"That is so nice. We enjoyed your company. Without you, I would have had to brave it with all these boys alone," my mom replies. You could see the tone change.

I was thinking, what just happened? Hello? Did Binki forget to ask?

Did Mom forget to be mad? I am confused. Women are a mystery. I just stood there. Before Binki approached the bridge, she turned around and started making her way back in our direction, "I about forgot. My mom, Mitch, and I are going out to eat tonight. Do you mind if Bo goes with us? It will be late because when my mother and I go shopping, it's an all-day event!!"

Laughing, my mother responds by allowing me to go and telling her that we should be back by 6 pm.

"Be ready, I will pick you up at 6!" Binki says to me and comes by to give me a goodbye hug. During the hug, she whispers in my ear, "Told ya."

She proceeds to give my mom and Stevie another bye hug and makes her way across the bridge. I was amazed. This girl is awesome. She just handled my mom like nobody I have ever seen. That was a work of art.

Chapter Nineteen - Mom Date

The tubing trip was the first time Phillip and I had time alone since the night I went to Devil's Head. Phillip was very much into hearing what happened. I gave him the tame version. Enough to get me in trouble, but not enough to get sent to exile if this story came out. We have always had a great relationship, but I believe having a secret like this only increased our bond. Made him feel important. The talk confirmed Mom's jealousy. He acts as the resident insider for me on family gossip. Thus, Phillip and I tried to minimize that jealousy by sanctioning a self-imposed Binki Ban! The only person who mentioned Binki's name in front of my parents was Stevie. Even then, we tried to make sure it was short and sweet.

We were giving our parents a reprieve from that name for as long as we could. Sticking with the family trip theme.

We enjoyed the day tubing. I worked hard to make sure I gave them a lot of attention. I know that my brothers and parents have missed me a lot.

Normally, we do everything together when we are on vacation. That has not been the case so far, and I wanted to do my part to make up for some of that lost time.

Tubing is always a lot of fun and very tiring, especially for my parents, who are trying to keep up with three boys. My parents threw in the surrender towel earlier than expected, which was OK with me. This gave me time to get back to the site and get prepared. Shower and shine up to meet Binki's mom.

Fear and doubt started seeping in more and more as date time drew closer and closer. What if she doesn't like me? Wait, she must like me. I must be a lot better than that bum Scott. My thoughts took another direction. What if she is crazy? I couldn't imagine the mom of Binki not being beautiful, but there is no way she is normal.

I walked towards the parking area in preparation for their arrival but stayed on our side of the bridge so as not to look too excited. Finally, an older burnt auburn two-door Yugo with a slender black stripe running down its side pulled up and parked near the bridge. The Yugo marketing team championed its automobile as being affordable. The public agreed somewhat. To its credit, this Yugo rightfully lived up to the Yugo reputation for being a cheap car. The missing hubcap that lay below the cracked window in the back of the passenger's side of the boxed-looking car allowed the Yugo brand to protect that affordable reputation. As the wheels came to a slow stop and the lights were terminated, fear rose through my stomach and settled at the top of my throat. I couldn't believe I didn't think of this earlier. I know my mom is going to ask about her husband, Binki's dad. If they said something about an abusive relationship, my mom might put an end to this right now. Or mom might bring out the bible and start having some form of prayer session that takes up the whole night. Or worse, just might scare her off. One thing is for certain. Anita Hawes is not shy about digging into the business of others and lacks the self-awareness to recognize this flaw. Not to mention that she has never been accused of being tactful. She is as direct as the day is long.

The fear of what might happen once the ladies met took a backseat once my eyes noticed the stunning creature that exited the passenger side door. On many occasions, I've looked at Binki and thought nothing could ever be more beautiful than the sight that my eyes have the honor of seeing at THIS VERY MOMENT. Then she goes and proves me wrong the next time I see her. I was certain that tonight was the masterpiece of all the visual collections I had assembled. The goddess, who rounded the front of the car in a pair of black sandals that covered very little of her feet, waved to the driver in an effort to hurry them up. She rested the light-colored jeans that were vented at the knees for creative purposes against the hood of the car ever so lightly. The way the jeans hugged her lower body was proof that the belt made to look like a cowboy tie was there only for show. My attention quickly made its way to the fitted black pullover crew neck short-sleeve blouse. It was cut low to allow the leather string that was laced from side to side to open or close the viewing area at the discretion of the person wearing it. Though the blouse was not suggestive, it did allow the imagination to roam. A matching black satin ribbon bow rested on her head. Restraining the hair from robbing the world of Binki's smile.

Her brother quickly took up post next to her. Mitch stuck to his collared shirt and khaki pants style. He was armed with a solid black belt, black dress shoes, and, as always, perfectly placed hair. If you told me he walked off the front page of a magazine, I would have believed it.

After a short wait, the driver's side door opened, and out walked an older version of Binki, who had short dark hair and was wearing a stylish baggy blue dress that extended to her ankles. It was paired with a white shirt that went up to the top of the neck and a matching black summer sweater that was perfect for a brisk night. She had the Jamie Lee Curtis look down pat. Once she got closer, I saw the remnants of scars that were buried within her beauty. Her eyes had a darkness that mascara was trying to brighten. I couldn't help but think that she once owned an exterior beauty that might have rivaled Binki's. The long sleeves that I assumed were part of her wardrobe undeniably were hiding another set of unhealed wounds.

The boards of the bridge stayed true to its history and crackled as they made their way in our direction. Almost step by step, the fear that had dissipated while observing Binki had returned and went into overdrive. I can't believe I didn't prep my parents. My parents will be suspicious of her wardrobe and the missing husband. They are understanding, right? Before the fear could turn into noticeable shakes or I just fell to my knees in prayer, begging God for help, the silence was broken by a yell of "hello" from Stevie. No chance of awkward silence with Stevie around.

Once the guest was close enough, I saw the suspiciousness in my parents that I was afraid of. That didn't stop the new traditional greeting, as Binki gave Stevie and Mom a hug. She proceeded to introduce her mom to everyone in my family, making extra effort to make sure she introduced everyone.

Stevie as her boyfriend, who gives everyone a good laugh and leaves Stevie beaming with pride.

Binki introduced her mom as "The Lovely Doris". The cause of my anxiety was resolved rather quickly. When it was Doris's turn to do her part of the introductions, and luckily, before my mom could ask, Doris told my parents that her husband Bill could not make it tonight because he had to return to Gastonia for an emergency at work. He might be coming back to join them sometime this week. She also apologized for the scars. She explained that she was in a bad accident not too long ago.

I was taken aback. Did she just lie that easily? That was too easy.

She must have had that story already in the queue. Ready to use. Then again, what did I expect her to say? Did I expect her to say I am hiding from my drunk, abusive husband, who is part of a biker gang? He beat the crap out of me, and that is why I have scars. I realized that the reason she had that lie so available was that she had used that same line many times before.

After all, it really is none of our business. OK, that works for me. That is a justifiable lie. I made a mental note to ask someone if God gives special concessions for certain lies.

The small talk that followed was not unlike my mom talking to some of the ladies at church. They seemed to hit it off. It started with Doris talking about the recovery from the accident that she said happened due to a drunk man. Maybe the lie isn't too far off. I mean, the accident was because of a drunk, and the recovery she is describing may actually be the steps she had to take. When she said she was still self-conscious of her appearance, I knew even Mom knew to let it go.

Both moms start thanking God and sharing how blessed they are. I understood my mom's blessings. But Binki's mom? I just didn't understand. How is she blessed? Once that thought entered my mind, the hypocrisy of that thought wounded my own self-awareness. Just the night before, I was telling Binki that maybe God had separated her family from her dad. To concentrate on the promise of tomorrow instead of the pain of yesterday. I guess that wasn't so original. Doris had already come to that spot in her life. That's the blessing that Binki's mom is talking about. Truth be told, we are all blessed to be alive. That blessing is just more real to her than most.

Eventually, the conversation included Doris telling my parents that she was taking us to the Bottomless Pond. The tourist destination that is nearby. A spot that birth many legendary tales of people falling in the water only to never be seen again. My family was familiar with it. We have visited the location a couple of times in the past few years. We would be dining at a restaurant on the site, which had tables that dangled over the pond. We said our goodbyes and made our way to the car that was missing one hubcap on the driver's side as well. I missed that upon the initial inspection.

Mitch sat in the front with his mom while Binki and I squeezed in the backseat. My appreciation for the Yugo finally surfaced due to the restriction in size that mandated that Binki and I sit almost shoulder to shoulder. I was careful to be respectful. I wanted her mom to see a different type of guy—a guy who treats her daughter like the queen she is.

I thought to ask Binki about her mom's story to my parents, but I wasn't sure which way we were going with this story. Am I supposed to know about her dad? Is the story that her mom told the one that Binki was supposed to tell me? I decided that until I get time to speak with Binki about the issue, I would just go along with the story told to my mom if questioned.

The goal was to make every effort to avoid discussing her father. That shouldn't be too difficult because I believe that was a topic they didn't want to discuss either.

Doris asked me every question imaginable during our time at the Bottomless Pond and at dinner. I'm not sure what I was expecting, but this felt very normal. Hard to comprehend that this is the same family that went through the nightmares that Binki had described.

Visiting one of the great wonders of the North Carolina mountains only got better when we discovered that the pond was full of ducks— ducks that we could feed. It was very satisfying to see the joy that one can have in such a simple task as feeding ducks. The night went better than I could have expected.

Chapter Twenty - The Macho Man

Doris brought the Yugo to a halt back at the site, and we said our goodbyes. Mitch and Doris disappeared into the camper, leaving Binki and me alone at the picnic table. I assumed that Binki was tired because I knew the day had been a pretty long one for me. With that being said, I still did not want this night to end. Our days together shorten every time the sun falls and the moon hangs above us. I thought something was up when she asked if I would walk with her to get a Pepsi. There is a cooler sitting just a couple of feet away. The look in her eyes confirmed my suspicion. Maybe this is her way of wanting to spend more time with me. Which I strongly welcomed.

The walk started with me telling her that I was impressed by her mom.

I made sure to compliment her mom's beauty and brains. Truth be told, I was very impressed by how well-composed and intelligent Doris appeared to be. It made me wonder how someone in her current situation could possibly be so composed, even for one night. So, I gingerly asked her this question, using it as a compliment on her mother's mental strength.

Before I got time to ask, words exploded from Binki's lips as if she had been holding them in the entire night.

"She is so brave. She was scared shitless!! She needed this. Get out and have some form of normalcy. When I went into the restroom, she told me that she was having fun. I can't tell you the last time she said this."

Binki beamed with pride. Without a moment's notice, the mood made a sudden change.

She continued, but this time more seriously and inquisitive, her face scrunched up on one side.

"She is amazing. It feels like Mitch, and I just discovered how amazing she truly is."

I agreed with her, and a moment of silence was given in an effort to reflect on Doris.

Then I went for it.

"I agree she is amazing. Hope you don't mind me asking, but she doesn't seem like someone that would be with the man you describe as your father. How does someone that amazing get into the situation she is in?"

Binki comes to a complete stop.

Oh Shit. I ruined a perfectly good night comes running across my head. I am such an idiot. I stop and turn my body to her with the goal of apologizing.

She surprises me in a matter-of-fact manner.

"I have asked myself that a million times. I know that Mom and Dad are different people today than they were when they first met, but could they possibly have been that different? I have asked Mom this before, and she just said she was blinded by love."

I was taken off guard by her frankness and very happy that she wasn't offended. Felt like I should say something but wasn't sure what the right words were. I quietly solicited the big man's help once again. But it was Oprah that came to the rescue this time. Or was it the big man using Oprah? Either way, I just regurgitated the idea from an episode about abusive spouses that I watched with my mom.

"I once heard that love and marriage could put people on the road to their own destruction."

I looked over and saw that I had her full attention.

"Okay," she said. "Please explain this."

I continued.

"Well, often, the destructive nature of a marriage isn't discovered until it's too late. Too late being one side of the marriage getting destroyed. People believe that being in love means you never leave. The prevailing thought is that once you are married, you are together forever. As the vows say, until death do you part. Oprah said the issue was not the act of marriage. That concept of marriage is not flawed. The issue is that love was not there for both parties. One was in love with their partner. The other was in love with the perceived power over their partner."

"Dang, that is deep. And really good. So, you know Oprah?"

I smiled and let her in that I watch it quite often with my mom.

Binki obviously bought what I was saying.

"I can envision it. You are probably right. Or Oprah? Mom was young, beautiful, and naïve. My father is a good-looking man. I bet he was a prince and was at her beckoning call at the beginning. She fell in love and married him. Only there was a monster disguised as a prince that didn't show until sometime after they were married. Sometime shortly afterward, the true colors showed. He turned into the monster we know today. She was so in love. Love was the excuse she used to allow the abuse. Wow. It feels so simple. But I never put it together like that. Love. Or the perception of love. That was the shield. That perception allowed the abuse."

She took a moment to let this sink in.

I couldn't help but think, what if he was a bad guy all along? Maybe her mom dug the bad guy back in the day. Something along the lines of Scott and Binki. Guess I will never know because I knew better than to ask.

The slow walking pace extended the time it should have taken to get to the office, but we finally made it to our destination. As I suspected, she didn't want a Pepsi.

"I have to make the call," she said in a tone that sounded more like a trance.

The office that neighbored the game room also housed the payphone; the payphone that she was staring at.

I knew "the call" was to Scott.

"I am scared," she mumbled as she climbed the steps to the wooden building with a wraparound porch.

You could see the phone sticking out of the building on the opposite corner of the entrance steps. I dare say placed so isolated to allow people to make calls in private.

I asked her what she was going to say. She said she was not sure. You could see that with every step, she was getting more and more nervous. The wood cracked as we stepped on the office deck, making our journey toward the game room. In between the office and the game room were two rocking chairs, and before we could reach the game room door, Binki sat in the first one she approached. More like fell into it and started to rock.

Slowly and methodically. You could see the thoughts bouncing from side to side in her skull. She was clearly stalling for time due to dread and lack of clarity in what she was about to say.

I joined her without questioning her. I knew that she was trying to gather her thoughts and put her words together. Therefore, we rocked in silence for a minute, and then I broke the silence. Maybe I should have appreciated the silence and not said anything. I said the words I wish I could take back before they finished leaving my lips.

"Do you want me to call him? I will."

Immediately, I questioned myself. Did that just leave my lips? What am I thinking? What would make me say that? Then I had an epiphany.

Could I be in love? That is the only thing I could think of. Yep, I'm in love! That just sealed the deal. I barely know this person and I am certain that I love her. Never really felt love before. I am not sure what it is supposed to feel like. But this I knew; whatever it is that is making me feel like I do, I love it! I don't want that feeling to leave. Even if it is short-lived, I would rather have this feeling for a couple more days than for it to end right now. If the cost is making a call to some loser and telling him that he is a loser, I am willing to pay the price.

Stillness hung in the air long enough for me to doubt even if those words actually left my mouth. Perhaps it was just thoughts that ran through my head. Then, I was called to the carpet.

"Would you?" she asked.

This false macho man act is not me. What in the world am I getting myself into? I think this is how murder mysteries start: crazy boyfriend, hot girl, and some country boy who is in puppy love. Yep, I have seen that movie MANY times, and it never ends well. Wait, I am just going to back out. She must understand that this is not my fight, right?

But my mouth and heart would not cooperate as the word "Yes" left my lips.

"That is so brave and honorable. What are you going to tell him?" Binki asked.

I have committed to this act. Now, regret with a huge dose of fear is really beginning to settle in. I am not certain what I would say.

But my mouth opens, and my heart speaks, "I will just tell him that you are too good for him. That you deserve better. You need someone to treat you with respect. To show you love, to hold you when you need to be held, and to protect you when you need to be protected. I will tell him that you need to live a life filled with love, not fear. I will tell him that Binki deserves someone whose life goals include making her the happiest woman alive. This person will know without any doubt that every day they wake up and see Binki beside them, they are the luckiest person on the planet. It needs to be someone who can't see their life without Binki being the point of their life. That you deserve better. You deserve love!"

My voice trails off as I finish by saying the last part to myself.

"Tell him that you deserve someone like me, who will always love you."

Or I thought it was to myself.

My mouth rests, and I focus on Binki sitting in the rocking chair with tears going down her cheeks.

"That's amazing. No, you are amazing."

She gets up and joins me in my rocking chair by sitting on my lap with her arms wrapped around my neck. I wrap my arms around her to return the hug and feel as if I am her great protector.

"Bo, those were the most amazing words I have ever heard. Hearing that gives me hope that I can do better than him. It gives me the knowledge that this is the right decision. Plus, the thought that you would get on the phone and say that to Scott is beyond words. But I must do this. I must call him and end this. Scott is a mess. My mess, not yours," she states as she gets up.

"Please, stay here. I must do this alone."

I tried hard to hide the great sigh of relief that left my body as she made her way to the phone. She reached into her pocket and pulled out a quarter that was noticeably weighted with dread. I watch her pick up the phone and deposit the twenty-five cents, which gives her access to do what is needed. I read her lips enough to see her asking for Scott. She turns facing the opposite direction making it impossible for me to intrude any further nor see her facial expressions.

Rocking back and forth in the chair, I was trying to envision how their conversation was going. Was she using my words? What could he say?

How is he going to react? Before long, I hear the phone slam back into place right after a loud "screw you" jumps from Binki's mouth. Her body fell limp against the wall, crying. Quickly, I make my way over to comfort her.

"Are you okay?" I ask as I begin to put my arms around her.

"I don't want to talk about it. I am done with that asshole!" she returns with authority.

She climbs down the steps and tells me she wants to go back to her camper. I wanted to comfort her but conceded to her wishes by walking beside her through the village of campers and tents. We never said a word the entire journey. I wanted to ask so many questions and find out so many details, but I thought she would tell me if she wanted me to know. Which I thought would eventually happen while we sat at the picnic table, but she never said a word. Mitch was coming back from the bathhouse and saw us sitting there. Her crying.

He asked me what I did in accusatory fashion. I could understand his reaction. Just a moment ago, all was fine. Obviously, that is no longer the case.

I explained to him what happened. For the first time, I saw a mature Mitch. He asked me to leave. Let him take care of it. He walked over and put his arms around his weeping sister.

With a peck on the cheek and a promise to meet in the morning, I left her in Mitch's care.

I had a lot of questions weighing on my mind. Why did she take that so hard? She was really upset. I thought she would be happy. Did she really love him? She seemed to know that breaking up with him was the right thing. I finally concluded the obvious. He is not a good person and probably verbally assaulted her via cursing and name-calling in a way that got her so upset.

One thing I knew for sure was that the call sabotaged what was previously a great day.

Chapter Twenty-One - Path to Love

My parents always had to get up early for work in everyday life back in Indian Trail. Thus, their inner body clocks never changed when we were on vacation. The routine of early rise and early bed continued. Going to bed early did not sadden me because I could just stay up as long as I wanted.

The getting up early maddened me! This morning was no different. Same as before, they woke me to join them for breakfast where they shared bacon, eggs, juice, and the plans for the day.

The excitement of yesterday's tubing left my parents yearning for a simple day. Therefore, simplicity was the agenda: fishing and swimming in the morning, and visiting the town after lunch. On our way to fishing and swimming, I snuck by Binki's camper to check on her. Nobody was there. The same was the case when I visited on the way back from the lake.

Before darkness thought about coming about, my family and I got fancied up for a night out in the small town of Chimney Rock. A night on the town for the Hawes required being back by 8 pm type of night. Which meant, it was mid-day at best when we left. Sticking with the Hawes theme of early arrival and early leave.

I quickly got dressed and received permission to see if Binki wanted to join us. Nobody was at the campsite or at least nobody would answer when I knocked. I tried opening the door and it was locked. This worried me. But I couldn't do anything except carry the concern back with me to join my family for our version of a wild night out.

Joe and Anita's night out in this area involved strolling down a nearly two-mile stretch that was within walking distance, but my dad insisted that we drive.

The exteriors of the buildings were created in the image of a Wild West community. The town leaders disallowed national chains and took great pride in filling these buildings with locally owned small businesses. Within 20 miles, there were no big-name restaurant chains, fancy retail outlets, or grocery stores. Just small, cozy local restaurants hidden in between unique shops, sitting very close to the 15-mph traffic that flowed down a two-lane paved trail.

There were always local magicians, people dressed as cowboys and Indians, and a local business that would allow you to mine for gold. The idea of mining for gold was always a favorite of mine. Never fail, the miner would tell us how someone found a piece that was worth $100. Enticing us to pay for $3 for a bucket of dirt. We would sift it and find fool's gold or other "Special" stones.

Music was a key contributor to the ambiance of the town. The sounds give the town life. From the moment we would get out of the car, either country, mountain music, or bluegrass was always within earshot. One band would drown out, and another would come to take its place as you moved from one experience to another.

It never fails that the night would end up with my mother making us partake in the magician's act or learn some line dancing. Phillip and I would act like we were too cool to participate in but always succumb to the peer pressure mainly because we both enjoyed it if we told the truth. Almost every spot that played music along the strip would do the broom dance. It was part of the Chimney Rock charm. This brought great joy to Phillip and me because it meant that we would get the opportunity to dance with someone from the opposite sex.

The broom dance was like musical chairs in theory. It started with two people of the opposite sex dancing to a song. The catch is that one person started out dancing with a broom. When the music stops, you must switch partners. If you were left without a partner, you had to dance with a broom until the next stoppage/switch came about. This results most of the time with the person dancing with the broom either being embarrassed or turning it into a one-minute comedy act.

The normal protocol was that they would do the broom dance, and then the next song would be a slow dance. This was a not-so-subtle effort to be matchmakers. They helped their guests find true love in the countryside.

I always believed that my parents had a connection with the mountains that started prior to my existence. But tonight, it was different. I saw my mom look at my dad with love and I noticed they walked as if they were 20 years younger. Cocooned inside the 40-year-old bodies were teenagers laughing and cuddling as if they were at the local drive-in. Dad bought mom a Big Red Candy apple. He got himself some local honey that he always uses on his biscuits upon his return to Indian Trail. A true Hawes family tradition. I pondered, have my parents always laughed and loved as they walked down the strip. The only difference is I never took the time to recognize it. Certainly, the past 24 hours have heightened my awareness. The path of how to treat a woman has already blazed me. Shame on me if I don't follow the road that my dad paved.

Stevie got his picture taken with an Indian. Dad purchased Phillip a knife, which caused Mom to question, but she eventually relented without too much of a fuss. Purchasing Stevie a small Indian Tomahawk with plenty of colorful feathers attached to the handle was the last festive act of the evening/day. The Hawes were done for the day, but part of the sun could still be seen peaking over the mountaintop.

I had planned to find Binki as soon as we got back to the site. I was worried and knew that I would never be able to sleep if I didn't get to see her tonight. My mind has been scattering into many different directions with each leading to a different scenario with regards to her mental state. Has she been crying the whole night? Has she been alone? Alone and crying? Did she call him back and apologize? Maybe Scott is on his way to Chimney Rock. Maybe she told him it was my idea, and he plans to try to beat me up? Maybe he is at the site waiting on me? Argh!! I had to talk to her tonight.

That was for certain.

I didn't have to hunt too hard. While we were emptying ourselves from the car, Binki walked up as if nothing was wrong.

"Somebody is looking pretty snazzy!!"

Trying to be cool I respond, "What this? Nah. We just went to grab something to eat."

"Oh, you thought I was talking to you. I was talking to the handsome man beside you with the tomahawk. He is looking fine."

Binki then winks at Stevie.

Stevie noticed that she was talking to him.

"Oh Yeah!! That is what I have been saying all night. That you are my girlfriend."

She plays along and agrees to be his girlfriend. We laugh as he runs across the bridge to tell Mom that Binki agrees to be his girlfriend.

Stevie's departure brought a change in mood as if a gray cloud had taken Stevie's place. It was not dark and gloomy but tense and strained. The moment obviously demanded that I give Binki my total attention. I put a hand in each of my jeans pockets while I slowly leaned back against the car to evaluate the scene.

"Are you okay?"

As she came closer, I could smell the unmistakable odor of cigarettes.

It was overwhelming. There was perfuming trying to battle for supremacy and losing. Bad. Dad is living proof that the nicotine-laced smell of cigarettes was oblivious to everyone except the smokers. Dad had gotten caught many times when he promised Mom that he was kicking the habit, only to be betrayed by this same odor.

Crickets. She was lost for words. Her lips would start to talk but give out before the noise exited. Binki looked more innocent and vulnerable than I had ever seen before. The burden she was carrying made her look older. The puffy eyes gave away that there had been a lot of crying, crying that had only subsided very recently.

This was my moment to follow up on the phone call. It's apparent that is what she is trying to say. For some reason, I choose a different path. The stumbling of words, the cigarettes, and the water-logged area around her eyes hinted that she didn't need that now. In fact, I could make a case that she had spent enough time today worried about that topic. She needed a change in atmosphere. A change in scenery. Something to allow her to escape the pressure that she is struggling to share.

"Wait right here," I instructed with purposeful excitement.

Binki did as she was told and placed her jean shorts that barely covered her hindside on top of the car hood. Just waiting for my return.

I returned with $20 dollars that I was able to borrow from my dad. He knew that I was good for the money. Our neighbor Stanley Turner often let me clean out his horse stables twice a month, giving me $25 for services rendered. Of course, mom being a mom. She reminded me that if I had saved my money, as she said, I wouldn't be borrowing money. I just conceded in the name of fear. Fear that it would turn into some long-winded lecture or, worse, an argument. The family time served earlier in the day allowed me enough goodwill for them to support my plan to take Binki back to the music and lights of the strip. Before I made my way across the wooden bridge, I gave Stevie a good-night hug and stole one of the yellow feathers from his tomahawk without him even noticing.

Still sitting where I left her, I asked, "Do you have plans for the night?"

I tried to be formal yet cute, mysterious, and creative without being too cheesy. It didn't work; it was cheesy. But the question and the manner in which it was delivered rescued her smile.

Responding in typical pre-phone call Binki fashion, she said, "Well, Madonna and I were going to party in New York unless you have something better."

"You want to walk to the strip?"

Staying in character, she smiles and raises one side of her cheek. She taps her index finger on her chin as if pondering such an impossible question, "New York with Madonna or Chimney Rock with some dude? Hmm…. That is a tough one. Hmmm…. By the way, are you asking me out on a date?"

I could tell the answer was yes and that she was playing with me, so I went for it.

"I don't have any flowers, so this feather will have to do."

I handed her the yellow feather that I stole from Stevie as if it were a flower and continued the playful banter.

"A date? Whoa, slow down. A walk to the strip is what I said. You are obviously making this into something more than just a walk."

She raises her eyebrows in a frisky way.

I gave in, "Okay if I must. Would you please be my date to the big town of Chimney Rock?"

My surrender allowed joy to find a home in her face as she returned with more playful folly.

"Since we only have a week, Madonna and I can go out anytime. I think a walk to the strip is the right answer."

I approached her, placing my hips between her knees.

"I think you have made the right decision. Anyway, Madonna is a material girl living in a material world. I am a genuine guy sitting in front of your eyes."

She was impressed that I had just used a line from a Madonna song, "Hold the phone. You know Madonna songs. I thought all you listened to were songs about drunk cowboys who drive old oversized pickup trucks that love to hug their hound dog."

I decided to pull out another Madonna song and blow her mind: "We are all just living on a prayer."

"That is horrible," she offered, breaking into laughter.

"Horrible but funny. But for the sake of my future friendship with Madonna, please stop."

She reached her arms out and pulled me closer by placing a soft hand on each side of my face. She cupped my cheeks as if they were the most fragile items in the world. Then kissed me.

"I needed that," she whispered into my ear.

What started as a soft kiss was taken to another level when she placed her legs around my waist and her arms around my neck while planting her lips as close to mine as humanly possible. I knew this was no normal kiss. This kiss told me that I was special to her. I meant something to her. Never have I meant something to someone. I mean, besides my family. But this was different. I have never felt more loved. More wanted or more alive. Whatever the problem is, I was destined to be a part of the solution.

"I'm guessing that's a, yes?"

She responded, "Of course, but you need to let me get dressed so we can do this right."

I reminded her that she looked beautiful and that changing was not needed.

My words were useless. She insisted on a change of clothes.

When we reached the camper, she asked me to stay outside while she changed.

Chapter Twenty-Two - The Promise of Tomorrow

Sitting at the picnic table, I couldn't help but see the irony in what had taken place. Before we were "dating", I could come in and see her in her underwear. Now that we are "dating", I must wait for her on the outside of the camper. The goal was to distance her thoughts as far as possible from that phone call, but I couldn't remove my thoughts from it.

What could that piece of shit say to her to make her feel so bad? How does someone like that have that much control over another person? How did she not see this piece of shit person being a piece of shit person from the beginning? Wait, did I just use the "Shit" three times in one thought? Back to Mom's words of wisdom. If you think it, you might as well of said it. Man, I have a lot of forgiveness to pray for. At this moment, I decided to take a moment and have a different talk with God.

I closed my eyes and prayed for God to look down on her, watch over her and her family, bring her happiness, and use me as an instrument to make her life better, if only for a week. Then, I made sure I threw in the part about forgiveness. I informed him that I didn't have the time to list all the actions and thoughts I needed to be forgiven for, but I reminded him that I am certain he knows them all since he sees and hears them all.

I opened my eyes only to see Binki looking at me with a mysterious smile on her face as if she had caught me doing something cute or precious. Standing before me was no doubt a wonderous creation of God.

"One second," I directed towards Binki.

I closed my eyes to add an extension to the previous prayer, "God, I pray I see this vision a million more times when I open my eyes."

Then I remember Mom saying that you should only pray for what you need, not what you desire. Oh, well. I thought.

The second time I opened my eyes was the same delightful vision as the first. Binki is wearing a yellow sun dress with one-inch straps lying across each shoulder. The dress tightened at the waist, which enhanced the hourglass shape of her body. The yellow cloth ended halfway between the thighs and her knees. Below the sun dressed were a pair of legs that had to be kissed by the sun. Sunflower designs on the strap of her sandals match in color and size with the purse that she was holding in her left hand. Her beautiful brown hair was pushed to one side, with the yellow feather placed behind her ear on the opposing side. The most noticeable feature was the smile that was genuine and carefree. Did my prayer come true that quickly?

"What you doin'," the mischievous beauty asked.

I grabbed her hand and rebounded with the words, "Just thinking of you."

I could smell the hypnotic scent of her perfume, which was once again somewhere between flowers and strawberries. There was still a trace of the cigarette smell that I noticed earlier. Her efforts to mask it worked to some degree this time. I gave her a kiss, let her know how amazing she looked and complimented her on her perfume.

My goal was to make her smile. To let her know how it felt to be loved and respected. My plan was to use the map that my dad had just given me. Who knows, in 20 years, it could be Binki and I bringing our kids to Chimney Rock. Start our own family traditions. If only, somehow, this week turned into something with more longevity. I will worry about the future later. This moment was too precious. Too important for me to worry about tomorrow. As my dad always says, that is what tomorrow is for.

We made our way from the campsite with her arm entangled with mine at a slow, purposeful pace. As darkness was beginning to show, the glowing lights confirmed the distance in which we were about to travel. The promise of the strip, along with the festive ambiance, began to come into focus with every step. The impending blackness of the summer night was starting to be lit by the moon. The summer air of the mountains held its reputation as being one in which new love could find roots.

Binki questioned, "Were you praying?"

I wasn't sure how to answer this remembering that the goal of the night. I was afraid this may go in the direction of being heavy and deep, which was not the objective of the evening. Light, fun, love, that is the hope. The promised, to be honest, slapped the ole membrane. Then the more pressing reminder that I JUST had a talk with God requesting his assistance. It may not be wise to lie about talking with God.

"I was."

"What about? Me?"

"Maybe?"

"The promise of tomorrow or the pain of yesterday," Binki recited my words from an early conversation. "That's my choice, right?"

"I believe that is everyone's choice. My dad is not a great philosopher by any means, but I do find him to be wise. My family always seems to have a daily struggle. Busted pipes, bills, car issues, or something. Our problems may not seem as be as big as the problems of others, but they are our daily struggles. No matter the challenge, my father always comes out the other side. Once, when our car broke down. My mom was stressed out and appeared to be overwhelmed. That night, when I went to bed, I remember worrying for them. The next morning, we woke up to the same problem. The car still wasn't fixed. Dad didn't seem so worried. I asked him why Mom was stressed out, and he acted as if nothing was wrong. He told me that he learned a long time ago that what happened yesterday is history. What happens today is a mystery. I like a mystery. Mom, not so much. I guess that was his way of saying we can't help what happened in the past."

A fictional light bulb came to light right above her head, "Did you steal that wise saying from your dad? The promise of tomorrow or the pain of yesterday."

"Honestly, I know you said you do not believe in God, but I have to give God credit for that. I am not smart enough to think of that on my own. Maybe a little too poetic for my dad."

Pondering whether or not she wanted to share, Binki replies, "First of all, do not sell yourself short. You are very smart. Whether that came from you, your dad, or God," pointing her fingers to the sky, "I will never forget that. As I told you earlier, I spent almost the entire night thinking about our conversation. Could there really be a God? One that really loves me? Could there really be a tomorrow with promise for someone like me? It is really hard to believe. Though I must admit, that would be nice."

Her stance on religion has started to crack, which opened the door for a hint of hope to make an appearance.

Breaking in with a victorious, reassuring, confident tone, "Of course, your tomorrow has a promise. And there is a God who loves you."

Binki senses my celebratory mood and makes an effort to bring me back to home base.

"Hold your horse's cowboy. I said it got me thinking. I still have a lot of questions. But you certainly got me thinking. I really like the idea of losing the pain of yesterday and love the idea that this is the start of my miracle. But can't grasp the thought that there really is a God that loves me. You can't love someone and then allow them to go through what I have been through. Beyond me and my struggles, I have a lot more questions. Sorry, but religion is more like a Fairy Tale than reality. Especially for me and my family."

The feeling of victory suddenly was a 2-touchdown lead that disappeared in the final 3 minutes of a game. As a believer who had been born and breaded to be a good God-Fearing Southern Baptist, I have always known the gospel that Pastor Simpson roared to the congregation as the truth. For the most part, at least. I have questions but never to the level of calling it a Fairy Tale. I believed because that was what I was supposed to do. I never questioned God. But is it possible the gospel is just an elaborate Jack and the Beanstalk-type story? I mean … there are similarities. Parting of the Red Sea, Sampson's strength from his hair, walking on water? Fairy Tales-like stories.

Not wanting to give in, "Please explain. I don't understand."

Before she began, she warned me that she would hold her questions to herself if her questions would ruin the night and put me in a bad mood. The prior statements caught me a little off guard and my confidence was starting to crack. I took a deep breath and accepted the challenge. I knew I had to be up to the task. This was my moment!! After all, I have been on a roll. A future famous televangelist like Jim Baker, Jerry Falwell, or Billy Graham, I just might be.

The thought that I could be like one of my heroes, Jim Baker, regained my confidence. Pastor Baker, along with his wife Tammy Faye, founded the PTL Club. This Club had to bring more people to God than anything I had ever seen. He is a true prophet who created a promised land on earth. The club's home base does double duty as a religious theme park and a church, which is more professionally called a Christian Resort. This resort is often referred to as The Christian Disney World but is officially named Heritage USA. I am not sure what heaven is like, but I think God would be proud of this earthly version. Christian fun with the word of God is never too far away. Gospel music sets the tone because the glorious sounds are blasted out of every venue and bleed into the streets almost no matter where you are. Ceramic Angels, replica Nativity Scenes, Bibles, and taped lessons are found in one of a dozen different gift shops. Events like Christian-based plays, gospel singing, and, of course, the live lectures seem to be on a daily loop. The fact that it sits less than 30 minutes from my house allowed us to make visits multiple times a year.

Every time we would pass the wooden sign welcoming everyone that entered the holy land of the Carolinas, Mom would proclaim, "The Praise the Lord Club is the best club in the world."

I bet I visited twenty times before I put together that PTL stood for Praise The Lord. The focal point of the PLT Club was a cable television network that was designed to share the word of God. I have heard non-believers call it a giant con. All the infomercials for Heritage USA and telethons to raise money for some grand adventure that God instructed the Bakers to oversee.

I was about to tell Binki about this place and the thought she would be one of the non-believers entered my head. Wait, do they have a point?

Should you strive to be a "famous" televangelist? Doesn't that demean the whole purpose of being a prophet of God? The thought gains traction as the thoughts of Jim Baker and another televangelist always wearing good clothes and having big houses. I remember asking my pastor about this, and he told me about a quote by my mom's favorite televangelist, Billy Graham.

"There is nothing wrong with men possessing riches. The wrong comes from when riches possess men."

I liked that quote. It stuck with me, and I was amazed at how he knew that quote right off the cuff. How to say that at the right time? God must have given him those words, not unlike what he has done for me several times in the past couple of days. When I get older, I want to have witty quotes like that in my repertoire.

Breaking me from my religious trance, Binki asked me, "How does someone know they are going to heaven?"

Boom! I got her. This is right up my alley. Anita Hawes's investment by way of demanding that my brothers and I attend every Sunday and Wednesday worship at Oak Grove was ready to pay off. I informed her that one must accept Jesus as your savior. My excitement started to wane when I thought that she had to know this already, right? Isn't that common knowledge? Doesn't every red-blooded American know this? I got the feeling that question was the setup to the real question.

"Do babies go to heaven?"

Thinking this was easy, "Of course?"

She said sounding miffed, "God is letting babies into heaven."

We slow the pace almost to a stop.

"Ok, I knew you would say that," confirming my previous intuition. "But how do you know? I mean, what is the age limit? Four, Ten, fifteen. What age do we have to be saved?"

There it is—the fastball I knew was coming, the question that let me know I fell into her trap. I was a squirrel in a tree, and grandpa's hound dogs were circling and barking. My termination was inevitable. She got down and dirty with the first question.

She stumped me, and she was just getting started. Binki drowned out the noise of the cars passing by, opening the floodgates with an avalanche of questions that blindsided me. Things I may have wondered about but subconsciously just reverted back to always being a believer based on blind faith, not facts, which is exactly how she described most religious people.

"Believers based on blind faith, not facts."

That was the nugget that I couldn't shake off.

"Why would God give a family a baby for such a short time? Aren't the parents his children, too? Why would he put them through this pain?" she asked.

Realizing that this was a debate that she has had before and was better prepared for than I, I stumbled for an answer. That two-touchdown comeback victory came back as a score recount, and I was never in the game. Jim Baker, Jerry Falwell, or Billy Graham never was I going to be.

Shoot, I am not even my Sunday School teacher, James Simpson. Wait, don't concede yet. If she's asking, she's wondering. She must be interested. She's not telling me not to believe—quite the opposite. She's asking because she wants to believe. There is hope.

Yet, I was shell-shocked. Nothing came out. I was waiting for God to put those magic words in my mouth. I was a deer caught in the headlights.

Binki showed no mercy. She was driving an 18-wheeler that was just about to hit the high gear. She was determined to push forward and run through this deer.

"Isn't there just one true God? Who promotes love and peace?"

The cracks are beginning to show.

"I. There. Hmmm," I stumbled on words. I can get the first word out, but nothing follows the first word.

She is just hitting her stride, "If there is only one true God, then why are there so many religions? Many different religions are very geographic in nature. Each country seems to have its own primary religion and they all are different. Then there are those that share in name, only to be different in translation. Don't you find it weird that religion speaks of peace and love, but the primary reason for most of the wars in the history of the Earth is because of religious differences? That sounds like religion is breaking us apart, not pulling us together. Right?"

She pauses for me to respond, but there is just too much for me to digest. For some reason, I bypassed the questions and was taken aback by the articulate way she made her argument. I always knew that she was deep.

She was smart. That intelligence just made its appearance and took center stage, no doubt in my mind. She has certainly presented this argument before, maybe a couple of times.

"Hello, McFly," she stated, referring to a character in the recent Back to the Future motion picture. "Over here. Remember me?"

Binki snaps her finger in front of my face as if to wake me up from some hypnotic session I was just in.

I felt the weight of the world. I was lost. "Please help" was a quick-fire signal I was sending up to God via the telepathic route.

I just took a deep breath. I opened my mouth, and out came, "I am afraid I do not have the answers to these questions. Or the rest to come."

I was humbled by my lack of knowledge in this field. I was dumbfounded that I didn't have the answer for a test that I had been studying for my whole life.

The smell of defeat spayed down as the apologetic "I am sorry" quietly left my lips.

Then, as if God Almighty himself whispered into my ears.

"Wait, I have an idea. Why don't we both get a list of questions together and I will ask someone better suited to answer these questions?"

Like a rat in a laboratory running on the wheel, my brain was in a never-ending loop of thoughts. I just opened my mouth, and out of blind faith, God gave me the answer. That is proof. This isn't blind faith. That is a fact! I know this to be true. Wait, did he give me the answer, or was that me just passing the buck? I mean, "Ask someone else" is not exactly getting quoted in the Bible. Did God just humble me because I was thinking about being rich instead of doing it for the right reason? It could be a test to show me that I do not know everything. Right?

To my surprise, her face lit up as she was excited about the possibilities.

"Wonderful," she exclaimed and informed me that there were more questions that she needed to have answered.

This time, the figurative light bulb went off above my head. Instead of the questions being statements to prove God doesn't exist, she is asking to confirm he is real. I have misread this the whole time. She wants to believe, but the devil is casting his opposition.

Satan would not stop as she hurdled another round of words of inquiry, "Why are people dying in such painful ways? Can't God spare them and their families the pain? Can people like my dad, who chooses to live an evil life, or those who murder someone, just accept Christ, and all is forgiven? Here is a golden ticket to heaven." She waves her hand as if she is handing me the ticket. "Someone like my mom who has been beaten and battered her whole life and never does anything horrible. If she doesn't accept Christ, does she go to hell? There is a chance that my dad could end up in heaven and my mom could end up in hell. How is that right?" She continues, "Why would God give me that man as my dad? How can my dad, Billy Ray Wallace, even have a shot at heaven? No way that man should be in heaven after the hell he put us through on earth."

It was very easy to see that her distance from religion is exactly the reason that I feel close to God. My home life is the key. My parents are believers, and I have a great life; thus, I believe. Her family life is wretched, and according to her, it's obviously God's fault. Thus, she does not believe it. But just like the night before, I can't help but think she has a reason to be mad at God. I don't have that reason. Why is the valley between our relationships with God so deep? This is going to be one of my questions to ask. Who are we asking these questions? I am not asking my parents. I am not sure what the hell is like, but I feel certain I will see hell on earth if Mom thinks I am questioning God. Maybe the camp has a preacher? They have sermons every Sunday morning. That is what I will do. Sunday morning, I will see if I can meet with him after we have church. Meet in confidence. I break into her rant and explain my plan that we will meet the preacher on Sunday morning.

Content with the resolution, she grabbed my hand, and we regained our voyage. The statement about her father going to heaven swims around in my head to the point that I constructed a vision. Imagine where Binki made it to heaven. There she is, walking on the streets of gold, long hair flowing over her white robe. Content as possible while the angels are playing the harp. The perfect scene. Then, she runs into her father. Could God let that happen? I know he forgives, but are there limits? Why have I never thought of this? Man, this is tough.

"I have a question," Binki offered.

Oh, Lord. No mas was my thought. My lips filtered out a better version.

"You mean another question. Heck, don't hold back now," I said with a laugh.

Hidden in the gesture was the notion that she was piling on just to re-confirm a victory in which the white towel was made visible long ago.

It was very much like when my Spartans were getting destroyed by Forest Woods High School 63 to 7, and they scored again on the last play of the game, making it 70 to 7.

"Where do you go to church? Do they have black people or people from other countries?"

I delivered the answer to her like I just fumbled in the end zone on the game-winning drive, and I had to go and explain to the coach why I lost the ball.

"No," felt uneasy coming from my mouth. Does that make me racist? It can't be; I have black friends. Angie, Clarence, Tyrone, Calvin. Hold up, isn't that the go-to saying for all racists? "I have black friends."

Oh lord! This girl got my head messed up. I know I am not racist. I know my parents aren't. I mean, we go out to eat with Danny and Tina, who works with my Dad at the mill. But we don't go to the same church. They have never asked us, and we have never asked them. Not to my knowledge.

I admit, "You know, I never realized this. That bothers me that I never thought about this."

"I have wondered this for years. Black people go to church with black people. White people go to church with white people. I think Hispanic people go to churches together. You get the point. Shouldn't church be the ONE place everyone should go and not be judged by skin color or social status?"

"I have to admit, you got me there. You are right. That makes no sense."

She is not letting it go.

"Last thing about religion. I promise," she states.

I believe she notices that I am not up to the challenge of answering all these questions and maybe throwing one last swing.

"I wonder if I died right now. Am I going to heaven or hell? A good law-abiding citizen? Not that I am, but I am working in that direction," she interjects with a smile. "What if there are good, honest people that just don't believe? Do they go to heaven or hell? My parents never took me to church or ever gave me a reason to believe. Am I going to hell no matter how much good I do on earth? Could the promise of tomorrow include me curing cancer and feeding every homeless person in the world be the make good to allow me into heaven? Or am I doomed? Just because I don't believe it. What if the doubts about God never leave me? Bo, what if no matter how much I want to believe, doubt never allows me to be a believer? What if?"

That was a lot to process. I gathered two important facts. One is that she is genuinely concerned about the afterlife and searching for guidance that I cannot give. This is miles over my head!! The second is that it became apparent that her father placed these doubts in her mind. Billy Ray Wallace may truly be the devil. He did make her life on earth hell. It made her feel as if tomorrow had no promise and took the idea of eternal life from her. Pure Satan!!

Everyone needs something to believe in, some place for comfort and answers. For me, it's God and family. For her, neither is applicable.

I just took a spiritual elbow to the head from the "Nature Boy" Rick Flair himself. My mind could not comprehend the onslaught of questions that were heaved in my direction.

Using my best tools to handle adversity, I change the direction of the conversation, "I surrender. I concede," putting my hands up as if I was reaching for Jesus himself. "Look, I plan to find these answers, but let's table this topic. Do what we came to do. Have some fun."

She knew that she had disoriented me but didn't respond in a gloating way. Her sly smile was her trophy for the evening.

"You are right. Let's have some fun. No more religion tonight. Sorry if I went too far."

We never revisited the topic verbally that night. We didn't need to. The damage had been done. She had shaken the very foundation I rested upon spiritually. Those were legit questions and now I needed the answers. Was I a blind believer? Nah...there must be practical answers to her questions, right?

Chapter Twenty-Three - The Dance

We got some ice cream, and the topic of the night became my wild night out with my family, leaving out no details. She persuaded me to make our way back to the area where people were singing and dancing because she wanted me to show her how to line dance. But it turned out, she knew how to line dance better than I and she was just showing off.

After we reached the dance floor, it was quite apparent that Binki had a lot of talent. Singing wasn't among them. She would act like she knew the songs only to destroy the lyrics with a humming sound or some crazy noise. That was until it got to the chorus. Then she would then blurt out every word very loudly. Her free spirit filled the mountain air as she got more comfortable in her surroundings. We did the Broom dance a couple of times, which brought special amusement to her every time I would end up with the broom. Binki, being so beautiful, never failed to find a partner and thus never had the task.

We would take a break every so often to get something to drink or walk into a shop to look. Only to always find our way back to the dance floor. The moon draped right over the peak of the mountain, hinting that the night was about to end.

Finally, the band leader confirmed the inevitable when he announced, "Friends, this is the last song of the night. Please grab the one you love, the one you want to love or grab someone who will let you grab them, and let's close the night out like a real cowboy. More specifically, an Urban Cowboy. So, men, bring out your inner John Travolta, better known as Bud, and find your Debra Winger, better known as Sissy and let's play Anne Murray's hit."

"Could I have this dance?"

She wrapped her arms around me and whispered softly into my right ear, "I have seen this movie 100 times. This is my mom's favorite movie."

I could feel the heat from her body through the cotton sundress as she placed her body close to mine. She laid her head on my shoulder so close that I could feel her breath on my neck. Her eyes closed as she was soaking in the moment. I could hear her softly sing as she had done several times tonight with the lone exception being that she was on key and knew every word.

When the song was drawing to a close, she lifted her head and looked me in the eyes as she recited the words, "Could I have this dance for the rest of my life? Would you be my partner every night? When we're together it feels so right. Could I have this dance for the rest of my life?" chorused Binki with true belief and conviction. Never allowing our eyes to come undone.

Never have I been clearer about anything in my life. I could see everything a man wants to see in a woman. In their soulmate. I saw total surrender. Someone who is willing to give you all that they are. Her mouth wasn't what I heard. It was her eyes that told the whole story. I saw love. A promise of tomorrow was coming into focus.

She leaned in towards my ear and whispered the words, "Wish this song could go on forever."

She then laid her head back on my shoulder and went back to dancing even though the music had stopped.

"Me too," I murmured, trying to absorb every second of holding her that I could.

We have successfully run from the problems that existed only a couple of hours prior, at least for one night.

When it became abundantly clear that we were the last two on the floor, she pulled her beautiful face right in front of mine and gave me a kiss. Then grabbed my hand and placed it over her shoulder as we walked off the dance floor, smiling and coddling. Not unlike what I saw my parents doing earlier in the night. Following my dad's path, I was.

We agreed to get ice cream for the second time tonight, with the only exception being that this time, we would share the cookies and cream in a cup before we started the trek back to where we began.

The pilgrimage back to our temporary homes was akin to dancing on clouds. The turtle style pace was a mutual subconscious partnership to make every effort to extend the night as much as possible. Each step was in perfect, non-rushed harmony that could not be topped by the greatest of dancers. Our bodies were powered by the constant contact by means of holding hands or her taking my arm and laying it across her back. The bud that was fated to be the flower of love had used the night as fertilizer and blossomed into magic.

Each glance in her direction made it clear that I wanted this for the rest of my life. The contentment, admiration, and, I dare say, love that

I saw in her face and felt from her body created an emotion that I have never had.

The fact was not lost on me that I would be on a constant journey for the rest of my life to duplicate this feeling over and over. This high I am currently on is my new addiction. Much like nicotine is to my dad. I can't live without this feeling. This can't be a once-in-a-lifetime feeling.

Our conversation matched our actions. Every sentence included the word love or best ever. "I loved that song. We loved that shop. That ice cream was the best ever?"

Not a cloud could be found, but the millions of stars appeared to be just a little more than an arm's reach away. A rare moment of silence allowed me to look heavenward and appreciate the splendid gem that was left for us by our creator.

The quietness was interrupted by the proclamation, "I love you."

The words were blurted out as if they were something that was supposed to be contained behind the walls of one's lips, but the force of the words "I love you" was too strong to be held prisoner.

I was caught off guard. I looked around to see where this came from. For one moment, I did a personal rewind to see if it was my lips that had committed treason, and I blurted this out without my brain's consent.

"Hello, don't look so shocked. I LOVE YOU, BO," she stated slowly and emphatically to stress the confidence in her words.

I wasn't sure how to answer but knew this moment wasn't being missed. This is exactly how I feel, but I wasn't sure if it was too early to announce those words.

Before I answered, she continued, "You don't have to say it. It's okay."

I grabbed her hand and pulled her off to the steps of the office.

"Listen, I'm a little afraid because I don't know how this will end when my family and I leave here in a couple of days. I honestly think I love you, but I'm not certain that you can love someone in just a short amount of time. What I know is that I can't stop thinking about you or thinking about how you make me feel when I'm around you. I honestly have never felt anything like this." Taking my thoughts from the previous night and putting them into words, "Is it love? I am not certain. I am certain that I love everything about you. Your long toes, the way your cheeks swell when you smile, or the fragrance of your perfume that lingers even when you walk away."

She interrupts, "Bo, listen. That is so nice, but this is not your moment to shower me with praise. That has been accomplished. My cup runneth over, as someone famous once said."

She smiles at her own witty joke. Then transforms back into serious mode.

"This is my time to tell you that these are not words that are spewing from my mouth. As you can probably guess, I have said those before and used them very recklessly. But never have I meant it. Mainly because I didn't know what love was. This is what I know. I know I'm a better person because of you. You make me want to be

214

better. You make me expect more out of myself. Bo, I promise you this, I will never tell another person I love them unless they treat me like you do. Make me laugh like you do. Most important, unless they respect me like you do. I have always felt confident in myself. But I never respected myself. That was until I met you."

I'm overwhelmed with emotion, but trying to keep the cool factor in place, "Wow" slips out, dripping with more emotion than I intended.

I was blushing. This is such uncharted territory. I have never had someone to proclaim their love for me.

"I am literally embarrassed because I don't have an adequate response. That is the nicest thing anyone has ever said to me. I... I just..."

Before another word escapes my mouth, she moves in and plants a soft, slow kiss. The kiss confirms every word that she just spoke. It is the kiss that no person could ever be able to forget. It is the kiss that kidnaps a man's heart. It is the one that gives him the conviction to travel the globe for just one more taste. It is the "I love you" kiss.

She tilts her head to one side.

"No new words are needed. I know," she slips between a coy smile, exuding every ounce of confidence that she is loved by me.

There is a saying about the look of a woman in love and how sweet it can be. This is that look. The look that Garth Brooks and George Straight write country songs about. It couldn't be more appealing.

Chapter Twenty-Four - Tides Turn

A car passed by with their lights temporarily, putting our kissing in full view. I used this as a sign to get back to my family soon. Or Mom would send out a search party named Dad to retrieve her oldest boy. I grabbed Binki's hand to walk her back to her site and drop her off for the night. But like a stubborn mule at our farm, she didn't move. She was planted in her place. I looked back at her, and with the quickest of turns, she changed. The mood changed. Just like that! I have heard my uncle say that women will turn on you in a heartbeat. I always thought he was crazy, and that's why he is single. But I think I just witnessed this firsthand. Maybe there is some truth hidden in there. We went from kissing to something very different in a matter of seconds! I was caught off guard.

With an apologetic look, she placed both arms around my body, directing me into the nearby rocking chair. The change in mood confused me. I was afraid the catalyst for the change was to discuss a topic that had eluded conversation the entire night. I mean, there was no reason to revisit that topic—not now.

Then the words came. Simple words, but they sounded like a siren screaming through my head—akin to a fire alarm going off while you are having a party—just wrecking the mood.

"We have to discuss the phone call," she said.

"No, you don't have to explain anything. Or at least, let's wait until tomorrow," I share, wanting to revert back to the warm and loving mood that we had just moments ago.

I could see the pain in her eyes as she said, "It can't wait."

I just didn't understand. Why now? Her festive mood was suddenly hijacked by the dread of the inevitable conversation that she felt had to take place—right now.

In an effort to trap me and keep me from moving, she took a seat on my lap, squeezing her buttocks between the handles of the chair. The base of the sun dress had risen to her upper thigh as she positioned both of her legs to dangle from one side by flipping them over one of the arms of the wooden chair. As any young red-blooded American teenage boy's eyes would do, they found a home on the temporary wardrobe malfunction exposing more of her leg than she obviously wanted to display. Binki caught my line of vision and quickly adjusted the dress, placing it back closer to her knees.

Very much like a perv being caught looking into the neighbor's window, I rapidly turned my head to the right, which ironically brought the impending topic at hand into sight. We are sitting just a couple of feet from the pay phone that had ruined the majority of the past 24 hours. Demanding my undivided attention, she grabbed my face as if I were a misguided kindergartener and turned it back to its intended position. Straight forward. Eye to Eye.

A tear starts to form in the corner of each eye as she tries to close them to hide the pain, but the pressure of the closure pushes the tears down her cheeks. More tears followed at a slow, steady pace before

Binki could organize her thoughts into words.   I sat quietly and the gravity of the moment that was weighing her down started to have the same effect on me.

Breaking the silence, "What is wrong? How can I help?" I offered.

I always think there is a way I can make it right, very much like my male role model. My dad always finds a way to make things right. I wanted to do what I had seen my dad do a million times. Take her problems and lay them on my lap. I will carry this burden for you. I will make it right.

That was the goal. "I want to help you but not sure how I can if I don't know the problem."

The words "You can't" come sheepishly out of her mouth.

"You may be right, but we will never know unless you tell me." She stayed quiet as the pain of her thoughts became evident. Sitting in the quiet of the night, I realized she wanted to tell me. Obviously!! Or we would already be back at the campsite. I decided just to be patient. Dad would understand why I was late. I am just helping a damsel in distress, I thought.

"Take your time. We can be here all night."

She took her wrist and wiped away the tears, only for the effort to be wasted because as quick as she pushed a tear away, another came in its place.

The words "I love you, and I am sorry" left her lips in a murmur.

"What?" was the only response I could muster.

Could all this be because I didn't say I love you back just a moment ago? My thoughts started to wonder that this is "the crazy" that everyone always talks about in the opposite sex.

"What are you sorry about?" I offer with pain and bewilderment sprayed across my face.

"I am afraid this is my last night here," timidly leaves her mouth but screams into my ears.

Not able to process what exactly this means, I found myself deep in thought. Questions were floating through my head like raindrops falling from the sky. It's over? When did she know? Why now? Wait, does "my last night here mean" she is going to take her own life?

Overcome by sadness, "Where are you going? You can't leave."

Desperation takes hold, and tears find their way into my eyes, too.

"You can't leave. I do love you. I love you. You can't leave me."

"You don't understand," meekly squirms out of her mouth.

My frustration is growing as my tone becomes more aggressive.

"What do I not understand?"

"I fucked up!! Once I tell mom," tears and fear cover her face, "We will have no choice but to leave?" she blurts out defensively.

More confused than ever before, I questioned, "Tell her what?"

Without answering the question, "He's coming," he quietly escapes as the weeping goes to the next level.

Being a churchman, my first thought was that "HE" meant Jesus. I have heard "Jesus is Coming" many times. After all, we have been talking about religion tonight. Is this about religion? Is this God telling me that he is taking her home?

A cold chill went straight down my spine, and my body filled with fear when I realized that she was not speaking of the lord, but instead. She is speaking of the Devil. I just wasn't sure which body the devil was going to inhabit. The Father or the Boyfriend.

I stood up out of the chair so fast that Binki would have slid to the ground if I hadn't caught her.

"Who's coming?" I say in a quick and very stern tone.

The shaking of my hands had become noticeable as I circled around her body to ensure I was standing in front of her. My words reach her quickly as we are less than one inch from touching noses.

"Binki, who is coming? When are they coming?"

Fear had taken full control of my body. This summer crush between two teenagers has now turned into something that could put me and my family's lives in jeopardy. Is Scott coming back for revenge on Binki and Mitch? And me? Will he take out my whole family? We are literally sitting under the stars where there is nothing to stop some psychopath with a knife or a little gun. Or is it the father? The man that is the cause of so much damage to his own family. Is he ready to inflict more pain? Is he coming to keep his promise to kill her and her family? Holy Shit!!! This is an unbearable situation.

She hugs me and lays her head on my shoulder to cry, but I must know the answer. Forsaking the effort to be patient. I put one arm on each shoulder and gave our bodies enough distance to look into her eyes.

"Binki, this is important. Who is coming? How do you know? When are they coming? Is it your dad? Is it Scott? Who is it? You must tell me?"

The urgency in my voice was evident. The fear for my family, Binki, and myself was to the level that I felt my heart coming out of my chest. I dropped my hands to my side as another set of car lights whizzed by.

The words "Both" almost sent my body into convolutions.

"What the hell? You have known this all night and are just telling me this now?"

She wiped her face once again and reached for my embrace.

I push her arms away.

"Binki, tell me everything. I mean everything."

She grabbed my hand and softly led me to a spot on the nearby steps.

She beings to give me the news that would change my life, forever.

Chapter Twenty-Five - Mom's Death Warrant

Two people holding hands under a hypnotic moon that hangs in the air on a perfect July night in the middle of the North Carolina mountains should contain an ambiance of warmth, romance, and hope for endless possibilities. But that was not the case because a cloud of darkness replaced all hope. A future that was destined to be limitless had just come to a dead end. The words that made it through her tears came out soft and tender but struck me like butcher knives being thrust into my skin.

She explained that when she spoke to Scott on the phone, he did not take the breakup very well. Cursed her one minute and then begged her not to leave the next. Right when she was about to hang up on him, he used his ultimate trump card.

"Scott said he was going to let my dad know where we were." This caused Binki to cry tears that became messy. "Damn, I need a cigarette," she said as if that was all that was needed to make this better.

It would be the magic potion. The great elixir.

I tried to put my arms around her, but she pushed me away. Said that there was more. Binki continued to share the reason for her anxiety. Her first reaction when she got off the phone was fear. She said she was scared and wanted to be alone. Needed time to think. Sort out what to do. Suppose he would really do this. After a while, she confided with Mitch about the call. They put together a plan.

Following the plan that they constructed, Mitch walked Binki back to the phone. She called him back and begged him not to. Told him that if he did this, he might as well sign her mom's death warrant because she was as good as dead. Binki broke down and started visibly shaking as she explained his response.

Scott said, "Like I give a fuck," and hung up.

She explained that for the first time in her life, she hyperventilated. Almost passed out from fear.

After numerous calls of him acting like an ass, he eventually calmed him down. She asked him to give her another chance. The only reason for the request was to give her time to tell her mom how she had created this clusterfuck. The plan was to never call him back once she hung up the phone.

Binki paused and took in a large amount of air in an effort to compose herself and continued, "I thought all was good when he said he would give me another chance. We talked a little, and I told him I was tired. He asked me to call him back in the morning. This gave us another day, but honestly, last night was rough. Mitch and I did not sleep at all. We discussed every conceivable outcome. Decided that this was the best plan."

She explains how this morning she called him back as he requested. Knowing that tonight, she was going to tell her mom. She said she was just trying to please him. Keep in his good graces. Instead of making it short and hanging up immediately, she strung him alone just to make sure it was believable.

"Maybe enough to get us another day or two. Now I realize I was just trying to delay the inevitable." She explained, "We started to make normal conversation. I was playing the part but screwed up royally when I told him that I missed him. I think he called my bluff when he asked to come up tonight to see me." Another deep breath. "I told him not tonight. Then he said, started calling me every name in the book. Said I was cheating on him. Then just hung up. Scott never answered another call."

I brought out my grandpa's go-to curse word and said, "Ah, Hell."

"So tonight, when my mom gets home, I have to tell her," she relented.

"So, you don't know if he is coming," I asked.

"I don't, but I wouldn't put it past him," she answered. "You know what kind of person he is."

This situation was overwhelming. All I could think to do was to put my arms around her. I wanted to hold her in my protective embrace for the rest of my life. I wanted to tell her that I would protect her. Protect her? How the hell am I going to protect her? I have no frickin' clue. Maybe I should share this with my parents. They would know what to do. Thoughts raced through my head at NASCAR speed. Binki's body was bordering on convulsions.

No way would Scott really tell her dad, would he? If he ever loved her, there is no way. That was my first thought. Suddenly, clarity came into view through the fog that was hiding in my head when I realized that this was my way of thinking. Not Scott's. His version of love does not match mine. Nor any other rational human being, as a matter of fact. My goal was to sound measured and controlled, just like my dad would. That was not accomplished. Scared and alarmed noises rambled from my lips.

"You need to tell her," I urged.

I knew the consequences of these words would no doubt be damning for our future, but the alternative would be much more tragic for Binki and her family. Especially her mom.

"When your mother gets home tonight, you need to tell her the entire story."

I was coming to grips with the fact that this most certainly would be the very last minute that we would ever spend together.

"I plan to. I just said that," Binki replied harsher than she intended.

I could not help but think that she may have already waited too late. My mind's eye could see Scott getting drunk or high and then doing something so dumb as to tell her dad. Not a care in the world for the repercussions of his actions. Heck, he already said as much.

"You need to call her right now. I don't think you should wait," I advise and then express my concern. "I think you need to give your mom all the time needed."

That was my way of saying you should have done this earlier.

Binki takes a moment.

"You are right."

I reach into my pocket in effort to find a quarter. Why did she wait? I had to know. Her response left me conflicted.

"I came to tell you this earlier. But the chance to have one more night. I thought. Just a couple more hours. Then it would be all over."

One side made me swell with pride. She wanted one more night with me. The realistic side noted that this one more night could have harsh consequences.

She wipes her face once again and starts to walk towards the phone.

"I am beginning to really hate this phone," she says in an effort to lighten the moment.

She returns and guides me to the steps of the porch. Once again, sitting under the moonlight. I have no doubt my creator placed it there to allow us to marvel at its beauty, but tonight, the moon had the role of the observer. It was watching young love end.

"Bo, once I make this call. Mom will be here in five minutes. That may be the last five minutes we have together."

My face could not hide that my heart was breaking. Her face, too, was a window displaying the pain that she was feeling.

She continues was a glimmer of hope. The words were said with love and hope. The delivery betrayed her with sounds of doubt.

"I have a million regrets. But the promise of tomorrow truly gives me hope. Once we get settled, I am going ...."

Suddenly, we noticed another pair of headlights. This time, the rusted red pickup truck with a dented front fender did not continue around the curb like all the other cars had done in the past. Instead, it hastily darted towards the office steps that we were occupying. The lights were blinding us, which left me a little disoriented. I looked at

Binki's face. Immediately, I knew this was not good. The terror in her face told me that the devil had just arrived.

Chapter Twenty-Six - The Devil

My pastor said millions of times that the devil can come in many images. This image was beyond all I had ever seen. A simple rusty ole red truck was carrying a world of horror. Binki's fear paralyzed me.

Almost simultaneously, Mitch came running around the opposite corner of the office porch.

"Binki, he found us. We need to..."

His words drowned out as he caught sight of the same vision that incited fear just moments before into his sister.

Instinctively, he finishes his previous statement in a murmur, "Tell Mom not to come home."

Binki and I get up and automatically start to backpedal onto the porch toward Mitch as a measure of self-defense. A 6 ft, 250-pound man jumps out of the truck. He gives a crooked smile and wipes his hands through his hair.

"Hello, Binki Boo. Mitch, my man. Missed me?" he says as if he is the Joker in a Batman movie.

I have never heard of an evil walk, but every slow step this man took in our direction oozed evil intentions.

"Mitch... Funny thing. I thought that was you running like a scared rabbit from that piece of shit camper."

The man's measured pace brings him up the steps and onto the office porch.

"No, Daddy, No!" Binki begs. "Don't do this!!"

"Y'all thought I wouldn't find ya. Didn't ya?"

He takes an exaggerated puff on his cigarette and blows the smoke into the air. He pinches it at the butt to recover it from his lips and then flicks it away into the darkness.

We are dumbfounded. Frozen. Which allows him to be right in front of Binki, Mitch, and I before we knew it. He was so close; I could feel the alcohol coming from his face and burning my nostrils.

His tone turns more serious and darker.

"Where is the bitch?" stating his purpose for the visit. "Where's the Bitch? Where's the Bitch? Where's the Bitch?" he says with the rhythm of some long-lost nursery rhyme.

"You know," he chuckles as if he is stating the obvious punch line of a cheesy joke. "She is going to die tonight."

He lunges towards Binki, and she hides behind Mitch and me.

The man wearing the stained white tee shirt, dirty pants, and dirty hands seemed amused.

"Well, well. What do we have the pleasure of here? We have a couple fucking heroes in our midst."

I reached behind me, trying to coral Binki between my arms behind me, but my arms were so weak I could barely raise them. I was prepared to say something brave and heroic.

The words "Fuck you" exploded into the atmosphere.

For a second, I was almost impressed that I could mustard that type of response but the realization that those words left Mitch's mouth instead of mine just confirmed that my body was numb from fear.

"You didn't tell me we had heroes amongst us," he says very loudly in a sarcastic, jovial manner.

The senior Wallace looks around as if he is talking to someone. Then it hits me. He got out of the passenger side door. He was not driving. I turn my head to see Scott standing right beside the truck. He was leaning against the hood, blowing smoke from a cigarette towards the sky.

His stance said, "Look what you made me do. Now you're going to pay."

That "I told you so" attitude was apparent by the smile that stretched across his face.

Scott's delight was affirmed when he responded, "Fucking heroes. Real nice."

Stars rang through my head as I found myself lying on the wood-planked floor of the office porch. I never saw the punch to the side of my head. I was not even looking. I regain my awareness enough to see Binki's dad reach into a leather knife holster with his left hand and pull out a knife. He yanked Binki by the hair with the other hand.

With no regard for having his daughter by her hair, he looks at me and says, "Listen here, you little prick. Do not move. This has nothing to do with you. If you move, I will cut a hole in your chest, pull out your intestines, and cram them down your throat. Just like I did that preacher that was fucking my wife."

I'm not sure if fear could reach a new level, but it did. I realized that his shirt, pants, and hands were not stained from dirt. Those weren't hard-working man stains. Those were blood stains. The blood stains of a man that he incorrectly thought was sleeping with his wife. A man who lost his life just because he was helping a woman in distress. Oh, Shit. That could be my story, too.

Emptiness and doom took control as I realized that this man had already killed someone today and just gave me a warning that I could lose my life for the exact same reason. It was clear. Whether it's me or not, he is not done killing today. This is not a threat. This man truly plans to kill his wife.

Still holding his daughter by the hair and looking directly at me, "You mind your own damn business." He finally acknowledges his daughter, "Isn't that, right?"

After a pause for effect, he adds the word, "Sweetie, we don't want your little Romeo to die tonight, too. Do we?"

I massaged where I was hit and noticed that blood was pooling and matting my hair. My thoughts were muddled. My head had a pulse as if it were a heart that was having a heart attack. Is that possible? Trying to gather myself or maybe in search of help, I looked around. Scott is smashing out his cigarette with the toe of his shoe, twisting the butt into the ground. Wait, do I see people? Someone right behind him? I used the back of my hand to rub my eyes and noticed that, just like water in a desert, it was a mirage. There was nobody. We were all alone.

My attention returned to my attacker, "Where is she?"

From the other side of them, Mitch shouts out, "Leave her alone," as he starts to get back to his feet.

"No, No, No… Mitch, my boy!!" the father says in a condescending tone. "Stay there."

Mitch stops as he sees his father press the eight-inch knife to his sister's neck.

The sick man uses a tone that makes it sound like he is giving his son a life lesson.

"You see, you are almost a man. As men, we have to make tough decisions." He turns his head to Scott, "Isn't that right, Scott?"

Scott confirms, "This is true."

"Scott made a man decision by telling me where you were? Isn't that right, Scott?"

Scott again confirms as if the puppy just did the trick for his master.

"Right again. You are on fire tonight, Mr. Wallace."

"Well, son, today's your day. You get to become a man. You get to make a man's decision. You see…" He takes a deep breath as if he just ran a marathon. He took a deep breath, and then the professor returned to his lecture. "You could be a pussy like Scott and make the wrong decision."

He looks in Scott's direction. No doubt to see his reaction to being called a pussy.

"Or you could be a man like myself and make the smart decision."

"The hell," an incredulous Scott says.

"You see, Scott thought just because he told me where you guys were that I was going to allow my only daughter to become his sex slave or something. But Scott is too stupid to know that no man wants his pathetic ass for their daughter, even if she is the shittiest daughter a man can have. Moral of the story. Even stupid people can make one smart decision. You understand? No matter how dumb you are, you are capable of making at least one smart decision. I mean, hell. You can't be dumber than that dipshit over there."

"Man, you can't talk shit like that about me," Scott says as he is walking towards the porch. "We had a deal."

Deal? I thought. What deal? Did they really make a deal with Binki being the bartering piece?

Scott is ignored as the elder Wallace continues, "Make a man's decision. Call your mom and tell her to get her worthless ass here. Right Now!" he says with a growl that seems like he is trying to hold a beast inside of his body.

He inhales through his nose like a yoga master would suggest as some sort of calming mechanism. He continues in a Mr. Rogers type of kindly voice.

"You can use that phone hanging on that wall right behind you. You know. Using that quarter you have in your hand. I have a feeling that you were about to do this before I interrupted you. Maybe give your mommy dearest a warning that death is here to get her?"

The tone changes once again. This time, Mr. Roger's pleasantries were replaced by Freddie.

Frueger's evil. He scrunches his face together to drive his point home.

"Or I am going to cut your sister's throat. Right here! Right in front of you."

Binki squirms and yells, "Don't do it."

He continues, "Do it! Or after I put an end to this miserable bitch, I will use this same knife and cut your throat. All with a smile on my face. Your mommy dearest is dying. That decision has been made. It's you and your sister's lives that are in question. One or three. Well," he looks down in my direction. "Maybe four, that is the question. You are not saving your mom; you are only prolonging her time on this Earth!"

Mitch is paralyzed.

"Move boy!! Call her RIGHT now!!" Mitch doesn't move.

"Okay, that is the way you're going to play this. I thought you were smart. You could have saved your sister. You are no more of a man than that sack of shit," he says, tilting his head in Scott's direction.

"I have about had enough of that," Scott's macho response still falls on deaf ears, and he starts to walk towards the porch.

The father then does the unfathomable. He slowly starts to cut his daughter's throat as she is screaming. The skin starts to come apart. The knife is moving slowly and precisely as if completing some demonic sacrifice to the masses. The slow pace was calculated for dramatic effect, which would inflict more pain on Mitch.

"Hold on! Hold on!" Mitch pleas. "Okay. Okay. Stop that!!"

The knife separates from her neck as blood starts to trickle from the incision. No different than he would a bag of trash, he pushes Binki to the ground. She cups her hand over the cut in an effort to try and stop the bleeding.

The agitated man roars, "Son, she has ten minutes. Not one minute more. Or your sister will be the first to die."

Mitch places the quarter into the pay phone. You can hear him ask for his mom.

Meanwhile, I slide over toward Binki and take off my shirt. Binki uses it to cover her wound. Protection is the goal as I put my arms around her.

"Aw! You really are a hero." The condescension was thick and obvious. "Binki Boo, I like this guy. Better than this POS over here. I bet this one actually would have tried to get you the 2.5 kids and the house with a white picket fence. Unlike that misfit Guns N' Roses groupie over here."

Once again, the father tilts his head towards Scott.

Billy Ray Wallace's harsh words obviously pushed Scott to his limits. He climbs the steps and walks towards Binki.

"Get your hands off her," Scott barks orders towards me. "Binki, get up. You are coming with me."

Scott turns his head towards the man holding the knife.

"Mr. Wallace," he says as if he had just completed a deal to buy a car. "It's been a pleasure doing business with you. But it's time for me to leave you with… well… you to sort out all this shit."

"Wait one damn minute. You ain't going nowhere," said the angry man with a knife.

Scott disagrees, "Oh yeah. We made a deal. I did my part."

He yanks on Binki's arm.

Binki holds tight to my body as Scott tries to collect his payment.

Before he can collect his prize, Scott discovers what happens when you make a deal with the devil. Binki and Mitch's father stabbed Scott right in the middle of the back. Scott falls face first on Binki and me, with blood spewing out of his body and on us.

I push him off and start to slide in the opposite direction.

Scott is trying to retreat as well. He starts to roll towards the steps, with blood leaving a trail, while Mr. Wallace admires his handiwork. You could see that he left us mentally for a minute. There was a new game to play. He was enjoying the dominance over someone else. Scott's body slowly falls down one step. Then the next and the next step as if he was a Slinky. Until Scott's body finally surrenders to the ground. Binki's father towers over him in a stalking manner every step of the way. Every step was accompanied by a curse word, and nothing was left to the imagination.

For a split second, I noticed that Mitch, Binki, and I were no longer his focus.

I gathered my courage and did the bravest thing I had ever done in my life.

I yelled, "Run!"

Binki and Mitch must have thought the same thing. Without thought, we were on our feet and off to the races. Mitch disappeared around the same corner that he had appeared from just minutes before. Binki and I jumped to our feet. I grabbed her hand as we started in the opposite direction that Mitch took. Before I could take the third step, something gave me a jolt as I lost control of Binki's hand. Binki had fallen to the ground. My body kept its momentum in the direction of freedom as my head turned to see Binki being dragged with her legs flailing back toward the center of the office porch.

Chapter Twenty-Seven - Self-Analysis

My pastor once taught a lesson titled "Who are you?" The gist of the sermon was a self-reflection lesson that required self-analysis. To look deep inside your soul and evaluate whether you are a consistent child of God. Are you different in front of certain people? Are you a better person in church than outside of church? Are you honest in the sight of others, only to be different if you think you can get away with it? Do you portray yourself as one thing and when that moment comes to be that person, you end up being someone different? I always thought of myself as a defender. A protector.

Just like my father. I know I will always do what's right, no matter what. I am certain this was not the situation he meant during that sermon. Nevertheless, here I am.

I stopped when I noticed nobody was following. The truth was, all he wanted was Binki. I am free. Nobody could blame me for not going back into a helpless situation to face a certain beating. Maybe even death. His threat of ripping out my intestines and feeding them to me is still fresh.

Plus, he just confessed that he had already killed one person. Then, I just saw him stab another, and he is openly advertising for a third victim, in which he is hell-bent that nothing was going to stop him from getting to her and doing the job. Bo Hawes would just be one more name in the morning obituary. After all, he is right. This is not my fight.

Struggling with my emotions and the gravity of the situation. I am fully aware that an ungodly man can care less about me. I watch him yelling at Binki and flinging his arms recklessly through the air. She is whimpering and cowering. The sound of her begging for her life is something I knew that I would never be able to forget. The sight of her recoiling away from her father with her hands outstretched in an effort to stop her father from stabbing her to death is something that will never leave my memory bank.

My plan is to go get my dad for help. He would know how to handle this. But … I knew if I did that, the odds were good that Binki would not be alive by the time my dad or the cops came. The pain of leaving her and not getting help in time is something that will haunt me forever. I would never be able to live with myself. The sights and sounds of her begging for her life will never leave me. They will not be able to be erased. The guilt will be with me for the rest of my life.

I found myself in the same man's decision that the wicked Wallace just gave his son. Either go get help and live with Binki's certain death. Or go back and help just to be killed myself. The voice in my head is yelling at me that I am free. Nobody will know. I will be a hero. Nobody will know that I made this decision unless I tell them. That is nobody but me. The person who holds me to the highest of standards.

In baseball, you are taught that a full mind equals an empty bat. That same thought applies here. The more I think about it, the harder it will become. I make the decision and go. Standing there does not help the situation, no matter the route I take.

I say a quick prayer, "God, I need you!!"

I reverse course and return. I must save Binki. The curtain of darkness allows me to get close pretty rapidly without the wicked man noticing. Picking up my feet and laying them down as if I were walking on eggshells, I cautiously make my way towards Binki. I could not believe the horror that was coming into focus with every careful step that was taken.

Bill had his hand above his head in a threatening manner. No doubt that hand was ready to plunge his knife into Binki's body. His hand continuously crashed down against her body. Again and again. More violent with every thrust. He is cursing and thrusting with no regard for mercy. I was perplexed that he was not calling her Binki. He is calling her Doris. He is either punishing her for her mom, or he has gone even deeper off the cliff and thinks he is killing his wife.

Then he stops when he sees the lights. The lights are coming from the same place that cars enter and leave at night—the same entrance that he used to use to get here. To his delight, a car slowly comes towards him.

I looked up at the sky and thanked God. He obviously brought Binki's mom here to allow me to save Binki. I used this opportunity to slowly creep up closer to Binki while his attention was diverted.

Terrifying thoughts clouded my mind. What if this car is her mom?

Could this save Binki but get her mom killed? Is he just going to kill everyone?

The intrigued man made his way off the porch to get a better look. Along the way, stepping over Scott's bleeding, motionless body. He has a look of disgust and irritation. As if Scott was dog shit that was on the floor, and he didn't want to get it on his shoes. Frustration resurfaced as the car continued along that path. I gasped. I could not believe it. It didn't stop.

Has God forsaken me? Us? Wait a minute. Could that have been her mom, and she saw her husband but was too scared to stop? Instant dejection. I wanted that car to have Binki's mom inside it. Cold chills ran over my body with the understanding that I wanted her mom to be in the car so I could have time to rescue Binki. Did I just choose her mom's death in hopes of saving Binki's life? Please forgive me, God, for that thought. Wait a minute. Where the hell is God? I need you. Right now.

Binki is lying on the ground with blood all over her face. Swelling and bruises were starting to show. That sight jolted me back into the moment.

She was lying there so helpless, as if she was the chalk line for a scene in a murder mystery. Crying or moaning between each deep, heavy breath.

My eyes caught sight of the knife that was lying a couple of feet from her. I never saw him drop the knife. The light bulb went off in my head. He wasn't stabbing her; he was beating her with his fist. I found relief that she was beaten, not stabbed. What the hell is that? She was beaten and not stabbed. That is the good news? There was no good news because the beating was brutal. He had pelted his own daughter with his bare hands with no empathy for her life. Even the devil could not be that heartless. Could he?

The deranged man once again changed his focus and made his way toward the side of the porch where Mitch had made his escape. He cupped his hands over his eyes to help his vision in the dark.

"Mitch, my man. I know you are out there. You can't leave your sister. Got some bad news. You know you running like that just got your sister and your mom killed."

He continues to bait his son as he ventures off the porch from the side entrance. He stretches out into the dark a short distance in search of his missing family member. Meanwhile, the rats were running as fast as possible on that treadmill inside my brain. I tried mightily to formulate a plan. There is no way Binki can get up and run. I could try to pick Binki up and carry her off to safety. But I would never make it. Maybe he is done beating Binki. Maybe I can go get help before he does further damage. That is what I plan to do. I just need to let Binki know I am not deserting her. Let me tell her that I am going for help.

The objective was to stay out of his sightline but get close enough to tell her that I was going to get help. I crouch down as low as possible.

I peeked over the opposite side wall and softly whispered, "Binki, are you okay?"

Crying and breathing heavily was the only response I received.

"I am going to get help. I am not leaving you. I will be right back," I inform her.

Heavy breathing with cries in between is all I got. Right as I was about to make my run for it, I realized that the heavy breathing was because he knocked her out. She wasn't crying. It was more like a snoring sound. Really loud. I have seen this before. When Mike Tyson knocked out some overmatched jaborandi. I ran to her side and tried to emulate what I have seen boxing doctors do many, many times. Damn it, I couldn't remember what to do first. I lifted her limp body into a sitting position. Put my fingers into her mouth to make sure she didn't swallow her tongue. Is this right? Continuing on, I softly smacked each side of her face in an effort to revive her. If I can wake her, maybe she can run. To my delight, it was working. The satisfaction that she was regaining consciousness suddenly felt hollow as I heard two large, overexaggerated footsteps on the other side of the wooden porch.

"Well, well. Mr. Hero is back," the soulless human said in a playful way as he bent his head from side to side like he was trying to stretch the kinks out of his neck. "You had your chance. I do not feel guilty for what I am about to do. You were warned."

My body was trembling. Fight or flight. The moment is here. I had to stay and fight or run like hell. I knew I could outrun him. That was the safe path.

I looked down and noticed the knife sitting almost within reach. My eyes betrayed me and gave away my plan. My sight path did not escape him.

"That knife won't help. But you can try," said the confident monster. "You don't have balls to use it. You are not a killer. You're the hero." Mocking me as he started walking my way. "I'm the fucking killer!" he added as he slapped his chest.

He got closer and closer, but I was frozen. I heard voices saying run. I heard voices say grab the knife. I heard a voice saying move before you die. But no matter what my brain was saying, my body was not listening.

He kept getting closer, and I never moved. The second time tonight, I just froze. What the heck?

In a sudden surge of adrenaline, I lunged for the knife with my fingers, getting a hold of the blade. But only for a second as my adversary's boot connected with my chin. The force of the kick rattled my brain and sent my body rolling in the opposite direction. Then, a large fist came crashing down on top of me. Followed by another fist. The onslaught of anvils being dropped on me with Mike Tyson-type force and Sugar Ray Leonard-type speed. It seemed to last forever as I caught glimpses of blood flying through the air with each connection. Suddenly, I thought he was walking away when he turned around and planted a boot in the side of my body. The kick felt like it dislodged my lungs as breathing now became a problem. Then he swung his foot again, again, and again. My head felt like an Indian chief was doing a ritual drum routine, and my membrane was the canvas. Thump, Thump, Thump! Taking one single breath felt like an impossible task. And now blood was spewing from my mouth. I'm not sure if it is bloody lips or blood from some internal organs escaping the traumatized torso. Or both.

He hissed at me, "I was wrong. Maybe you are not the hero. You just got a death wish. You are just a dumb shit who didn't know how to mind his own damn business."

He casually makes his way over to the knife. Starts to whistle as he reaches down. Once he picks it up, he throws it in the air and catches it by the handle in an effort to show me that I am no match for him. He has decided that my time has come.

"Didn't have to be this way. You are just a …"

He stopped in his tracks when he heard the car horn blow as a set of headlights came barging in our direction.

Chapter Twenty-Eight - Yugo

The car abruptly slams to an immediate halt and parks on the left side of the truck, which brought the evil. I recognized the car. It was the same Auburn two-door beat-up Yugo that I rode in earlier in the week. The lady that exited may be in her work uniform, but she looks ready for a fight. She is wearing the local pancake house issued employee uniform. Shirt, apron, and even the nametag stating the name Doris. But the item that she had in her hands did not come from the local pancake house. She was not holding a spatula; she was holding a shotgun. The anger and rage in her eyes said that she was ready to dance with the devil.

"Billy Ray Wallace. Look at me," she demands. "You have fucked up," she explains.

Her voice sounds confident, but the shaking of her hands says otherwise. The confidence in her voice is justified. Maybe for the first time in her life, she has the upper hand in a fight between her and her husband.

She continues to give him directions, "Bill. Get in that truck and drive away. Or God as my witness, I will blow your worthless head off its shoulders."

There is an old country saying that says you must match crazy with crazy. I got the feeling that is exactly what she is doing. Good for her, I thought. I bet she has practiced this confrontation in her head a thousand times. Doris had probably hoped upon hope that he would never find her. But her having a shotgun on demand meant that she most likely knew that she could not always hide from this sadist. She knew this day was coming and was going to be prepared.

Quickly, we discovered that this man was not crazy. Describing him as crazy is like calling the Grand Canyon a hole. Crazy was the pre-school stage for the level of insane this man was. He gives his wife his undivided attention as he slowly turns his body to face her as if he is trying to be John Wayne from the movies. There is delight in his voice.

"Looky, Looky! Who just decided to show up?"

Doris responds, "I am not playing. The police are on the way. You decide. You could leave here before they come or leave here in a body bag. That is your choice."

He chuckles.

"Bitch… I don't care about no police. Make no mistake," he hisses. "You are the one leaving here in a body bag. The question is, how many people will be lying beside you in that body bag?" using a slow, taunting cadence, he continues, allowing his knife to be the pointer.

He aims the knife in the direction of each person as he does the roll call, "Scott, your daughter, Captain America over there."

Then he pointed the knife to his own chest.

"Hell, maybe even me. I am prepared to die. Don't really want to. But if that is what it takes… But you…. Yeah… You," he directs the knife in her direction. "I am for sure sending you to hell tonight. Just like I did, your preacher lover!! Bank on that!!!"

He walks to her with no fear. He sees death and is walking right to it!

Doris is suddenly shocked. Though she may have practiced this scene in her head no less than a thousand times, there is no way this carnage was ever in that vision. Especially the one with Binki barely breathing.

"Bill, I am telling you. STOP!" Doris pleads. "Just get in your truck and leave. Please. I need to get your daughter help."

Chill covered my body as blood continued to drain.

I made an effort to encourage him to stop, "Just stop and leave. Please."

That is what I wanted to say but I was not sure if I said that or just thought that.

Then, I realized that I could not have uttered those words. I can barely breathe. If those words left my lips, then I wasted my breath on words when what I need is air in my lungs. No matter, he does not leave. He does not stop.

Without warning, two images came racing from the darkness. They were coming from the campsite side. I could barely see them. My vision started to fail me, but it looked like they were coming closer and fast.

One could be heard screaming, "Leave her the fuck alone," from quite a distance away.

That was most certainly Mitch. But I could not make out the bigger frame right behind him.

Wait. I know who that is. The very instant that my eyes could confirm that my dad was the second image, horror robbed me of any relief because my attention was regained by the actions of the senior Wallace. He had raised the knife over his head. His pace had quickened. He was walking with a purpose and making a beeline straight to Doris.

The curse words were getting louder and closer. It only added to the mayhem of the moment. Fear had made its way to everyone. Everyone, that is, except for Billy Ray Wallace. All Billy Ray Wallace was hearing was white noise, and he was long beyond feelings. He was a missile that had its target in sight. His mission was at the point of no return.

The chaos was beyond maddening as we heard the first sounds of sirens from the police cruiser echoing in the background. Bill remained focused and gathering steam. Doris yelled with her tear-filled eyes for him not to make her do it but insisted that she would. Binki was moaning in pain.

Scott lay on the ground. Most likely dead. Mitch and Dad rapidly joined the mayhem. I thought about trying to get to my feet, but that thought did not result in action. All I could do was just sit there slumped against the building. The world was revolving around me. I concentrated on trying to make the turning stops. The earth slowed down long enough for me to see Bill almost at Doris. Then…. BOOM … The rifle went off.

Chapter Twenty-Nine - Last Dance

It is remarkable how much damage can happen in less than one second. A single shotgun blast only lasts a moment. Yet that is all it took. One second! Actually, less than a second. Sound moves at 1,125 feet per second, and a shotgun pellet goes around 1,100 feet per second. Since the body was about 20 feet away, the shotgun pellets found a home in less than one second. The damage was done before my ears could make my body aware. Before I could react, though, there was nothing I could have done.

I was in a haze. Could not comprehend what had just happened. I thought my eyes were deceiving me. His body recoiled in the opposite direction he was originally going. It lifted him off the ground only to discard him to the earth in a crumpled pile of flesh.

Billy Ray Wallace had made it to Doris almost at the exact same time as she was able to pull the trigger. Though Doris hit someone, she missed her target. Bill's aim was much better. He hit the person he was trying to inflict deathly damage to, but not the spot he was aiming for. The knife was intended to hit the middle of her chest. Either her trying to protect herself subconsciously or the violent jolt from the shotgun twisted Doris's body in a manner that her right arm caught the blade. Not her chest, which was the intended target. The sharp steel lodged deep into her bicep. Almost going completely through her frail arm. The shotgun, or more important, the bullet, was redirected.

The shotgun fell to the ground due to the sudden blast of pain coursing through her body. Doris could not see what she hit. Bill's aggression grew. He was a shark and could smell blood in the water!! Doris did not even try to pick up the gun. She was too busy retreating as Bill secured the knife from her right arm and raised it to inflect more destruction. He brought the knife above his head and, with all his might, forcefully directed it towards his wife. Trying to end her existence with this one blow. His second swing did not find its home as Doris fell to the ground and frantically scooted her body in reverse. The life-or-death situation was dictated by how fast she could move. She hurriedly crawled under the truck in an effort to evade him. Just when her body went out of sight, it reappeared. Bill grabbed her by the ankle and violently pulled her back into his path. Dragging her from under the truck with her face sliding on the pavement.

The sirens were getting louder as the blue lights could be seen coming into sight.

A wicked grin crossed his face. He was pulling her body as if she were the rope in a game of tug-a-war. Doris was screaming as desperation echoed with each sound. She was digging her fingers into the ground, trying to find something to grab hold of. But to no avail.

"You ain't goin' nowhere Bitch" escaped from his lips.

Bill got Doris fully withdrawn from underneath the truck. He picked up the knife and started finishing what he was here to do. He thrust the knife into her back. He did not immediately take it out. But instead, the evil poured out of this creature one more time. Torturing and taunting her, he left the knife in and slowly twisted it from side to side. I felt the pain in her screams, but you could hear the satisfaction in his voice.

"Hope this hurts like hell. I told y…"

A loud thud rang out. Bill collapsed to the ground before he could finish the sentence. Above the devil's body stood Captain America. The real one. My dad had picked up the gun and used the butt as if it were a bat, and Bill's head was the ball.

The swelling was immediate as blood was pouring from the side of his head. Bill quickly gathers what had just happened and accesses the scene.

"What the fuck? I'm going to kill you."

Calm as I have ever seen him, Dad replied in a language I have never heard before.

"You sick bastard. I want you to come towards me." Dad slowed his words and said them as clear as day, "I promise this, Mother Fucker. That step you make will be the last step you ever take."

The sirens were closing in and starting to ricochet in small sound ripples. We could see the lights flickering brighter and brighter, bouncing off the surroundings.

Bill slid back away from my dad and towards the truck. Holding his head as if he could stop the blood from dripping out of it. He gingerly got to his feet with his hand never leaving his head and his eyes never leaving my father's body. Once he reached his feet, he brought his hand from his head. He achieved the confirmation that it was covered in blood. By this time, the blood was falling down his face. The sight of his own blood recaptured his rage once again.

"You will regret this."

Bill slowly started to make his way towards my father. Dad was ready. He brought the butt of the gun back into the air in preparation to swing again. With the same badass tone that Charles Bronson had used many times in the movies, Dad served him another notice.

"One more step. I will hit you again. But this time, I swear to God I will knock your pathic head straight off your shoulders." Just to drive the point home, he added. "Try me, you son of a bitch! Please. Try me."

Billy Ray Wallace stopped in his tracks. The sirens were now blaring, and the lights were approaching rapidly. He reconsidered and abruptly reversed his direction in a hurried, drunken swagger, jumping into the truck. The truck's taillights dissolved into the darkness.

Chapter Thirty - Blue Lights

Dad stood there in a moment of disbelief. Motionless. Most certainly relieved that the man had decided not to press the situation and instead cower away. I wanted to run toward my dad and give him a hug. Shower him with praises. But I, too, was in disbelief as tears were falling from my face. Just overwhelmed by the actions of the night. My head was still ringing. What once were small lines of blood is now a full-fledged faucet leaving my head and falling onto my bare chest. For some reason, I found myself trying to figure out which of the blood that covered my chest was mine and which was Binki's. Or Scott's. Snapping out of it, I tried to get up but fell to the ground. My breathing was getting more painful with every intake and exhale of air. My body was too weak. I just sit there. Leaning against a porch pole with my eyes, trying to follow my dad's every move.

The spinning of the campsite was not helping me. I felt like I was about to go to sleep. Perhaps, pass out.

Dad transitioned from freedom fighter to paramedic seamlessly.

While kneeling down to attend to Doris, he directed me not to move because help was on the way.

I heard him talking to her but could not make out the words. No doubt he was trying to get her to respond. As I had done for Binki earlier, he took off his shirt and tried to use it as a plug to stop the bleeding from the large stab wound in her back.

I shifted my head toward Mitch. He was lying lifelessly on the ground. The shotgun blast had punctured so many places on his skin that it was impossible to spot where the blood was coming from. Was it his head? His Shoulder? His neck? Blood covered all the spots.

The scene was one Wes Craven would have been proud of. That is if this were one of his movies. But this was not the case. This scene was a real nightmare. Doris was bleeding with a large hole in her back. Looked like it was disconnected. She was making noise but not making sense. Binki was moaning. Bruises and cuts hid behind the red liquid that covered her body and was starting to pool around her. Mitch was not moving. Scott was most certainly dead. The world was getting grayer by the second for me.

The approaching lights illuminated the scene but only added to the thunder that was erupting in my head. Each siren blast had a constant ringing. The sound was not that of a throb but a heavy pound.

The police cruiser raced to a stop, and the young officer leaped from his vehicle. I could see the shock on his face. After a moment of assessment, he immediately pulled out his gun. Pointed the police-issued revolver straight at my dad and yelled for him to put his hands in the air.

Dad did not move. He yelled at the officer. The officer was in no mood to listen. Instead, the officer responded with the same instruction as before, only louder this time. The yelling continued, but the pulsation of pain that was beating in my head refrained me from making out the words.

In a moment of clarity shining through the foggy haze that was in my brain, I started to put together the situation. The officer received a call about a domestic violence situation. He sees a woman lying on the ground, bleeding from being stabbed. Mitch, Binki, Scott, and I scatter throughout the place in different states of consciousness. All were critically injured, and a couple of us could be interpreted as possibly dead. Then there is my dad with blood on him. Hoovering over the intended domestic violence victim with the gun and knife lying near his feet. "Oh shit," was my thought, but my head was getting heavy. My breathing became more troublesome, and words could not form loud enough for them to leave my lips. The dark night was getting darker in my head.

I thought I heard the Police yell, "I am not telling you again."

Time was eluding me. I knew my father needed my help, but my body could not move. I was stuck. Just watching in-between moments of consciousness. It felt as if someone was placing a dark tarp over my eyes and then removing it. Only to put it back. Life was flickering on and off. The last thing I remember seeing was a body being put into the back of an ambulance.

Then gray that clouded my eyes went totally black. My body fell limp.

Part Three

Chapter Thirty-One - Alice's Dismay

The horror and dismay in Alice's eyes didn't match the serenity and stillness of the hospital halls near midnight. Bo Hawes's room was most certainly one of the few in the building that still had guests this late at night. Due to Alice and Marcus's status in the complex, nobody was coming to evict them from the premises.

The storytelling injured man stopped to make sure that his audience was still committed to hearing the entirety of the account of events. The events led him to be lying in a hospital bed, fearing a letter bearing his name.

"I told you this may take a while. You guys okay?"

Before the last words broke free from his mouth, Alice responded, "Are you kidding me? I gotta hear the end of this. What happened? Is your dad or mom, okay? Did they catch that horrible human being? Did the girl, Binki. Did she make it? How about the brother? I could not sleep now unless I knew the ending."

Marcus stood and walked towards the window, giving his legs time to get the blood flowing and his head time to gather what he just heard.

Marcus took the approach you may expect from a man of God as opposed to Alice who was responding like she just watched the cliffhanger of some Soap Opera. Marcus's words were measured. The thought that he put into them was almost visible.

"You are here. So, I assume that is one miracle for sure on a night the devil was certainly present."

Bo Hawes took this as a "Please continue from both parties."

Alice could hold her composure no more.

"Son, you need to tell me what happened?"

Bo smiles as he shares that his father was originally placed into custody because the police had mistaken him for Billy Ray Wallace. Once they put the pieces together with the help of a very loud Anita Hawes, he was released.

"That's good," Alice says. "Good, he was white. If that man was black, he would have been shot, and they would have asked questions later."

"Alice Lucielle Wilson," the suddenly angry Marcus responds.

"My bad," she responds. The follow-up of "You know it's true" gets a death stare from Marcus.

"Maybe. But that ain't what God put in this room to discuss," he educates. "Mr. Hawes, please continue."

Bo takes in the moment. This is the first time he put it together. Alice and Marcus are married.

"Y'all married?" he inquires.

Marcus gave me the hand caught in the cookie jar look. "Yes, sir. Twenty-seven years and counting, I have been blessed to have this lady as my bride."

Bo's eyes wandered towards the window, but his vision was somewhere out in space.

"Hmm...if my father hadn't died, they would have been together for 27 years, too."

A confused look landed on both Marcus' and Alice's faces at the same time.

They were both thinking about it, but Alice was the first to ask, "Didn't you say your dad lived that night?"

"To be honest, my dad was the only person I was certain that made it out until recently," Bo revealed.

Frustration is being shown on Alice's face.

"Son, I have been sitting here for a couple of hours, and I have more questions than I did to begin with. What happens to all those people on that night? How did your dad survive that night but is not alive now? Still nothing about this letter or what put you in the hospital, to begin with?"

Right on cue, Marcus starts, "Alice."

But before he finishes, Alice finishes for him. "I know. I know. Corinthians 13 dash 4. Love is patient. Love is kind." Alice leans towards Bo and whispers, "He tells me that all the time."

Marcus chuckles at his wife and confirms, "This is true." He turns his attention to the man lying in the bed. "Now, Mr. Hawes, if you would please continue."

Part Four

Chapter Thirty-Two - Triple Murder Charges

Summer of 1989

The details are foggy, but my parents told me that I was originally taken to the local hospital. The Police advised us to change hospitals once I was stable and granted permission from the medical staff. One that wasn't close to the scene of the chaos. So, they decided to bring us closer to home. Charlotte Medical Hospital.

I suffered 4 broken ribs, several stitches, and a concussion. All healed in time with no lingering effects, with the exception being the concussion.

Which has led to periodic migraines and an intolerance to really loud bangs. I asked about Binki and the others, but my parents kept telling me that they did not know.

Miraculously, Billy Ray Wallace was not caught that night or even the next week. Even though the police felt certain that we were not in danger, it still caused my family a lot of anxiety. There was comfort in the police's position that Bill Wallace did not know any of the Hawes family names or where they were from. No matter, it was still a lot to take in.

My parents tried to keep me from the news. Though I was old enough to stay by myself once I was healed to a certain extent, one of my parents always felt the need to stay with me. One evening in the hospital, Dad and I were watching wrestling. Dad fell asleep, and the news came on right after World Championship Wrestling and Rick Flair and the Horseman putting a beat down on Dusty "The American Dream" Rhodes.

That is when I saw it – the lead story. A picture of Billy Ray Wallace wearing a gang jacket, slicked-back hat, and cigar sticking out of his mouth. Megan Johnson, Channel Nine's Award-Winning News Anchor, said, "The hunt for Billy Ray Wallace is still on. If you see this man, please call Crime Stoppers or dial 911 immediately. This man is wanted in connection to a list of crimes, including three homicides. More right after the break."

Stupid teases. I do not believe news programs should tease news like this. But it worked. Here I am, watching every commercial, waiting until the news comes back to my TV. That was the longest commercial break of all time. Three homicides? The pastor and Scott. Who was the third? His wife, Doris. His son, Mitch. I could not bring myself to name the only other person. Not even in my own mind. No way. Binki? Maybe he killed a police officer trying to evade capture. Maybe he committed another murder before the pastor. Am I wishing for another person to be dead just so Binki would not be? Is that a sin? It can't be. Megan Johnson already said three homicides. That is not on me.

Finally, Megan's face came back into view, and she mercifully went straight to the lead story. She recited the open statement once again, but this time, she shared a picture of the three individuals who were killed by one Billy Ray Wallace. The first picture was the preacher. Megan informed everyone that he led a church just outside of Charlotte and was loved by so many.

Then there was Scott Snuffer. Megan reminded everyone that he was Billy Ray Wallace's daughter's boyfriend at the time of the murder. She continued to share that Scott was a loving son and will be missed.

Which I found as bullshit. But I am certain someone will miss him. The news left out that it was HIS fault that Bill found his family. It was his fault that all this occurred. I am not certain if you could pray someone into hell. But I just tried!! He better have a front-row seat in the pits of hell, I thought. Not that it was my position to judge, but I am pretty sure he was an agent for the bad guy!!

Megan continued. "This man is considered dangerous!! Not only is he wanted for the murder of a preacher and his daughter's boyfriend, but he is also wanted in connection to the murder of his own child. My emotions are wrecked when I see Mitch's picture come on the screen. What I thought would be a relief because it was not Binki, transitioned to a wailing cry. I cried so hard that I woke up my dad. Felt the air in the room evaporated. I could not breathe! Instant nausea led to vomit projectile over the side of my bed.

The vomiting scared my father to the point I saw fear. Which calmed me down in a weird way. I am not used to seeing fear in my father. He literally battled a killer, and I never saw fear. His son was vomiting, and fear was front and center. He came to my rescue once again by calling nurses and moving aside to allow the professionals to do their jobs.

The nurses took my father into the hall far enough away that I could not hear them, but I could see them. I was certainly the topic at hand.

Joe Hawes walked in to have a conversation I could only imagine he dreaded but knew was inevitable. We stayed up the entire night as my father tended to my every need and filled in every gap that I was not aware of.

He informed me that the police said it would be wise to distance ourselves from Binki or her family, just in case Bill Wallace was stalking them and recognized them. We did not want any chance encounters. This was a pointless recommendation because we didn't know where they were. It was even more pointless when Mom and Dad discovered that the Wallace family had also been moved from the original hospital for their own safety.

Dad answered THE question even before I asked, "Son, I was told that Binki is going to live. She and her mom are going to make it. But they are in bad shape, and it will be a long and tough road to recovery. I am not certain what you were expecting." He chokes up, and the vulnerability that makes him such an amazing man comes to the forefront. "Son, I hate to tell you, but I am certain we will never see them again."

Part Five

Chapter Thirty-Three - The Bench and the Bottle

Monday- May 8, 2000 – Seven Days Before Injury

The bench sat between the tombstone with the name Joe Andrew Hawes engraved on it and a lake with ducks splashing about. This bench has been serving as my safe haven as of late. A place of hiding from the problems of the world and chaos of everyday life. A place where I find comfort. Much needed comfort ever since my father's death just six months ago. Nothing makes sense anymore. The world is just closing in on me.

Spring Lakes Cemetery offers the stillness that allows me to reflect on exactly how my life has turned into such a mess.

What has become routine and a key part of my reminiscing, I pull out a small bottle of Smirnoff Vodka from my coat jacket and take a swig in hopes that the bottle will ease some of the pain. Give me answers. Though this path has been tested many times, the bottle never seems to have long-lasting solutions – just short-term remedies that end up compounding the wreck that is my life.

With this in mind, I find myself returning more and more. Mainly because this allows me to talk man-to-man with my father. Our conversations have become more one-sided lately. Anger!! Feels like even my father is getting tired of hearing my voice. Unlike my wife, he cannot tell me to go away. Though I am certain he never would have. He would have the answer. He always did.

Which is why I am getting pissed off more and more with every visit!

I am mad. Why did he leave me? Leave me here to watch over Mom?

That is his job – a job he has done so well for all my life. Now, Mom is alone, and I can't fill the void. Lord knows I have tried. Flowers, dinners, trips. All are bringing her a smile for the moment, which results in her being alone every night. Sad and heartbroken.

Often, I remind him that if he didn't leave me, he could help me with my mess of a marriage. How could I possibly be married to Kimberly Simpson? Of course, I married her years before his passing. But marriage is different now. It has never been as hard as it is now. She is so critical.

Bitches about everything, and the birth of our daughter was a death sentence to our sex life. Sex, hell, she doesn't even want to hold my hand. Little less get naked together!! She goes to bed without even saying good night. No good morning kisses. No random hugs or hand-holding. We are roommates, not lovers. We are convenient to make ends meet. Plain and simple, there is no social life. All she does is go to church and do things for our daughter. I am just there mainly to be the one who can be blamed for anything that goes wrong.

A smile comes across my face while another taste of the problem-solving drink hits my lips. My smile is brought about due to me envisioning my wife's beautiful face yelling at me when she smells the alcohol on my breath. Wait. Is that a vision of the future or a memory of so many scoldings from the past? I get them confused these days. I only take a couple of sips, yet she rants and raves about me always drinking the devil's juice. She reminds me that we could use that money to catch up on our house or car payments. Any generic conversation is always followed by her throwing the bills into my face.

My life sucks. The constant theme. This thought resurfaces once again. More of a confirmation than an opinion these days. Without fail, my father's voice resurfaces in my head. I remember asking him once why he worked so hard. He looked towards Mom and my brothers and said, "That picture right there." Mom and Phillip were cooking while Stevie was licking the cake mix bowl. More cake mix on his face than in his mouth. He continues, "When she said, "I do", I knew I always will. I will always love her and do everything possible to make her happy. Be the man she married. Which ironically matches with being the man I want to be."

How the hell do I live up to that? This hopeless goal just provides me another invitation to ask the bottle for more assistance. This time, I finish the bottle off and stretch my body across the bench to rest my tired eyes.

Chapter Thirty-Four - Too Much

The blue lights illuminated the night as the moon hung brightly in the backdrop. Upon opening my eyes, I notice that more time had elapsed than I thought.

"Shit, not again" came loudly from my lips.

I must have drunk more than I thought.

I heard my dad say, "I was thinking the same Damn thing."

I sit up and recognize the figure in front of me. The image was that of my father's, but it belonged to my uncle. Buster Hawes was a Union County Police Officer and the new resident family patriarch. His time in Germany during the Vietnam War afforded him unquestioned respect within the family and a spot in public service once his duty to his country was complete.

Never one to mince words or beat around the bush, he reprimands, "What the hell are you doing? I can't keep getting these calls!"

Shame takes over my body, but words never left their place. I sat with my head hung as my chin rested on my chest. Emotion has seized my existence, and I can't stop the tears no matter the effort given to hold them in.

My dad's brother drops his body beside mine and puts his arm over my shoulder.

"Trust me, I know the pain."

A moment of silence passes, and he continues, "But son, you are not the only person hurting. I am not saying this to ease your pain. That pain cannot be addressed by words."

Buster's body language became more erect and proper. His voice was more aggressive and sterner. No doubt, these are problem-solving characteristics that he learned during his time in the military and what makes him such a great officer of the law now.

"But son, you got to get your shit together!! Your mom is hurting. Your brothers are hurting. My brothers and sisters are hurting. His friends and family are hurting. Your father's death is the most painful thing I have ever experienced, and I served in the military and lost many friends. I have lost both of my parents, your grandparents. But your father was my hero. He quit school and worked in a cotton field and mill just to help our parents put food on our table. Not only did this feed us, but his sacrifice allowed us to graduate from high school. Hell, we may not have a college degree or some fancy title, but we had a fighting chance that your dad didn't. But no matter the setback of not finishing high school, he married a wonderful woman and built a beautiful life."

Tears swelling in his eyes. They are threatening to escape as the recollection and pain are greater than the heart of the man in the public service attire.

He gathers himself and continues, "But as I said before, you got to get your shit together. You are killing me. Coming here and seeing you in this condition."

272

Buster stops long enough to put flames on his Marlboro. He points to the nearby liquor bottle that had slipped to the ground.

"That has to stop. This self-pity has to stop."

"I think I am going to get let go from my job," I blurt out.

Not letting him continue his good ole country chewing out. Pretty much the same message I heard last time and the time before, with each message getting louder and more forceful.

Buster takes another puff and looks at me. And chuckles.

"By God, I can see why. I think you are lucky that you're getting fired instead of not already gotten fired!! Just look at you now." He does an exaggerated look up and down my body. "I am surprised you still have a job. Getting means you have time to change the situation. I suggest you get your shit together."

Knowing he is right and that he has been right every time before, I choose not to challenge him.

"Com'on! I am going to drive you home," Buster says as he uses his spotlessly clean, government-issued shoe to snuff out the cancer stick.

I find it ironic that he is lecturing me about getting my act together, yet he is still smoking. Years of smoking assisted my father in being diagnosed with cancer, the cause of his death. But I have not consumed enough alcohol to be brave enough to say that to his face. I have a sneaky suspicion my uncle has killed people either in the line of duty or on foreign soil. And that he would not need the gun on his side to kick my ass despite the 20 years or more he has on me.

"I got it," I challenge.

The bewildered policeman responds, "Got what."

I straighten up as much as possible and confidently respond. "I can drive home."

"Son, you have got to be shittin me. If you don't get in that car, I'm gonna–"

"OK. OK!" I concede. Not out of fear but instead knowing that we have had this same conversation numerous times and I have never won. As standard procedure, I give him my keys to allow him to have one of the patrolmen to drop the car off at my house later.

The same route to my house led to the same counseling session. How my dad would be hurt if he saw me like this, and how I have a wife, child, mom, and brothers that are depending on me. He is right about everything he is saying but does not realize that I understand this. My issue is living up to the standards that all the people expect from me. It is just too much.

As we drive up to the house, Buster correctly assesses the situation.

An assessment that police nor military training was needed, "Boy, she looks mad."

"Nothing new," I respond.

I open the door to get out.

"Bo."

I stopped getting out to see what was happening now.

He hands me a stick of gum and says, "Stop giving her reasons to be mad. I mean, even a dumbass like you can see why she is mad. Right?"

"Yeah, thanks," I say as I slam the door and put the gum in my mouth. Take a deep breath and walk towards another lecture about how I am a fuck up!!

Chapter Thirty-Five - Dave's Burger Barn

Word around the office at Trigg Foods is that we may be bought out by a larger restaurant group called Glad Foods Inc., which traditionally means that the employees who work in the restaurants are safe, but that is not the case for the team members who work above store level. Often, the new company does not need the old company's administrative team. They already have a team that does payroll, marketing, and HR. Word is my Real Estate Department Team is most likely one of the groups that will be relieved of their duties.

The change is not because my current company is struggling. Quite the contrary. David Trigg started the burger chain in 1977 known as "Dave's Burger Barn". Now, there are 300 company-owned and franchise locations throughout North and South Carolina. The company is growing strong and has plans to develop in neighboring states. Which is why they hired me a couple of years ago as a Real Estate Consultant. My responsibility is to find people with the money, resources, and desire to buy and operate their own Dave's Burger Barn franchise.

Sifting through the candidates is actually tougher than I originally thought. Dave accurately told me that finding people who can afford the $50,000 franchise fee is not too hard. They will find us. All of them will show desire, or they would not have contacted us. The secret to this being a career for me boils down to two things. One is how comfortable I am telling rich people that they are not rich enough.

People will see the $50,000 fee and think that is doable. They will save or have the means to borrow enough to buy a franchise such as Dave's Burger Barn. But it takes more than the $50,000 price tag. Much more. Especially for Dave.

Dave wants to make sure the prospective buyers have enough discretionary income to pay payroll and food for six months. Which is close to a million dollars and finding people that have an extra million dollars lying around is not so easy. Once again, Dave accurately shares that not all restaurants come out of the gate making money, and he does not want people going broke just because they don't get an immediate return on their investment. He selfishly does not want his company to be associated with franchisees who can't pay their employees or vendors. That would be a black eye on the Dave's Burger Barn brand.

Thus, upon my taking this position, Dave shared, "I have told everyone in your department this exact same thing. This is a great responsibility. You could ruin someone's life. If Dave's Burger Barn allows someone to be a franchise, only for them to claim bankruptcy, I will hold you and your department accountable."

That is the only time I have worked for this company that I have ever heard Dave be hostile. Therefore, I make sure they have the money.

The second secret to success, according to Dave, is to make sure they have the right people in place to build a successful restaurant. Most people who have the money do not comprehend the hard work involved in the restaurant industry. And since they have money, they often lack interest in working all the hours it takes to run a restaurant, most certainly not a chain of them. He emphatically pointed out that they should make sure they have a proven operator. It is not an easy conversation to tell someone with money that they do not understand how a restaurant operates or the hours it takes. Plain and simple, too many people oversimplify the complexity of operating a restaurant and the people skills needed. Making sure each company has this is critical to the brand's growth, and I understood that fully.

I have found my niche and was looking forward to making this my career. Then, the snowball of bad news kept growing when I discovered that old man Dave Trigg put in 22 years and was looking to enjoy the fruits of his labor. Glad Foods Inc. seems to be the company that desires to make this happen by buying him out and taking the concept all over the United States. Most likely, without me.

The direction given to everyone in the company was clear. No matter the rumors, we are still obligated to do the job we are being paid to do.

Giving every effort to stay within the company's graces, I am doing my part by heading to Asheville, NC, for the company summer retreat. When the retreat is over, everyone will be driving back to their homes and resume everyday life. Everyone that is except for me. I will leave the meeting and head to Knoxville, Tennessee, to meet with a potential client that evening.

This was extra credit on my part. When I heard that another person in our department could not make the meeting, I volunteered to step in. I needed the sale. I needed all the money possible. Plus, the good mojo might be needed, given the uncertainty of the future.

The three-day retreat in Asheville is a team-building exercise and the brain trust of HR specialist Calito Thompson. Calito has been with Dave for almost as long as Dave's been in the business. Calito started as a grill cook, and Dave helped him through college, understanding that when he got out of college, he would help Dave run his business. Calito has proven to be a valuable resource. He sold Dave on the idea that if you get the store leaders out of the store a couple of days each year, they could mix a companywide training session under the umbrella of team building. To Calito's credit, it has been a wonderful success.

The format has been the same every year. The company invites every General Manager who runs a Dave's Burger Barn, along with the company's administrative team, to some resort for two nights and three days. The location is normally somewhere in the Carolinas, with the locations shifting from beach to mountains for every conference. No matter the location, the agenda remains the same. People check in at noon on the first day , and the company starts with the first training session or break-out classes for the next couple of hours. That night, they have a companywide dinner in a ballroom with some form of entertainment. The following day has more breakout sessions, but the second night ends with an awards banquet and entertainment. To their credit, the entertainment is normally very good.

The entertainment, too, follows the same footprints. First, there is something motivational, and then normally a musical group that lasts for a couple of hours. Allowing the company to mingle and put their hair down a little. The last day brings a morning training session, and then everyone gathers to allow David Trigg to speak and remind us how amazing and blessed we are. Closing with a yearlong theme resembling "Be Better" or "Don't Settle". The company then provides a farewell lunch, and everyone is gone by 2 pm, allowing everyone to be home before dark. That is except for me. I will be heading to Knoxville in an effort to get what maybe one of my last "$5,000 Finder Fee Bonuses" that is given if I find a franchisee that stays for 3 years or more. I must wait three years to get it, but it is still paid whether I am with the company or not.

The convention is held during the week because the weekdays are the non-peak days in the restaurant industry. So, the meeting starts on a Tuesday and ends on a Thursday. This scheduling allows the General Managers the opportunity to get back home in time for them to assist their units with the chaos of restaurant life on a weekend.

Being in an administrative position, my schedule this week is not different than that of a typical week for the most part. I spend about four to five days a week on the road. Which I admit does not help my marriage in a relationship-building way, but it does help me pay the bills. Well, pay enough to be behind but not evicted. I guess. Holding my head above water is better than drowning, or am I just drowning? Just a slower death. To think about it, would it be better if someone just tied an anchor to me and dropped me to the bottom of the deepest part of the ocean?

Chapter Thirty-Six – Drive Time

Tuesday -May 9, 2000 – Six days before Injury

It is a three-hour drive from my home in Indian Trail, North Carolina, to Asheville, North Carolina. Since Asheville is the destination of the day, I decide to leave at eight am in order to compose myself and hobnob with upper management upon my arrival. Which suited me just well. I was up and gone before Kimberly was awake and complaining.

I like the drive time. It gives me time to think and look out the window to appreciate what wonders God has placed here for us to admire and enjoy. The moment God enters my thoughts, I cannot help but wonder why he has forsaken me. I have always been a good man. Treated people right. Yet it feels like he is just constantly throwing challenges my way.

When I speak to any church representatives, they always say the same thing. God would never give you more that you can handle. I wish he would consult with me because I am not only overwhelmed, currently I am stuck under an avalanche.

I have bills I cannot pay. A mom that is lonely. And I have a marriage that is nothing like I wanted. Just when I think that is as bad as it gets, I find out that I may not have a job to bring in money for the bills I already cannot pay.

Reverting my thoughts back to my marriage, I am confused to where it went wrong. I honestly can't find the moment, but I know this is not what I wanted from a marriage. She is not bad, just not interested. She is a good God-Fearing person and a great mom. But there is no excitement. If we are not doing church events or things for our daughter, we are just sitting at home. Two different rooms, watching two different TVs. I watch sports, and she watches some religious channels. There is no sex life. Hell, I don't even think there is a love life. Never a "Love You" randomly leaving either mouths or a show of affection. In fact, I think when we accidentally touch, we are more likely to apologize for inconveniencing the other than acknowledge that this may be cupid, giving us a chance to ignite sparks. Sex is an obligation via our marital vows. No different than someone who has to pay the rent every month. We paid on time because we were supposed to. But nothing extra is given.

As fate would have it, my Nokia 3310 started to ring. The company issued cell phone was one of the first to hit the market and Dave made sure his team had one. He said because he wanted his team to keep up with the times, I swear it is because he wants to be able to reach us no matter the day or time. My house number shows up on the screen.

I have told Kimberly that the company doesn't like me using the new cell phone for personal reasons, but I swear she doesn't even seem to listen. Or maybe she knows this is not the truth. Dave has told us many times that since people in my position stay on the road so much, to make sure we keep in touch with those we are working hard for. Our family. Dave truly lives the family motto he preaches. Guess I am fortunate in that regard.

Either way, I am not answering this call. Pretty sure this will be a good ole fashion earful about my actions of the night before. Kimberly has had time to call daddy and speak with God. Now she is ready to rain down a verbal punishment that any southern Baptist preacher would be proud of.

This thought reconfirms the original plan. I choose to ignore the rings and go on my marry way. If it is important, she will call me back. Or call the resort because I told her where we were staying. Either way, I can't handle her right now. I'll just blame it on the connection. She won't believe me, but it allows me to defer the bitching for a little while.

Before long, I find myself pulling up to a sign stating that I have reached my destination. The Hiwassee Club and Resort did their part in making us feel appreciated by placing several banners along the path to the registration desk that welcomed all Dave's Burger Barn employees.

The resort had villas and rooms that spread along the beaches of Lake Junaluska. Every thirty feet were piers that stretched across the top of the water with benches, some of which ended with the pier being covered by a Gazebo. The villas were often reserved for upper management, and since I had not achieved that status, I resorted to a room on the third floor of the hotel portion of the campus.

Upon registration, I went to the room and gathered my notebook, which I would use to collect the teaching for each breakout session. I grabbed my Dave's Burger Barn embroidered notebook and was starting to walk out when I remembered that I had forgotten the agenda and map that was given out as part of the welcome package. The yellow page had information that covered both sides of the paper. One was a huge map of the place. The second was the itinerary for everyone. I must admit that the schedule for the day did not seem too bad. After two breakout sessions, we would finish our night with a Lakeside Luau. The directions in bold italic were to "Dress comfortable but not provocative for the Luau". There was a live band called "The Hawaiian Party People" and an open bar.

I peek to see what is scheduled for tomorrow evening's events. After four breakout sessions with lunch occurring in the middle of the training classes, once again, Dave's Team is having the evening event outside if weather permits. The menu includes maple glazed pork or oven-roasted salmon as the main course, with each being partnered with a salad, roasted potatoes, and seasoned vegetables. The dessert is strawberry and cream white cake. I have to admit, that is pretty strong. Dave and his team are going all out. After the awards banquet was a guest motivational speaker, a North Carolina-born author named Ann Chaney, and a musical group out of Tennessee named The Rusty Bucket Band.

The awards banquet made me think. They often give out awards to different departments in the administrative branch. If they give my department an award, I might be the winner. This would be a very nice addition to my resume if I get laid off. Even better, it would be a feather in my cap if they are looking for people to stay. After all, I have had a very nice year with regard to gaining new clients.

Chapter Thirty-Seven - Awards Banquet

Wednesday – March 10, 2000 – Five days before Injury

The restaurant business is filled with hard working, decent people that are just trying to make a living and provide for their family. The average person does not realize the work and intelligence it takes to operate a business that makes two to five million dollars a year. Some restaurants even more. I once heard Dave tell a group of managers to go out and ask their friends if they manage a company that serves 100,000 customers per year or does two million dollars annually. Nobody could ever argue that Dave valued his team. The resort he had this convention at was confirmation of that appreciation.

After two days that included seven breakout or team-building sessions, the team was looking forward to the final night of the events, and the company obviously worked hard to make sure our last night together was a memorable one. The Awards Banquet portion was our company's version of a black-tie event. It is a night to shake off the world's perception of just a burger flipper and embrace the stance of businessmen and women who operate multi-million-dollar making machines.

Tonight, everyone came dressed in their most elegant or professional attire. All were smiling as we stood along the lakeside entrance to the outside theater. You could see the lights reflecting off the water and hear the soft music of Kenny G effortlessly free flowing through the air.

As we gained entrance, every person was given a goody bag that had a lot of company swag like towels, pens, and notebooks that all bore the Dave's Burger Barn logo. Along with the swag came the seating assignment. I stepped into the outside theater and immediately felt the appreciation that Dave was trying to share. His message was that we were more than restaurant employees; instead, business leaders were heard loud and clear.

The large patio had tables covered in white cloth and waiters that looked like they were borrowed from the White House Staff. Each table had a beautiful flower bouquet that was sitting inside a vase that probably cost more than my weekly salary. Stringed lights and soft music only enhanced the ambiance. The cost of this had to be outrageous. I could not help but think this was Dave's farewell and thank you dinner.

The tables sit below a cloudless star-filled sky between the lake and the stage. The image was something straight out of a glamour magazine. My table was 5A. What I gathered was the fifth seat on the front row, and the "A" was for the first row of the aisle. Nevertheless, it was in a corner away from the action of the stage but close to the restroom and the lake, which was okay with me.

As per protocol for anyone that has been assigned sitting, I make a quick incognito check of who and where everyone was sitting at my table. To the right was Trevor Mantz, the head of Public Relations.

"Okay, he is a cool guy," I silently say to myself.

He likes to talk. Not best friends, but we talk. I look to my left, and there is Calito Thompson, the HR specialist. Awe hell!! Now, I really have to watch what I say and make sure I do not partake in too much of that devil's juice. I kept inspecting and see the nametags of guest speaker Ann Chaney, then Stacy Roberts and Alora Long, who were store operators from Gastonia and Tabor City, respectively. Man, I really got to be on my best behavior with Calito sitting near me.

Recollecting a conversation once with my supervisor, I was reminded that the company often would put people winning awards closer to the front to help expedite the evening. This had me thinking whether or not I was sitting in the award-winning section of the audience. After all, Calito was sitting near me, which had to help my chances. Didn't take too long before I convinced myself that I would be receiving an award tonight. No way they would have me at this table without good reason. I am contemplating what award I could receive.

It felt weird that Alora, Stacy, and I were the only ones sitting at the table. We acknowledge each other as the crowd starts to hush. The images of Dave and Calito on the stage signaled that the events of the night were about to kick off. Calito addressed the group with a quick welcome and thanked everyone for showing up. As if we really had an option. He made a couple of jokes that could be best described as dad jokes and then turned the audience over to Dave. Who reminded everyone how blessed we are to be working with so many amazing people and in a company that is thriving. He reminds us that this success is all due to our hard work. He thanked everyone from the bottom of his heart and then went into his traditional pre-congratulatory speech.

The celebration moves forward as the MC of the evening and Calito's right-hand man, Sabastion Carr, told everyone the agenda for the evening. He shared that hors d'oeuvre and drinks will be served through the first two portions of the event. Then dinner and dessert will be served and followed by the main attraction, The Rusty Bucket Band. I felt like he was looking at me with the reminder to drink responsible and that this is a corporate event.

Calito finds his chair for the first time tonight. He takes off his coat jacket and asks me where my friend is. I was not sure how to answer.

Though I know Trevor, we are not friends. I'm not sure why he thinks we are friends. I did not want to get him in trouble with HR, so I just responded that I am certain that he will be here soon. He looks at me weirdly and then turns his conversation to Alora.

A waiter came over and whispered something in Calito's ear, and he seemed relieved.

Calito leaned over to me and said, "Your friend is running late. They will be here before the awards banquet ends."

I want to say, dude, I really don't know Trevor that well, but I feel that correcting someone in HR might not be the wise move. Especially when my department is already on shaky grounds. I need every good reference possible.

I choose to show restraint and say, "Thanks. I was worried."

"Me too. Holy Cow," Calito responds.

I give Sabastion my full attention because I do not want to miss my name being called out. Each time the waiter asks if I want a drink, I just stick with the sweet tea. Especially with Calito literally sitting a couple of feet from me.

The entire awards ceremony came and went without my name even being mentioned. What the hell? Not sure why I was so hurt. I am not sure what award I was expecting to win. Then I think, just my luck. I do not have any idea how I thought I could win anything. I managed to gather enough courage to ask Calito if anyone in my department had ever won an award. I turned my head to ask, but that same waiter was talking in his ear once again. As soon as the waiter left, Calito followed. He got up and bolted through a door that led to the backstage area.

Chapter Thirty-Eight - Vodka Tonic

The depression enflamed me. The waiter came by once again and asked me if I would like a refill of tea. This time, sweet tea will not do it. A Vodka Tonic is in my hand, and I slam it as fast as possible. I catch the waiter and tell them to bring me another.

I heard, "Dude, slow down."

I looked around and saw Alora looking at me, but Stacy's attention was on the stage. That was a man's voice.

She didn't say that. I turn to my right and Trevor is taking off his jacket to have a seat.

Trying to play it cool, "Hey, man. What's going on?"

"Not much," Trevor responds. "I'm not trying to be nosey, but you can't slam drinks here, man. This is the wrong place and definitely the wrong table."

I look around again and see Alora looking at me as if she agrees with Trevor.

I respond, "Don't worry. That was just my first of the night." Deciding he was right, I add. "One more is all I'm going to get, and back to sweet tea it is."

Trevor is apprehensive but concedes, "Good. I have seen a couple of good people through my years lose their jobs at events like this. I wasn't here, but I bet they put out a reminder that this was a company event at the beginning."

Calito's voice comes across the stage, recapping the events as I responded, "No, you weren't here, but you are correct."

Timed almost perfectly, the waiter brings the second Vodka Tonic and puts it in front of me. Trevor gives me the "watch it" look.

Changing the subject, "So where have you been? Missed the whole awards ceremony."

Trevor laughs, "I wasn't winning, first of all. That is why they sent me to pick."

Calito's introduction drowned out Trevor's voice, and I could not make out what he was saying. All I could hear was Calito saying, "Please welcome motivational speaker and author Ann Chaney to the stage."

Everyone in the company stood to their feet and gave a standing ovation. Which is the customary greeting for our company, no matter the guest. While joining the crowd in the applause, I asked Trevor to repeat what he said. This time, Trevor leans over to me and repeats it loud enough for me to hear. This time, I heard what he said but did not understand it.

"I had to pick up your friend. The one on the stage."

He nods his head to the guest speaker, Ann Chaney.

As I turned my head to see my unknown friend, I heard Calito say, "Ann wrote the best-selling book, 'The Promise of Tomorrow'."

All blood left my body. I fell to my seat and had the Vodka Tonic in my hand before I knew it. Draining the entire glass without a care who was watching.

My ears heard, "Dude, what did I tell you."

But my focus was on the speaker who was on the stage. Of course, I did not know anyone by the name of Ann Chaney. But I did, in fact, know this woman. I knew her as Binki Wallace.

Chapter Thirty-Nine - The Return

She was absolutely stunning. Dressed in brown business casual slacks with a black belt and a thin white V-neck shirt. Her gold watch around her wrist, and the necklace that hung around her neck implied recent success.

She stood proud and looked in total control.

Ann thanked the crowd and started her speech, "My name as a writer is Ann Chaney." She looks directly at me. "But my friends call me Binki."

I thought I saw tears building in her eyes. But I am certain that I was mistaken. My vision was too clouded by the shock that was erupting from my eyes. She explains that her real name is Billy Ann Chaney. After the events that she is about to recant, she drops her dad's last name and adopts her mom's maiden name.

She informs, "By the end of the night, I think you will understand why."

She diverts her vision away from me and finds the crowd discovering her professionalism as a speaker and hits her stride. She tells the story of her life. Just as I remember it. Meanwhile, I ask the waiter for my third Vodka Tonic of the night. Much to the displeasure of Trevor. Pretty sure Alora's accusatory glare was not one of support either. But right now, I could not give two shits. I needed vodka to come in and rescue me. Give me the momentary support just like it had done in the past. To hell with the long-term problems it caused. I need to get through the night.

Within a matter of minutes, my next serving of the devil's juice was in front of me.

Trevor gets up and disappears. This had no effect on me because my body could not find the ability to move if I wanted it to. It was in shock.

There she was. Truly the woman of my dreams, walking back and forth across the stage. Totally captivating the audience. Telling her story. Wait, that is our story word for word.

Trevor returns and leans over to me. Waking me up from my trance.

"So, how do you know her?"

Before I could answer, Calito interrupts. For some reason, taking it upon himself to answer for me.

"Be quiet. We can talk afterward. Let's hear what she has to say. We can discuss this later."

Am I taking that long to answer questions? Wait, did he say "We"? What part of "We" is he? How the hell would he know about "We"? As I down the glass of liquor in front of me, I decide that Calito is right. I think I need to hear what she has to say.

The scenes that were buried in my mind were brought to life with every word that came from her mouth. It was not an audible story I was hearing, but instead, a visual movie that was being replayed in my head. The account was perfect. Not one detail was left out. The only difference was the names. Instead of Bo Hawes, my part was played by someone named Brad Harvey.

She shared parts even I was unaware of. For example, I learned that the night she made "the call," and I had no idea where she was, she went to the cliff called Suicide Slide with the goal of taking the plunge. She was just going to jump. End all the pain. Life was too hard. All the drama was just more than she could stand. But before she took the dive of death, she decided first to say goodbye to all those she cared about. She shared that she had already written the note to her mom and Mitch. Brad Harvey was her last stop before she was going to make the fatal jump.

She said when she went to say goodbye, Brad (ME) brought her a feather and asked her to go out and dance. She said this made her think. She was going to have one last night. Then leave this screwed-up world. Afterall, "Hell could wait a couple more hours," was her exact thought.

Binky said this night saved her life. More precisely, the talk along the walk toward the dance hall did. She openly recants every topic and every insecurity. Then she opens up and shares that this one talk, one walk, saved her life spiritually and physically. She learned about the possibilities with God in her heart. And the promise of a better tomorrow is indeed possible, through God. She shared that she thinks God spoke to her that night through me when she heard that she has a choice between the "promise of tomorrow or the pain of yesterday." That was the moment. At that moment, she knew that God was real. She felt his arms embrace her. The sounds of the night were coming from my mouth, but the voice she heard was that of the almighty. She said that simple, caring talk was her way of knowing that destiny had her on the right path.

The emotions started to make eyes puff throughout the crowd.

Napkins being used to gently wipe cheeks were a common site. Just like rain on a hot summer day, tears were inevitably coming. I was no exception.

After reciting the horrific reunion with her father that led to her brother's and ex-boyfriend's death, she speaks of the unimaginable physical damage done to her and her mom. She has the crowd captivated. Feeling every emotion as if they were there that hot summer night ten years ago.

Feeling the terror, then depression and hopelessness. They, too, had the infections from the rusty knife. The punctured lung, broken wrist, broken blood vessels, and nerve damage to the brain kept Binki and her mom in the hospital for almost a year after the attack. She informed the crowds of physical damages that to this day need attention.

She also shares that even though her dad was caught six months after the attack, it took years for Binki and her mom to feel comfortable. She admits that they both still may struggle with trust. Her psychologist said that she suffers from derealization. A feeling that one's surroundings are not real.

Derealization. That is the state that I am in right now. Is this real?

Chapter Forty - Q & A

To hear this story brought to life through Binki's words was mesmerizing. The crowd was awestruck and thought her story was about over. In reality, she had truly saved the best for last via visual proof. She reached under the podium and revealed a dark brown 8 by 10 picture frame.

"Anytime I wonder if God is real, I just look at this frame."

She turned the frame so the image was facing the crowd and held it above her head. Most of the crowd had no idea what was in the frame. Which only had them anticipating what was to come next.

She starts, "This is a simple 8 by 10 picture frame that I got from Wal-Mart. But inside this frame, behind the glass…. is a reminder of where I was. A reminder of the road I was heading down."

She turns the image towards her as if she needed some form of reminder. Does a dramatic pause before starting back up. Everyone could tell that something very special was being held in her hands.

"That was before I felt the warm embrace of my savior."

You could see tears running down her face. She gathers herself.

"Every night, I promise myself I am not going to cry. Every night, I cry."

She laughs and wipes away the tears.

"You see. Inside this frame is the suicide note that I wrote to my mom and my brother. A nurse found this blood-stained note inside my pocket the night I was beaten almost to death by my dad. Science says it is my blood. I see the blood of Christ. Forgiving me of all my sins. Showing me that he loves me. Allowing me to be reborn. To have a new life. One of purpose. This is why I stand here today."

Binki brings the story to a happy ending. Afterall, her story truly is a happy story. She finishes her speech with the prevailing thought that love outweighs hate. Love is strong enough to overcome any obstacle. Giving love is something we should strive to share daily. Because it is the love of a person, she only knew for less than a week, that gave her the promise of tomorrow. That love introduced her to the ultimate savior. The only man she now calls father. And that is her heavenly father.

Her last words being, "God is real. I would like each of you to choose the promise of tomorrow over the pain of yesterday."

Some eyes were filled with tears. Most mouths shined with smiles. No doubt, every heart was touched as the crowd stood once again to give her a standing ovation. An ovation that she genuinely deserved. Dave walks to the stage and asks for the book that she had been holding during the entire speech. He holds it up to the sky and proclaims that proceeds for every book sold goes to help victims of spousal abuse. Then shares that he has agreed to purchase each person sitting in attendance tonight a copy of the book, "The Promise of Tomorrow". This gains a shocked look on Binki's face and another round of hand clapping. This time even louder with some people yelling "Thank you" and "Praise God" as hands lifted into the night air.

298

Dave informs everyone that dinner is almost ready, and the staff will be bringing the food around. While the wait staff is setting each table for dinner, Ann Chaney will be taking questions. Hands appear in the sky faster than a cat with firecrackers tied to its tail.

Trevor leans over, "How do you know her?"

I did not respond. I wasn't sure how to respond. I heard her in the background answering a question about her mom and how her mom is doing now, but I did not hear Binki's response. I had questions, too, but my first question was to my company. How did she end up here?

This puzzles me. It didn't make sense! I have never shared this aspect of my life with anyone outside of my best friends and immediate family. Hell, my own wife only knows the bare minimum. How dad saved someone's life.

"How did she…. I mean, why?"

I had so many questions for so many people. I was not sure which one or who to ask first. Everything was running together.

Trevor was waiting for the answer, but I decided to go a different route. Maybe it was the vodka taking control, but I had to know. With an accusatory tone, I direct my attention to the head of the HR department.

"How did she end up on that stage? How did you find her?"

Calito responded with excitement. This time, sharing the news with the entire table.

"It's quite an interesting story," he starts in a loud enough voice to gain everyone's attention.

299

This was not needed. Everyone was already interested.

"She found us. Every year, our team searches for a motivational speaker to do this event. We did not have one this year. Ann's..."

I interrupted to correct him, "It's Binki."

"What?" Calito questions.

"Her name is Binki," I realize I said more aggressively than needed.

"Okay?" Offended, Calito continues. "Binki's agent called us a couple of months ago. Said she had a motivational speaker who has spoken all over the country and would like the opportunity to speak to our company. That is not too unusual. After all, we use these types of people every year. She asked if we ever did corporate events."

He looks towards the stage and sees Dave waving him to come and take his place.

"Duty calls. I will share the rest when I return," Calito says as he runs to man his position as Dave's replacement.

A lady in the front asked, "Have you ever seen Brad since that day?"

Binki looks at me for only a moment, then back to the lady, "I have not been that fortunate."

Everyone in the crowd sighs in disappointment.

The lady's response was the one I should have made, "You should find him. You know. I think you were meant to be together."

Binki blushes and says nothing as she smiles. Not before taking another glance in my direction. I smile back. This time, I think Trevor caught the interaction.

With a curious glance, "Dude. How do you know her?" Trevor asked again.

Once again, I ignore him. I needed isolation but wanted to hear her answer the questions. Also, I knew that Trevor's suspicion would only grow if he continued to catch our non-verbal communication. The communication that I now was seeking. I excused myself without looking in Trevor's direction. I caught her following me to see where I would end up.

I found a bench near the lake. It was away from the tables and Trevor and yet still part of the crowd. Most important, close enough to hear her voice. That same voice that has echoed in my head for ten years. The voice of an angel.

Now Calito has a helper. A buff kid named Dawson from his department. Dawson is walking through the crowd with a microphone in hand with the goal of allowing the people on the stage and the crowd to hear the questions without having to be constantly repeated. I cannot help but notice her beauty as she so elegantly answered each question. Taking time to be attentive to everyone in the crowd and the crowd eating up every word that left those lips.

Those lips. The set of lips whose touch has never been matched.

Never did I doubt that if things were different, we would be together. I waited years for her before I finally agreed to marry Kimberly. Years I waited. All that time. Wondering where she was and the uncontrollable misery of not knowing. To this day, she has provided a love that has never been equaled.

Negativity once again shows his face. My mind drifts. Is this God's way of playing a mean trick on me? Is God punishing me? I am here all miserable. Trapped in a loveless marriage, and there she is. So happy. So beautiful. Looking so content.

The questions keep coming, and I am pissed off that people are asking questions about my life. I think if anyone deserves answers, it is me. Why didn't she ever look me up? Then the realization hits me. Maybe I was the only one who thought we were meant to be together. Maybe I was just the boyfriend for the week.

Calito tells the crowd that it is time for one last question as he reminds everyone that Ann needs to eat too. There are still a large number of hands in the air. I make the decision to allow my hands to join the others in the air. My bench is sitting in the back of the center aisle. Hands are all around me. All in front of me. I raise my hand higher. Swinging it side to side. He has to see me. I see Dawson running in my direction. My heart is pumping, and adrenaline is flowing.

Boom, the Bo Hawes luck kicks in!! Dawson hands the microphone to someone I am not familiar with. The short, stocky woman shares her appreciation for Binki and thanks her for her bravery and words of wisdom. She tells her that God must have his hand on her in order for her to be sitting here today, sharing her story with everyone. Then she asked the question.

The question I should have thought of. The question that was better than the one I was going to ask.

"If you were to see Brad today, what would you tell him?" the lady asked as if she were reading some teen love magazine.

Without hesitation, she smiles and looks straight down the middle of the crowd. The crowd thinks she is looking into the lake or into the darkness of the night. But they are all wrong. Her hypnotic eyes were no doubt on me. Her voice is bypassing my body and talking directly to my soul.

"Thank you for asking. I would tell him that I love him." Her voice starts to shake as she continues, "Tell him that I always have. Not one day has passed that he wasn't in my every thought. Tell him that he saved my life spiritually and physically. If he stood before me today, I would tell him that my wait for him is over. If he were here right now, I would tell him to come home with me. Where he belongs. No matter what is happening now, our promise for tomorrow is so much better together than apart."

Those words license the crowd to give a unified "Awe". The tears flowing down her cheeks imprisoned their hearts as they once again showed affection by giving her another standing salute via pounding their hands together.

The whole situation was almost too much for me. It engulfed my heart with love. Love that I was meant to receive. Love that I have been missing for ten years. That was said on my behalf. She wants me. That is my love story. I wanted to run up to the stage and hug her.

Tell her that I, too, love her. Always have. Always will. And yes! Tell her yes. Yes, I want to go home with you.

But it's not that simple. Instead, Calito is the one hugging the woman of my dreams. Though professional in nature, he is hugging the woman that is supposed to be mine. Talking to the lips, that I have longed to touch. I fall back to the bench as she makes her way across the stage. Exiting the same side that she entered.

Chapter Forty-One - Dinner Time

I sat on the bench for a while, gathering my thoughts, and then I noticed some of my co-workers were starting to look at me weirdly. I jumped to my feet and was making my way to my table when I saw Binki already there, shaking everyone's hands. I decided I would make a pitstop at the restroom to compose myself for the introduction. I splashed water on my face and was trying to envision how exactly this reunion was supposed to go.

Obviously, they do not know I am the "Brad" that she is speaking of. Wonder how she told them she knew me. I decided that I would go and act like a friend and somehow allow her to share how we met. If the question comes up, which is almost certain with Trevor, I will allow her to answer. I checked myself once again in the mirror and walked out to reintroduce myself to the woman of my dreams.

Before I even reached the table, I heard my new best friend, Trevor, announce my arrival.

"There he is," he said.

Binki got up and gave me a quick hug, and I could smell the hypnotic scent of her perfume once again. The smell was somewhere between flowers and strawberries.

She whispered in my ear, "I missed you. Don't be mad. Let's talk later." Then, louder and for the benefit of the people at the table, "It's so nice to see you again."

"I was just telling them that I haven't seen you since high school."

As she had done several times in the past, she seemed to know my concern and put it to rest rather quickly. So, we went to high school together. Hmm... Works for me. I confirmed her story and took my seat.

Being so close to her and not being able to ask what I wanted or hold her like I wanted was like being stranded in the desert, dying of dehydration with a bottle of ice-cold water fingertips away. But you just cannot grab it! It felt like hell. Like torment. She was just smiling and answering every question as the salmon and salad were quickly disappearing from my plate. I learned that she lives in Charlottesville, Virginia. Volunteers at a shelter for battered women. The book has done very well for her and is making her a lot of money. So well, in fact, that she has reached a deal with the publishing agency to write three more. The deal came with an advance and was enough money to allow her to quit her job at UPS and focus on becoming a writer full time. Her next book will detail the lives of some of the battered women who live in the shelter she is working at.

Meanwhile, I am a mess. How could she say that on the stage and then just sit right beside me? Like I am just another person in the crowd. Another person at the table. Then again, what did I expect her to do? Jump on me and make love. Confess her undying love in front of everyone. Well, I guess that is exactly what she did. Confess her love. That brought a smile to my face as I took a bite of the seasoned vegetables.

But the smile was temporary. What does this mean? Does she really expect me to just pick up and leave with her? Then, a peaceful, relaxed, cold breeze came over my body when I realized that I think this is exactly what I want to do. After all, I have a loveless marriage. Bills I can't afford. And a job that may soon be kicking me to the curb. The thought excited me and scared me at the same time.

I lean over to Trevor, "Man, this waiter stinks. I am certain that I have asked about my Vodka Tonic three or four times, and they keep saying they forgot. Who the hell forgets that many times?"

"Dude, don't be mad." There is a nervous tone to his voice. "But I told them to stop. I was worried about you. You were slamming them down."

I was offended. Steaming mad. I was about to scold him when I heard Binki say something that totally derailed me. She was answering a question from Alora. I did not have to hear the question to know it. The answer told me the question.

Binki was looking at Alora, but she was talking to me, "As I said on the stage. I love him. But if I met him and he was happy with his life. I would move forward. I would not like it, but I would accept it." A moment of silence passed. She gathered her words and continued, "But if…" She left that hanging. Did not continue.

I couldn't help myself.

I asked, "If what?"

Noticing that Binki was enjoying this game, she answered, "Well. I will cross that bridge when and if that day comes."

With a smile on her face, she gives the food her attention and stabs her fork into the salad.

A vodka tonic was no longer needed. I just realized that I found my vice. The thing I need. The thing I have been needing for the past ten years of my life.

While we were eating, a team transferred the stage from an awards banquet to what could be a country music dance hall. It is a scene straight out of the Old West. Full of every stereotypical item that you might see on Gunsmoke or Bonanza. The spotlight came to life with Sebastian standing in the middle of the stage.

"Ladies and Gentlemen, it is my pleasure to welcome Buddy, Richard, Bobby, Jeanette, and Celina, better known as 'The Rusty Bucket Band', to the stage. Let's show them some love."

As the crowds welcome another form of entertainment to the stage, the band hits the stage and starts out with a bang, playing "Nothing but the Taillights" by Clint Black. Which immediately got people's hearts racing. It is a fun, upbeat song that generated excitement and movement.

People started getting up and mingling. Some were dancing in the open spot near the stage while others moved back towards the lake to get more room. But it was obvious that people were ready to move around. This included everyone at our table except for Binki and I. Weird that we had been sitting at the same table for an hour. The entire time I wanted this. Just her and I. Now I had it, and words escaped me. She was just sitting there.

Being beautiful but quiet. Then I understood. Her appearance tonight was her move. She found a way to tell me how she felt. Now it's my turn.

With all that weighing on my mind, "Hello" was all that left my mouth.

She laughed and said, "Let's get out of here. Go somewhere we can talk."

For the second time in an hour, she seemed to know my concern and came to my rescue.

Chapter Forty-Two - Gazebo

The music was dancing in the air. The moonlight majestically reflecting off the lake with North Carolina's greenest trees as a backdrop was a sight and ambiance that could only be described as picture-perfect. But all was not right. Though the image from the outside of my body was picture-perfect. Calm and serene. Tranquill beauty at its best. Yet, the action happening inside my body was anything but calm. Every part of my body felt as if it was moving at the speed of light. Hands noticeably shaking and mind racing. Questions were popping into my mind so fast. I could not settle on one question before a better one came to the forefront. I decided to be patient and not bombard her. After all, we have all night. I think.

We walked along the waterline of the Lake slowly. Making small talk about the conference and the people that I work with. Eventually making our way onto a pier that hung over the water with a Gazebo sitting where the wooden structure stopped. The randomness of our conversation made it apparent that we were both avoiding the topic. The topic that we both wanted to discuss. I needed to discuss this. But neither could find the transition. Instead, we stayed safe. Raved about how good the band was. Agreeing that they are destined for a bright future that no doubt will sell out stadiums all across the country.

The conversation got more personal when she inquired about my position with the company and exactly what were my job responsibilities. The stars that were hanging in the sky were almost at arm's reach. The Rusty Bucket Band version of Tim McGraw's 'Just to See You Smile' was loud enough to hear, but far enough away not to infringe on our conversation.

"Ironic, isn't it?" I asked. "Here we are. On top of the water, under the stars, in the mountains of NC. Again."

Binki smiled and said, "Unbelievable. Kinda like God wanted this."

For ten years, I have wanted this moment. Wanted to hear those words. My body felt the excitement. The same attraction and feeling it possessed when I was a fifteen-year-old boy. The words "Kinda like God wanted this" crept through my ears and landed on my heart. She was right. For the first time in a long time, I feel like I am where I belong.

I wasn't sure what to say next but instantly wished I would have chosen something better than, "You know a lot has changed."

"I know," she responded with a deep exhale.

An exhale that unveiled the tiresomeness of the long journey she has traveled the past ten years.

After a moment of thought, Binki directed an inquisitive eye in my direction and added, "Obviously, a lot has changed."

For a moment, all was still as we both pondered the changes internally. A fish jumping in the distance, causing a ripple in the water, seemed to break the stillness of the night. We had so much to discuss and could not find that starting point. I wanted to tell her so much. To tell her I missed her. That I did wait. Ask her if she meant it when she said she loved me?

Does she really want me to go back with her? More than anything, I want to tell her I want to go back with her. But that remains in my voice box.

Instead, I went safe again, "Seems like you are doing well."

"I am so blessed. My book did better than I could imagine. I have a deadline, but not a boss. Mom and I have a renewed life. Things are good. And honestly, all because of you."

Not really feeling like a hero, I wasn't sure how to respond. It was weird hearing someone say something positive about me. Recent times have been filled with a whole world of problems, and everyone has chosen me to blame.

She continued down the path of memory lane. I realized that revisiting the past allowed us to become comfortable with the present.

"And though I miss Mitch, I found peace in knowing that he is in a better place."

She is so strong. In such a good place in life. Full of purpose and hope. Has a defined direction and vision for her life. Not me. Self-pity grows inside of me. Ten years ago, I was the strong one. The one in a good place in my life. The one with a great relationship with God. I had the world in the palm of my hands. Had all the answers. Not so much these days. The light that once glowed with every word I said and gave direction to every step I took has been replaced by darkness. I feel so much stress. I often dread waking up for a new day of despair. Grief is heavy in my heart.

Always angry. Pissed off at the world. I am lonely but never alone because I am surrounded by bitching, moaning, and complaining. Whether it's my wife, my job, or my so-called friends. Then there is God. He obviously has turned his back on me. There was a time when I felt like he fed me words of wisdom.

Here lately, I feel like God doesn't even know my name.

I really don't understand how we know Mitch is in a better place, but I agree with her thoughts. That's the nice thing to do.

"Your Dad, too," she says.

I was about to say I know. Knowing he was in a better place, but I don't think that's right. Could not bring myself to say this. I know, there is no place my Dad would rather be than here with my Mom and his boys. My dad was never about walking the streets of gold, hearing angels playing harps of glorious sounds, or seeing some majestic gate. He was simple. He never cared about those other things. He just wanted to love his family. Instead of proclaiming my Dad was in a better place, I just shared about his death and how my mom, family, and I have been struggling to adjust. Especially my mom.

There is genuine sorrow as she shares her apology, "I am so sorry for your loss. If anyone was meant to be in heaven, it is your dad. My mom nor I would be alive without your dad. He was a great man."

Emotions start to flood in.

She continues, "But I think you know that."

I felt really uncomfortable and got quiet. I did not want to go down this road. The sorrow/full of self-pity route. Silence filled the air, with

313

only the sound of the band playing in the distance. The first notes of Randy Travis's 'Forever and Forever, Amen' echoed about, and I grabbed her hand. Let's dance. She smiled and stood. Without saying a word, our bodies swayed from side to side and moved in harmony underneath the moonlit sky. As if it was always meant to be. Just like God wanted.

I looked down and noticed that Binki was humming the words. Eyes closed. Absorbing the moment.

As the song was coming to an end, she put her face in front of mine and said the words, "I'm going to love you. Forever and Forever, Amen."

Then kissed me.

That kiss. That touch. The one I have been longing for. For… years.

That kiss sent my body into an inferno of passion. I embraced the kiss. Until… for some reason, I pulled away. Only for a second. Then I cupped her face in my hands and kissed her on the neck. She rolled her head back to allow my lips access from her neck up to her lips. Then, my consciousness took control of my body. I took a step back. Not sure what I was doing.

Binki said, "Something wrong?"

I shook my head and said, "Nothing is wrong." Stumbled for words. "You are perfect," I respond.

My guilt was getting the best of me. I am a married man and needed to let her know.

"Binki, I have something…"

Before I could finish, she interrupted me.

"Stop!" she insisted. "I don't want to know."

Confused, I respond, "But…"

"No", she insists. "Truth is. I don't want to know. That would make this too hard."

Even more confused than before, "What too hard?"

"Bo… I need you to know that I can't move forward with my life unless I know you have moved on. Tonight, your eyes. Your body. Your hands." She reaches out and touches the center of my chest. "Your heart tells me that there is still something there. Something that has been there for ten years. I meant every word I said on the stage. I love you. I want you to come to Charlottesville and live with me."

I am taken aback by her frankness. Goose bumps cover my body as I suddenly remember how it felt to be loved. To be wanted.

Binki continues by grabbing my face. Allowing us to be nose to nose.

Then, once again, she kisses me on the lips.

"I love you. Always have."

"Me too. I have always loved you."

Before I realized what I had said, the words were out. My emotions betrayed my consciousness once again.

Part Six

Chapter Forty-Three - Condemned

Charlotte Medical Hospital – May 20, 2000 – Five days after Injury

The look on Alice's face was that of a witness to a murder.

"Tell me you did not tell a woman." She stopped for a second and took a deep breath. "A woman that is not your wife."

Another dramatic pause.

"You told a woman that is not your wife that you loved them!" It was not a question. But instead, an accusation. Alice continued, "Son, please tell me you didn't say that."

"I did," Bo said. Doubling down, "I said it because I meant it."

Alice seemed visually upset. Marcus taps her on the leg and reminds her that they are here to listen. Not judge.

Marcus apologized and encouraged the man to continue, "Son, I am a patient man, but how does all this result in you lying in this hospital tonight."

She could not control her disgust.

"I bet that wife of his bopped him on the head. Tried to knock some sense into him. Telling another woman that he loves her," Alice offers.

Marcus gives her a stern, "Alice!"

This time, Alice notices the man's frustration. Feeling good and scolded, Alice apologizes and asks Bo to continue.

Bo tells them that his wife did not cause the injuries.

"No bopping happened," he says matter-of-factly with his eyes directed in Alice's direction. "The injuries occurred because of a car wreck," Bo offered. "The perpetrator wasn't my wife.... It was either the devil or the hand of God. Not sure."

"Son, God would never do this. It is totally the act of the devil," Marcus proclaims with certainty.

"With all due respect, I ain't so sure," Bo said.

"What would make you say something so silly," Alice interjected. "Well. I would say don't judge me, but I guess we are passed that."

Bo taking another shot at Alice.

"Son, we are not worthy of judging others. That is the job of the good lord," Marcus says with confidence. "Please continue."

Bo gathers his thoughts and continues, "Binki and I spent the rest of the night together on that pier."

He looked over and noticed Alice's lips were smacked together, head shaking in an 'I bet you did' manner. A blind man could see the look in her eyes had him already condemned. No matter, he proceeded.

Part Seven

Chapter Forty-Four - Farewell

Thursday – May 11, 2000 – Four days before Injury

Four days from now, I have to decide. Monday, May 15, 2000. I must choose. Whether to stay or go. It just doesn't seem real. The decision is easy. Go. Be with Binki. Live happy and full of bliss. Live the life we were meant to live. The images are playing in my head. We meet at the fast-food restaurant called Bojangles' across the street from the Billy Graham Library, just like she said. We get into her car and ride away together. To a new life. To a better life.

Without a doubt, I would have said yes last night. I would say yes right now. Not sure what waiting four days will do. But she insists. Said she wanted to give me time to think. She said that at this location, she would tell me everything. She said she wants me to walk into the future with "eyes wide open". Exact words. Wants to make sure I understand everything I am getting into. Not sure what more needs to be known, except I have lost her once and will not do it again!

Then, doubt creeps into my head. What if she changes her mind?

What if she backs out? Doesn't show up. What if she didn't like what she saw? Heard? No, that can't be. Then, she wouldn't have prolonged it. She was the one who insisted on the meeting. Maybe she was just giving me time to back out. That is precisely what is happening here! Or maybe she is the one that needs the time to think?

My thoughts were a million miles away; my body was stationed at the final assembly of the retreat. The traditional gathering of the masses for lunch is followed by a farewell speech. This entails Dave and the corporate head honchos telling everyone how proud they are of everyone, accompanied by the obligatory pep talk about how the company's future is so bright. This speech was no different, except everyone sensed that this maybe the final farewell talk Dave would be giving. It was awkward and somewhat tense. Nostalgia hung in the air. The hugging and handshaking had a little extra meaning with the knowledge that this maybe the last time we will all be together. Finally, the congregation dispersed and hurriedly made their way to their cars to start the long journey back to the hustle and bustle of everyday life.

All but me. I was in no hurry. I sit with my car running and the radio on low. My car was ready to go, but I was unable to move. Can't make sense of what had occurred to me in the past twenty-four hours. I can't see a map of where to go next without her. Last night, Binki gave me the ultimate chance at a restart. Or is this God bringing her back into my life. Giving me a second chance. I want to chase her down and spend more time with her.

But who am I kidding? I am a married man. I need to start this car and head to work. To a job that no doubt is in serious jeopardy. Then, go home to a marriage that feels like a bottomless pit. Then, simply no-show the meeting with Binki in four days. Live the rest of my life wondering what could have been.

Or I could embrace the actions of the past twenty-four hours. See it as the sign it obviously was meant to be. Twenty-four hours ago, I felt unloved and unwanted. Hopeless about almost every part of my life. Suddenly, that all changed. The love of my life literally walks back into my life and is ready to save me. She has given me hope. The opportunity for a future of happiness. All I have to do is say yes. Yes, to all the questions. Yes, I will promise to love her forever. Yes, I can leave my job. Heck, my job is about to leave me. Yes, I will leave my wife. This marriage has been devoid of love for years. None of this seems difficult. The voice is saying "yes". This has to be God's voice. Giving me direction. Giving me a second chance at life.

Finally, I put the car in reverse and started the two-hour drive to Knoxville. I was regretting the decision to be a kiss-ass and take on a client that I didn't have to take. The idea of accidently forgetting crossed my mind. Only for a moment. My mind quickly drifted back to the previous night. So much had happened that I kept jumping to different portions of the night.

The recollection of the last night together as teenagers jumps into view.

How horrifying her father's return was and how scared we were. A recollection that gave both of us cold chills. I can still hear his evil voice and her cries for help. As bad as it was, we agreed it still would have gotten much worse if it wasn't for my dad showing up. Made me swell with pride for a moment. Which allowed me to share with her that cancer took him and how it impacted my life. I opened up about my current emotional state. The lack of self-worth and daily struggles. How the daily routine of my life seems far from what I wanted. I feel as if I am a ship without a destination. I am just wondering abroad. Aimlessly. I saw the pain in her eyes. The pain for me. For my family. Genuine love and empathy.

This led to a lot of conversation about the long battle back to health physically and mentally for Binki and her mom. It was obvious that the loss of Mitch was the toughest adjustment. She shared several stories about Mitch that made both of us smile, which seemed very therapeutic for her and allowed me to find some form of peace.

I had to ask if she really would have taken her own life. Binki said we never will know if she would have gone through with it. But believes with all her heart that she would have killed herself that night, had I not asked her to go to town and we had the talk. The journey that injected God into her life. The talk that gave her a promise of tomorrow and the endless possibilities that came from that promise.

My brain quickly jumped from the words that were spoken to thoughts of the physical joy that my body felt every time she smiled at me. The lust overtook me with every touch. How each kiss completely filled every void, yet always left me craving for more. My mind's eye took me back to the gazebo, holding her in my arms under the moonlight. The words "I love you" being replayed in my eyes while the pound in my heart has yet to cease.

Chapter Forty-Five - The Call

Crossing through the Blue Ridge Mountains from Ashville to Knoxville in a car is a visionary gift from God that every person should be blessed enough to see at least once in their life. There are spots where you are so high in the sky that you can't help but think you can just knock on heaven's door. Treetops and valleys capture your field of vision for miles. I swear, you think you can see where the Earth starts to the east and ends to the west. The scenery allows for an ambiance of thought and perspective. Just when you think the sights can't get any better, the sun starts to decline, and the constant images of mountains and valleys are presented in a different but equally amazing beauty.

Normally, the initial meeting with a new potential franchisee goes quickly. Either they are such a trainwreck, that the answer is an obvious no. Or they have their stuff, so together, they pretty much just tell you how they are going to be successful. Fortunately, this group had a lot of promise.

Which meant they had the two most important ingredients for success. People and Cash. The two-hour meeting included a very nice dinner at a local steakhouse, but I pleasantly declined the after-dinner cocktail in an effort to get home tonight if possible.

Meetings that end late in the evening mean driving in the direction of home with every intent to make it there. Often, I end up stopping at a hotel for the night once I discover that I can no longer drive. Worst case scenario, this allows the drive home the next morning to be shorter. With it being 9 pm at the start of the journey and a four-hour drive ahead, that was the plan tonight. I was fully aware that not getting much sleep last night, means that a hotel a couple hours down the road is inevitable. Four straight hours in the car and getting home after one am, would not be much of an issue on most nights. But my sleep-deprived body most certainly can't make it the entire trip home.

True to my belief, a little over an hour in, my eyes were beginning to feel heavy. I made the decision that the next hotel sign I see, wins my business for the night. That was the plan until I heard a sound. The company-issued cell phone rang. That ring changed the course of the night. Well, not the ring but instead the person who is causing the ringing. It made what I thought was a simple decision become an impossible decision.

Very few people have this number and only one person would be calling me this late. That call would be coming from my house. From my wife. I decide that it is too late to be dealing with any antics from Kimberly, so once again. I ignore it. One more day won't hurt.

The phone stops ringing. Just as quickly as it stops, it starts up again.

I am tired and just want some sleep. But as human nature goes, my mind goes to the worst possible outcome. Catastrophizing everything! What if something serious happened? If she is calling back-to-back, something must be wrong. I quickly decide to answer, but I am going to play it off like the signal is bad.

One word changed all of that. The one word that made my heart melt.

"Dad?" And just like that, everything changed.

Chapter Forty-Six - One Good Thing

My daughter is the one good thing in my life. My god has forsaken me. My marriage is in shambles. My job is on its last leg. The weekday problems are atrocious. But a Friday at the movies watching "The Adventures of Elmo in Grouchland" or our monthly "Dad Date," which allows us to go out skating and eat ice cream with my sweet princess, has saved my sanity many weeks. Plus, the added bonus of allowing Kimberly to have a night of peace. Which I know is well deserved. For all her complaining, she is a wonderful mom. If I had to be honest, she is a good wife. She works a part time job cleaning the church and still keeps our house clean and cooks almost every night. Often, I don't know what the issue is, but it seems like we just don't see eye to eye anymore.

I feel certain that if Brianna Victoria Hawes was not part of our lives, we wouldn't still be married. Well, that and Kimberly's belief in God, which frowns on divorce. I reckon that this is the main reason that she hasn't packed her bags and left. Almost any other woman would have. She believes that once God puts you together, there is no separation. Honestly, I used to believe this as well. So maybe Brianna is also the reason I have never just walked away. Or could it be that I have this same belief? Hell, that is exactly how I was raised.

As tumultuous as our marriage may be, we happen to be great parents, and both of us recognize that skill in each other. We both love Brianna and would do anything for her. Even stay together in a marriage that is broken. On many occasions, I know without a shadow of a doubt that I only drive to our house because I know Bianna is there. Tonight is no different.

I believe I was born to be a father. My dream is just to have a beautiful wife, a house worth $100,000, and be a father. Being a father is my purpose in life. I have always felt that way. But it feels like I can't get it right. The parenting is simple; it's the other aspects of my life that are troubling. My marriage, the bills, my profession, and have no relationship with God. I am done with religion, to be honest. Well, I think I am. But it seems like I am still asking God for favors. Or thanking God when things go right and blaming him when things go wrong. My relationship with my God is very similar to my relationship with my wife. Very dysfunctional.

A sweet voice sings in my ear, "Hello... Are you there?"

"Of course, my princess," I return. In my best cheerful voice, I remind her, "Aren't you supposed to be asleep?"

"I miss you. When are you coming home?" the four-year-old asked, totally disregarding the question.

My heart falls apart. I feel selfish. I have been feeling like my life is voided of love, yet that question is dripping with love. "Well, I was hoping to make it home tonight, but I am getting very sleepy."

The dejection was noticeable by the deep breath that was exhaled loudly through the phone. "So... does this mean you won't be coming home tonight?" she questioned.

Trying to interject some hope, "I am going to give it my best shot.

But it has been a long day, and I am driving by myself. So, I may not be able to make it."

"But Dad…" she whimpers.

"Princess, I will give it my best effort," I assure her.

"Dad, if you were riding with someone, does that mean you could make it home?" she inquires.

"Most likely. Because this means I would be talking to someone, and it wouldn't be so quiet. I may not get so tired," I explain.

"Hold on," she says with excitement. Then before I can respond, I hear the phone slam onto the table. A couple of seconds expire, and she returns. With renewed hope in her voice, she begins the interrogation. "How long before you are home?"

"I am in Boone," I say.

Not realizing she has no idea where Boone is from Charlotte.

"No, No, No!" she says in quick succession. "I mean how long before you are home?"

I say two hours, and before I can ask why, she has already said, "Hold on," and I hear the slam of the phone once again.

"Okay, Dad. You will not be riding along no more. So, you can drive straight home tonight," she says with the resolve of an adult.

She sounded just like her mom. No, talking about it; she already has it figured out.

"Girl, have you gone crazy," I say in a playful voice. "How am I not driving alone, when I am the only one in the car?"

Glee explodes through the phone.

"Mom said I can stay on the phone with you until you get home. So... you won't be alone."

This was an offer I couldn't refuse. Especially when she added, "I have a surprise for you. When you are about home, let me know."

I promised her I would, and for the next two hours, we talked about everything from Grandma making the best tomato and mayo biscuits ever to her friend Madison getting in trouble for throwing eggs at her brother. She did her part and talked every possible minute. Every so often, she would ask me if I was sleepy or okay. Which waited heavily on me because I am the one who is the parent. The one that is the protector. Yet, she is the one watching out for my safety.

One of our favorite topics was to reflect on our many "Daddy Dates". We agreed that our favorite "Daddy Date" was the night we got dressed up, with me in a suit and tie and her wearing the beautiful yellow dress that her grandma bought her just for this event. She looked like Belle from Beauty and the Beast as we got dinner at a sushi place and then went to watch "Beauty and the Beast on Ice" at the Charlotte Coliseum. Sushi has always been our thing and we did that together quite often. Mainly because Kimberly didn't care for sushi too much. But this night was different than normal visits to the Oki Sushi Palace because we were a living version of Beauty and the Beast.

Numerous people made comments on how cute we were, with Brianna taking her rightful spot as the star of the show. The goal of making her feel like a princess was accomplished in spades!!

Ironically, a night that was made to make her feel like a princess, gave me the greatest sense of satisfaction a man could possibly have. Never have I felt like a better man than every time I caught her laughing or smiling. This night was so special that I kept a picture of the two of us with the Belle look-a-like in my work folder. When things get shitty or the day starts to go awry, I will just look at this picture and remember my purpose. To be the best dad in the world. To make every dream she could possibly have come true.

During the entire two-hour phone call, her energy never wavered. As I rounded onto Potter's Road, I informed her that I was mere minutes away.

With joy transitioning from her lips to my ears, she hurriedly says, "BYE!! I got to go get your surprise ready."

As she had done twice before, she slammed the phone down. This time, disconnecting the call.

I walk into the house with my computer bag over one shoulder and carrying my luggage in the other hand. Both quickly made their way to the ground as a four-year-old missile made her way to me. She jumps in my arms and gives me the hug that every father wants when they return home. Kimberly has quite the opposite reaction. She gives me a hug and kisses me on the cheek as she makes her way to turn in for the night. She's tired.

The lack of excitement from Kimberly is noticed but I quickly shift my attention to Brianna grabbing my hand and dragging me towards the living room. I turn the corner, and there is a towel on the floor with two cushions from the couch removed and placed as backstops on each side of the towel. On the towel is a bag of chips and a bowl with Salsa already poured into it. Then I noticed the flower vase with fresh cut flowers that normally sit on our dining room table, right beside it.

"We didn't get to do our Daddy Date this week, so Mama helped me put together a date."

She instructs me to sit down on the floor. I took my spot on one side of the towel and eased back against the cushion that was propped against the base of the couch. She disappears, and I notice that the TV is prompted to start playing something once the command is given to the remote.

"Here you go, sir," Brianna says in her best effort to speak sophisticated.

I return a "Thank you, Kind Lady" with an equal effort to sound proper in my best English accent.

Though the accent was enough to offend any true-blooded British, Brianna always found it to be amusing. She handed me a can of Pepsi that was so cold that I wasn't so certain she didn't get it out of the freezer instead of the fridge.

She took her seat on the other side of the towel and said as if she were an announcer from the local circus.

"Now, on to the main attraction. The Cheetah Girls." Easily her and Madison's favorite show.

In a playful tone, I ask, "Why do I get a feeling you have already seen this?"

She giggles and says, "Because I have. With you, silly."

We laugh and let Raven Simone and the gang do their thing.

I was certain that I would be the first to fall asleep, but that was not the case. Ten minutes into the show, she came on my side of the towel and fell asleep with her head on my lap. The idea of just laying there on the floor the entire night crossed my mind, but the recollection of how my back felt the last time I fell asleep on the floor put an end to that thought rather quickly. I picked her up and headed to her bedroom.

Walking into her bedroom instantly brought back memories of when my marriage wasn't so cold. The pink walls brought images of a barely pregnant Kimberly dipping her fingers in the paint and drawing a heart on the front of my white Tee Shirt. Or the memory of me really struggling to put together the first baby bed that we bought. In the midst of my struggle, Stevie came over and walked into the room, only to break into immediate, thunderous laughter. The reason for the laughter was only divulged once he called me an idiot and explained that, somehow, I had put together the bed upside down. When it was time for the bed upgrade for Brianna to a canopy bed, Stevie insisted that Kimberly call him to do the work. For the safety of Brianna.

I laid her on the bed and covered her in the Little Mermaid bed covers. Gently leaned over and kissed her on the forehead.

Followed that up with another secure tuck of the blanket and said quietly, "I love you".

As I was starting to straighten up, I heard a soft return of "I love you too, Daddy."

I walk across the stairs and slide in bed with Kimberly. I realize that she played a big part in making this night so special for Brianna and me.

Leaning over to give her a kiss, I tell her, "Thank you for doing this for us."

She responds, "Please stop. I am trying to go to sleep."

"What the hell," I say. "I was just trying to say thank you."

"No, you weren't. I know what you are wanting!" she says in a raised voice. "I am too tired tonight. Just get some sleep," she continues her scolding.

"It pisses me off that you think I am so shallow to only think about sex. I actually could have been genuine in my appreciation," I respond.

She turns to the other side and commands, "I am done with this conversation. Go to sleep."

I decided that the couch wasn't so bad after all. I get up and go back into the living room and open my suitcase to get out the Buffalo Trace Bourbon that I had hidden inside. In my search for the whiskey, I came across the book that Binki had given me. An autographed copy of "The Promise of Tomorrow". I couldn't help but think, is this God or some other universal force of love giving me a sign? This is too much of a coincidence. I walk to the kitchen and pour some of the bourbon into a glass. Find my way to the couch and read the story of my life.

Chapter Forty-Seven - Stench Shower

Friday – May 12, 2000 – Three days before Injury

"Get up. I can't believe you did it again!" an animated voice rings in my ears.

I try to open my eyes, but they feel like they are welded shut.

Shooting pain was pulsating behind each eyeball. My mouth's as dry as the desert, and my head feels as if it is filled with quicksand.

"Your daughter is still in her room. Get your drunk butt up before she comes down. I can't believe you did this again."

"Stop yelling," I say.

Loud enough that one could consider me doing the exact thing I am accusing her of.

Kimberly lends down to my ears and whispers softly in a condescending tone, "I am not the one yelling. You are drunk. Well,… hungover. No matter, you are not in a good state. Unless you want your daughter seeing you in this condition, get your butt off the coach. Go hide either in the bed or in the shower. Do not come back out until you change clothes and use mouthwash. You smell like a drunk straight off the streets of Charlotte."

My thoughts are having trouble reaching their destination but once they hit their spot, I gather that Kimberly is right. There is no way I want Brianna to see or smell me like this. I give up the fight and put my body into motion. Just sitting up is a challenge. I decided to take my time and not rush it.

The first time that Kimberly found me in this state, her anger was uncontrollable. She called Stevie to come and pick me up. Took me about a week to get her to let me back into the house. And that was only after a colossal religious intervention by the leaders of the church, with her father as the lead advocate. Then it happened again. And again. I guess she has built a tolerance for it. Or she is afraid to tell her daddy that the intervention didn't work.

"What's this," Kimberly says nonchalantly, pointing at the book lying on the floor beside the couch.

Words were still struggling to make their destination in a timely manner.

I was thinking how impressed I was that I was sitting upright.

"Hello," Kimberly says. "When did you start reading?"

Finally apprehending what is being said to me, "Oh" is the only word to come out of my mouth.

"Oh?" Kimberly mocks. "How messed up are you? Get yourself together."

"My bad. This is the book the company gave us at the convention," I recover.

"The Promise of Tomorrow. Hmmm… Sounds good. I might have to read this when you are done. What's it about?"

The question totally took me off guard and quickly sobered me up.

I wasn't sure how to answer but knew, whatever happened, she couldn't read this. I have told her this story too many times. The story of my dad's heroism. How my dad took down a criminal.

Just to make sure I am not digging this hole any deeper, I respond, "Not sure. Haven't really read much."

I grabbed the book and made my way toward the bathroom to wash off the stench of the previous night. To allow soap, water, and a couple of Aspirin to transfer me from the hopeless drunk who slept on the couch to a man worthy of being called dad.

Part Eight

Chapter Forty-Eight - The Devil's a Lie

Charlotte Medical Hospital – May 20, 2000 – Five days after Injury

Darkness is covering the moonlit skyline of Charlotte out the hospital window. The recently completed Bank of America building is the centerpiece as stars appeared to be dancing around it. Most nights, this was a calming force to those in need of that serenity. This was not the case tonight. Well, not for Bo Hawes. He has discovered that it is hard to find calm and serenity with Alice Lucielle Wilson anywhere nearby.

"That's what I was talking about. Exactly!" Alice booms as her head shakes, and her index finger cuts through the air like a sword preparing for battle.

The confusion is apparent on the faces of Marcus and Bo. They couldn't figure out "Exactly" what she was talking about.

Marcus is the first to ask, "What in the world are you babbling about?"

Alice takes a deep breath and gathers herself.

"I was wondering when you would get to that little girl."

Now Bo is confused, and his protective spikes start to show, "What do you know about Brianna? How do you know her? You can't possibly know anything about my daughter."

"Son, you must have bumped that head really, really hard. Remember me telling you that there have been a lot of people coming in here. All worried and stuff. None more than that beautiful little girl you just described. I saw her standing over you and crying. It broke my heart into pieces," Alice explains. "I mean, I can't stand to see any of God's children hurt. But especially one so precious."

As Alice continues her reflection, Marcus's eyes wander over to the patient, and he notices tears going down his face. But Alice is oblivious and plows on through. Every word she spoke matched by a tear sliding down Bo's face.

"I knew it. Her mother. Now I know her to be Kimberly. I'm betting a dollar to a doughnut that she hit you with a frying pan or something. She must be feeling pretty guilty. That is the only reason I can see her crying over you, too. Not sure you are worth those tears."

Bo's tears come to a halt, and anger comes to the forefront.

But before he says anything, Marcus comes to the rescue, "Now Alice, that's enough."

Bo pipes in, "Enough! Enough!! That is too much. First of all, that is not true."

Alice can't contain her anger, "The devil's a lie. And you my friend, I don't need to hear anymore. I ain't gonna call you the devil. But a wolf you just might be!"

"Alice!" Marcus scolds.

"Alice?" She scoffs. "Don't Alice me. This man is telling me that he is a good man in a tough situation. This is a man who put himself in a bad situation. He wasn't put into anything. He got a good God-fearing woman. A beautiful wife. And he's here lusting after another. If that ain't a picture of the devil, I don't know what is."

Her words cut deep. Bo knows that Alice's assessment might just be right on point. Maybe he is a wolf. Or the devil. The realization is too much for him to handle. His body can't hold in its disappointment. The shame is too much to bear. His head drops to the opposite side of his guest.

Alice could see that she may have gone too far as the man started to shake. Alice's words come to a halt as she wonders what he is shaking from. Does he need medical attention? The nurse side of her jumps to her feet and moves to him. Ready to assist. She grabs his face and turns it in her direction. She checks his pupils. Ready to see if some form of medical assistance is required.

That's when she sees it. Medical help isn't required. She looks into his eyes and sees a broken man. His trembling is not because of a physical issue. As broken as his body may look, his soul is the one in need of real repair. The image before her gives her flashbacks to when her husband Marcus lost his mother. The only time she has ever seen the strongest human she knows to ever ugly cry. The patient's crying is so intense that his face appears to be warped or disfigured. This immediately reverts Alice's tone from one of admonishment to one of caretaker. She takes his head and brings it to her bosom. Hugs him like he was her child. Marcus stands and watches his wife. Knowing that this man needs a lot of things right now.

Love and understanding are on top of that list.

"Let it out, son," Alice pats, holds him, and then continues, "Tonight, we are giving this problem to God. He gonna take care of this for us. You just let all this out."

Once he noticed the man starting to settle down, Marcus reached out to Bo and grabbed his hand.

"Son, you don't owe us anything. You don't have to continue. This is between you and God. If you want, I would like to say a prayer with you."

The acknowledgement by way of a nodding head had the three holding hands and bowing their heads. Marcus said the prayer that resembled that of many southern Baptists. One of thankfulness and glory. Then, asking for understanding and mercy. Then guidance. A unified "Amen" from Alice and Marcus was followed by a humble "Thank you" from Bo.

Marcus takes a moment to contemplate his next move. He knows this man is fragile mentally and physically. He knows that not only is his body fighting the pain, but his soul is trying to battle its own demons. After much thought, he concludes that this man is tired. He is a beaten man. Rest is needed. So, he tells the man they are going to leave him alone because he's in God's hands now.

Marcus reaches into his billfold and gets out a business card.

"Here is my card. Once you get some rest, I suggest you talk to someone. Even if it is not me, please, son. Take my advice and talk to someone. But know this. I will check back with you later. After you get some rest. Also, note that I can always be that someone to talk to. Feel free to contact me at any time. Day or Night."

Bo starts to regain his faculties and lands back closer to normal. But he doesn't say a word. Just nods his head for approval.

Alice reassures the man once again that God is going to take care of him as she grabs her jacket and makes her way to the door with Marcus by her side.

Chapter Forty-Nine - Who's Knocking

A common belief is the average person has an estimated 45 thoughts per minute. Bo is not aware of this, but he feels like he just set a new record for the most thoughts one human can possibly have at one time. Alice's words? Brianna? Kimberly? Binki? His marriage? God? How horrible of a person he must really be. Just too many thoughts to get any kind of rest. He has no idea what direction to go. He has no idea what he is going to do. But he knows he does not want to be alone.

"Hold up," he squeezes meekly between his lips as the door closes behind Alice and Marcus.

They didn't hear his feeble plea for help. The doors slowly come to a rest, and they are gone. He is alone to drown himself in self-pity. To reflect on all his mistakes. To wallow in misery. He once again takes up the action that started it all. He stares at the envelope bearing his name. More scared than before. He feels certain that the letter is an invitation from Binki. He can feel it in his bones. Why else would she have given it to Phillip? He is afraid that he can't let her go. He is afraid of himself. From his own willpower or lack of willpower. He knows he is weak. How could he possibly have to choose between the love of his life in Binki and the life he loves of being a dad? It's just not fair.

This is too much. Bo has missed his father a million times, but never more than this moment. He reflects on what his father would do. He closes his eyes to ask his dad for a sign, but it somehow turns into a prayer.

Almost like his dad meant for this to happen. No matter the reasoning and who was in charge, Bo just relented. For the first time in a long time, Bo opens his heart and talks to God. Just like he used to do many years ago. Asking for guidance. Asking for a sign. Asking for help.

Bo sat momentarily with his eyes closed, and it felt like a load had been lifted from his shoulders. That maybe the problems weren't so heavy.

But once his eyes opened, "Oh Shit" jumps off his lips.

The sight of the letter ends the temporary peace, and the mountain of worry and confusion catapulted back into place. Bo knows that the letter can't be sitting here when Kimberly comes in the morning.

Her last words were, "See you in the morning", right after she gave me a kiss on the forehead. A thought that sends absolute terror through his body and into his spine. For some god-forsaken reason, Bo just came to the understanding that time was running out. He has to read this letter now.

Bo reaches for the envelope gingerly. His hands are quivering in fear. As if he was putting his hands into a fire, which strikes him odd because that is exactly what it feels like he is doing. Holding the envelope in his hands, he decides to say a second quick prayer. To take Alice's advice and give it to God. To take Marcus's advice and talk to someone. For the second time since being left alone, he closes his eyes for prayer. He closes his eyes, but this time, a talk with God never happened.

Bo hears a knock on the door and opens his eyes to see who it is. His heart almost stops at the thought this could be Kimberly. Surely, the hospital allows wives to come and go as they wish. Then he thought, could this be Binki? Instant shame overrides his emotions. No married man should feel that excited to see another woman. But he can't hide it. The joy the thought of Binki brought him was out of his control. The knock happens for a second time and the door starts to open.

The opening of the door doesn't stop the knocking. Instead, the knock becomes even louder and more aggressive as the door crept its way open.

As soon as he hides the letter, he feels the act is unnecessary because it couldn't possibly be Kimberly knocking. She would have just walked straight in. But it could be Binky. I mean, she would knock. Right?

The door slowly opens, and his heart races.

Suddenly, a black bald head peaks around the door threshold.

"Sorry to bother you. Hoping you weren't already asleep. I took the chance of returning since I just left."

He makes his way over to the area where he was sitting just moments ago as Alice makes her way through the door.

"I forgot something," Marcus said.

"He would forget his head if wasn't already attached," she says in an effort to bring some levity to the room. She continues her lighthearted attack on the pastor. "I always tell people that's what happens to his hair. He forgot it somewhere."

Alice laughs at her own joke, and Marcus playfully reprimands her, "Alice, don't you see the man has had enough of us. Leave the man and my bald head alone."

Bo gives the obligatory smile but says nothing.

Marcus picks up the can of Diet Coke and extends it in Bo's direction.

"I wouldn't come back for this, but it is almost full. Hope it wasn't too much of a bother. We are getting out of your hair now."

Alice seemed to be the person who always got the last word in, and this time wasn't going to be any different.

"I keep telling him that Pepsi is not healthy. He needs to be drinking water. But his stubborn butt always tells me that water gonna rust his pipes. Can you believe that nonsense?"

Cold chills run through Bo's skin. He can't believe what he just heard.

"What did you say?" a trembling set of lips asked.

Confused about what was going on, Alice repeated her last statement, "I said that Marcus is so silly. He always says that he can't drink water because it rusts his pipes. I just think he's stubborn."

Bo sits like he is in shock. Then tears begin to fall down his cheeks once again.

Marcus noticed something just happened. Makes his way back to the bedside.

"Son, what is it?"

Bo is astonished and mumbles, "I think God just spoke to me."

Alice laughs. Thinking the man is finally going out of his mind.

"That was Marcus."

Marcus shoots her an evil eye, and Alice quickly realizes that the comment may have been out of sorts.

Marcus senses something powerful is happening and gives him a verbal nudge to continue his thought.

"Do you mind sharing? How did God speak to you?"

Without hesitation, Bo talks quietly in a trance-like state. He speaks as if he is trying to figure out a math problem.

"Rusty pipes. You walking back into the room. I just asked God and my dad for guidance. Then, you walk back into the room. My dad used to always say water rusted his pipes. He said this even on his deathbed. No matter how much the nurse and our family would beg him, he wouldn't drink water. He said he couldn't drink water. He said because it rusted his pipes. He only wanted his Diet Coke. That's weird."

Silence fills the room for a moment. Then Bo turns his head to Marcus.

"Could that be a sign? I mean, isn't that how God talks to people?"

Alice's eyes light up as if she were a Christmas tree. Joy is filled with every emotion as she whispers, "I think I just witnessed a miracle."

Resolve falls across Marcus's face. Not the sheer joy that Alice is expressing, but a sense of calm. The pastor no doubt has seen his share of miracles, but he isn't so quick to know the answer.

"Son, all I know is that God works in many ways. Only you know. But it sounds pretty convincing to me."

The bewildered Bo says, "Well. What is he saying? I feel like I just got a sign, but I am not certain what the sign is saying."

Marcus doesn't respond and like a well-trained advisor, allows the patient to try and answer his own question.

With clarity, Bo says. "I was about to read the letter. First, I prayed, then I was going to read the letter. But you walked in. I think God wants you to be here when I read the letter. So read the letter to me."

Alice is eager to accept the job. "Okay, I will."

But Marcus wasn't so sure, "I am not certain that was the message."

Alice retreats, "I mean, only if we are supposed to."

"Then what is the message," Bo shot back. "That's what I understood."

Alice's anticipation builds, "Marcus, you heard the man. That's what the man heard, Marcus."

Marcus still not sold.

"We don't know what's in that letter. Could be too personal?"

"Personal?" an offended Bo states. "You have been sitting here all night, and I have told you things that I haven't told anyone else. Personal? We passed too personal a long time ago."

Marcus stumbles for a response. For the first time tonight, Marcus is at a loss for words.

After much thought, Marcus goes to his comfort zone, "I know you said you just prayed, but let's pray one more time. After the prayer, if that is still what you want. Then that's exactly what we will do."

They all reached for each other's hands and closed their eyes. Peace and serenity overtook the room as each bowed their heads.

When someone prays and they are totally invested in the prayer, the one emotion that comes dripping from that effort is one of love. Bo could tell that Marcus was a man filled with love. Words of praise and requested for guidance were requested in every way a good Southern Baptist man could possibly express. Marcus was praying for a man he barely knew and prayed as if it was his own child that he was seeking advice. Marcus prayed as if he was begging God to give him the answer. Not the answer to his own problems but the answer to a total stranger's problems. Bo couldn't help but think, why did he care so much? How could someone be filled with so much love?

Chapter Fifty - Time to Read

It was a unanimous decision that Alice would be the one to read the letter. This was a job that she was only too happy to do.

Bo sat up and tried to get as comfortable as possible. Ready to hear the words that are no doubt from the heart of the person he has loved over half his life. The person who has dominated his thoughts all week. The person that he was sure he was meant to be with.

Alice asked, "Are you ready?" looking at Bo.

Bo responds, "I guess?"

Alice opened the envelop The noise of the paper tearing was the only audio that the room had to offer.

Alice was in the process of removing the contents when she heard, "Wait, Alice!" The tone was loud and direct.

Alice was startled by the tone. A little shaken, Alice did as she was instructed and looked around for the source of the request.

Bo continues, "It's not fair. I just want you to know. Thank you for the conversation. You guys have helped me so much. But…"

Marcus says, "Son, we understand. You don't need to explain."

Alice's face says differently, and her mouth verbalizes the objection.

"Nah… We don't understand. I am lost to what just happened."

Marcus's calm demeanor quickly soothes Alice. Without saying a word, he tells Alice I got this with just one look. He instructs Alice to lay the letter on the table.

"No, No. You got this all wrong," Bo says.

Marcus is now the one perplexed, "What do you mean?"

"I don't want to read the letter."

Renewed excitement enters Alice as she says, "Okay. So, you do want me to read it?"

"No, I want you to take it with you. I don't need that letter. I misunderstood the sign. I mean, I was right about it being a sign, but the sign wasn't that I needed you to read the letter. The sign was meant for you to take the letter with you."

A smile appears on the face of Marcus. One of satisfaction.

Alice's face said the opposite.

"I don't understand," she said. "I am certain someone gave you too much of that crazy juice!! You don't want to know what's in the letter. I mean, you need to know. Right?"

The tone was one of conviction, "Not at all. You see. It doesn't matter what that letter says. I have already decided."

A bewildered Alice blurts out, "Decided what? When?"

The unfazed patient answered, "You see, Kimberly doesn't watch a lot of television."

Marcus and Alice looked at each other in confusion. "Where did this come from?" was on their minds, and "What the heck?" was displayed on their face. Unbothered, Bo continues before either says a word.

"But one show she watches regularly is the Oprah Winfrey Show. You know the lady. The show I am speaking of. The lady that's all positive and gives things away."

Both Marcus and Alice shake their heads in acknowledgment.

Alice gives verbal confirmation, "Of course! Everybody knows Oprah." The tone displays some agitation.

"Well, I'll sometimes sit down with Kimberly to watch it with her. Often, I'll get caught up in the show. Of course, I don't tell her, but it intrigues me. One of Oprah's shows, in particular, just came to mind. She said that people often have 'Aha moments'."

Bo looks to his audience, seeking approval, and asks, "Do you know what I am talking about?"

Alice shakes her head, yes, but Marcus looks as if he needs more information.

Bo says, "Well, Oprah explained that an 'Aha moment' is that moment when something becomes clear. When the proverbial light bulb goes off above your head. Something that has been foggy becomes more comprehensible. Makes more sense. She explains that it is not something that someone has taught you, but instead, it's remembering something that you already know."

Bo turns his head to Marcus, "During your prayer, I had my 'Aha Moment'. Just like Oprah said!"

Excitement is exploding from his voice, "You... you helped me remember something I already knew."

Chapter Fifty-One - What I Already Knew

Bo worked his body up as straight as possible and spoke with clarity and conviction for the first time tonight. He is a man who just found the map. A man who knows where he is going. For the first time, in a long time, he can see a path out of the hell that he calls life. He now can see the answer to the impossible question.

He explains, "Remember me telling you that the Friday prior to my injury, my wife woke me up and told me to go take a shower before Brianna came down."

Marcus shakes his head in affirmation.

"During your prayer, a vision came across my mind."

His eyes watered up as he took a minute to gather himself.

"In your prayer, you said, God help this young man be the man he is meant to be. My mind went back to that Friday morning before my accident. To that very moment. The moment I grabbed the book and made my way toward the bathroom to wash off the stench of the previous night as Kimberly directed. I dropped my book and looked back at my wife as she was dutifully cleaning up my mess. No fuss. As if that was her purpose. To clean up after me."

Bo stopped to gather himself once again. Marcus and Alice stay quiet because they realize that the troubled man is finding his way through a troubled life.

Bo continues, "That moment, I remember feeling something. Something weird. At that moment, I thought… I felt déjà vu. I chalked it up to the alcohol from the night before. But when the words, "God, help this young man be the person he was meant to be," left your lips during the prayer. It hit me! That moment surfaced in my mind's eye as clear as day. That thought reentered my mind. Now I realize, it wasn't déjà vu or the alcohol. No, it was my conscious. It was guilt."

Bo stops once again. As if he is waiting for the painter to put the final touches on his masterpiece, before the big reveal.

A single tear leaks down his cheek as he resumes, "She was there. The hair was a little messy. Wearing my old Dolphin's tee shirt and unmatching plaid pajama bottoms. Nothing special."

Bo sits stationary. In a trans-like state.

Alice breaks the silence, "I don't understand."

Marcus nudges her on the arm and wrinkles his forehead in an expression that says be patient. The quiet communication was understood.

"Nothing special. But it was everything. Everything I ever wanted. Everything I ever asked for. It was all sitting there at that moment. A million times, I prayed and asked a simple request. All I ever wanted was a house worth $100,000, a beautiful wife, and to be a father. Not to be rich. Not to be famous. Just to be a father and a husband. To have an all-American family. There it was on full display at that moment. Everything was there. And I didn't. I mean, I don't even appreciate it. That moment, I now realize why I can't dispose of that sight. That moment. I realize now that I am not currently the man I am supposed to be. At that moment, I realized that I was holding a book called The Promise of Tomorrow, fully realizing that I was breaking a promise to the woman I had committed all my tomorrows to. Instead of working to be the man I was meant to be, I … Well, I guess …"

The room once again goes silent. Until Marcus smiles and turns into a soft laughter. Not haha laughter. More of a religious sound of happiness. This is not the stone faced, serious man full of wisdom that has been sitting here for the past couple hours. He was almost jovial. His happiness takes Bo and Alice by surprise.

Alice calls him out on it, "What in the world are you smiling at?"

Bo joins in, "I was wondering the same thing."

Marcus obliges with the reason for his giddy mood, "God is good."

Alice on que throws in a "Hallelujah" without thought.

No doubt something she does subconsciously and has done a million times.

His smile disappears, and the philosopher once again makes his appearance.

"Sometimes, we are our own worst enemy. We just can't get out of our own way. And sometimes, we have all the answers. Yet, we don't recognize them as such. Often, we look past the obvious."

A bewildered look is planted on Bo and Alice's faces. Alice has proven that patience is not one of her greatest strengths.

Once again, she lives up to this repetition, "What in the devil are you talking about?"

Marcus continues in his all-knowing tone, "Bo, we have sat here all night looking for answers. Son, you have had the answer all along. What are you going to do? Are you going to embrace the promise of tomorrow or the pain of yesterday?"

Marcus waited for the comment to find its spot. Resolve settles into Marcus when he observes the 'Aha moment' hitting its intended target.

"Son, you are young. Your marriage is young," Marcus says as a prideful Alice shakes her head in acknowledgment of every word.

"Every marriage has its opportunity. But in order for your marriage to work, you must let go of the past. Don't allow the hope of yesterday to interfere with the promise of tomorrow. Have you ever considered that you actually might be on the right road? I challenge that maybe God gave you Kimberly, because maybe Kimberly is exactly what you needed. That's not for me to answer. That is between you, God, and Kimberly. But maybe the greatest gift God gives us is the unanswered prayers."

Marcus takes a dramatic pause once again to allow this thought to soak in.

Then continues, "No matter. What I am certain of is that you must resolve this issue with the past for you to move forward and become who you are meant to be. Or, more importantly, the man you want to be. Because I know you want to be a good man. But you must decide. Son, you can't ride two horses at one time and most certainly can't ride two horses heading in two different directions. For the sake of everyone, including yourself. Pick a horse. Pick a direction. You must decide who you want to be. I'm not going to tell you which direction to go. But let me give you a recap. Everything you ask of God is there for you to accept. You have a wife that obviously loves you. You can't convince me that she doesn't love you. I mean, by your own description just a moment ago, you have put that woman through the wringer."

Alice can't let this go by without putting her two cents in, "Ain't that right."

Immediately realizing that the thought escaped her mouth. Marcus gives her the evil eye and then turns his focus back to Bo.

"But... She's still there. That's my point. Son, you have described yourself as a man who has not been easy to love. Almost like you are trying to run her off. And yet, she is still there. I believe that the man you want to be is the man she knows you can be. That is why she is there. I suggest to you that you are her promise for tomorrow. I bet that has been the case since day one. You are her horse. She has chosen. You are the one. You have been too selfish. Feeling like you are unloved. Son, have you thought that maybe she feels the same way."

Alice puts her hands in the air, "Speak the truth."

Marcus doesn't break stride, "Then there is your daughter. I heard how much your parents mean to you. How your father worked tirelessly. You spoke of how their marriage was your ideal marriage. If you can't be the man, you are supposed to be for you. Or for your wife. Please, son, be the man you are supposed to be for your daughter."

Bo quickly strikes, "I am a great father."

"Didn't say you weren't," Marcus quickly counteracts. "You are missing the question. Are you the father you are meant to be? Are you showing your daughter how a man is supposed to treat his wife? Just so she knows how it should be when it's her turn to pick a husband. Like it or not, you are setting the standard. I don't know the answer, but can you say with 100% certainty that she is getting your best effort as a father? Are you continuing the circle of being a great dad? Man? Husband? Like your father was. Or are you breaking the circle of being a great dad? Ask yourself those questions."

Bo's eyes can't hide the mountain of emotions that is building. He falls back onto the bed as if he was just stabbed in the heart. Defeated, depressed, and full of self-pity.

Marcus notices this.

"This is not all bad news. You have a chance. You can make this right. Just like you said to that young lady on the mountaintop many years ago, you just have to choose. Do you want to dwell on your past mistakes, or do you believe in the promise of tomorrow? Your words, not mine."

The silence is so strong, you can hear Bo's heartbeat. Marcus knows he has said his part. He is about to explain to Bo, that he has laid out the situation. Now the ball is in his court.

But suddenly, the word "God's" squeaks out Bo's mouth.

A confused Marcus asked, "What?"

"Those are the words God gave me. I remember. I asked for guidance on that mountain years ago. I asked God for the right words to say to Binki, and God put those words in my mouth."

"Allow no man to destroy what God has put in place," Marcus said.

Fully aware that this is often the verbiage in most marriages.

This reference didn't pass by Bo. Because he remembers this being said the day he promised all his tomorrows to Kimberly.

"Son, I think you got a lot to think about. I would like to say one more prayer with you and then I think it's time I take my beautiful bride home for the night."

So, they all held hands and bowed their heads for the final prayer of the night.

Chapter Fifty-Two - The Hitman

Bo was the last to open his eyes, but when he did. Something was different. Different enough for Marcus to notice.

Enough difference for Marcus to ask, "Hmm, are you alright?"

"In your prayer, you prayed for me to get healthy," Bo got right to it.

"Of course, son," Marcus stated.

Alice is looking at the letter and almost squirming. Bo and Marcus ignore her.

"I never told you, but I think I was purposely hurt," Bo stated.

Marcus' jaws almost hit the ground. "Hurt? On purpose?"

"Who would do this?" Alice's attention went straight from the letter to the new juicy detail. "Someone put a hit out on you?" a curious Alice asked.

"A guess it could be called a hit," he responded.

"Do you know who? Have you told the Police?" Marcus looks around. "Are you still in danger? There are no police."

Alice interjects with wide, conspiratorial eyes. "Was it your wife? I knew it. It's always the good people. They say the spouse is the first person you look at."

"No. Not Kimberly. She had no part in it."

Alice offers another option. Her eyes get even larger, and she takes in a deep breath.

"Was it Binki? Or was it Binki's dad's old gang? You said he was in a gang, right?"

"Yes," Bo said.

Alice and Marcus are stunned by the confession.

Bo immediately noticed his mistake.

"No, no, no. You got it wrong. Yes, Binki's dad was in a gang, but no Binki nor a gang had anything to do with me being in the hospital."

Alice offers a final scenario, "The father-in-law. Oh lord. Please don't let it be a man of God."

"It is a man of God. You just got the wrong one," Bo states.

"Son, just tell us who did it, and we will call the authorities for you. You may be in danger." Marcus says.

Bo takes a deep breath and says one word, "God."

Both Marcus and Alice are flabbergasted at the accusation.

"Son, be careful. Why would God... I mean, if God wanted you gone, you wouldn't be sitting here."

"That's the thing. I am not certain he wanted me gone. But I do believe he wanted me to be here. You see, I grew up with the notion that God works in mysterious ways."

The two shake their heads in acknowledgment as Bo continues, "I have always been curious as to whether God had boundaries or not.

Does God really strike people dead? If so, why wouldn't he strike down that serial killer before they killed? Can God really heal the sick? If so, why doesn't he just heal all of his children? If he does strike people down or heal the sick, how does he choose who to heal and who to kill? I have never fully grasped this. But looking back into my wreck. The reason I am here, I can't help but think that God had something to do with me getting t-boned one mile from the place where I was supposed to meet Binki. Is this just a coincidence? Or is this an example of God working in a mysterious way? His way of telling me I am going down the wrong road?"

Marcus has consulted hundreds of people. Never has anyone accused God of being a hitman. He is dumbfounded by the accusation.

Trying to choose his words wisely, Marcus responds, "I, too, believe God works in mysterious ways. I do not know the reason for everything. But this, I believe. It's God's will that the three of us are sitting here today. I have felt the presence of the holy spirit many times, and I have no doubt that we are in the presence of the Almighty. You are a loved man. Whatever path brought us to this point, it is up to you to decide where you go from here. I feel comfortable that my work here is done."

Marcus and Alice stand up to exit the room. Marcus shakes Bo's hands and wishes God's good graces, while Alice takes the more traditional southern woman's approach and shares a hug.

As they approach the door, Bo notices the letter is still sitting on the table.

"Hey, Hey… Don't forget the letter," Bo instructs.

"Are you sure?" Alice questions.

"I am all about tomorrow. I am certain. I have chosen my horse. My direction," Bo proudly says.

A totally different man than just a couple of hours ago.

Alice picks up the envelope that was ripped open despite its contents never being removed. Marcus and Alice left the room, giving a final wave. Bo never read the letter, and the two of them never saw Bo again.

Chapter Fifty-Three - Didn't Tell

They quietly walk down the hall of the hospital, with Alice holding the unread letter in one hand and Marcus's hand in the other. She is squirming like a child that needs to go to pee.

"Oh, Lord, my Savior", Alice proclaims.

Marcus has heard this a million times from his wife during their long marriage. He knows that this wasn't a grateful noise unto the Lord. But more of a sign of stress.

Marcus's puzzled look is followed by, "What's got you using the Lord's name like that? Up in a tizzy? I thought you would be happy. Why are you shaking like you got the jitters?"

"Marcus, we might have to return. He's got to read this letter. There is something he doesn't know," Alice says.

"Nah, we ain't. God has spoken. The man is at peace. We have done our part," Marcus returns.

"Marcus, I am telling you. He needs to read the letter. I know there is something in this letter that he needs to know," Alice says.

"How do you know what is in the letter?" he questions.

"I don't know the contents, but I have a pretty good idea. And he needs to know," she shoots back.

A confused Marcus responds, "What is it that he needs to know?"

Agitation has begun to show.

"Okay okay," Alice continues as they stop outside of the elevator. "Get this. I saw this Binki girl."

"What? When?"

Alice says, "Just hold your horses. Listen, I saw that Binki girl give that man's meaty brother the letter."

A bewildered Marcus says, "Okay. So? How do you know it was her?"

"Oh, I know. I saw the brother's reaction. I saw that beautiful lady crying. I wasn't sure what was going on at the time. But now I know. She's the one!" an excited Alice states.

Marcus pushes the down arrow to the elevator.

"So? I don't think that changes a thing."

"That's because you don't know. That same lady had a young boy with her," Alice stresses with a raised eyebrow, and a smirk stretches across her face as if she had just uncovered some conspiracy.

"So," Marcus says. "She has a son. That is possible. They have been apart for 10 years." Marcus turns towards the elevator as the door opens and starts to enter.

Alice grabs his arm and pulls him back out.

"What if the son is about ten years old, and she called him Bo?" A dumbfounded Marcus relented and stepped back off the elevator as Alice continued, "What if this letter is her telling him about his son?"

"Well. That changes everything," Marcus said. He contemplated the situation and then came to a conclusion. "Here is what we will do."

The eager wife listens as he continues, "We will read the letter. If there is a mention of a child. Then we will pray on it tonight. Most likely, take it back to the man. But, if no mention of a child. We throw the letter away as he requested and leave."

The lady thinks about the proposal. Only for a couple of seconds, and then she agrees. Alice enthusiastically walks over to an isolated corner and pulls the paper out of the envelope in such a hurry you would have thought it was about to self-destruct.

In her hast, she spots a chair that is meant for people who are waiting for the elevator and allows her body to come to a rest. Marcus perches behind her so he can read the letter over her shoulder.

Before too long, an emotional Alice stands up and takes a deep breath and says, "Well be. Ain't that just something." Then puts the letter back into the envelope and repeats her amazement, "Ain't that just something."

Marcus pushed the down button one more time. The button calls for a ride. The boxed ride arrives and takes Alice and Marcus down to the bottom floor, allowing them to wander out into the darkness. Stopping just long enough for Alice to discard the letter that started all the commotion in a nearby trash can. Walking in the direction of the parking deck, never to see or speak with the man ever again.

Part Nine

Chapter Fifty-Four - Destiny

Summer of 2019

Paintings of Elvis Presley, Lenny Kravis, Jimi Hendrix, Michael Jackson, Louis Armstrong, Johnny Cash, and other music legends of every genre strategically hung on the wall, which helped give the cool, relaxed vibe that the Artful Bean Café was known for. Though Queen City has its share of national coffee chains, the locally owned and operated shop that sits in the heart of downtown Charlotte was by far the favorite amongst the Charlotteans. The café was within walking distance from the legendary GB Music Factory that housed some of the greatest music performances in the history of Carolinas, if not the United States. GB was short for "Guitar Boogie," which was the name of the guitar instrumental that catapulted Carolinian Arthur Smith into the national spotlight in 1945. After some time in the US Navy, Arthur hosted the first nationally syndicated Country Music Show on television called the "Arthur Smith Show". The GB Music Factory sits on the site where he would open the first commercial recording studio in the southeastern United States. Though it has been remodeled several times, including a total tear-down and rebuild in 2009, the nostalgic feel of the place is still enough to attract some of the top stars in the music industry.

No Carolina born musician is legit unless they have been able to do the Guitar Boogie on the stage of the GB Music Factory.

The slightly graying Bo was a regular visitor to the Artful Bean Café. Per protocol, he took his normal table under the painting of Conway Twitty and Loretta Lynn singing on stage at the Grand Ole

Opry and connected to the Wi-Fi after he opened his laptop. His best friend Mike Holmes owned the café and bought that specific painting for Bo after his dad passed. Mike knew that Loretta and Conway were Bo's mom and dad's favorite singers.

Bo loved it but insisted Mike put the painting up in the coffee shop, right by his favorite table. Their friendship started in the sixth grade when Bo offered a Don Mattingly Rookie Card in exchange for Mike's Dan Marino rookie card in the back of Mrs. Sell's class. Their love of sports, music, and wrestling has held true for the past 35 years.

The morning ritual held to form as Mike brought an extra-large cup of coffee with 2 pumps of sugar with light cream and a liver mush with cheese bagel smothered with Duke's Mayo out for Bo along with his own bagel and coffee.

"S'up Hawes," he says as he grabs a seat.

Mike is the only person that calls him by his last name. Bo reminded him that he does this because Mrs. Sells would address everyone in middle school by their last name. "Hawes, Holmes, etc."

"God's good. The line is to the door, and your team is moving the line," Bo replied.

"God. That ad in the newspaper. Or my new manager Addison. Or all three. Seems like the perfect storm," Mike replied. "We are up over 12% over last year. Man, things have been booming." He takes a bite out of his bagel. "So, what's on your agenda today."

Since Bo took the position as Vice President of Real Estate Development for Glad Foods Inc., he travels to potential sites Monday through Wednesday. He reserves Thursdays and Fridays for meetings. He conducts meetings that are follow-up in nature, casual, or personal at the coffee shop. For any clients that need professional dress attire, he uses the corporate office off Woodlawn Road.

"Well, I have a full agenda today. I am meeting Phillip to discuss refurbishing my dad's headstone. Mom's all up in a tizzy. Hard to believe that he has been gone for more than 20 years."

Mike's head shook in acknowledgment. He continued his breakfast while Bo continued the rundown of today's events.

"Then, the group from Staunton, VA, is coming by later today. Sometime soon, Rick from the office will be dropping by. You know Rick? The tall bald guy from accounting. We have been working on this project in Jacksonville for about six months, and we think the group has finally got their act together. They've always had the money, and all signs point to intelligence. They have degrees and success in many different areas. In almost every field imaginable with the lone exception being restaurants. Which is what they want to open. To move forward, we need to make sure they have an operator that can run the business. As I have said many times, money starts the business. People run the business."

Mike laughs because he has heard that so many times, and he knows it to be true.

"Brother, you can say that again." A moment of silence, and then he starts back, "Hmmm… Rick…" Mike scrunches up his face as if he is thinking hard. "Is that the guy who talks and talks and talks?"

Bo shakes his head in the affirmative motion as he takes a bite into his bagel.

He laughs and pokes at his friend, "Pot meet kettle."

Mike smiles and adds, "Okay, you got me there."

Bo's attention is suddenly diverted by the striking lady entering the coffee shop. He can't help but to notice several men whose heads turned to grab a glance at the beautiful woman dressed in business entire as she took her spot in line.

"My first meeting just walked into the door."

Mike turns his head to see the person in question. A smile stretches across his face. He recognizes the lady that Bo is referring to.

"Why does she insist on standing in line? Please tell her she does not have to wait. She can just text me, call me, or just walk up and ask me. That is not necessary."

"She insists on waiting. She said that she feels guilty cutting in front of everyone," Bo said.

Mike scoffs, "Anything that beautiful should not be waiting."

"Watch it," Bo says with a jovial smile.

The lady in question waved towards the men but shifted her attention back to the phone in hand. The phone conversation held her attention until Mike grabbed the trash from the table, threw it away, and walked over to her. Mike has always had a fondness for her. As Bo's best friend, he knows that Bo's life revolves around the young lady who stands before him. That is why he agreed to be her

Godfather. You could see him playfully scolding her right before he gave her a kiss on the cheek and made his way back behind the counter to help his team.

A couple of minutes later she emerged from the line and set her coffee on the table. Brianna gave her dad a hug and a peck on the cheek before she took a seat beside him.

"Hello, Princess. You know it drives him crazy that you keep standing in line," the smiling father said.

Brianna blows on her coffee to cool it down.

"I always think of taking him up on the offer, but I just can't. I guess now I have extra motivation now that I know it bothers him."

"I guess we need to discuss something important if you are getting up before work to meet with me?" Bo asked in part out of concern with the goal of getting right to the point while throwing a jab at her affection for sleep.

"Yeah…" she continues to blow her coffee.

Shaking his head, Bo offers, "You know there is this new invention called ice. They can put this in your coffee to cool it down if you want."

"Nah… I think I like cooling it down myself." She makes an inquisitive face. "I just realized how weird that is."

They both laughed as she continued. There is a moment of silence as Bo sips his coffee, and she works to cool hers down.

"So…" says the impatient dad, trying to pull out the purpose of the meeting.

Seriousness covers her face.

"Dad, the last couple days…. I feel lost. I am not certain of my purpose. Where am I supposed to go?"

Brianna has always been a confident, independent woman. She graduated from Radford University with a degree in business and was immediately able to find a job in downtown Charlotte with an investment group making close to $60,000 a year. Her job has allowed her to travel all over the US for business and often allowed to stay extra days for pleasure if the business ends on a Friday. In Bo's eyes, she must be the envy of every person we know. This confused and concerned him.

"Am I missing something? Did something bad happen that I am not aware of?"

"No… This sounds silly, but …." She takes a deep breath. "I feel like there is something else I'm meant to do."

This brings Bo's heart at ease. He knows that he has had this talk many times with his daughter in the past twenty-four years. Brianna has always been that person who believes she has a defined destiny just waiting for her. Bo would always tell her that when she accomplished a goal, it was destiny's way of telling her she was on the right path. In elementary school, she was destined to read the most books. Every year. Accomplishing this goal gave her great grades, which was destiny's way of letting her know she was on the right path. After the first year of cheerleading, she was destined to be the captain.

When she was a tennis player, she was destined to be a starter, then a captain, then get a scholarship. By the age of nine, she was destined to be Mary in the church play when old enough. Brianna's destiny was her way of setting a goal. Bo knew that if it was "destined", she would work tirelessly to make sure she fulfilled her destiny of staying on the right path. For this very reason, he never altered this verbiage, but instead, he fed it. Or better yet, Bo knows that he was the one who put her on this constant chase for destiny. He would always tell her that she was destined to be the first Hawes ever to graduate from a four-year college with a degree.

Destined to be a leader. So on and so on.

Bo feels certain that he knows where this is going but is not sure what brought about the concern for her destiny this time. When she was in college, she was destined to graduate. Then destined to land a great paying job in the city she loved. Now that she has accomplished this, does she think she has no destiny? She has not been at her job long enough to fulfill her destiny or achieve whatever goal she can achieve on their career ladder.

Could this be the issue? Often, things that troubled her are caused because she takes these short-term issues way too seriously. These "serious" problems are ones that 99% of the people in the world would love to have as their number one issue. No doubt, she can be a drama queen and overreact to the most basic of issues. Bo knows that it is not her decision-making that is at fault. She is golden. Things always come out right for her. Her issue is not the decision; it's the over-analyzing that goes into making the decision.

She looks at every angle.

Bo did not want to patronize her or minimize her feelings. But he felt he was obligated as a man of God and as a father to remind her how good she had it. Before he got too far in the speech that she had heard millions of times, she interrupted.

"Dad, Stop. I know I am lucky," with a boring, drab tone that instructs him that he is missing the point.

Bo thinks for a minute.

"Okay, man to woman." As soon as he said this, a moment of déjà vu sent cold chills down his back as Bo's talk with his dad almost 30 years before eerily came to the front of his mind. He realized that he was about to have a similar talk with his daughter that his dad had with him. His dad told him what he was destined to do as if his dad had already laid out the map. Now, Bo was about to walk in his father's footsteps once again. All he needs to do is follow the map.

"I am proud of you," he says before she breaks in and tells him to stop all the mushy stuff.

"I know," she says.

"Let me finish. Brianna, you have accomplished what I think you were destined to do as far as I am concerned. But God has more in store."

Bo tells her the story just like his dad told him about the oldest Hawes in each family having to support the family about the Hawes always working in fields and mills. He reminded her that by getting a degree from a four-year college, she allowed him to accomplish his destiny. Allowed him to fulfill his promise to his father through her. Both swelled with pride as she reached over and hugged her dad.

Once again, Bo's attention was diverted to the door as he noticed Rick in line. Rick was living up to his reputation as he was talking to a middle-aged man who had a bible tucked under his arm right in front of him. The man seemed to be smiling but he kept looking at his phone in a way that was hinting for Rick to end the talk. Rick was oblivious and kept talking.

"Dad, I love that story. But you have told me that before."

Bo searches his mind and can't recall that conversation. Before she continues, he concedes that his wife's constant reminder that he can't remember a darn thing maybe accurate.

"I know you are proud. I understand my role in this family. I share that story with pride."

Bo adjusted his focus after coming to grips that he was way off. He has no clue.

"Is something else going on? What brought this talk of destiny right now? Am I missing something? Work not going right? Carson and you having issues?"

Her facial expression told him that he hit the magic spot.

"Yeah... Hmm... I think Carson is going to ask me to marry him," she blurts out, but not with a smile.

"Is this good or bad?" Bo asked. "I thought it was good buuuttttt..." he says in an exaggerated dragging of the word. "The way you said that didn't send signals of rainbows and unicorns."

She gives him the obligatory laugh.

"It's good. We are fine. But I don't know if this is my destiny. If he is my destiny? How do you know?"

Bo realizes that he isn't totally off. She was overanalyzing, per protocol. She's looking for approval. Looking for her dad to validate her own conclusion. Brianna is a successful woman who has accomplished a lot in 24 years. But her destiny. Her goals. Her direction has always been heavily influenced or flat-out given as a command by him. He is about to speak when she changes the subject.

She motions her head towards Rick, "Hey, doesn't that guy work with you?"

Bo looks and confirms with a yes.

"Isn't he the one that is a little strange? I mean, he talks and talks."

Bo cannot help but laugh and comes to his defense, "He is different. And he certainly likes to talk. But that is one of the reasons he is so good at his job. He is not afraid to ask questions. He will know more about a person in the shortest amount of time than anyone I have ever met. This is a great quality when our company is trying to figure out if the stranger that is wanting to join our franchise community is worthy of being a part of the fraternity. Financially and ethnically."

Bo notices that Rick is still talking to the same man he was talking to earlier. Obviously, the well-dressed man conceded that Rick was not going to stop talking and had his phone out of sight.

Bo wants to get back to the previous conversation.

"I am meeting him in a moment, but he will be okay. Something tells me he will find someone to talk to until we are done."

Brianna is ready for the answer, "So. How do you know? You and Mom have been married for more than 25 years. What is the secret? How do I know this is my destiny?"

Bo takes his hands and rubs them through his graying hair.

"There is a lot to unpack with that question," he says.

He knows that Brianna has lived her life seeing their family living a good life. She was raised by two loving parents who worked hard not to disagree or argue in front of their only child. They always made God and family the top priority. But he also knows that the picture shown does not always tell the story. She remembers good times because Bo and Kim shielded her from the problems.

"First of all, know that your destiny is to be happy. You do not need marriage or a man to be happy. That is between you and God."

She shakes her head in an act of confirmation.

Bo continues, "As far as Carson goes, I think he is a good man, but I am not sure if he is your destiny."

Shock jolted to her face. The sudden hurt was obvious as tears almost instantly came into vision. Bo paused purposely to see the reaction that the harsh statement would cause.

Then he continued, "Of course, I am not saying he isn't your destiny either."

She smiles as if she should have known that was coming. Her dad always communicated as if he was in a dramatic reading when giving advice. Like some wise professor sitting in front of a room.

"Brianna, I love you and want to protect you. But I cannot make that decision. Nor do I care to."

She smiled and said, "I know. I guess I was just wanting your thoughts."

"Ok", Bo concedes. "Here is what I know. A moment ago, I thought your heart broke into a million pieces when you thought I did not think he was the one. That tells me you love him. That is huge. But here is the other part: you need to make sure he loves you. Love cannot be one-sided."

Bo stops himself to gather his thoughts as he wonders how to describe love. Is love a summer day lakeside with a beautiful girl sunbathing next to you or dancing in the moonlight as if you were the only two people on earth as he felt with Binki? Or is it love seeing someone believe in you and love you no matter the challenges? Be at your side no matter the battle like Kimberly? Or is love watching your daughter grow up to be the wonderful person she is today? A smile crosses his face as he realizes the beauty of God's world and that love can be found in so many forms. So many places.

Brianna waves her hand in front of his face, "Hello, Dad. You were saying?" bringing him back to reality.

He apologizes and recovers, "Sorry. I just want to make sure I share the right words." He readjusted and continued right where he left off, "Love must be greater than lust. It cannot be a one-sided commitment.

Every disagreement cannot be a threat of separation but instead a new lesson on where the common ground can be found."

She was soaking in the information as if she were a sunflower in the middle of a Union County field.

"Marriage is not easy. Marriage is messy. Marriage is the ultimate partnership that is based on respect as much, if not more, than love. One person must balance the other." There was a pause, and Bo reflected on a talk that his father had with him, "I think my father told me the best definition of marriage. He said that no matter what happened in his life, he believed in my mom. Because no matter what obstacles came about, my mom always stood by his side. Believing in each other – Trusting in each other - is loving each other."

With a giant smile and a bit of blush on her cheek, Brianna said, "That is beautiful."

She brings her wrist up to her face to see the time.

"Ah crap, I got to go. I am going to be late."

Bo can't help but smile because this is Brianna. Always in a hurry. Always with somewhere to go.

"I am certain this would not be your first time late," he says in jest.

She agrees and reminds him that this is exactly why she must leave now. She gives him a kiss on the cheek and tells him they can finish this conversation tonight. Which he knows, probably will not happen. Because she is always busy and has somewhere to go.

Brianna hastily makes her way past Rick, who is still talking to the same man at a table closest to the exit. Bo notices that this time, the man has his bible out, and they are deep in conversation. Instead of waving him over, he activates the laptop and scans the thirty or so e-mails that he received overnight.

Chapter Fifty-Five - The Return of the Hitman

Before long, he notices Rick walking his way toward him.

"Made a new friend," Bo remarks as he motions his head to the man with his nose buried in the bible, sitting at the same table as before near the door.

"That is one interesting man. I must admit. I was impressed," Rick says, almost gushing.

"What makes him so interesting," Bo offers, indulging in the fascination.

"Well," Rick says as if there is so much to tell. "He is an evangelist who travels all over the world telling his story. He just visited the Billy Graham Library. He said he visits the library every so often, but when he does, it is always on March 18th. Which I found fascinating."

Bo bites, "Okay, what is the story and why March 18th?"

"Well, I am glad you asked," Rick says with excitement. "This is a great story. I told him he should write a book about this."

They both awkwardly look towards the man. His return glance left no doubt he knew he was the topic of their discussion. They witness the man close his bible and start writing on a tablet.

"Here is the cliff note version that he gave me. He was raised by a single mom who had him when she was very young, and they always went to church," Rick says.

"Rick, that is the story of a lot of people in the world," Bo scoffs.

"Nah… Be patient. He said his dad was an amazing man, that he had never met."

Bo rolled his eyes.

"Maybe we should get to work," Bo recommended.

"Hold up. You want to hear this."

Bo relents and nods his approval for Rick to continue.

"He lived the first ten years of his life, with no dad. His mom never knew where his dad was. Suddenly, when he was around 10 years old, his mom finally found his father and brought him to Charlotte to meet his father. They drove to Charlotte, sat, and waited. He never showed. She thought she got stood up but later in the evening discovered that his father was t-boned at an intersection on the way to the meeting spot. Literally, a mile before he was to finally meet his dad. He even went to the hospital to see his dad. But his dad died before he got to meet him. That was March 18, 1999. He said he never forgot that day because his mom was so broken hearted. Could you imagine being so close to seeing his dad, only to never get to see him?"

Rick dropped his head and frowned in sadness. Then, in a dramatic fashion, he shakes off the sadness and returns to the uplifting state that he was in just moments before.

"This is the amazing part. He said that night, he went with his mom to a revival that none other than Billy Graham was preaching. He said the ultimate eye-opening experience. They met some people who changed their mom's life. Gave her a purpose. Though they had gone to church quite often, now a church and God were the center of their life. He said they never missed church again after that. Well, for the most part. That revival had such an impact on his mom, that he wants to pay it forward and hopes to impact others the way he and his mom was impacted that day. So, in a way, his dad saved his life."

He was intrigued.

"That is pretty amazing," Bo declared as he took a glance back at the man who was now gathering his stuff, no doubt about to make his exit.

"I thought so, too. That is a great story, but it gets better. I asked him if being one of God's children allowed him to forgive his dad for being an absent father for the first ten years of his life. You know, before his dad died and all. He corrected me. He said, his father was not some sort of deadbeat dad. But the exact opposite. He said that his mom had him when she was 16 years old. Said his mom had an abusive father. Meaning his grandfather would beat everyone in their family. His grandma one day was fed up with it and took her brother and her and went in hiding from her dad."

The smile was falling from Bo's face. Déjà vu had a grip on his spirit.

Rick did not miss a beat and went on with the story with great urgency, "Unbeknownst to them, his grandfather got word that they were hiding somewhere in the NC mountains at a campsite. And the devil was in that man, and he was seeking revenge. He found them with one goal in mind. His sole purpose was to kill his family, including her. The man said that his father was only 15 years old. One night, it all came to a head, and his grandpa was beating on his mom something serious. Punching and kicking his mom until she was unconscious. Then, his 15-year-old dad jumped in to save his mom. But his dad was no match for his grandpa. His grandpa beat his dad almost to death. Then, his grandpa pulled a gun from his waistband and took aim at his grandma. Before he could fire a shot." Rick adjusted himself in the chair as he was really getting into the meat of the story. "The boy's other grandpa, his dad's dad, shows up and somehow dislodges the gun from the evil grandpa. But not before his grandma took a bullet. But the good grandpa ended up running off the evil grandpa."

Déjà vu was gone. Was this a strange trick his brain is playing on him. Bo was lost.

Per standard, Rick continued, "Said that night, his grandpa had killed three people, including his uncle. Destroyed his grandma's life. Really damaged his mother. Here is the kicker. He said that after that night, his mom never saw his dad again until they met somewhere back in 1999. This led to the second meeting in which they drove to Charlotte from Charlottesville, Virginia, to tell his dad about him. Tell him that he has a son. But that car wreck took his father before he even knew he had a son. Man, that is some powerful stuff right there!!"

Bo was in the twilight zone. He was in shock.

Rick, totally oblivious to Bo and forgetting that this was supposed to be the cliff notes version, continued, "That man said that amazing story is all he has to remember his dad by."

Rick shakes his head in pity, "His father died, never knowing he was alive. Just a shame."

There is a moment of silence as Rick notices for the first time that his friend has not said anything.

"Told you. That is an unbelievable store. I am not sure I believe all that, but he is a man of God. So, I tend to think that is true."

Bo's body is paralyzed from head to toe, except for his lips whispering, "It's true," so low that Rick barely catches it.

Rick starts up again. "I agree. It must be. Oh… My bad. Let me be thorough. His mom told him of a saying that she said his father told her. He said this gets him through the hard times because it allows him to choose "The promise of tomorrow or the pain of yesterday". Said that she wrote a book with that title. I wrote it down. I am most certainly going to read that!! Oh… the saying, the promise of tomorrow or the pain of yesterday. He said he was very helpful a couple of weeks ago when his mom died from cancer. It just tugged at my heartstrings."

Rick's mouth kept moving but the words were no longer reaching Bo's ears. Bo was frozen. He knew the story. That is his story. Cold chills overwhelmed his body, and he went numb. "The promise of tomorrow or the pain of yesterday" – That is what he told Binki that night. That is what Binki said she remembered. That didn't come from a book or movie. That came from God's voice directly to her ears.

"Physically and spiritually, that's how his dad saved his mom's life," Rick finished. "Isn't that unbelievable? I mean, this is a Hallmark movie on Christmas Day if I have ever seen one."

Bo's head is spinning. The letter in the hospital was dated March 18th.

The one he never read. "Physically and Spiritually" – Binki's exact words. 16 years old – this can't be. Bo was dazed. Felt like he was about to lose consciousness or throw up. Or both. The room was spinning.

Rick babbles on.,"Oh, I thought you may find this just cool. His name was Cameron. Can't remember the last name. But he goes by the name "Bo", just like you. I told him that was what everyone called you. He thought our meeting today was destiny's way of knowing he was on the right path."

Those last words awakened Bo from the trance he was in. He looked over to the table where the man sat. But the man was no longer there.

The commotion caught Rick off guard, "Hey…Where are you going?"

Bo got up, sending his chair yelling a loud bang as it bounced against the floor. As if he was Carl Lewis in the Olympics, he sprinted out the door. Startling everyone in the café. Every head in the building turned to follow the action. Bo's body came to a stop in the middle of the sidewalk as people gawked at him. He stands outside the door, looking both ways, but cannot find the man that just left. Hope left his body. He was deflated. He wants to chase but doesn't know which way to go.

Rick runs out the door frantically with Mike on his heels, only to find Bo looking for something. As if it was life or death.

"Dude, you alright," Rick questions out of concern.

"Man, you scared the Jesus out of the customers," Mike adds but notices that something is not right.

The sudden burst out the door should have been enough evidence, but the tears falling from his friend's face confirm that his friend needs help. Bo's knees start to give away as Rick comes over and puts his arms around him.

"Hold on, Big Boy." He motions towards Mike. "Grab the other arm."

Each man grabs an arm as they lead him back to his table. Bo does not say a word despite both men's interrogation Bo hears white noise because he is lost in his thoughts.

"What the heck is this about," Mike turns his questioning towards Rick. Not minding one bit that Bo was in between them. They were talking over him as if they were parents discussing why a two-year-old was not in bed on time.

"Nothing, really. I was just telling him about this person I just met," Rick replies. "It is a good story, but not all this. I just met him 30 minutes ago. Sitting right here in your shop."

Mike is puzzled, "I don't understand. Did something happen?"

Rick shakes head and mouth moves simultaneously, "Not that I saw. That was weird. If I didn't know better, I would think he's on drugs."

Though Mike is not one to cuss, he couldn't help himself.

"Shut your damn mouth. You shouldn't say things like that."

Rick back petals and in an effort to say what he meant.

He stutters, "I'm... I didn't say he was on drugs... I just..."

Mike's frustration is showing, "Forget it. Just don't say that again."

Rick agrees as if he were a child being scolded by his belt-waving father.

Mike instructs Rick to sit with him while he goes and to get some water and a cold towel.

Before Mike is out of sight, Bo turns his head to Rick, not unlike a robot. Stiff and mechanical.

"Where is the mom?"

"What," Rick is bewildered. "Where is your mom? I don't know, but I can find out."

Rick starts to walk away. Bo grabs his arm with force.

"No, No, No," an irritated Bo exclaims. "Where is the boy's mom? The man you were speaking to."

The realization that all this is about the man he just met has Rick perplexed.

Before thinking about the ramifications of his words, he nonchalantly responds, "She's dead. She died a couple of weeks ago. Remember, I told you that. That is why he came back this time. The Billy Graham Library is the closest he said he could possibly be to his mom, his dad, and his God all at one time."

Life leaves Bo's lifeless body as he sinks into the chair. His chin drops like an anvil until its descent finally makes its place, landing firmly upon his chest. He is in his own thoughts. Numb and overwhelmed. His motionless frame is blind to the pain that creeps through him, with the tear that is sliding down his face exhibiting the only evidence of consciousness. A small glimmer of life was spotted as he squeezed his eyes together.

Suddenly, the one tear that was once alone now has plenty of company.

Without moving any part of his body except his lips, "He took her. God took her. The hitman returned," quietly escaped his mouth as sorrow captured his heart.

Part Ten

Chapter Fifty-Six - The Janitor

Charlotte Medical Hospital – May 20, 2000 – Thirty Minutes after Marcus and Alice Left

Drake was doing his normal janitorial duties at the hospital, which included circling the hospital and collecting trash. When he reached the trash can by the entrance of the elevator, he noticed an opened envelope sitting on the ground beside it. Could be someone was trying to throw it away and missed the can. Then again, someone could have dropped it. Drake looked around and couldn't find anyone close by who may have dropped it. Never one shy about being nosey, the fifty-two-year-old man picked up the envelope and found a nearby bench.

Bo,

My country bumpkin. The words that I am about to write will never allow me to express my love for you. I can honestly tell you that you are the greatest love of my life. You saved me – physically and spiritually. Ever since you shared the words "The promise of tomorrow or the pain of yesterday", my life has not been the same. The dance on the mountaintop will always be "The Dance" to me. The night in that camper will never leave me. I am reminded of it daily. Not one day has passed that I didn't want to be with you. That I haven't thought of you. I know you are my person. You will always be my person. God put you with me when I needed you with me the most. It breaks my heart that we spent ten years apart, and I desire more than anything to be with you for the rest of my life.

You are the most gentle, caring, and honorable person that God has ever put on earth. Every time we were together, I was better. You made me want to be a better person. You made me want for a better future. Your love is something I have never felt – before or since. You have created a standard for love that I have been seeking. I know compassion because you showed it to me. I know God because you introduced me. I know passion because we shared it. I know love because I felt it. I have a life and a life worth living, thanks to you.

When I saw you at the company retreat, I found the answer to the age-old question of whether or not time can hinder love. I know now that love can most certainly stand the test of time.

A few days ago, I drove to Charlotte. I sit. I waited. My heart broke when you didn't show. I couldn't believe you didn't show. Then I got a call from Calito at your firm, sharing that you were in a serious accident. He had no idea that it was me you were coming to meet. It was me that you were going to ride away with. We were so close to finishing our promise of tomorrow. So close to letting go of the pain of yesterday. So close to bringing to life the fairy tale that I have dreamt of a million times. The one I waited ten years to achieve. But I am afraid that it is because of love that each of our tomorrows will have a different path.

Two days ago, I went to the hospital and saw your banged-up body. Every intention to claim you as mine. Tell the world I am here, and once healthy, I am taking my future – YOU - Home with me.

I remember when we were talking about God, you often spoke about God putting words in your mouth. You spoke of signs from God.

I am close enough to God that I can relate. I have had the pleasure of having God put words in my mouth. I have seen signs of his existence. But none stronger than two days ago. No sign stronger than when I walked into your hospital room and saw your beautiful wife crying. Holding a little girl in a yellow dress. Looking like Belle from Beauty and the Beast. My heart melted when I heard the little girl say, "Daddy, please don't go."

Those words were put in her mouth by God. The tears streaking down the face of your wife were put there by God. I was meant to walk in and see that image. Of all the times I could have walked in, that was the time. God put me there. It took less than thirty seconds, for me to see exactly what God was saying.

It was all too much for me to take in. I left immediately and found a church. I prayed. I sought guidance.

When I started this journey to find you. The goal was simple. To find out it, we were meant to be together. I have my answer. I believe there was a time when we were meant to be together. But that time has passed. On this day, you were meant to be a father. You are meant to be a husband. Meant to be the husband and father your dad was. I realize that we both need to move on. To allow you to be the man you were meant to be. To allow me to be the woman I am destined to become. I believe with all I have; this will happen. It just can't happen together.

Please understand that my heart is breaking because I have to say goodbye. But you have promised your tomorrows to someone else. A tomorrow that can't include me.

But know this! You will always be loved. Always. The impact on my life is beyond comprehension. There are memories and lessons that will last me a lifetime. I promise to break the cycle of my family and ensure that God and family are at the forefront. That is where everything will start and end for me.

I wish you all the happiness the world has to offer. But most of all, I hope you know that God put you on earth for a reason. There is no doubt you are an angel from God. God put you on that mountain that week for me. I am convinced you are my angel. What I came to realize was that I was just borrowing you. You were on lease. Your work is not done. God has a lot more in store for you. There is a little girl and a woman who needs that angel now. With a tear in my eye and a smile in my heart, I must let you go. I refuse to steal someone else's angel. She - well, they - are your destiny. You are their angel, not mine.

This is goodbye in body – But you will be in my heart forever.

Love

Anne "Binki" Channey

Made in the USA
Columbia, SC
19 September 2024